TREACHEROUS SEAS

Chronicles of Evil:

A Freighter, a Woman and 22 Men

Based on a True Story

Gerri Simons Rasor

ISBN: 1501059955
ISBN 13: 9781501059957
Library of Congress Control Number: 2014915933
CreateSpace Independent Publishing Platform
North Charleston, South Carolina

Dedication

To my darling husband, Wen.
We romped around the world together on land and sea,
Delighting in our youth, our fun and, best of all, our love.
You were my safe haven and inspiration.

Acknowledgements

For your support, encouragement and energies in helping bring this book to fruition, I thank you humbly and sincerely:

Joyce Hill, Friend and Editor Par Excellence: You are not only smart and fun, but also kind and tenacious.

Patrick McBiles, U.S. Merchant Marine Academy graduate, seafaring expert, friend and, incidentally, darling relative: This little tale sure jogged some fun memories, didn't it.

My wonderful Readers, Editors, Helpers and Friends, who thought this book stuff would never end: Barbara Emerson, Jan Rains, Kay Loftin, Bill Shover, Sue Mack, Marge MacDougall and Dave MacDougall, and to all you other kind friends, who dished out support by the carload – thank you, thank you. What a team! Also, thanks to Dr. Rowe: 'Evil' sneaked into the title, after all.

Jumbo hugs to my two sooper-dooper guys who were REALLY glad they didn't have to experience the blue air. You missed a great performance, my cutie-pies!

To the men of Markship Mexico: We had a wild ride, kids. Especially to Ion: A satisfying outcome, my friend!

And to the Managing Director, who saw what must be done and did it!

Abrazos y besos a todos, Gerri

Table of Contents

Treacherous Seas

PART ONE

PRELUDE

Author's Note

This tale is set in the Year 2000. Economies, attitudes and viewpoints have experienced drastic changes throughout the world in subsequent years, and today's may be completely different from those Dark Ages of Year 2000. Many things in my story may seem dated, but are true to the period. Yet, even as we dart forward with the speed of light, it's difficult to dismiss the old adage: "The more things change, the more they remain the same."

The term 'Freighter' is familiar to us all, but is frowned upon in the modern world of sea commerce. Cargo vessels, containerized ships, sea-going vessels are amongst a host of upscale appellations that bring smiles to mariners' faces. Feel free to substitute your choice.

The freighter MarkShip Mexico's full complement for a trans-Atlantic voyage is a crew of twenty-two hardened men from Captain to lowliest deck hand, each man adhering closely to his duties and ranking in the insular seafaring world.

This particular one-month crossing, however, adds a twenty-third, a passenger. Into the midst of tight-knit Eastern Bloc officers and Filipino deck hands, who have never known an American, is thrust an American! Woman!

CHAPTER ONE
MarkShip Mexico,
November 2000

I had become their pet, their mascot - the barrier against their Captain. Twenty-two pairs of eyes followed my every step.

As I walked the narrow passageways between ship's railing and the mountain of tightly lashed, turn-buckled, creaking cargo boxes, the Filipino deck hands stopped their back-breaking work for the slightest moment, each carefully measuring, each with a hello and smile, which not so long ago had been derisive, each with a flicker of hope peeking out of their brown eyes. When we met in the superstructure hallways, they stepped aside and smiled shyly, eyes sliding away. But, for that brief moment, real smiles, like I was a real person. Only Bosun looked directly at me, his wiry body tense, his eyes flat and uncompromising, a man who had been disappointed often and trusted no one.

The officers smiled readily, waiting. They knew they were beyond the pale, having taken me into their confidences, having confided more than they should. Their eyes held more than a flicker of hope. Theirs were assessing, frankly hopeful, body language pleading, although they spoke not a word of their expectations, looking to Chief Officer to articulate their hopes.

On the Bridge where I rode often with the duty officers day or night, bracing nonchalantly against the rolling sea, used to its pitches and yaws, we chatted about families and pets and laughed at sea stories. Should an off-duty officer stroll onto the Bridge, we three would indulge in a real gab session, always alert to the radar, array of dials - and the sea. It was relaxing and fun.

Unless The Peasant staggered onto the Bridge, a rare moment when even the air seemed to freeze, an illusion of hoarfrost glazing the massive Bridge windows. An icy breeze of distrust and disrespect shot a sick, flu-like chill up the spine. The silent duty officer would become engrossed in the blinking radar screen, the off-duty officer would melt away, and I would say, "Hello, Captain. Having a nice day? Looks like Force 4 sea today." He would grunt at my contemptuous gaze, drop his red-rimmed eyes and shuffle his feet, swaying in a liquored cloud, then glare around the Bridge from under wild, bushy eyebrows, as though his presence was important. After a few mumbled words to the duty officer, he would disappear through the narrow Bridge stairway door, its vacuum seal whooshing behind him, his thick body banging against stairwell walls as if unused to the sea. The duty officer would dart a quick glance at me or look calmly into the sea, his body language screaming, "WELL?"

On the deck or Bridge, in the Dining Room or Lounge, air crackled with tension, underlying anger crisp and demanding. At night in my darkened cabin, ship's running lights flickering far below, air from the companionway popped and snapped, sparks exploding like electricity running along high-tension wires in a rainstorm.

How could a mere passenger, a woman amongst twenty-two men on a cargo ship, this microcosm of humanity floating on the empty, endless Atlantic Ocean, have come to a moment such as this?

Officers, deck crew - Men of MarkShip Mexico: Stop waiting. I cannot do anything! I would if I could, but I can't. I just can't.

***

So I will tell you my seafaring tale - from beginning to end - just as it happened, leaving nothing out and adding nothing.

How I ache to imbue the men with dash and gallantry, the women with glamour and sophistication, the circumstances with bonhomie, the surroundings with luxury, the surfaces with less grit, the edges with less razor sharpness. Foremost, I would like to infuse my own person with nobility and majesty-of-self instead of the self-absorbed, ignoble character that emerges from these pages.

Temptation's siren call is difficult to resist. Telling it like that would be easy, fun; living with it impossible. I have only one proof: It must be told as it was lived.

Why embellish? Landlubbers will shake their heads and exclaim, "Honestly! These things just don't happen in today's world." Seafarers will twitch their shoulders, defensive eyes skidding around me, and vow nothing like this ever occurred on their ships

Nobody is going to believe me anyway.

Except - maybe - the Director of The Company who owns the vessel, MarkShip Mexico.

PART TWO

JOURNEY TO THE SEA

CHAPTER TWO

Valencia, Spain,

October 15, 2000

"**L**ook, Mr. Agent," I hiss into the telephone, switching from my barely-passable Spanish to English, "I'm not the one who is responsible for your ship's erratic schedule, an entire week early as it turns out. You now tell me that you cannot even guess as to its future departure. I'm in Valencia at your request, which I almost missed since you e-mailed at the last minute, and I ran long and hard across Spain to get here on time. The hotel here in Valencia, where I was lucky to get a room for a few days, is fully booked for the holiday weekend. I need a place to stay WHILE YOU DIDDLE AROUND FIGURING OUT WHEN MARKSHIP MEXICO IS (a) going to ARRIVE and (b) going to LEAVE Valencia. Find me a hotel somewhere in the area tonight because I have to move tomorrow!"

My telephone conversation at the hotel lobby desk has caused no concern until this moment, simply another low-toned Spanish conversation. Until I switch to English and raise my voice. Now all faces swivel from the view outside the lobby windows to the desk telephone, all bodies turned away, but leaning backwards, trying to translate the petite, blond lady's angry English words, the tone raw and sharp.

"But, Senora, this is a holiday weekend," oozes the telephone voice. "We cannot take responsibility for you."

"You damned well better take responsibility. You are totally responsible for cargo on the ship you represent. I AM A PAID UP PASSENGER.

JUST LIKE THE CONTAINERS, I AM CARGO – and you are responsible."

"Pues, vamos a ver lo que podemos hacer," says the oily voice.

"No! We are NOT 'going to see what we can do.' *You* are going to do it. Call me here before 10 PM tonight with a new hotel. By the way, should I charge you for taxi fare and something extra for all this inconvenience?"

All right, Ms Self, keep it down. I take a deep breath, at the same time leaning toward the windows to watch the last rays of the dying sun illuminate the cathedral spires in the plaza. Espectacular! Not one lobby denizen is looking directly at me.

"Look, Mr. Agent," I say in a wheedling tone, "the ship leaves from the Port. I am now in the exact middle of Valencia, one block from the plaza. Why don't you find a place for me close to where the ship leaves so that if you are, um, tarde (and I stress the Spanish pronunciation) in your advisement as to day and time, I can be near enough to walk to the ship, if necessary?"

He laughs. *I may not be sleeping on a park bench, after all.* "OK, I'll call you later tonight."

"Mil gracias por todo. Estare esperando tu llamada," my tones dulcet. *Aw, Ms Self, remember you can catch more flies with honey than with vinegar.* I laugh out loud. *But first you have to smack 'em in the head with a 2-by-4 to get their attention.*

When Mr. Agent finally calls, he is full of instructions, good cheer and hail-fellow-well-met, practicing his very precise English, then lapsing into Spanish. So charming is Mr. Agent, so nauseating.

CHAPTER THREE
Port of Valencia, Spain, October 16

N ext morning, in a car sent by the agent as a peace offering, I'm off to the beach hotel to await still further instructions from my new best friend as to the departure of MarkShip Mexico.

The car passes the shipping terminal entrance, behind which a long line of cranes jut into the air like giant gallows, containers (which I love to call 'boxes,' to the despair of my shipmates) swinging between ship and trucks, which once loaded rumble in all directions. Hustle-bustle is the order of the day; a shipping terminal is not a place for lolly-gaggers. "Do your job; we are all on a tight schedule." The car continues along the beach for a couple of miles to the hotel, and I am content to know that I can crawl to the terminal if worse comes to worst.

My new hotel, slightly faded elegance in a rambling two-story beach-front manner, is very pleasant with its shiny white paint and French doors. The wide white beach is only a step from the veranda, and the ambience of seclusion is broken only by seagull cries. It's odd to be so close to the terminal and not see one crane. I enjoy every moment, even as I become increasingly worried that MarkShip Mexico is lost at sea or Mr. Agent has forgotten me. As the days roll by, enjoyment turns to anxiety.

To pass the time, I pound my computer keys to catch up on my journal for the past five weeks – has it really been that long? *Lazy, MsSelf, better get to it. So we're back in the USA and…*

Some months ago, my friend, Alisha, convinced me that we 'just must' float by self-propelled narrow boat through the canals of England, a country I never wanted to visit, but I caved to her compelling "Puullleezze." So here I was at her house in broiling Bakersfield, California in mid-August to complete the trip planning, the many glitches frazzling my nerves. I cursed myself for agreeing to this trip, which would begin and end with a hated trans-Atlantic flight. I much preferred a ship's cabin to being jammed together in a 747's, not once, but twice. 'Ship's cabin' brought fond memories of my husband's beaming face and trim body dancing a jig on one of our many cruises, singing, "This is my favorite, the only, way to travel, my darling wife."

THAT'S IT! SHIP! MY BELOVED SEA! *Visit England with Alisha, put her on a nice big plane to the USA and you, MsSelf, take a freighter home.* Brilliant visions of last year's around-the-world, three-month cargo ship voyage rose before me tantalizingly, a hint of fresh sea air wafting through Bakersfield's heavy smog. *Wait, you wanted to spend the winter at a Spanish school in Mexico. Well, why not do it all? Wander through Spain and Portugal, as you're so close, then get on a freighter from Spain to Mexico. Perfect!*

Clicking computer keys recording every nuance, I relive the fun of England, where we were deluged with rain on the canals, then toured the countryside, each traveler's problem sending us into fits of silliness and gales of laughter. Onward alone by ferry, bus and train, just meandering across Green Spain and down the length of Portugal, where the fun stopped in Coimbra and Lisboa when I contracted the national fever epidemic, nearly becoming one of the people dying in droves.

"Can't be, Doctor, a person is dead at 105 degrees," I mumbled through fevered lips.

"You're not, we'll save you," came the anxious reply.

Maybe I shouldn't dredge that up.

Now, suddenly, on the warm Spanish beach watching the serene rollers kiss the shore, the familiar bone-chilling Coimbra shiver runs up my spine. Instantly, I am covered in sticky cold sweat, and my eyes won't focus as I frantically wipe the rivulets of sweat running into them. I steel my body and grit my teeth but am nonetheless transported to Portugal where fits of coughing and wild shaking had set my bed to dancing a tattoo on the marble floor, twisted soaked sheets, flashes of light and dark… No, don't think of it! Get to your room now, take a blazing hot shower, pull the covers tightly, adding sweatshirts and jackets from your suitcase. Let this pass. How could this be happening after a week of normalcy? Don't look in the mirror at the delineated ribs and hipbones protruding. Tonight I will eat bunches of food. Tomorrow much more. Right now, just find all the blankets and heap them on. Hurry, now, hurry. What has caused this - anxiety and worry? Who knows? Just get warm.

In the twilight before sleep, I wonder yet again if I have some form of malaria. It is just like described in novels, except for the coughing. Visions rise up of us kids playing 'Panama Canal' amongst tall grasses in the large field behind my childhood house, using pieces of rhubarb as quinine. We 'doctors' would holler at our unseen victims lying so still in the waving grasses. "We'll save you. We've got quinine." And the victims would chew the rhubarb we forced between their teeth and were instantly recovered, immediately jumping up and demanding their turn as doctor. Please, somebody, give me a piece of rhubarb. Tomorrow…

Tomorrow is here. The weather is delightful, and I slowly walk the broad beach into town, hopefully gaining strength with each step, stopping often in an attitude of admiring beach kiosks and sunlit sea, begging my body to cooperate. I gag down pastries, ice cream, an apple. Eat! Returning to the hotel, two glasses of local red wine help mask the problem. A few bites of steaming chicken soup and I am again ready to collapse in my bed, blankets, sweatshirts and jackets at the ready. The night passes slowly.

Yippee! Today, I'm almost normal. Like a miracle, I am restored. Greeting the morning sun and drinking scalding, sludgy-black coffee, I yet again ruminate on how MarkShip Mexico can be so iffy in its arrival and departure.

Remembering the tons of information, both printed on paper and imprinted on my brain received from last year's container ship voyage, one thing was paramount as I rode on the Bridge, engines pounding if we were running late, faces tense, body language screaming: Regardless the problem - at the mercy of bad weather, mechanical failures, port strikes, pirates, the port authorities did not care - get to the berthing on time. With the Bridge deck, seven decks above the Engine Room, vibrating, the message was clear: Be there! No refunds were allowed and maybe no place to berth your mammoth ship, maybe anchoring in the roads for days, scrambling for pilots and crane time, begging for bunkering, if you were late. Run hard, no matter how much fuel it took. If you spent days waiting for a berthing at this particular port, paying berthing and other attendant fees twice, all the future ports would be delayed with identical consequences.

Pilots, docking crew, crane operators, truck drivers, chandlers, schedulers, shuttle busses and tens of auxiliary members were all poised to receive your ship. A cargo terminal is like a city, but with only one purpose - load and unload. They are all there waiting for you, keeping their part of the bargain. Now you keep yours. Run hard!

What is with MarkShip Mexico?

A week early is as bad as a week late, isn't it? Is someone on board now scrambling day and night to revise the berthings for an EARLY rather than a late arrival? Would that be the Chief Officer, sitting in his miniscule office just off Hatchcover Deck, computer fired up, papers covering every square inch, cursing and muttering "Why me?" Why me or not, he will do it, day and night, because he is The Go-To Man, The Big Kahuna, for ship's cargo and ship's day-to-day activities.

What has caused an EARLY arrival? Lack of cargo? Missed ports? And because of that, no money for fuel? *Novice, novice, you don't really understand any of this.* Still, I suck in my breath. *Am I going to get to Veracruz without rowing?*

As the days unfold on dry land, body cooperating, mind clear, checking with the hotel desk nearly hourly to ascertain if I have a message (the hotel staff courteous, but becoming bored with my inquiries), anxiousness to get to sea coloring every moment, I ask myself that question often, *What's with you, MarkShip Mexico?*

My hotel room window looks out onto a sunshiny expanse between beach and town. The wind has picked up dramatically, and I am pleased to be on the landward side of the seafront hotel, although each day I present myself at the hotel desk to inquire (a) if they have heard from the ship's agent as to when MarkShip Mexico might arrive and (b) if today might be the day I can finally occupy a sea-view room.

"Es hoy el dia puedo mudarme a una habitacion donde puedo ver su mar espectacular?"

The answer is always (a) "No, nothing from the ship," and (b) "Maybe tomorrow a seaside room will be available so you can see our spectacular sea."

I snatch the loudly ringing telephone, and the desk informs me that just such a room, their very best, is now disponible (available). I quickly pack bags and dutifully follow the chatty (in Spanish and hesitant English) bellman to the seaside room. The room indeed has a spectacular view. However, the wind, which could not be felt as severe in the landward room, is nothing short of horrifying in the sea-view room, whistling through the floor-to-ceiling French doors, sand sifting in little drifts through every crevice. And cold.

Leaving my bags by the door, I hug my jacket around me and walk to the French doors. The wind's screech is ear-shattering, and, to escape it, I flee into the spotless, tiled bathroom, close the door, sit on the closed john and think, *What next?*

The telephone rings. *Should I tell them that I really don't want this room after all of my badgering? Oh God, why me?*

"Your ship has arrived in port. They expect you onboard by 3 PM." The desk clerk's tone is excited and congratulatory. *Can't wait to get rid of me, hmm? Don't blame you.*

"De veras? Really? I'll leave immediately. Can you call a cab for me? I haven't unpacked or even sat on the bed in my new room. Will I owe you for the room? Never mind, I'll be right down. Gracias, gracias. Thank you."

They say I owe not one cent more, wish me well and all come out to see me into the cab. "Adios. Gracias, gracias," I wave through the cab window, wind blasting sand in my face.

PART THREE

UPON THE SEA

CHAPTER FOUR

Hello, MarkShip Mexico.

October 22, Valencia, Spain

The cabbie is unused to entering shipping terminal gates. I am used to it. My ticket, passport, a few pleading smiles and the Powers-That-Be surprisingly allow the cab to deliver me directly to MarkShip Mexico. "Siga esta camioneta (pickup). Entonces…"

The cabdriver nervously follows the pickup so closely through the maze of stacked containers, rumbling trucks and screeching cranes that I think we might rear-end it. At last, I spy the looming bulk with emblazoned name 'MarkShip Mexico' on its dull black beam. Cranes are working some seventy-five meters forward, containers swinging with precision onto waiting trucks. Good. They aren't near the superstructure.

"Parate!" The cab screeches to a halt. "Estamos aqui." (The cabdriver sags with relief that we're finally 'here.')

"OK, Mr. Cabdriver, stay outside the tracks and stop by that gangway going up the side of the superstructure. When I get out, you turn around and go back exactly the way we came in. Do not get between the ships and the crane tracks. Todo va a estar bien, mi amigo. Me crees." The cabbie smiles weakly as I shove money across the seat, adding a substantial tip, hoping that will make him believe everything is going to be fine and he should believe me.

Quickly pulling my bags off the road and across the crane tracks, keeping a close watch on the cranes, I arrive safely at the bottom of the gangway. I look way up to the top of the superstructure, which contains all the rooms and spaces for living and working, the Engine Room and that all-important place, the Bridge.

This superstructure, six decks high, is located about two-thirds back from the bow, leaving on-deck space both forward and aft for containerized cargo, five boxes high. The forward hold is open, and the crane is removing a box from its depths.

MarkShip Mexico is some seventy meters shorter than my first 'freighter,' in fact, smaller all around than that first behemoth. *Hmm, a little ship*, I nearly sneer. *Stop that, right now!*

Still clutching my bags, I stand alone on the windy pier, having a heart-to-heart chat with myself. *NO-NO-NO comparing this ship with that fabulous first freighter, The Other Ship. Remember how you used to do that with cruise ships and how it took a lot of fun out of the first few days with all that comparison crap? Take this ship as you find it. Take the personnel as they are. NO COMPARISONS – Different is Good! Got it, MsSelf? Are you sure?*

"Okay, Baby, here we go. Think good thoughts," I whisper. And with that I place my bags close to the gangway for someone to hopefully haul up later and begin to climb the cleated metal stairs that sway with each step, clutching the rope handrail, trying to ignore the dirty water far below, glimpsed between the open risers, lapping in the narrow chasm between ship and dock. Up and up those shaky stairs, the dull black ship's bulk my only companion, trucks rumbling, cranes shrieking, the ever-present shrill claxon signaling movement on the tracks.

At last, my jelly knees support me that one important step onto the cluttered deck. People and machines are in concentrated motion from bow to stern. Checking in all directions, I leap across the deck's expanse to what appears to be the Hatchcover door of the superstructure. Yep.

Hello, MarkShip Mexico.

A tall, well-built, thirty-something man in rumpled khaki shirt and pants stands just outside the door, totally focused on the clipboard in his hand. If not for the a miniscule roll peeking over his belt, he would be a perfect specimen with his short dark hair, square handsome face, small ears, jutting jaw and broad shoulders above a compact, fit body.

"Hi," I chirp. He jumps, although how such a small sound in this mass confusion and cacophony could startle him amuses me. "Uh, are you First Officer?" Although I feel he is just that, his manner of dress in port is way too casual and slightly sloppy. Capt R. of The Other Ship would have had a cow. Everybody on his ship was pressed and polished in port. *Oh dear, I haven't been onboard two minutes and I'm already doing the verboten thing: Comparing. NO!*

Wind rustling his dark hair, he smiles, round brown eyes crinkling, "Yes. And how would you know that?" We measure each other, both obviously approving of what we see.

"Well, you look like the man in charge." He looks very pleased. "I'm your passenger, Cari Lindley."

His pleasure fades in a heartbeat, replaced by a barely concealed scowl, previously languid body now tense and prickly. Obviously, I am not the passenger he was expecting.

"And I'm Ion, Chief Officer." He eyes me carefully, unsuccessful at hiding his disdain. "Welcome aboard," he adds abruptly, lips pulled back tightly.

"Could you tell me where my cabin is, please?" I ask so very sweetly, ignoring his frown.

"Sure. Alex, the steward, will show you. No, never mind, I have a few minutes, I'll show you myself." He scans the deck, noting crane and personnel positions, steps through the open door and places his clipboard on the cluttered desk inside the tiny room directly to the right of the Hatchcover door. Jammed with computers and papers, this is obviously the Chief Officer's office, where all ship's business takes place.

I follow, stepping high over the raised threshold, glad to be out of the chilly wind, rain suddenly threatening. "Aha, the First Officer's Den of Iniquity." I try my most winning smile, hoping to get past the cranky attitude.

"Yeah," he mutters. "It's a mess, as always, but everything important on this vessel manages to get done in here."

"I'm sure you're very efficient." He glares, turns his back to me and starts down the hallway. "By the way," I call, skipping to keep up, "do you prefer to be called Chief Officer or First Officer? I don't know why, but somewhere along the way I became stuck on First Officer."

"Ion, Chief Officer, First Officer. Take your pick and it'll suit me fine," he throws over his shoulder. Then he stops and wheels around with me practically running into him. "I'll quickly show you the, shall we say, amenities, then your cabin and you can come back and investigate more thoroughly by yourself later. And if we see anybody of interest along the way, I'll introduce you." He shares his 'Oh dear God' grimace with me again and charges forward.

"Here is the Dining Room," and as we begin to enter, a very tall fifty-year-old man, his bearing regal even in greasy clothes, steps into the hallway from a door opposite the Dining Room. "Ah, Stan, this is the passenger, Mrs. Lindley. This is Stan, our Chief Engineer."

Stan's deep-set, dark brown eyes fill with shock. Yet he offers a clean right hand to be shaken. "I understand we are to be dining companions. That will be pleasant. Excuse me, I must rush off. There are many things to be accomplished whilst in port."

I shake his hand, marveling at his precise speech, measuring him as closely as he is measuring me, which causes his shoulders to twitch. "I look forward to being tablemates, Chief."

The Dining Room, on the Main Deck, turns out to be a mousy room. Indeed, drab would be considered a compliment. Upon entry, a gloomy, cluttered sitting room with two short, gray couches, two upholstered muddy-brown chairs, coffee table, TV set and bookcase holding five books is described by First Officer as the Officers Lounge. The Dining Room is divided from this dismal place by latticework beyond which are round tables seating six, a few framed, innocuous prints on dull gray walls that match the Officers Lounge. Beyond is the service area, then the galley, which I am not invited to see. On the other side of the galley will be the crew's Dining Room I know, but again no invitation to see it. *Whoa, we need some happy paint here.*

Apparently, I will be sitting at table with Captain, Chief Engineer, Chief Officer and any other visiting dignitaries who might wander off the sea and into our dining area.

24

"You will barely see me." This seems to greatly please First Officer. "My watch is from 1600 to 2000, so I rarely come to the Dining Room for dinner – or any other meal."

We move along the Main Deck narrow hallway.

"The pool." He throws open the door onto a dingy room with a bathtub-sized pool, now devoid of water in port. "If you want it filled, we can do so. Nobody uses it. Don't know why it's taking up space. Bad smell in here, too." Both noses wrinkle.

"Trust me, I won't be using it either." He actually smiles. Is he happy at the thought of my discomfort?

Come on, MsSelf, get a grip.

The Hobby Room, very hot with no windows, is in the 'basement' next to the Engine Room. A beat-up ping-pong table and dart board complete the amenities. Again, a quick glance tells me I won't be spending any time here.

We trudge silently up three decks, where he abruptly opens another door.

"Here's the washer. And an iron, if you need it."

"No dryer? And does one washer work for all of you guys?" A sullen stare.

A smiling young Filipino boy bounces into the hallway. "Alex, the steward, this is the passenger."

"Oh, our passenger, Mum. Mum, I'm happy to meet you. I can do anything you need, Mum. Just call on me and I will come running. Happy, happy to see you, Mum. I will halt at your cabin later, Mum, to make sure everything is fine for you."

"Great, Alex. I'm sure we'll get on very nicely together. Thank you."

"And thank you too, Mum." He rushes down the stairwell.

"Seems like a nice kid," I say to his departing back.

"He is. Badly overworked. And mistr…" The First Officer stops short and frowns at me, eyes suddenly brimming with rage. "He's a good boy."

We climb up the stairwell to Deck 4 and turn right.

"Here's your cabin." He flings open the door, stepping aside to allow me to enter.

"Oh," I manage to squeak after one sweeping glance at the small, murky gray room with single bed, a couch covered with a blue sheet, desk with telephone, two cupboards, a wardrobe plus drawers under the bunk. No TV, no VCR, no radio/stereo, no refrigerator – nada. Five steps and I'm in a very nice bathroom, (goodbye bubble baths), shower only, of course. Cabin is situated aft, not forward as advertised, with a sealed window aft and a window opening to port. The stack is right outside my cabin aft and starboard. It will be interesting to smell and hear what goes on with it – heat and smoke, no doubt. "And what does one do for a refrigerator?"

"Refrigerator! Why, one goes without," he parrots, smiling evilly. "Not what you expected?"

"Well, not really. But I'll make do." He frowns. "Before you go, First Officer, I have a really important question." I hesitate, looking at him nervously.

"Say it, please."

"About The Captain's Bridge Policy. That is, can I ride on the Bridge?"

He snorts, "Ride? But, of course." He regards me as some kind of nut case, then shakes his head. "The Captain's Bridge Policy. Heh." He's getting quite a yuck out of me, but still I persist.

"I mean, whenever I want. Even in and out of ports."

"I'm sure the Captain's, um, Bridge Policy will permit all of that." His accent overtakes his English, and it's all I can do to understand that goodie! I get to do what I want.

"And secondly, about the other passengers. I understand there are staterooms," I sweep my arm disparagingly at the woeful room and roll my eyes "for three passengers. How many will there be? Booking agents never tell you anything." I laugh.

"That's the truth," he mutters sourly. "No other passengers. You're it."

"Oh. Well. Oh." This is an unexpected and unwelcome surprise. "Uh, thanks for the tour. Hope to see you at dinner."

"Very doubtful. I must get back to work. Enjoy your ship, ah, ride." He seems to thaw for just that moment as he smiles and shakes my hand, fingers barely touching mine.

The afternoon is spent unpacking and arranging my computer on which I shall keep my detailed daily journal. I run between my chores and the port window facing the harbor, since we are backed into our berth, watching tugs berth and unberth ships in the now-pelting rain. MarkShip Mexico shakes with the weight of the boxes as they come on. Either this is a very small, frail ship or the crane driver needs some lessons. Hope it's the latter since I'm about to cross the Atlantic on this bugger.

Another solo tour of the superstructure takes me to the pool (nope! again), Hobby Room (what a misnomer!), Dining Room and dreary closet called the Officers Lounge. I tread the inside stairwells, noting in every room, every stairwell, every hallway many signs, advisements and placards on the evils of booze and drugs. No hard liquor allowed to crew ANYWHERE ON THIS SHIP. Wow! It's a deluge of information and warning.

The main advisory board on Hatchcover Deck displays a letter from Management to The Master with regard to a problem between Cook, who wants to be paid for hours he works, and Master. Management advises Cook is out of line and will be reprimanded. How do we suppose our food will taste with this going on? Oleander salad with hemlock dressing? Cook spitting in the soup? And why is this posted? Isn't it enough that Captain and Cook know their problems have been addressed from on high? Do we all really need to know the details, Captain? Maybe a tiny refresher on personnel relations and managerial skills is in order. I haven't even met Captain and his image carries a slight tarnish. I return to my cabin, #403, Superstructure Deck 4, amid the barrage of booze and drug signs.

Two soothing cocktails made from that forbidden booze I had so blithely carried aboard relax me. Wind and rain continue full force, and I stand at my window, evil brew in hand, watching harbor sights.

A ship across the way is receiving bunker, and I smile, hoping he is not receiving bilge as we almost did on The Other, where luckily Chief Engineer tested the fuel in his small lab and stopped the bunkering just as they were about to pump pure bilge into our tanks.

Chief Engineer chuckled, "We were late to berthing, so we lost our turn with our regular bunker barge. There was something funny with this guy, so I told him to hold up until I tested. By the time I got back to where his barge was, and steaming mad I was, he was long gone, lost in harbor traffic."

When I think of the disaster such an act could have caused not only to engine but the ship's safety in high seas, I shudder. Aw, the human species' greed for just one more free buck, consequences be damned.

With the second drink, I mentally review my shipboard vocabulary learned previously. *All right, from The Other.* Last voyage, I noticed when back amongst the landlubbers and relating what I considered to be an exciting sea tale that they were puzzling over some words – just when I wanted them to be honed in on the grand finale. *So, MsSelf, make sure you don't misspeak at the dining table on your first night. Review, idiota, review.*

Superstructure – wherein we all dwell and all ship's business gets accomplished.

Bridge – place from whence the ship is charted, guided and steered. The Holy of Holies.

Bridgewings – normally open terraces from the Bridge to port and starboard.

Engine Room – where the real action is and the absolute most important place on the ship.

Dining Room or Officers Mess – where we hopefully are going to choke down the food, maybe even tasty at times.

Galley – where the above is prepared.

Companionways/hallways – where we walk from one place to another. Hallways, in my vernacular.

Starboard – right-hand side of the ship looking forward. Even looking backward, starboard is the same side.

Port – left hand side of ship looking forward. Even looking backward, port is the same side.

Bow – the pointy end where the ship comes together in front.

Stern or beam – the blunt end where the ship comes together in back.

Forward – anything in front of the superstructure.

Aft (abaft) – anything in back of the superstructure.

Main mast – the pole sticking up above the Bridge where all the necessary flags and clanking gadgets that sometimes replace flags are affixed.

Forward mast – the pole sticking up on the pointy end. Normally has a nice light attached, called the steering light, which all good seafarers naysay and vow they never use. (Oh, puulleezze use it!)

Cabotage – sailing between points in the same country, say, Valencia to Barcelona.

Pilot – that guy who comes out to the ship in a tiny fancy or rickety boat in all weather to guide your ship into port, normally coming aboard by climbing the rope ladder hanging over the side of the bouncing ship and arriving on the Bridge as if from a fancy ball. He has an intimate knowledge of the harbor and its entrance and his guidance is required in every port in the world. Snacks for this vaunted presence are advised. But Captain is not under the control of Pilot. No, no, no. Captain is always responsible for his ship. Except in one place.

Agent – the guy on land that brokers all cargo and arranges everything for the ship while in port.

Bunkering – taking on fuel, whether heavy fuel or diesel. Delivered via bunker barge in port.

Bilge barge – that floating sewer that pumps bilge from ship's tanks and takes it away. I've often wondered where. Dumping most sewage into the sea is verboten, although the list of what can and cannot be dumped is somewhat iffy.

Chandler – the guy who supplies all foodstuffs and other incidentals to ships. In the beginning of time, chandlers were actually candle-makers and supplied only candles. They branched out over time, and today can supply practically anything a ship requires.

Stores – food and where it is kept onboard.

Provisions – food and other things used onboard.

Slopshop – a kind of canteen open to crew and passengers on a fixed schedule, say, once a week for an hour, where specialty snacks and beer can be purchased by crew and booze by passengers, if any.

Force 1-12 – the height of waves and roughness of seas. '1' being glassy calm and '12' being fifty-two-foot-and-above waves, actually knowing no height limits, capable of wiping out entire large islands.

That's part of it. Tonight I'll learn bunches more. And every day thereafter. Gonna have fun, MsSelf, lots of fun and learn a lot. Captain still hasn't shown. Hope this isn't a bad omen.

Dressed casually in slacks and a cashmere sweater, I present myself in the Dining Room at 5:30 on the dot, ready to meet the gang. Except there is no one there. I stand uncertainly in the middle of the room until Alex comes bustling in.

"Mum, you sit here at Captain's table," and he sweeps his arm with a great flourish, smiling importantly. "Here, here is a nice seat for you, Mum. Captain sits right across from you, Chief Engineer next to him, then Chief Officer between him and you, Mum. To your right, there are two empty chairs, one that should be for 2nd Off…, for guests," he giggles. *Ah yes, where the other non-existent passengers would sit.*

"I see. Thank you, Alex."

"And thank you too, Mum. Will you start dinner?"

"No, I'll wait a bit." And I do as the minutes tick by. We're in port, everybody's very busy.

At last, Chief Engineer arrives, bows slightly and slowly seats himself, pulling the chair to some precise spot in his mind, arranging his long, fit body just so in the chair. He scrutinizes the table setting, the army of condiments grouped in the middle, fidgets once more to align himself with the physical attributes of the chair, sits absolutely erect, nods, then raises his eyes to mine. "Good evening and welcome aboard. Shall we begin?" He smiles slightly, lips barely pulled back, the light never reaching his eyes, indicating the forthcoming adventure will not be to his taste. The food or me I can't fathom. But I am so entranced with the seating performance, I can barely respond.

"Shouldn't we wait for Captain and First Officer?"

"I think not." Then he parrots my earlier thoughts, "We are in port. Everyone is busy." I am fascinated by his precise speech, English perfect but with a definite, very pleasant accent.

The door bursts open, and four young men come in, jabbering loudly in a language I cannot detect. They spy me and their laughter and talking cease. They parade by me and sit at the far table against the wall.

No introductions, but obviously officers of some rank, although their clothes are rumpled and not too clean. *Oh dear, more Other comparisons.*

Chief Engineer makes no move at introductions, and, although I know I should go over and introduce myself, I find their blatant stares with giggling asides to one another, off-putting, hostile, and I don't move. Although I nod and smile at them, they simply nod and continue staring. I hear a hushed, "A woman! My God, a woman!"

I turn my attention to Chief Engineer as the food arrives, and we begin a desultory conversation about ship facts. He seems reluctant to release this precious information into my incapable hands. "How many horsepower is the engine?" I ask.

"1.36 times 12,000." What? Tonnes or ? I wait for horsepower and receive none.

"Something less than 17,000 horsepower, Chief?" *Now, Chief, why couldn't you have figured that for me.* He nods blandly, but looks at me sharply. *What's the matter? I can multiply.*

"How fast can we go?"

"Sixteen knots maximum."

"Sixteen knots!" Then, I boast of The Other's 55,000 horsepower and twenty-six knots maximum. "That's for a ship over 300 meters long." Immediately, I clamp my mouth shut. Although Chief Engineer's eyebrows rise dramatically and he looks impressed, I chastise myself for talking about The Other yet again.

Over barely warm chicken thigh (yuck), tepid boiled potatoes, green peas like BBs, cold conglomeration of onions and canned mushrooms, toasted white Wonder bread and tasteless cheese, Chief Engineer and I struggle with conversation, where I finally pry out of him that ship's officers are Polish and Romanian with one Filipino officer, the deck crew Filipino.

"On a German ship?" I ask, puzzled.

Well, it is a sort of German ship. Huh? – but I don't ask. Okaaay. Food's the same – shitty.

Finally, I put down my fork and ask, "Is your food warm? Mine is ice-cold."

He regards me sternly, then surprisingly bursts out laughing. "Yes, Madam, to use your expression, ice-cold." I guess the Captain/Cook issue cannot be resolved, and Chief Engineer confirms that with his next sentence. "We shall have a new cook tomorrow. We can only hope for improvement."

"Amen to that." And we both laugh (which draws keen attention from the other table), the ice broken at last.

Four more young men enter and sit at the next table with no acknowledgement to anyone. Chief Engineer eyes them but says nothing.

"My God, how many officers do you have on this ship?"

"Oh they are not our officers. They are a part of the team sent by the shipbuilder to address any final problems before the ship is out of warranty. You see, this Polish ship," he sits up straighter, if this is possible, "is one year old and will pass out of warranty next week. We really do not have any problems, just some machinery to be replaced. They joined us here in Valencia and will travel with us to Italy, during which time we will accomplish all."

No problems? What does one call 'machinery that must be replaced?' I look around the dull, plastic Dining Room and speculate that this piece of crap will never be around long enough to be called 'a jolly old tub.' It's only a year old and could be easily mistaken for a well-used ship. John Glenn's quip made when a reporter asked him how it felt to be the first man to ride in the nosecone of a space rocket jumps into my head. "How would you feel to be the first man ever into space, riding in the nosecone of a rocket built by the lowest bidder?" This ship reeks of lowest bidder – minus.

Two more young men come in, look around, see Chief Engineer and sit at our table. More of the warranty team, I presume. One sits in Captain's chair. I open my mouth to point it out, but Chief Engineer smiles at me slyly and turns to ask the young man a question. *Well, hmm.*

The Dining Room, which has so recently been like a tomb, except for the giggles and smirks directed at me from the other table, is now a beehive of conversation. No laughter, I note. Surreptitious, astonished glances at me are delivered from each new arrival. Still no introductions and few smiles.

The Dining Room door swings open with a loud bang, and a very short, rotund, but heavily muscled man enters, his face stern, a mask of displeasure. Fifty-ish, a shock of gray hair, huge bristling mustache with eyebrows to match. Our Captain, I presume?

He glances around the room, glaring at each set of startled eyes, then turns in my direction, his runty, sausage legs in tight, dirty white jeans propelling him toward me. I stand.

"Welcome aboard. I am The Captain, and my name is Romick Kzzzzzzkkkk (a buzzing sound, which I cannot make out.) In a harsh bark, "You won't be able to pronounce my last name."

"Shall I call you Captain, then?"

"No, Romick."

Really! I think not, but utter not a sound.

He shakes my hand, his hand hard underneath, but soft on the surface. Once a wrestler, perhaps, for his head sprouts directly from his muscled shoulders. On second glance, he was and is a street fighter, a groin kicker, without the discipline of a wrestler, but the requisite to defend his short stature.

"I hope you are enjoying your food."

"It's okay, but cold." Heedless of my reply, he looks beyond me to the next table and mumbles he hopes I will enjoy the ship.

"Oh, I shall, Captain." Our exchange is followed with utmost interest by all fellow diners, their eyes never leaving us.

He regards the two young men sitting at our table with distaste, and I wait for the explosion at the one sitting in his chair. Nothing. The one in his chair desultorily says he will move. Don't bother, Captain has business at the next table. Holy cow! I can't believe this whole scenario of sloth and disrespect.

Indeed, Mr. Captain does have business at the next table. Much angry conversation as he discusses in loud, caustic tones, both in Polish and English, the ship's problems. "I cannot be responsible for that and will not be," he shouts. "Everything I've done has been right - by the book. This Master has done nothing wrong. This Master knows vessels."

Most of the Dining Room denizens sit in utter silence as the tirade runs on, although the two very angry team members, recipients of this hollering, retort, hard-faced, bristling but determined, trying to keep control. Something very bad is going on here. Why is Captain making this scene in the Dining Room; why not the Engine Room, Visitors Lounge or Bridge where it is appropriate?

No time for a lowly passenger now. In the midst of his next outburst, accompanied by a banging fist on the table, I give a brief wave to Chief Engineer. He glances at me sorrowfully – embarrassed, his color high – ashamed, barely nods and looks down at the table. While the men are riveted on the wild exchange being played out before them, I make a fast exit out the still-open door into the hallway. *Whee! Are we having fun yet?* My heart is pounding, and I, too, feel embarrassed for this wild man, whose suddenly vicious language echoes in the hallway.

Get out of here, and I literally run through the hallway and up the stairwell, smack into a tall, lanky, overgrown boy with an unruly thatch of black hair standing on end, wearing a striped T-shirt under bib overalls. A happy smile lights a smooth, nearly vacant face. *Why is everyone on this ship so young?*

"Hi, I'm Roberto, the electrician."

"We didn't see you at dinner," I croak.

"Nope. Couldn't make it. Busy."

"Be glad for that," I mumble.

"What?"

"Nothing. I'm Cari Lindley, the passenger."

"Do you want to see the laundry?"

"Laundry? Well, I've already… Sure, why not?"

"It's right here. I just fixed the washer, you see. Always breaking down. Lots of trouble."

"No dryer, I see," for the second time that day.

"Oh sure, we've got a dryer," and he propels me down three stairwells to the Main Deck, then to a stairwell just opposite the Officers' Mess, where the door is thankfully closed, but anger can be heard spewing behind it. Roberto's smile vanishes, and he looks at the door apprehensively. *Scared*, I think, but his smile reappears as we descend to what I remembered was the Engine Room (and Hobby Room) stairway and along the hallway to the steward's washroom.

"Here's our dryer," he says happily. "Mornings are best."

"A long way to lug a load of laundry, my friend." And I make a mental note that lots of hand-washing will be in my future. "By the way, I presume there are outside stairways from the Main Deck to the bridgewings? I haven't been to the Bridge yet, but somehow missed seeing the stairways when I came in."

"Oh sure, come on." He steps into the hallway, then suddenly stops, gazing fearfully down the hallway to the stairs, which will deposit us just outside the Dining Room door.

"Do you want me to go by myself? You could stay here, you know. Maybe hang out in the Hobby Room for a while." I see him debating the merits of my suggestion. Then he straightens and walks purposefully toward the stairs. The shouting from inside the closed Dining Room door has changed to an angry buzzing, but we hurry by the safely closed door as he glances furtively at me. I smile weakly. *Why is he so frightened?*

I walk up and down the outside stairs, crossing the open bridgewing to the Bridge, remembering as I try the door handle that the Bridge is always locked in port. Moving fast on slippery, cleated outside stairs, staying well away from the working cranes, stinging rain soaking me, I am at last calm. A hot shower is in order, then maybe a nap until unberthing, a nebulous time somewhere between midnight and 2 AM. But before the nap, I'll just peek at the Bridge - have to know how to get there at the appointed wee hour.

First Officer is on the Bridge, busy with charts. He greets me curtly. I want to tell him that he really missed a scene in the Dining Room, but hold my tongue. He'd probably tell me to mind my own business, which I certainly intend to do.

I glance around the scaled-down version of The Other, which was luxurious and reeking of dollar signs. This is plain and reeks of saving dollars, but has all the important equipment. The Bridge is where I want to be. I can put up with monochromatic dining rooms, drab cabins, bathtub pools and many inconveniences; they are not important. This expanse of windows, computers and radar screens is why I'm here. The Bridge. Hopefully I will ride along on it with the same pleasure as I rode on The Other. After a cursory stroll from port to starboard in utter silence, I simply leave, no good-bye, nothing. Two can play the silent game.

Goodnight, MarkShip Mexico. Goodnight, and I hope I will be awake in time for sailing. Surely I will feel the engine start. No one said they would call me as I was used to on The...no! Why would they? The Powers-That-Be have barely spoken to me. *But it's OK – give it time. I've done this before. Time.*

As I drift off to sleep, I remember I am still in possession of my ticket and passport. Guess they don't need it for the authorities. It also occurs to me that Roberto never asked me what was going on behind the Dining Room door. Never mind, he, like First Officer, will know nearly every word in record time. The Jungle Drums are very timely on a ship. *Lordy, what have I got here?*

CHAPTER FIVE

The Bridge

Monday, October 23. The Mediterranean

The rumble of engine and whine of mechanism reeling in berthing ropes awaken me at 2 AM. It's dark and cold, and I wonder whether I should really present myself on the Bridge without Captain's express permission. I smoke and watch the tug pull us away from the dock. *To hell with it, I'm going to the Bridge.*

The narrow silent stairwell to the Bridge is illuminated sufficiently by a caged yellow overhead bulb to easily read the large red-lettered No Admittance sign. Standing on the small top landing, I take a deep breath and yank hard on the vacuum door, holding its inside handle so it will click only softly. I needn't have bothered. No one turns around, and the exchange between men on the Bridge and radio covers all. Captain calls the headings, and Helmsman, both hands on the surprisingly small wheel, turns it a tad, repeating.

"081."

"081 suh."

"Dead slow."

"Dead slow, suh."

"082 midship."

"082 midship, suh."

I would normally position myself next to the black-curtained Chart Room, where I know 2nd Officer is hand-charting every foot of ship's movement, but now I dart far to port on the darkened Bridge, illumined only by outside distant harbor lights, control panels and radar glowing eerily green.

Captain, First Officer, 2nd Officer, Helmsman and Pilot are in attendance. I stand in the dark, watching MarkShip Mexico slowly propel forward. Pilot is off before we even reach the heads, and we pick up speed.

First Officer stands without speaking or moving, legs apart, hands behind his back in the standard sailor's stance, a luminous green statue in the radar's reflected light.

Captain rushes back and forth between his chair near the middle of the deck and starboard, then back across the Bridge to a control panel covered with buttons near me, calling coordinates and mumbling, loudly but incoherently. Back and forth, trying to give the impression of great responsibility, but appearing frazzled. *Such frenzied activity*, I think, used to slow movement and clipped instructions on the Bridge in port. *Maybe he is working off the hyper-energy induced by his earlier pyrotechnic display.*

Finally, after we've left the heads, he acknowledges me. "Who is it?"

"Captain, First Officer said I could be on the Bridge for unberthing. I hope it is all right."

"Sure, and you're welcome to be here." Very laid back and I breathe a sigh of relief. We ride along in silence, watching the giant windshield wipers scrape away the rain, peering into the black sea.

2nd Officer snaps off the light, opens the Chart Room blackout curtains and steps around the enclosure that looks ever so much like a bar, complete with a couple of high stools.

"So," Captain says to him with scathing sarcasm, "your friend, the cook, left tonight. We have been missing lots of provisions, lots."

2nd Officer, whom I can barely distinguish on the darkened Bridge, but I know to be Filipino and who prefers to eat with the crew (*now where did I pick up that info?*), says not a word, simply seats himself in front of one of the radar screens and stares into it.

"Yes, lots of provisions," Captain chuckles. "What you think, huh, Ion?" he asks First Officer.

First Officer continues to stand unmoving and does not answer. A few minutes later, I look around, and he has left, surprisingly without a word of farewell or instruction, followed shortly by Captain, who also vanishes without a word. *How odd! The departing officer always wishes the one on duty "A safe/good watch." It is a courtesy of the sea.*

I don't move from my dark port position, but ride along silently for fifteen minutes, watching the sea, feeling resentment and anger emanating from 2ⁿᵈ Officer. I want to chat with him, find out about him, somehow lighten his load, but dare not. The stony silence previously between the three officers leaves me unnerved.

"Good night, 2ⁿᵈ Officer, have a safe watch." I head for the inside door.

"Thank you." He sounds startled, at my words or simply my being there I cannot tell. "Yes, thank you."

I'm in bed again by 4 AM.

At 9 AM by my trusty travel clock, which, thankfully, was in my luggage since nothing resembling the luxury of a clock resides in my cubicle, uh, cabin, I awake to cloudy skies and heavy swells, ship rolling.

Starving, I run down for coffee and breakfast, only to find I am too late. Alex delivers the official spiel: Breakfast at 0730 to 0830. If I am too late, he will bring me a thermos of hot water to which I can add instant coffee that is in a drawer in my cabin.

Mindful of Alex's Herculean schedule, "No, you need not bring it up. I will come down and get it. I'm sometimes on the Bridge until very late, you know, for berthing and unberthing. Thank you, Alex." *Why do I think he already knows where I've been?*

"And thank you too, Mum. Would you like to meet the new cook?"

And how! "Yes, Alex, very much." He smiles and dances ahead of me through the galley door.

"And thank you too, Mum."

Cristori is a small, trim Filipino, maybe 40, clad in a sparkling white smock and full of friendly smiles.

"We re-provisioned from the ship's chandler in Valencia, and I will have many nice things for you to eat." *Well, thanks to all the gods.* "I was a chef on cruise ships – Princess Cruises."

"Really! My husband and I cruised often on Princess." We are both delighted with our new-found link and chat amiably about the Princess Line.

"I am very good cook, Mum. You will see."

"I can't wait," wishing he'd give me a taste of something right now. Never mind, I have snacks in my cabin. Long ago, a traveler's need for nibbles was impressed upon me, and I am never without some goodie in my ditty bag, however humble.

After yucky instant coffee in my cabin, I attempt to exercise for the first time in two months, the result sadly lacking. Tomorrow will be better. I must still be weak from the Coimbra fever. If only I could rid myself of this constant tiredness and hot, red eyelids – plus lined washed-out face. *You're a mess, MsSelf, face it.*

A knock on the door and Abey, an able-bodied seaman, requests my passport. *Better late than never. Maybe Barcelona officials are more picky than Valencia's.*

Heavy spray on deck, which rides low in the water, makes walking there impossible. Maybe we took on enough cargo in Valencia to pay the bills – and hopefully not sink. So I run up and down the outside stairs, ignoring my protesting body and the hostile stares of the deck crew working on top and around the boxes, their bodies stiffening as they regard me.

What is SHE doing on our ship?

Stopping at last on the Bridge, I meet 3rd Officer.

"Please don't call me 3rd Officer, Mrs. Lindley. Call me Marius."

This makes me edgy since my personal rule is to address officers by their ranks, not their names. Something about using a first name implies a closeness that I don't want on a ship with twenty-two men, and I say so.

"Ah, Mrs. Lindley, I understand your position with regard to the higher ranking officers. Although I take my responsibilities on this vessel very seriously, I am but 3rd Officer and your constant repetition of '3rd Officer' would only serve to remind me of my, shall we say, lowly position. Everyone calls me Marius because I request it. It is who I am, who I wish to be. It would please me greatly if you would call me Marius also."

He smiles appealingly, and I cave, knowing I've been sucker-punched, but not seeing an easy way out.

Reluctantly, I acquiesce. "Okay, then call me Cari."

"Deal." He feels my hesitancy, but rubs his broken-nailed hands together as if he were shaking my hand to seal a pact.

Not a bit shipshape, so to speak, his tall, powerful, oddly out-of-shape body dressed as though just of out of bed in rumpled faded Levis, clean T-shirt advertising some product tucked in, he keeps pushing long stringy black hair off his face that sports a rubble of black beard and penetrating black eyes.

He is very friendly, for which I am VERY grateful, and we chat about inane things, those black eyes alert to all gadgets and dials. He has a most interesting, insightful way of expressing himself, and I wonder what really lies behind this rambling wreck that would have driven a furious Capt. R. on The Other to disgustedly send him below for shower, shave, press and polish.

I seat myself casually in the Captain's chair and put my feet up on the slender rod in front of the radar screen.

Marius looks amused. "You've done this before, I see. Perhaps, often."

"What? Oh, sitting in the Captain's chair." I remove my feet from the rod.

He laughs. "Putting your feet up is very little to what I believe should transpire with regard to this Cap..." He looks away, then points out an interesting swell. "That one will move us a lot when we cross her." And she does, the ship bouncing over the wave with many a creak and groan.

"I didn't see you at dinner last night," wondering if he will refer to what he has surely heard of last night's fracas in the Dining Room.

"No, I rarely take my dinner in the Officers Mess, preferring the solitude of dining alone in my cabin. My books make much better company."

"Aha! We will miss your pithy comments."

He smiles and adjusts a knob.

CHAPTER SIX

They Hate Me

Now begins a parade of folks appearing on the Bridge, lounging about. The Jungle Drums beat out, reverberating throughout the ship: Meet the freak.

With perfect cordiality, Marius, obviously well-liked and enjoying his role as ringmaster, calls each over and presents each to me. They regard me askance, eyes hard and wary, treating my hand as if it were a viper.

A Woman! Even worse, An American! Aboard our ship. Scarcely polite, their rigid body language says it all. "How did we get saddled with this monstrosity?"

Trying to maintain my cool, I greet each with as much aplomb as I can muster. *Why don't they just holler out their wrath to the scudding clouds – or to my face?* No, their closed faces and barely touching fingers tell it all – "We don't want you here." *Now, have I met them all? More to the point, how did they all get away from their jobs?* Even Bosun, Helmsman and a couple other 'privileged' deck crew are allowed on the Bridge for this circus. And I had thought I was going to pop in for a few minutes to meet the duty officer after a brisk stair-climb.

After the parade leaves, I jump up and start dejectedly toward the bridgewing door.

"Please acknowledge, Cari, that we are unused to passengers. Some of these people have been on board on continuing contracts for nearly a year and have rarely been exposed to anyone outside their workmates. Please try to understand our quirks as we will yours."

"They really hate me, don't they?"

He sits back abruptly in his chair. "No, not hate. 'Don't understand' is more precise. Your presence here is much more than they can deal with. A woman? Their women are safely at home with the babies, always ready and willing to receive the breadwinner when he struts triumphantly home, not sailing with them on treacherous seas. An American? Most have only heard about Americans, never actually met one. Everything evil to them is American. They've been taught that under Communism, you know, and not that many years have passed since those people ruled us. We are all Eastern Bloc people who have spent most, if not all, of our lives under the repressive boot of the Communists. We are just now figuring out how to live comfortably with the rest of the world." He shakes his head as if he wants to disbelieve his own words.

"You won't find that so with the Filipino deck crew. They are more used to American ideas. Yet, they, too, have spent contract after contract on board, don't really know Americans and are very suspicious of a woman traveling alone. Not in their culture, either. However, if you can get 2nd Officer, who is Filipino, to talk to you, you will find him well-educated, urbane and very interesting."

I fidget under this barrage of information while he stares out to sea. Then he adds with great solemnity and a hint of warning, "You also must take into account the Superstitions of the Sea. I believe you are probably aware of some. They are to be reckoned with at every turn, taken very seriously on board a ship. Perhaps we can review them sometime in the future."

"Ah, Marius, you are a wizard with the English language. I look forward to seeing you and riding with you again." I wave my arm at the Bridge expanse. "Thanks for all of this."

He smiles, sweeping lank hair off his forehead, pleased with my compliment. "Please, ah, ride, yes, ride with me any time. You know my watch."

I trudge down the stairs, marveling at Marius' insight and use of the English language. What other astonishments hide behind that crude exterior? Why don't I - and the preponderance of my American and Canadian friends - speak such lovely, interesting English as Marius and Chief Engineer?

Lunch is taken with Chief Engineer only. No Captain or First Officer. I don't know where they eat, but sure as hell not with me. Bony fish is accompanied by a few miniscule potatoes, ten peas and an apple, barely ample to chase away the hunger pains. So much for the culinary skills of the new cook. Perhaps he has not yet dug into the new provisions taken on in Valencia. Nobody is going to get fat on this ship, except maybe me with my stash of shore goodies, about to be augmented in Barcelona this afternoon.

When Chief Engineer enters, he greets me, performs his fascinating seating ritual, then announces, "You must call me Stan."

Astonished, I manage, "Well, Chief Engineer, I kind of have a personal rule that I call officers by their titles. It seems so much easier that way."

"Of course, I am sympathetic to your preferences. But, if you can refer to one officer by his first name, your rule is broken, and it follows that you allow yourself to call others by their given names. You are calling the 3rd Officer Marius, are you not? Therefore, I am Stanislaus - Polish, of course, shortened to Stan."

I stare at him, open-mouthed. The Marius business had transpired barely an hour ago. He is amused by my amazement, but valiantly tries to hide it.

Trapped, I close my fly-catching mouth, rearrange myself in my chair and say, "Stan," and I dip my head, "you must then call me Cari."

"Perfect. Shall we lunch?" We chat about the ship and do not touch on yesterday's debacle played out only feet from where we now sit. He watches me closely to see if I will bring it up. I do not, although I certainly want to.

Stan eats very properly, in an almost finicky manner, knife and fork softly clinking in perfect cadence. His table manners are exquisite, and his elegant long fingers with buffed nails hold the knife and fork at a precise angle, no doubt taught at his Countess mother's knee. Every bite is chewed well, and he never opens his mouth to speak until every crumb has cleared his throat. Occasionally, he stops his fork in mid-air to eye that which he is about to put in his mouth, a perplexed look on his face as though he cannot ascertain whether this is the bite that will put him beneath the sod or whether, in fact, that which the fork holds is actually edible. It is quite a production, and I bite my lip to keep from giggling.

I wonder what he eats at home in Poland. I must ask him sometime in the future.

In the hallway, I meet Captain. "Good afternoon, Captain. We missed you at lunch."

"Mmmph. Yes. Good afternoon." His wrinkled pants and shirt with a large tear in the sleeve match his mood.

"We'll be in Barcelona soon, I guess. Will it be OK for me to be on the Bridge for berthing?"

"Yes, of course," he answers, irritation bristling. "I'll also arrange with the agent for you to go into Barcelona, if you want."

"Wow, that would be great."

"Umhmm. And I should probably have your ticket." He walks away, his gait an odd mixture of mincing and strutting, upper body slightly forward, chin jutting. *Spoiling for a fight. Oh dear, and I had so hoped for friendly folks.*

Misty Barcelona comes into view at 1300. We slow for Pilot to board, turning partially broadside to the wind to create a lee for the pilot boat. I run out to the bridgewing to lean way out and watch him transfer from his bobbing, forward-moving pilot boat to the rope ladder hanging over the side of our ship. The sea swells, and he nearly misses his grip as the ladder swings far out from the ship, then he climbs it like a monkey, sure-handed and –footed. I am always in awe that such a feat can be accomplished in perilous as well as calm seas by pilots of all ages, some nearly as old as me.

I had inquired more than once before about such a risky business and was informed, rather smugly, that it was a tradition of the sea and was unlikely to change. But, in Tokyo Bay, a helicopter delivers pilots to ships big enough to receive them (and willing to pay extra). Yet, I suppose, in really bad weather, the traditional pilot boat would be employed, incredibly dangerous or not.

Once in Malaysia, a typhoon threatening, I had grudgingly been allowed to don a large yellow slicker and follow 3rd Officer down to the Main Deck into the wild storm to watch from a relatively safe haven as he helped guide Pilot, swinging out over the sea as if on a trapeze, to safety, all of us hanging on for dear life against the pitching ship, the gale and driving rain. An experience I never begged for again.

It doesn't make any difference how they get there, no port in the world allows a ship to approach and enter the harbor without a pilot aboard to direct the visiting ship through the treacheries lurking both above and below the restless sea. Although heeded carefully by Captains, Pilot is NOT in charge of the ship while aboard, Captain is. Rarely are there disagreements, but when they occur, it is not a pleasant sight.

I watch the whole berthing procedure.

"Steady 080."

"Steady 080, suh."

"Stop engine."

"Engine stopped."

"Starboard 20."

"Starboard 20, suh."

"Dead slow."

"Dead slow, suh."

"Midship."

"Midship, suh."

"Hard on starboard."

"Hard on starboard, suh."

"Dead slow astern."

"Dead slow astern, suh."

"Shore crew stand by fore and aft."

We are berthed at 1400, the tugs pushing us snugly into what appears to be an undersized space. During that time, Captain, still dressed in the torn shirt, comes over to my perch well out of the way and asks if I've been to Barcelona before and how I like Spain.

I ask him why so many ships were anchored in the roads; he shrugs carelessly, mumbling, I think, that he doesn't know, then abruptly walks away. *Well, at least we've spoken a few words.*

A nice snooze will kill some time while the agent, port authorities and other mucky-mucks, who regularly come on board, complete their business.

Two hours later, I am still awaiting word of the agent's ride into town. Nada. At last, seething, I go down to the Main Deck and find Captain talking to a tight-lipped, disgusted man in the Visitors Lounge, a very small cubicle housing a cramped conference table and chairs. A spindly table beside the door barely supports three large, brown paper-wrapped boxes, taped and tied with string, addressed, I briefly note, to Hannah K. somewhere in Poland. They are talking rapidly in Spanish, and I catch only a few words, "Send today. Bill the ship. I take responsibility."

The man steps to the table and lifts the top box with a grunt. "Muy pesada." Sure looks heavy, and he looks very unhappy, but picks up the first box and staggers out the Hatchcover door. Must be important stuff.

I clear my throat, and Captain jumps. "Ride to town, Captain?" I say tightly.

"Oh. Agent is busy now and can't take you. Get your passport from Chief Officer and walk into town – only a short walk." *Great! I could have done that an hour ago.*

Stepping to First Officer's office next door, I ask for my passport.

"No ride with the agent into town, hmm?" he asks as he warily watches the unhappy man cart another heavy box past his door. "Never mind, there's a van to pick up two signing-off technicians. You can ride to town with them, but you're going to have to get a cab or walk back."

"Fine," I snap and extend my hand for my passport. He takes it out of the drawer and is about to hand it to me when his total attention is drawn again to the unhappy man carrying the third box.

"So, it's three today," he mutters, pulls down a yellow pad, notes "Barcelona – 3" and hands me the passport, his face a sudden mask of impatience and anger, turning away abruptly. *Oh lovely, more good times on Markship Mexico. But, at least the rain has stopped.*

The technicians and I wait interminably for the van. I try to chat but am unable to break through their obvious distaste for me. Their excitement at being off Markship Mexico makes me smile in spite of their stinging animosity. At last, riding in the van, I try to identify terminal landmarks for my return walk, noting especially our position to the low castle spreading across the escarpment above the city.

The van drops me in front of a small supermercado, where I intend to spend my leftover 3,000 pesetas on vodka, Scotch, chocolate and cookies, since the ship provides no dessert. Lack of dessert is a usual occurrence on a freighter, but the palate sometimes appreciates a little sweet with an after-dinner drink. The crowded, dirty market reeks of salted mackerel, huge boxes of which I locate in back near the meat market. It reminds me of an evil-smelling stew that a French Canadian was brewing over a campfire in Nova Scotia. To my inquiry, he said it was mawk-aw-roh. Yup, it was mackerel, all right.

Maybe for the first time ever in my many travels, I have no wish to explore a city. I'm done with Spain and its many marvels and want only to return to the ship. Walking the short distance to the terminal, lugging my grocery sacks, I worry that the cool but very close weather will become rain again before I get home.

Through the terminal gate with little difficulty, I dodge trucks and spreaders. The drivers look at me as if an alien from outer space. What's this blond doing in the busiest part of the terminal? I try to appear nonchalant, but also ask myself what the hell I am doing here, since I'm very lost. At last, a person afoot appears near an important-looking building. He whisks me inside, looks very amused while making rapid telephone calls, then points me to MarkShip Mexico, which is close enough for both of us to spit on. We have a good laugh while I relate my freighter adventure to his interested, amazed face.

"Si', soy una pasajera en el barco, rumbo a Veracruz, Mexico. Vamos a llegar en un mes, mas o menos. No, no problemas con los trabajadores en el barco. Son muy amables. Gracias, mil gracias, senor. Adios." What a story he has for his wife over dinner about the lady who is a passenger for a month on a freighter bound for Veracruz, who says the twenty-two male workers on the boat are very nice.

I make it on board just in time for a drink and dinner, which is taken alone in a vacant Dining Room, except for Alex, who bounces and smiles while we chat. He is thirty-six years old (but looks fifteen), Filipino with two kids, the first one a mistake which made him get married, which he guesses is all right. Perhaps that's more information than I needed. He thinks I'm thirty-eight or -nine. *Wow! He needs eyeglasses or is a very good fibber.*

"Thanks, Alex."

"And thank you too, Mum." *What a sweetie! Must remember a good tip for him.*

Midway through dinner, the door bursts open and in breezes a young man, rosy cheeked, blue-eyed, a shock of blond hair falling onto his forehead and a shy grin.

"May I sit with you?" I nod, and he chooses First Officer's chair. "I'm Adam, here to introduce the Internet to your computers and having a heck of a time since a lot of screwing up has gone on in the past year with those computers."

"I'm Cari, a passenger."

"Passenger? Didn't know these ships took passengers. Who'd want to ride around on this thing? Yes, well, of course, you do." He laughs with me.

Adam is a breath of fresh air, blowing straight ahead and fast. "I'm a Manxman, from the Isle of Man, a Manxman. Have you ever heard of Manx cats? They're from my home, an island thirty-six miles long and about fifteen miles wide. Seventy thousand people, 130 of whom speak Manx fluently and seven, no eleven, golf courses. Cold all year, although no snow, just freezing wet wind off the North Sea. Manx is a Gaelic language, kind of a cross between Irish and Scottish Gaelic, although its origin is Irish. Some people say it sounds like Russian spoken backwards."

He stops and looks at the plate Alex has set in front of him, and I try to catch my breath, fascinated by both man and speech. Alex stands rooted to the spot, mouth agape, as he listens to this exuberant, bubbling fountain of information. I smile at him, he dips his head and grins back.

Then Adam plunges on between bites, words tumbling over each other. "Few people really speak Manx all the time, although many use some of it. English is the language of choice and even it is spoken in a kind of shorthand. A few English words, depending on how they are spoken, mean a whole bunch of stuff."

"Like what? Give me an example." He looks suddenly unhappy. "Come on, just one example."

"OK, don't know why my mind is suddenly blank, but here's a weak one. 'It's not a fair day.' That means, with just the right inflection, 'It's not nice outside now, but it will be nice later on.' Well, I'd better hurry up and eat, I've got five hours to get these computers rolling – and what a mess."

"Then I'll leave you, darling young man, to your dinner." He grins happily.

"But you must visit The Isle of Man, Cari. June, I think, is the best month. You can visit all the golf courses, five castles, many one-lane roads and fascinating museums. You are sure to enjoy it. And we're sure to enjoy having you."

"I will. Nice to meet you, Mr. Manxman, Adam. Good luck." He wriggles with pleasure.

And I'm very sure to enjoy my visit if every Manxman is as delightful as this one. Not an evil or self-serving bone in his cute young body. Boy, I've never met a Manxman before and sure did like what I saw. *Isle of Man here I come. Well, maybe not. Remember that cold wet wind from The North Sea?*

The weather has turned balmy, and I have a go at the outside stairs

"Sailing," says Roberto, whom I meet at a turn on one of the upper decks, "somewhere around 2300." *Gadzooks, this guy is everywhere.*

Maybe I'll have a nap so I can be on the Bridge at 2300. This is the loosest ship. The person who seems to know the most is Roberto, the electrician. Everybody else kind of shrugs.

We say adios to Barcelona at 2300, sea calm, stars peeking through clouds. Everything goes without a hitch. Captain, First Officer, 2nd Officer, Helmsman, Pilot and I are on the Bridge. Less helter-skelter than during berthing, Captain is calmer, in fact, quite crisp and nautical. First Officer speaks in clipped phrases only to answer questions, and 2nd Officer speaks not at all. It is an odd feeling to know that they have to be working together to unberth this mammoth ship, yet rarely speak to each other. *Whatever is going on?*

The radio squawks in what I know is English, although it is barely discernable, and Captain and Pilot exchange coordinates, as do Captain and Helmsman, in English. All communication on the Bridge and between port and ship, in fact, even between ships must be in English. Sometime in the 1950's, in a meeting of all nations of the world, English was selected as the International Language for international transportation (such as ships and airplanes), communication and conferences. The use of any other language carries a heavy fine and dismissal. There is no alternative or excuse. Even the deck crews of all nationalities speak English.

When one considers the safety factor alone, it makes sense that all international workers speak one language. (Although, I'm sure the proliferation of computers was the driving factor.)

A dear friend, whose father worked as an iron miner in the 1930s in Michigan's Upper Peninsula, told me that a huge sign over the dry, the place the dust-covered miners showered and changed clothes after their shifts, proclaimed in two-foot high letters: IF YOU CAN'T SPEAK ENGLISH, LEARN IT. IF YOU CAN'T LEARN IT, GO BACK TO WHERE YOU CAME FROM.

My friend, a little boy at the time, knew that his neighbors were miners from all parts of the world and thought the sign very harsh and rude. One day he said just that to his father, who sat his small son down and explained, "For the men working 1,000 feet below, the smallest problem can turn into disaster if those men can't understand each other. It's not harsh and rude, son, it is essential for our safety in that very dangerous place that we all speak the same language."

And so with ships and planes.

First Officer and Captain wordlessly disappear shortly after Pilot-off. I ride silently along with 2nd Officer, trying a few words here and there with little result, certainly nothing to tell me who this guy is: His life, his hopes, his dreams, or even his name. How strange to think of The Other where Pilot-off meant we were off to romp on the open sea, the rigid port formalities of the Bridge banished, and conviviality flourished amongst the Bridge denizens.

"Good night, 2nd Officer. Have a safe watch."

"Thank you very much. Sleep well."

PART FOUR

JOURNALS

CHAPTER SEVEN

Day by Day

Tuesday, October 24, The Mediterranean.

Lying in bed, focusing on the cloudy sky, I think 'Med' and jump up to find out why we're rolling about. Force 5 seas, maybe Force 6 the waves white-tipped and sea frothy. I force myself to remember the excellent U.S. Coast Guard book on sea forces, complete with pictures of corresponding seas and clouds plus written explanations. Bet that book is on board. I'll look. In the meantime, memory supplies: Force 5. Description: Fresh. Wind speed: 17-21 knots. Sea appearance: 6-8 foot moderate waves. Many white horses. Maybe small spray. Force 6: Description: Strong. Wind speed: 22-27 knots. Sea appearance: 9-13 foot larger waves. Spray. White crests. We're rocking along somewhere in the middle.

Alex is as good as his word again, and the yellow thermos of hot water is outside my door. I must remind him at lunch that I will go down myself for hot water.

Even the instant coffee is beginning to taste OK. After the previous months of early-morning dragging myself down to residencial (Spanish/Portuguese small hotels) breakfast rooms or out onto the street to buy coffee, this hot water thing at my door and instant coffee is just fine, thanks very much.

The day is a bit of blurry disinterest, although I sit at the computer and start my journal, catching up from Valencia. *There will be no more sloth — experiences will be recorded daily. When this voyage is complete, I will have detailed memories of fascinating events and glowing, friendly personalities. Got it, MsSelf?*

I wander up to the Bridge and spend a half-hour kibitzing with Marius, marveling yet again at his turn of phrase as he tells me stories about Romania.

Lunch by myself, nary an officer in view to stare and snigger about the American! Woman! I chat with Alex, remembering to tell him I will come down for hot water in the mornings. "And thank you too, Mum."

Cook still hasn't found the new provisions, although a very large beautifully carved radish resides beside the gruel on my plate. I am delighted and rush into the galley to thank Cristori, who beams at me over a huge, evil-smelling pot of something thick. "The crew's lunch. Very busy now. Will talk later." And I return to my lunch.

By the way, I wonder, *where are those guys from the shipbuilding crew?* They're riding around with us, but sure are invisible in the Dining Room and hallways. Where are they sleeping – the Hobby Room? If they are in passenger cabins on my deck, I hear not one peep or footfall – nor angry shouting reverberating up the stairwells.

No need to exercise this afternoon, since my laundry and its need to be dried sends me scurrying up and down, up and down five decks to the fabled dryer.

Captain, all shiny clean – body and clothes – all hairs in place, is sitting at table when I enter for dinner. Stan appears, also very spiffy -but then, he always is - bowing, and placing himself gingerly beside Captain, nudging his chair inches toward First Officer's chair, who once again is not in attendance.

Our "Good Evenings" accomplished, I say, "You grace our table Captain." He looks non-plussed, and Stan smiles wryly.

Rasping and harsh, he bellows, "Alleexx! bring the wine. NOW." Alex rushes up with the bottle, opens it and stands back at attention. Stan and I glance at each other, while Alex cowers tableside. I try to catch Alex's eye and smile, but he refuses to look at me.

"When Captain is at table, there is wine," Stan remarks. Stan and I lift glasses (Captain declines, "I'm a beer man."), then apply ourselves to the 'old' provisions. I am the only one to have two glasses of wine. I try not to look too dismayed at the food on my plate, which is beautifully presented with yet another carved vegetable, but is tasteless and sparse. Captain eyes me, then looks away.

Although Stan talks directly to me, he rarely talks to Captain, looking somewhat surprised when Captain asks his opinion. He also does an odd edging away, nearly imperceptibly leaning away from Captain, so that his rigidly erect body tilts slightly to the right.

I am fascinated by Stan's perfect manners and his occasional quizzical inspection of the food on his fork contrasted to the hunch-shovel-chew-sprawl-hunch-shovel-chew taking place at Captain's chair, an overflowing forkful disappearing in record time. I am determined to like this man, remembering how I had originally disliked Capt. R. on The Other (and how that changed to admiration and friendship as time passed), and chat brightly of Valencia and Barcelona. *Just getting to know these people, MsSelf, be patient.*

Captain and Stan excuse themselves and adjourn behind the latticework to the Officers Lounge, where their English gives way to Polish, and Mr. Captain drinks beer. I am surprised at such rudeness, but assume that Polish and beer take precedence over passengers. Still, my resoluteness reigns.

On my way out, I stop to thank Captain for the wine and say I hope we can talk soon since I have a million questions. He beckons me to a seat. Before I can start on my questions, Captain says importantly, "I am planning a barbeque for you after Italy."

"Barbeque!" Stan and I say in unison. Stan grins like a kid, his long, mournful face lighting up. *Man oh man, what even the hint of a party can mean to people on board ships for many months.*

"Thank you."

"And you will be receiving wine and fruit in your cabin. Specialty things. Everything for the passenger." His tone is subtly mocking, making me edgy. He opens another bottle of beer, which he has retrieved from a small refrigerator within his reach, and waves it haphazardly in the air.

Stan's grin disappears, and he stands suddenly, excusing himself.

"So soon, Stan. But we're just getting to know our passenger. Come on, stay and have a beer with us. You want to know our passenger, don't you? Don't you?" His tone is sly, rudely suggestive, and I feel uncomfortable.

"Good night," Stan says stiffly and leaves. But angry or not, I know that within the hour the whole ship will know about the planned barbeque.

"No boring questions tonight. Now, don't you go too. Here, finish off this wine. Let me tell you about the stowaway."

"Have you had many stowaways?"

"No." He is irritated at the interruption, but continues, opening another beer. "But this wasn't a regular stowaway, forlorn and scared. No, this guy had two suitcases in very good condition and when he was found between some forward boxes and presented to me, he brazenly told me he wanted something to eat now. But no rice. He refused to eat rice.

"'You refuse to eat rice?'

"'I don't want rice! I won't have it.'"

"'Fine, no rice.' So, he subsisted for three days on water only. I mean, I couldn't let him get away with telling me what to do, how he wanted his meals served, now could I? Not to The Master.

"The problem with stowaways is not so much that they have some-how sneaked on board, have to be guarded, etc., but when you put them off at the next port, there are hundreds of sheets of paperwork. And, worst, the ship pays for his hotel, meals, even pocket money, plus trans-portation for repatriation, in one case $3,500. A few years ago, the annual stowaway cost to owners was over $5 million U.S. Some ports rule that after a ship leaves, stowaways cannot be returned to port. The crew is to inspect the ship and containers before leaving port, otherwise the ship is responsible. What do you think of a system like that?"

"It sucks."

"Well," heh, heh, "I fixed him with the no rice thing, don't you think? He didn't much enjoy the diet of water."

His eyes narrow introspectively, and, in a split-second, his entire demeanor changes from a benign, pudgy teller-of-tales to a seething lump of malevolence. "I can think of some others who would benefit from that." He looks at me with eyes unfocussed, shifting aimlessly in his chair.

Startled, and suddenly scared, I force myself to ask blandly, "Where was this?"

"Not New York or I'd still be filling out paperwork." He is back to the jolly Captain. "But I really like New York, it's my favorite port." And he is off on a litany of the pleasures of New York, opening another beer, making it his sixth since I sat down, and looking bleary. Other ports of choice follow with his strange observations: All the women have frizzy hair. Lots of new cars, but they all need to be washed. Flowers in the parks are all red. Every tall building seems to lean. Too many pink sticky things sold by street vendors. Girls look exactly like their mothers as if they had no fathers to contribute to their looks. No big dogs, only small yapping ones, running everywhere like rats. Girl students are taller than boys. The young women are fat, the old ones skinny.

Now he is leering, and before the discussion further deteriorates, I stagger off to my cabin full of three glasses of wine, passing the barrage of No Liquor or Drugs signs in every stairwell and hallway. I sleep like a log the entire night. *How long has it been since I've slept the night through? Can't remember. Long before the UK, Spain and Portugal.*

Wednesday, October 25, The Med.

Let's see. On our way to Italy, so we're in the Med. Calmer, maybe Force 4. Description: Moderate. Wind Speed: 11-16. Sea appearance: 3-1/2-5 foot waves. Clouds are breaking up and maybe we'll see sunshine today. Hope, hope.

Regardless of what I told Alex yesterday, the yellow thermos is again outside my door. And shortly after coffee, Alex appears with clean sheets and towels. "Once a week, Mum."

"Just once?"

"Yes, Mum, Captain's regulations."

"Alex, what can we do about the bathroom smell? I can't stand it."

"Oh, Mum, all the toilets stink like that." Yet he dutifully scrubs the bathroom with bleach as I request, while I mutter about how strange on a new ship.

"And thank you too, Mum."

I walk the decks, ignoring the hostile stares and disgusted head shakes, shower and present myself at lunch. Food and its timing seem to be the ship's clock. Everything revolves around meals. It's a good thing that the portions are so small and that I rarely eat breakfast, a habit of many years.

Lunch is a gorgeous surprise of perfectly done steak, potatoes and cauliflower with some kind of red garnish. (Captain tells me later that this is special treatment for the passenger, which apparently all officers are sharing since they are regarding their plates appreciatively, so engrossed that I hear no whispers or titters of American Woman.) There is wine (in the middle of the day!) and Stan, spit and polish, joins me at table and a glass of wine. I regard the wine apprehensively, knowing that it will surely be the cause of a siesta post-haste. *Why not? It's not like you're going to be driving or – ugh! – working. And you can nap when you darned well please. Rest and peace is why you're riding around on this big boat.*

Stan and I discuss canal boats in England, from whence I have recently come. He has a friend who owns one, and Stan and his wife have spent time on the canals. Maybe even on the same route. He is very pleased with this scenario, and his sad eyes light.

We turn to heavy fuel and its joys and problems and bunkering

"Taking on heavy fuel is not like putting gas in your car, where you fill the tank and drive away. The shortened version of heavy fuel is this: It is normally the consistency of liquified asphalt, has to be heated to 60 degrees C to transfer into our tanks. Transferal to the engine takes heating to 140 C. Then it is put through three purifiers plus pumps, where it enters the injectors at 133 C. The viscosity must be just right. Water in the fuel and fuel expansion as it heats require separate calculations. The processes are very complicated, both for taking on bunker and using it, checking at every stage. Each trip we get about fifty tons of residue from the fuel plus slop water, which goes into settling tanks. Remember, this is the short version." Stan smiles gently, his sensitive face displaying amusement at my wide-eyed fascination. "But it must be right, otherwise this ship does not go forward." *Wow!*

He prepares to leave for the Engine Room. "It is difficult to join you at lunch since this is the hour I must make my daily report. Still, I like the break if I can manage it."

Just before Stan leaves, Captain comes in carrying a sack, disappears into the galley and reappears with a plate stacked high with buttered French bread and a tin of anchovies.

As he walks by the table, headed for the Officers Lounge to indulge alone, I say, "French bread! How nice. Did Cook make it?"

"No," he says sourly. And I wonder where it came from since we've not seen French bread or anything even close to it.

"Well, maybe he could be persuaded to do so."

"I don't think so! Cook has problems with baking," and he continues on past the latticework. Stan's hungry, wishful eyes follow the plate, then he stands abruptly and takes his leave, not looking at Captain as he passes to the Dining Room door, leaving me to wonder how a chef has problems making a simple loaf of bread.

On my way out, I stop to thank Captain for the wine. He motions me to a chair, swigs beer and munches his goodies. He tries to snag a few other officers to join us, but they shoot him an incredulous glance and refuse, which blows me away. I should think everyone would want a few leisurely moments with his Captain.

Finally, Marius and a tall, blond, handsome young man, whose name is Tom and is head of the shipbuilding contingent, join us. I remember he was one of the stalwarts listening to Captain's tirade some nights back, but he seems pleasant and cordial.

Now that he has a Pole and Romanian as audience, Captain initiates a discussion on problems of Poland and Romania. "Of course," he says disparagingly, waving at me, "she can't possibly understand what is happening in newly-repatriated Communist countries." He lectures us as if in a classroom, throwing in many personal opinions. Marius disagrees often and Tom, who is being treated like a child, disagrees more.

Wine is poured, beer is consumed, and we practically have a fistfight. I drink wine and listen to the conversation swinging wildly between English and Polish. *Wow and double wow!* Captain eats bread and anchovies and consumes eight beers, breaking into his tirade every so often to

61

announce, "See, Cari, I'm smiling. You said I never smile. Well now, by God, I'm smiling." Or, "She can't understand any of this. Women just don't grasp this important stuff." Marius and Tom regard Captain with horror and me with sympathy.

Well, in fact, I do understand more of what's being said and implied than he thinks. He has been a part of the 'high earning class' of Poland for a long time and cannot grasp today's realities. He brags of having a swimming pool. "Very few people have pools in Poland, you know. But I do!" He makes $60,000 U.S., which is a fortune in Poland, he crows. Marius adds that American Captains make $150,000 and nearly sniggers.

I have no reason to disbelieve what is being said, but it's difficult to realize that the 'mentality' of the post-Communist worker is so blasé. Captain pounds home that under the Communist regime nobody really had to work. Everybody was equal, so the smartest and the dumbest both got equal pay. Thus, no reason to excel. For example, a 3rd Officer who went to sea and was therefore expected – required, if you've ever watched ship crews work – to work his tail off received $1.50 more per week than the shore-bound worker, who didn't even have to show up. Captain bangs his fist on the coffee table causing glasses and plates to dance.

Since the collapse of Communism, outside interests have tried to collaborate or introduce factories and investment into Poland and Romania, but in the end, have simply given up due to lack of interest on the part of government and the work force's attitude.

The three men finally agree on one thing: The stupidity of it all is mind-boggling, but their guess is that it will take one to four generations to change the mentality. They throw their hands in the air.

Appalled at my ignorance of what's happening in the year 2000 in post-Communist countries, I don't touch my full glass of wine and listen dumbstruck to their wild disagreements, which seem to really be agreements, just stated in different manners.

In the meantime, Captain rages, companies cannot afford to pay their workers a salary so they pay them with the goods they produce. For example, a lamp factory pays workers in lamps which they then peddle on the street. It is sheer madness, but either no one wants to or cannot figure out how to change the system. They say the main problem is government, which still thinks in old regime terms. Corruption is rampant, and any outside help simply goes into politician's pockets.

I butt in and say that education is the key to change. They agree, but point out that teachers still think in the old terms and are teaching the kids in the same manner, the same useless tactics.

"When the Communists pulled out, they took everything with them, down to the last typewriter and paperclip. They left us with no food, no machinery, no structure, no viable work force and no hope," Marius says.

Then we add the complacency of the people, who don't want to look for opportunity outside of the country where all their countrymen live. They are afraid, don't want to take risks, don't know how to after forty-five years of Communist control. Better to have a few crusts to eat and a 50-cent bottle of wine (surprisingly called Arizona) with your friends and relatives than try to improve yourself, however one goes about doing that. Romania has twenty-three million and Poland forty million of these people.

"Ask him, ask him," Captain yells at me, challenging me to ask Tom how he thinks, how he can live on $400 a month with a wife and three kids, a gas-guzzler car with gas at $4/gallon and a new plot to hopefully build a house. *Aha! They have been somewhat civilized together in the Engine Room or wherever for Captain to know these facts.*

"It's our phenomenon, it's our phenomenon," he hollers, spittle flying. "Nobody can figure out how people are living, yet they are. Tom should be making as much money as I am, but he subsists on only $400 a month. Yet he won't leave to find better work in another country. Tom's very smart and very skilled, in fact brilliant, so could get a work permit in any country. Ask him! Ask him!" he yells, bouncing on the couch, sausage legs and square feet flying off the floor.

Marius, very embarrassed, Tom, open-mouthed, and I stare at him in disbelief as he reaches to the refrigerator for another beer.

So I do ask Tom. Gathering all my forces, I calmly turn to Tom, "Why do you do it?"

He tells me that he manages to live within his salary. There is no money from outside, except the government's payment to his wife to stay home with a child until it is three years old, then the payment stops.

His wife worked in the financial section of a hotel, but now is home with the kids, receiving a high percentage of her hotel pay from the government. She will obviously go back to work after three years.

(Yet, as he talks, I note that their kids are seven, four and two-and-a-half. That means seven years of not working outside, but being paid for it. So maybe she will have another child when this latest pension runs out? Maybe she's pregnant now? Kinda of like our welfare system - the more kids, the more free money.)

"Where does the money come from to pay her for staying home?" I ask.

"Now you have it, the crux of it. Now you have it!" Captain yells, looking at me approvingly. "It's that same phenomenon – where does the money come from when everything is broke?"

"Captain, please don't interrupt. You asked me to ask Tom and I'm doing so. Give him a chance to answer." A black, mean look flits across his face (and I shiver, thinking of yesterday) as he glares at me, then he smiles and shrugs.

Tom never takes his eyes from me. "I don't know." Then he goes on to admit that he likes the way things are. Even though he graduated first in his class and is a highly-skilled shipbuilding engineer, he does not want to leave Poland to improve his lot.

Captain hrrmmphs, looks very satisfied and smiles at me crookedly. "See?" Point taken.

Tom is becoming more and more agitated with Captain, but dares only disagree with contained vehemence, although he is very angry. Captain is making a fool of him, and he hates it.

"If all the brains and skilled people left Poland, as is sometimes demanded even by our own people," he pauses, but does not look at Captain, "where would we be? There would be no way to pull ourselves up, to start over. The damned Communists will have won. How could I take my brilliance," he snorts, "and work in other countries, making piles of money, when I know people like me need to stay and help with our reconstruction. Without us, we are doomed. I can't allow it. What would happen to my Poland?"

Tom's eyes, still boring into mine, are misted. I look away so he cannot see my amazement at his patriotism, as if Americans had a corner on patriotism. Nor my shame that I, the world traveler who smugly thinks she is in sync with the world, am so out of tune to the realities of what is actually transpiring on this planet.

As Captain reaches for another beer, Tom says softly, "Captain is so proud of his money, but his kids have grown up without him. Who is the wealthiest here?" Ah, a question worldwide, even in poverty-stricken Poland.

"Captain," looking straight at his wandering eyes, "I believe Tom. What he is telling me is the truth. He is doing what is right for him."

Tom looks at me gratefully, and we are instant friends. Although I want to shout at him, *I didn't say I agreed with you, because I don't. Captain has valid points, and I am more in agreement with him, although I salute your commitment to your country.* But I clamp my mouth shut and await the next episode.

Captain starts making coarse jokes about the drink, Tom and Jerry. "Tom and Cari, just like Tom and Jerry. All mixed up together." He blathers on. Tom, Marius and I look at each other disgustedly.

This donnybrook breaks up at 1500 with Captain mostly in the bag, but still willing to give it another go. "See, Cari, I am smiling because what I say is right." He sways on the couch and Marius, Tom and I file out silently, with him laughing, "Tom and Jerry, Tom and Cari. Lots of funny, nasty jokes about Tom and Cari."

I turn right out the Hatchcover door and rapidly walk the decks, trying to absorb all I've heard. The world is a mean place.

Upon return to my cabin, I find three nice bottles of red wine, a tin plus a large box of cookies and a basket of fruit. Whew! Captain is really trying to make up for these rather humble accommodations. Maybe his ridiculous behavior.

I shower until my skin crinkles, trying to wash off the poverty, hopelessness, sadness of what just happened, then ready myself to eat again.

This time some kind of meat so tough it's inedible. Both Stan and I have one small glass of wine and talk about upcoming Italy, pushing food around on our plates.

Chief Officer surprisingly appears, but no Captain, who is presumably sleeping it off getting ready for Gio Tauro Pilot at 2030. Although he directs most of his conversation to Stan, I assume Chief Officer is here to maybe have a decent word with the passenger who has ridden with him only during port times, during his mute hours. The Drums must have told him that Captain wouldn't be here. So we are cordial, if stilted. The rest of the nearly full Dining Room is very quiet, all eyes and ears on the Captain's Table. First Officer is in the Dining Room for the first time in forever. What does it mean?

The sturdy young man says in an oddly apologetic way, "I must get back. This is my watch, I'm sure you know, and eating at Officers Mess means I must get someone to sit in for me. It's Marius this time."

"Nice of you to join us, First Officer," I say in my brightest, most cordial tone. "I'm sure Stan appreciates it, too."

Brows drawn together, he and Stan exchange a glance, then he turns steely eyes on me. "Good evening." *Oh my, I've certainly fallen down in the charm-'em-make-'em-like-you department here.* Conversation at the other tables resumes, and Stan and I finish our tough whatever-it-is.

Gio Tauro comes into view at 2230.

2nd Officer is just appearing from behind the Chart Room blackout curtains headed for the Bridge stairway door, when Captain, without turning around, barks, "2nd Officer. Pilot. NOW!" We all jump, including Helmsman. 2nd Officer hesitates, and I swear he is going to come over and sock Captain, who richly deserves it, but he continues down the inside stairwell. Captain turns to me and grins. I turn stiffly to watch the pilot boat disappear from sight under the bow, where I know he will continue around the back of the ship and pull alongside starboard.

Now that he has shown his mastery, Mr. Captain is full of ebullience, stopping to ask, "How do you like this?"

"I love it!" and watch us do a fancy spin-around thing at the end of the harbor. "Wow, Captain, that was slick as can be." *You ARE going to be cordial. You ARE going to like this man, MsSelf.* He smiles in the dark. Pilot is Chatty Cathy, but First and 2nd Officers maintain their silence. We are berthed at 2330, an unpleasant heavy smoke haze, reflected in the harbor lights, covering the port.

I hope to have a few pleasant words with First Officer, but he is off the Bridge like a shot. This is his busy time, I know, since he is responsible for cargo and all the deck crew. The cranes will start unloading seconds after berthing. Somebody has to direct the cranes and that someone to direct or direct the director is First Officer. Still, just a word or two…

In bed at 2400, the distant noise of cranes working outside. There is a big advantage in sleep terms to having most of the boxes forward – no cranes working outside my window. Although it never ceases to amaze me how tightly screwing down the window literally shuts out port noise. Yet, it is only two-paned.

CHAPTER EIGHT

Melting Ice

Thursday, October 26, Gio Tauro, Italy

Heavy clouds and misting rain hold the gray-green smoke over the port. A truly nasty-looking place, and I decide to stay onboard. A good choice since our time is shorter than I realize.

The morning is spent exercising and washing the cabin walls with soap and bleach, plus every square inch of toilet, shower, under and into every crevice, hands covered in my hair- coloring plastic gloves. I am determined to rid this cabin of smells.

Bleached to a fare-thee-well and reeking, eyes stinging and bugging, ears ringing and metallic taste in mouth, I sit alone at lunch, listening to boxes banging and ship trembling. Bad crane driver.

I ask Cristori if he will show me how he makes those wonderful carved vegetable flowers that appear on my plate. He will be delighted to do so after La Spezia. We chat a moment, and I suddenly feel us moving. *Bloody hell, why didn't somebody tell me when we were leaving. Shrugs are NOT specific times.*

Grabbing a piece of bread, I gulp my wine, which is now served at both lunch and dinner, and bolt up the outside stairs to the Bridge. We are barely underway, so I watch the oncoming sea plus Gio Tauro fade out of sight. No loss there; I'm glad I wasn't left on shore. I had been warned there was absolutely zero to see in port, so I didn't miss a thing.

Captain is grouchy this morning and gets grouchier when I snap, "Why doesn't anybody tell me anything?" He growls something, then leaves me shivering on the bridgewing.

Half an hour later, I come upon him playing solitaire on the computer and ask if we have a bowthruster. "No," he grumbles, "Why do you think we need two tugs?" Snarl, growl – at the lack of bowthruster or that I have caught him playing solitaire I can't say. *What a great guy!* I disappear onto the bridgewing and down the outside stairs.

Calm seas accompany my stair-walking. Five rounds are almost an even 1,000 stairs. And I sure do need the exercise. As from the first day, I feel the hostile eyes of the deck crew drilling into my back. If I come upon them suddenly, they drop their eyes, say "Mum" and scurry away, shoulders twitching with irritation and animosity.

Alex arrives at 1500 to clean my carpet, although the arrangement had been for 1300. With a clean carpet, I cannot think of one more thing to do for this poor old/new cabin, except keep after the bathroom. Keep those bottles of bleach coming, Alex.

What a blah day. Think I'll sit in my cabin and get drunk. I deserve it, although the Scotch tastes like bleach. I set my tenny-stompers in the slightly open window. They need to be aired out, even if it's misting outside. Wish we had some sun.

Dinner with Stan and, again a surprise, Chief Officer. Both are witty, charming and full of glee. *Wonder why.*

An officer walks by our table and hands me a piece of paper, which is a copy of a funny e-mail. I leave the Dining Room and sit on the stairs to read it, pondering what could have caused this tiny show of friendship, this thawing.

Returning to the Dining Room, I walk to their table. "Very funny," I say. "Did you get this by e-mail today? The Manxman told me he couldn't install the Internet before he left."

"No, it's a copy," says Florin, 2nd Engineer, he the loudest of the giggling, twittering and growling about the American! Woman! In fact, the whole group I'm facing is guilty of same.

"I have a bunch of very funny ones on my computer, if you guys can enjoy English humor." Their faces show shock. Computer, you have a computer in your cabin? How come we didn't already know that via the Drums?

"Yes, yes!" they say as a group. "Save them to disc."

"I've never done this before with e-mail, but I'll try." I run up to my cabin to do so, leaving the door open in my haste.

A brief rap at the doorsill and three guys enter, standing behind me watching my feeble efforts. We try all kinds of stuff, the shaved-headed 2nd Engineer finally sitting at my request. We have "ignition," to wit, a meeting of minds and energies that have nothing to do with the blond American! Woman! We're talking computers here. They howl at the video of the guy getting mad at his computer. Haven't we all wanted to kick the hell out of our computers? At last we think we have it, and they file out, leaving me with all the crap that this computer can generate.

With a few fun e-mails in hand, I run up to the Bridge to ask First Officer to print, which the computer whizzes assured me he would. We look at my stuff first and see some of it is dots, dashes and funny letters. "I'll fix it and come back tomorrow."

"That will be good, we want to see it." He tries a watery smile, and I hurry out.

Overripe fruit is smelling up my cabin, so I take it down to the Dining Room, sure someone will eat it during the night or for breakfast, thinking no one would be there. Wrong. There are folks everywhere. I tell the computer guys what has happened and that I will clean it up tomorrow. "Hurry."

Marius is in the Dining Room, which nearly knocks me off my pins. So I sit with him and get into a rousing conversation of officer's duties.

"In a nutshell (Marius is smugly pleased with this American expression), Captain is the ship's highest officer, acting on behalf of the ship's owner, which is why he's called 'Master,' and is legally responsible for day-to-day affairs. Chief Officer, or First Officer, as you like to call him, is second-in-command after Captain and primarily responsible for cargo operations, safety and security of the ship and also the welfare of the crew; in fact, he's the guy who runs the ship. 2nd Officer is in charge of navigation, and 3rd Officer, me, is in charge of the safety of the ship and crew. Chief Engineer oversees the engine department and is responsible for all engineering equipment. An important man, but he cannot assume command. 2nd Engineer is responsible for the daily maintenance and operation of the engine department and is normally the busiest guy onboard. 3rd Engineer assists the 2nd and sometimes is in charge of bunkering. Then there's Bosun, not an officer but a really important guy, too, who is in charge of everything on deck. Want more?" I shake my head.

"I'll bet you, Marius, that the only place in the world a Captain is not responsible for his ship is the Panama Canal."

"Impossible! Captain is responsible everywhere."

"I'll bet you money." He looks doubtful. "All right, a bowl of olives," looking down at the bowl of green olives that Stan earlier sniffed were inferior. "Unless I'm sure, I never bet." Marius sweeps the long hair off his face. "I'll bet you, I'll bet you," I chant. He grins uncomfortably. "Who can we ask?" I prod.

"Captain. He will know these things." I am astounded. I thought he had no time for his Captain, but I am obviously mistaken. "Also, there are many reference books on the Bridge."

"Good, you will consult the books tomorrow, and we will discuss this again." Now he is really looking nervous. *Come on, you, the mariner, should know these things.*

"We'll look at the books together," he says primly.

"Good night, Marius, see you tomorrow," And I swagger out the door. *Gadzooks, what a day. What crazy thing will tomorrow bring?*

Friday, October 27, The Med

Sunshine! Calm sea. Force 2: Light breeze, 4-6 knot winds, ½-1 foot small wavelets.

So impressed, I cannot go back to sleep, quickly drink coffee, don pink shorts and top to celebrate the spring-like weather and begin a marathon walk of the decks. And discover the spotless 'Monkey Island,' the mainmast deck above the Bridge. Never have seen this deck before, and I'm intrigued.

I stop by the Bridge to ride along with Marius, chatting about the sea, volcanoes, the horrid ship somewhere ahead of us that is throwing plastic into the sea, resulting in bobbing bottles and trash. "There are rules," Marius grumbles. "This is not permitted."

"Um, Marius, did you consult the book regarding Panama?" Innocently.

"No," he says, throwing me a nasty look, then smiles. "But we'll look right now."

"While you're looking, see if you can find the U.S. Coast Guard book on sea forces. It's a really good one with pictures of the seas at a certain force, cloud formations, precise pictures with meticulous explanations, etc. I've been told it's here someplace, but I can't find the thing."

"Sure. I know the book you're talking about. Every ship has one on its Bridge." He walks to a cabinet on the bulkhead, opens the door with a flourish and grunts loudly in surprise.

"There. Are. No. Books. Here." He rushes to the next cabinet and rummages around, then the next and next. "All the reference books are gone. We need those things. Some of them were new – the latest version." He looks around in exasperation.

"You probably hid them so you don't have to look up Panama." We laugh, but he looks concerned and is fidgeting irritably as I take my leave.

Lunch is a raucous affair, beginning with Stan's approving view of my pink shorts. "You look beautiful. Just like my Eve. She is a blondie, too."

Roberto stops by the table to ask me how I'm enjoying the weather and how far I walked today. "Five rounds of the ship and five up and down stairs. I counted the stairs yesterday and there are 100 in each direction, so five rounds up and down equal 1,000 stairs." Roberto looks impressed, then alarmed as Captain enters, ducks his head and scurries away like a scared rat to join Marius, who is yet again in the Dining Room. *What's going on, Roberto?*

I smile at Captain and say, "I want to thank you for two things. One, for arranging the beautiful day. I knew you were powerful, but didn't know how much." He laughs. "Second, the wine and cookies in my cabin. The cabin smiled all over, and so did I." He laughs again, something apparently new to him, since he does it self-consciously.

He sits, and Stan does that weird leaning-away thing, shifting his chair unobtrusively. I find the whole scenario fascinating since Chief Engineer need not kowtow to Captain because he makes as much money as Captain, has vast authority, although not in the management and control of the ship, but because he's the guy who makes the whole thing work, and is treated with great respect by all those aboard. Without the engine running, a ship and its crew are not worth the powder to blow them away – and everybody knows it. Stan, of course, knows all of this, but seems to prefer to downplay his importance in favor of a Captain he obviously does not admire. But as a mark of his true elegance and gentility, he says not a word, but leans and quietly moves his chair away from his Captain. All to keep a facade of peace and ease of day-to-day living, I presume.

"About the deck above the main mast…"

"Ah, you found Monkey Island. Eons ago, cargo ships also carried animals and that is where they put them."

Stan asks how come I didn't see the monkey up there. "Ask Alex, he feeds her every day." He smirks, very pleased with his little joke.

Talk turns to La Spezia coming up this afternoon. Stan says slyly that perhaps Captain will show me the nightlife in La Spezia. "Oh, do you know it well, Captain?" He smiles.

"Sure he does," Stan says. "He does know it well." Then giggles, so unlike him.

Frankly, I hope he does suggest running about La Spezia with Stan and whoever else since it's our last port for a month, but doubt it will happen. Still, one never knows. It now enters my mind to suggest he be the 'show-er' and I be the 'payer' as thanks for the wine and cookies. We'll see. We are going to be there two days and nights.

After a couple more Tom and Cari jokes, just slightly off-color, which Stan and I endure with no comment, Captain takes himself off to the Lounge, and Stan excuses himself for the noon report.

I glance at Marius across the room and stop by the Lounge on my way out. "May I sit?" Captain looks at me as if he hasn't heard, just offers me a cigarette.

I say loudly, "Remember our conversation about Panama?"

"Yes," and he spiels off just what I want to hear. "It's the only place in the world where Captain is not responsible for his ship. Pilot is."

I stand, walk to the latticework. "You owe me a plate of green olives, 3rd Officer." Marius laughs and waves his fork, returning to his lunch.

"Hmmpphhh! Betting on my ship. I never gamble, but I do like computer games."

"I've got a bunch on my computer. I'd put them on disc for you, but I don't have any with me."

"Solitaire is what I like. I win all the time. I know how to do it."

"You cheat," I laugh.

"No, I just know how to do it."

"Bull, you know how to cheat." We laugh.

"Pilot at 1400. See you on the Bridge then."

I am startled. So he took to heart my grumbling yesterday. "I'm off to walk the decks. See you at 1400." I walk in the lovely sun, the pleasure of laughter and camaraderie of sorts accompanying me. *God, I hope this lasts. Please, MsSelf, don't screw it up. Please, gentlemen, continue being pleasant.*

I shower and change, placing my shoes on the sill in the sunshine. Maybe dry, at last. Can't have stinky feet. If I could count on the dryer working, I'd throw them in the washer with tons of bleach and soap. Everybody says don't do that. Yeah? How do YOU get your shoes clean?

Tom and his four co-workers are on the Bridge for the last time, as they will leave us at La Spezia, their work done. Tom and I talk and talk about Poland and life.

"Cari, I want to explain about Poland. There are opportunities there. There are."

"Be happy, young man. Remember, it's what it's all about."

"Could I have your address?"

"Of course, Tom. We'll e-mail, but here is the whole thing, including telephone number, if you ever come to the U.S." He hands me his very impressive business card with some grand title plus his private e-mail.

"Oh, and Tom," I say loudly so that Captain can hear, since we rarely speak to each other on the Bridge, "just think, Captain won't have the opportunity for any more of his Tom and Jerry jokes. He's going to miss you as much as I will." We laugh, Mr. Captain tries not to, but finally gives in.

Although he dresses casually on the Bridge in white levis and pullover sweater stretched to the maximum over his ample belly (enough to drive Capt. R. on The Other into a frenzy), Captain can be very official on the Bridge when he wants to. Today is crisp commands, pleases and thank yous, his portable telephone an appendage to his ear, obviously for Tom's and my benefit since the other officers look startled. Where Capt. R. on The Other entrusted his First Officer with many Bridge duties, this Captain does not. He's in command, mustache bristling, rotund body propelled by sausage legs in an important military manner with that funny, mincing gait. I can't help smiling.

Tom tells me that the company van drivers, who are coming from Poland to pick up the crew, are bringing two suitcases of special Polish food for Captain. Nice touch, I think, believing that the food is a gift from the shipbuilder. He will be overjoyed since he doesn't like to eat the food on board. (But then, heaven knows, neither do the rest of us.) He has mentioned more than once that his wife is a good cook. *Then why don't you change the shipboard food to suit yourself. You are, after all, God on board. And what do you eat at home that is so special?*

Berthing at 1530.

"An hour before I can get off?"

"Sure, time enough for the agent."

As I dress to go to town, I ponder again the incongruity of time, the hour, always addressed by the 24-hour clock on the Bridge and occasionally AM/PM time elsewhere. It's getting too confusing. 24-hour clock for me, and I'll always be on time.

I present myself at the Ships Office, where Captain says to the agent, "Passenger would like to go ashore."

The crisp young man in tailored suit, reeking of expensive aftershave, stares at me. "This is the passenger?"

I can feel Captain's insides chortling. "Yes. She can go ashore, correct?"

"Correct." He continues staring at me in a sort of stupefied shock, his Latin smoothness having flown.

Captain turns to me, barely managing to hide his evil grin. "Tell Chief Officer to issue you a shore pass." A shore pass is required for a merchant ship passenger to go ashore, since the passenger is considered a part of the crew for simplicity reasons and all ports seem to go along with it. In actuality, in the many ports I have disembarked for the day, a shore pass was rarely in my hands.

Chief Officer is outside, laughing with the Filipino crew.

"Everybody's happy. Are you going ashore?"

"Yes, Mum. Tomorrow is Saturday and then Sunday when we only have watch duty, so we're almost all going to town." Bosun, usually dour, jokes about the expensive taxi ride (we can practically spit on the gate and town is just beyond). Then, suddenly realizing to whom they are talking, they step back almost in unison and regard me with vacant eyes, lips pursed.

I follow Chief Officer inside to get the pass and nearly collide with two uniformed officials, all gray serge, gold buttons and epaulets. Aha! Earlier I had strolled past 3rd Officer pulling stuff from an outside closet. "What are you doing now, Marius? I find you in the most interesting places."

"Captain thinks we might have a safety inspection, and I'm readying everything."

Good on ya', Captain, for guessing correctly. Maybe you do something other than drink beer, cause distress and bark orders.

La Spezia is very nice with wide boulevard, trees, lovely park across the boulevard from the sea, and very special piazza with its cathedral, specialty shops and narrow streets winding away through centuries-old buildings. As one stands in the flower-studded park, it seems odd to see but not be dismayed or distracted by the cranes jutting into the sky. Beauty and business living happily together. And business seems to go well with La Spezia because it feels very upscale.

I am slavering for a pizza and red wine. But, restaurants don't open until 1930 and I'm used to eating at 1730. No time to wait, so I buy a pizza in a to-go place with a wood burning oven, thinking to take it to my cabin. I drink a beer as I wait, listening to the chatter of the friendly owner and a customer, realizing that my Spanish assists me in easily reading the signs, but that I can't understand a word they are saying. They eye me from time to time, and finally the customer comes over and speaks in English, "Not many tourists in La Spezia at this time of year."

"Well, I'm only a tourist for a short time. I'm here on a ship." I gesture to the port.

"Ship? We receive no tourist ships here."

"A container ship."

"By yourself?"

I nod assent.

"What do you do to pass the time?"

"Walk, read, write." *And most importantly,* "Listen. Learn."

"Aren't you afraid? No?"

I want to shout, "How can I be afraid of people who won't come within 100 feet of me and when they do, act afraid of *me*, as if I might contaminate them?" I just smile.

Dark streets and too much attention paid to the pizza box in hand combine to make me very lost. The pizza smells delicious, and I can't resist, so I eat while I walk. Stupid idea, but the pizza is great. Where do those nutcases get off saying that pizza in Italy isn't good? I wish I had two of them.

Back on board, I see Tom in the Dining Room, and we hug and hug like old friends. Maybe the crucible of Captain has burned a friendship into our souls. "I'll e-mail you, Tom. Remember, be happy."

"Thank you, Cari, thank you." He hugs me tightly.

Just as Captain enters. "Oh," he sing-songs leeringly, "I guess I was right about Tom and Jerry. My, my, what a sight. Tom and Cari hugging in public."

"Oh be quiet," I snarl, although I want to scream at him, "Shut up!" *Must his every thought and statement be smarmy?* He blips his head like a cartoon character and steps back sharply. Message received.

"OK, cute young man, have a lovely life. When you and your wife come to the U.S., call me." And Tom and I hug again.

"We leave in an hour. Can you be at the gangway?" and I shake my head, eyes indicating Captain. Tom hurls a disgusted glare at Mr. Captain, turns on his heel and leaves. Attempted cordiality with the Master is absolutely at an end. Not even a so long, been good to know ya'.

I turn to Captain, "Did you get your Polish food?" I try to ask pleasantly, sure it's coming across as an accusation.

He looks startled that I know about it and tries not to frown, still smarting from the "Be quiet" barb. Then, "Yes." He cannot contain himself and smiles – he is very pleased with the idea of Polish food. "I'll share a bite with you."

"No you won't. I wouldn't take one bite out of your mouth." He looks surprised, but giggles. Whatever came in those suitcases made him a happy man.

We are berthed to port, so I stand at my window in exactly one hour and watch the shipbuilding crew leave, first a trip down the gangway with suitcases and another trip with familiar heavy, brown-paper wrapped, string-tied boxes in hand. Five. I guess everything that goes to Poland is wrapped in brown paper and tied with string, even if it is old machinery parts. Maybe it's a rule.

I fix a drink and watch a cab pull up. Stan and Captain get into the cab. I am amazed that Chief Engineer is going anywhere with Captain. Obviously, nobody is going to show me La Spezia tonight. I holler out the window, "Stay sober, Chief." He looks up but can't see against the ship's bright lights, so hurries into the taxi, eagerness to be off-board literally sparking from his lean body. Can't blame him, it's been a tough week.

A couple of hours putting my fun e-mails on disc and I'm again at my window in time to see a cab disgorge Stan only. What? Did he murder Captain? In a flight of fancy, I picture the tall, elegant Chief Engineer, garbed in royal purple velvet with ermine-trimmed cape, one Italian glove-leather boot placed next to the ruby-encrusted sword protruding from The Peasant's body, his long, aristocratic face sardonic, "I told you to employ better manners at table." I giggle myself into bed.

Not tired enough to sleep, I get up and sit in my window, smoking, watching the lights of La Spezia. A cab rolls up, and Captain staggers out, empty arms out slightly in front as if to ward off an oncoming train. A little too much vino, Captain?

Saturday, October 28. La Spezia, Italy

Sun pours through my window, and I rush to open it, warm breeze pouring through into my pores and soul. Aw, sweet Italy.

I lunch on board, thinking about a long La Spezia adventure. Captain joins me, shoveling his Spartan lunch into his open maw. Between bites, we discuss La Spezia.

"What will you do tonight?" he asks.

"Why, take you to dinner."

He frowns.

"Look, Captain, I'm not asking you for a date. I thought it would be fun to gather up you, Stan and whoever else can go ashore and treat you all to dinner at a nice restaurant. Only to be friends and enjoy pleasurable company in a civilized setting." *Now, why I would spend time and money to sit in a fancy restaurant across the table from this boor, watching him shovel food into his face? Pleasurable? Still, company in town would be fun. Could Old Spare Tire be fun? Doubtful.*

I'm about to rescind the offer when he says, "Cannot. Too much work on board. Many inspections and officials. You've seen them. There are more coming. I have lots of time at sea, but not in port. Much work," Polish accent growling the "rr's", almost like gargling.

"Whatever," I breeze. And chat brightly for a few minutes, then excuse myself. "Have to inspect all interesting things in town."

"Well, maybe…"

"No. I invited, you declined. I never offer invitations more than once. But, then, except for this very moment, you will never have the opportunity to know that. Look, I have worked with men all my life – traveling, working and dining together. Just that, nothing more – planes, business and food. What did you do in town last night? I can almost guarantee you that I will NOT be doing anything even close to whatever it was. See you." A very bright red suffuses his face, and his mouth opens and closes like a hooked fish.

Climbing the stairs past walls covered with No Liquor posters (are they breeding?) it occurs to me that Captain is requesting only half portions of food. Alex looks nonplussed, but dutifully, if hesitantly, places the scanty plate before his Captain, pulling his hand away quickly, perhaps fearing it might become part of Mr. Captain's lunch. Do we think this has something to do with the drunken Tom afternoon, where Captain joked about his 'spare tire' and I regarded it kindly, but distastefully, remarking about the need to exercise if one wishes to keep fit. So much time alone at sea must make mariners very intuitive. Thus, half portions. *Nonetheless, Captain, you will not lose that spare tire between here and Veracruz. Maybe by running stairs and starving, but I doubt it. God, one would think that the stress of mastering a ship would keep one thin as a rail.*

And then the light bulb: *Pop, pop – you dummy. He's got two suitcases of Polish food sequestered in his cabin for his consumption, surely washed down with a six-pak or two. Why eat the vile gruel ordered up by him for the rest of us (Cook reports to Captain) on MarkShip Mexico? Oh well, what the hell, the Polish stuff is a gift from the shipbuilder. Or someone said he said it was from his wife. Think it was him.*

I walk the entire town again, very pleased with La Spezia, thinking all the time of what I shall eat. Spaghetti. No, fettucine with cream and parmesano. No, pizza.

I've got piles of money from yesterday's ATM stop and can't seem to find anything to spend it on. What did I think I was going to do – run over to Rome for the day?

Into the ditty bag goes vodka, grapefruit juice, parmesan cheese, the best supermarket grade of Sambucca, grappa (which I have never tasted), surprisingly, tortilla chips, a can of pinto beans (no refries available), grapes and a few other goodies. I'm so hungry, I'm salivating for totopos y salsa with refried beans. Not now, somewhere at sea.

I scout for chocolate shops, remembering Rome and Venice, but come up blank. The only chocolates are in fancy boxes at the pasteleria and tabacari, probably years old, wrapped in stunning gold wrappers and in fancy little cups. I buy them anyway, thinking I'll spring them on officers and crew some dark Atlantic night. Surely they'll satisfy the crew if not the officers, who talk non-stop about food delights while cleaning their plates of the sparse stuff presented. There are three for each — sixty-six in all – which I might string out like Hansel and Gretel's crumbs, hoping that maybe a chocolate will make them like me.

Loaded with sacks, I now really plan dinner. I find the perfect place with outside tables in the balmy night along the wide, tree lined boulevard. When I finally drag my sacks onto the veranda, it is not a place to eat spaghetti or fettuccine, it's a drink place with horsey-doos and snacks. Damn!

I hoist my sacks and trudge toward the ship, meeting Cook and a seaman on the street not far from the port entrance. They are looking for town, and I direct them. Cook insists he will accompany me back to the port entrance while his companion dances about, wanting to go toward town. No, I have walked this street many times, Cristori, I can get there by myself. Reluctantly, he leaves me. Such gallantry! Wish I could bring that out of the rest of those folks on board.

Walking toward the ship, I think of the trattoria across from the port entrance, but when I get there, it is jammed and noisy; maybe not a place for one old lady. So, I return to MarkShip Mexico, eat a roll with parmesan cheese, grapes and wine. Very tasty. I try one of the sure-to-be stale chocolates, hand hovering over the box until just the right one calls to me, and find it exquisite. Yippeee!

After reading a Tony Hillerman book, which I found in the Officers Lounge 'library' of five books, I am in bed, cranes working all around, their screaming sirens and claxons denoting movement along the track. I jump up and secure the window. Ahhh. Early to bed, early to rise…

Then I think of Edna St. Vincent Millay's poem, "Grown-Up (A Warning on the Passions of Youth),"

Was it for this I uttered prayers,

And sobbed and cursed and kicked the stairs,

That now, domestic as a plate,

I should retire at half past eight?

Sunday, October 29, La Spezia, Italy

At 0700 (0800 yesterday. For some reason we are retarding clock in port. Maybe Italy has Daylight Savings Time?), I jump out of bed, open the window, shiver slightly and am dismayed by the clouds. No matter, all I can think of is bacon, eggs, toast and hot black coffee.

At exactly 0730, I present myself at table, expecting to breakfast by myself, but find a full Dining Room. So this is when they eat. Everyone looks at me in surprise since this is my first meal at the breakfast hour, but no one comments. As we go west, I will surely be at breakfast. We will lose some nine hours, so my stomach will think I'm ready for dinner at breakfast time.

First Officer and I share the table. "We sail at 1600, right?" He butters his toast as if he has not heard me. "Yes or no!" I snap, and his head swivels toward me.

"Yes."

"Thank you."

He looks repentant. *Good. Enough of your youthful mumbling*, I grouse to myself. *I don't give a shit whether you like passengers or not. You've got one, and we are tablemates – rarely. And even more, if you hope to be Captain, as somewhere along the way you told me you do, you'd better change that sullen attitude. Start now, my boy, by the numbers – One, Two…*

The other surprise in the Dining Room, Marius, jokes from the next table, "You'd better be back on board before 1600. Ships have a way of sailing at odd times."

"Don't you worry, my dear, I have no plans of hiring a jet ski to catch you. I'll be here with bells on my toes." We all laugh, even First Officer joining in.

Atlantic weather is the next topic. "Bad, rough, gray," says First Officer.

Marius says, "Why don't you think optimistically? Sun, smooth, beautiful." *Aw, Marius, so like you.*

"That's just what I am going to do, 3rd Officer. Have a good day, gentlemen."

I step into the galley to thank Cristori for the breakfast of eggs, hash and toast. Everything delicious.

"Will you be on board for lunch, Mum?"

"I don't think so."

"Good ribs, Mum, I'll save you some for dinner."

"Thanks, Cristori and Alex", who has run into the galley, smiling hugely.

"And thank you too, Mum."

La Spezia's church bells are going nutsy at 0900 as I change into black stockings, plaid skirt, red turtleneck and black vest. *Hurry along, MsSelf. Sailing at 1600, so must be back on board 1400 latest.*

La Spezia opens its Sunday charms to me. A Sunday custom, remembered from past Italian visits, is that nearly every third person, hurrying through the charming piazza on their way home or to a friend's house, is carrying a lovely Sunday gift of flowers in a pot or a bouquet elegantly wrapped or a plate of fancily-wrapped sweets from the pasteleria, which is doing a land-office Sunday morning business. It makes my heart sing, even as I feel very lonely.

Walking the town, I plan my lunch at the restaurant by the park, but the restaurant is closed. Even though it is early, I begin to worry about time. What if the ship's loading has been accomplished early? With Pilot and tugs ordered, they couldn't wait for me while I sipped red wine and ate spaghetti. And, if out of the kindness of the Captain's heart (now that's a hoot!), they waited (which, of course, they couldn't), what a persona non grata I would be henceforth. Bad enough being the only Woman! American! on board. They watch me like hawks, waiting for the big screw-up and are only now accepting that I can hold my own, don't request special treatment, including me with a tiniest degree of equality and laughter.

Is our shipboard retarded time different than on land? With that in mind, I stop for two last boxes of chocolate and hurry to the ship for lunch. Good thing – none of the restaurants along the way are open. Sunday in Italy.

The gangway is swaying against my first step, when I retreat, put both feet on the dock, then one foot on the cleated stair, one foot still on land. This will be my last step on land for many weeks. Neil Armstrong's famous moon quote pops into my head, "One giant step for Mankind." What an odd thing to think about.

On deck, I look up to the main mast, checking out something that has been bothering me. And sure enough, there is neither an Italian flag nor a red flag signaling dangerous cargo. Now that is weird! Surely rude, since all ships fly the hosting country's flag in port as a courtesy, but it's probably illegal, since dangerous cargo must be indicated by the red flag. 'Dangerous cargo' can be cargo as dangerous as bombs or innocuous as paint. Practically all ships carry paint to keep the ship in good order, but it is considered dangerous cargo, so up goes the red flag. I'll ask about it later.

Cook's ribs are every bit as good as advertised – indeed, spectacular. With garlicky pasta and carved vegetable gracing my plate, I rave and rave as Cristori and Alex dance about with pleasure.

Captain comes in, and they flee, disappearing through the galley door with only one fleeting backward glance.

"How do you like the new cook?"

"Very much. Not only is his food delicious, but he is a very nice man." Delicious may be an overstatement, but what the hell. Cook reports directly to Captain, and I want our Atlantic dining hours to be pleasant and full of good things to eat, as those hours seem to be the only time when I'll see most of the ship's inhabitants.

Strawberry ice cream for dessert (funny taste). Dessert is served only on Sunday; other days, only fruit. Hence, my chocolates. Now, here's a dilemma I hadn't thought about: Need I ask Captain for permission? I don't want to – won't – do that. I refuse to ask permission from this guy to share a treat. Oh well, the boxes of gold-wrapped chocolates residing in my cabin will be eaten somehow, I have no doubt.

The spiffy agent comes in, nattily dressed, and says we have clearance to sail at 1500.

"See you on the Bridge later, Captain."

"And you are welcome there." Wow, old boy, spare tire or not, do I love those words.

A few hours later, I am arranging with Alex which refrigerator to use to store my cheese and grapefruit juice.

"Perhaps here in the galley, Mum."

"What about the refrigerator in the Officers Lounge?"

"Oh no, Mum, it is always locked. Captain keeps his beers and other good things only for himself in there. Only Captain and I have a key, and it is always locked, always," whispers Alex. Before we can settle anything, Cristori joins us, and I tell him what I told Captain earlier.

"Thank you, Mum. Thank you. I try to do the best with what I have."

"What do you mean? What about all the new provisions from Valencia?"

"Well, you see, well, I didn't do the ordering, so I just thought certain things would be here, but, well, uh, normally I can, uh, but…" He is very uneasy, eyes darting from side to side, and I want to let him off the hook.

"Tell me about your years on cruise ships, Cristori."

He launches into a monologue, ending with the fact that his current onboard contract is for ten months with no days off, daily hours 0600-1300 and 1500-2000. I make that twelve hours every day. *Whooh!*

Alex is on his third contract on this ship and in all that time has seen only two male passengers, well, he thought they were passengers. Anyway, two men were on board for only a short time each. *No wonder,* I grump to myself, *with the oh-so-lacking accommodations. Another no wonder that the crew and officers are astounded at this blond person in their midst. Little did I know when booking…*

On the stairs, I meet a young Filipino, and he asks shyly if I have been in town. "Did you go to church?"

"No, I didn't."

He looks alarmed. "Are you Catholic, Mum?"

"No, but I used to be."

"Used to be? What religion are you now, Mum?"

"None."

"NUN! YOU ARE A NUN?"

I double over with laughter at his astonished face, finally catching my breath. "No, I am not a NUN!"

Leaving his confused face, I continue up the stairs, past the barrage of No Liquor signs, which reminds me that Alex and I never settled the refrigerator issue.

1500 comes and goes. I finally say the hell with it and go down to the galley to resume our chat about refrigerator space. Captain is sitting alone in the Officers Lounge, looking like he is in dire need of a drink. *Lordy, this guy spends a lot of time by himself.*

"We're late," I say.

"As always," he grumbles.

"Captain, since I don't have a refrigerator in my cabin, I'm wondering if I can have a tiny bit of space in yours here in the Lounge."

"Mine! It's not Mine! It's for all the officers' use. They can use it any time they want."

"But it's locked."

He looks at the padlock guiltily. "Oh, only in port, yes, only in port." *Uh huh.* "Alex," he yells roughly. "Unlock that refrigerator and don't lock it again while the passenger has her stuff in it."

Alex, who looks like he is about to be whipped, turns away and smiles hugely, merry eyes meeting mine. "Right away, Captain."

"Rain coming," I say from the porthole.

"Rain? No rain." He hurries to the porthole. "Maybe rain." *Damned ship captains. They only accept what they themselves predict.*

We sail at 1800, RAIN misting as I stand on the bridgewing to watch the unberthing, running from side to side watching the tugs work and the receding lights of Italy. Then, pouring rain, sound sweet and clear, smell clean and of the sea. *Man oh man do I love this riding around on big boats. And do I adore standing on the Bridge to see it all. What would I do if I were not allowed? Probably knife Captain since we are not allowed guns onboard.* As it is, I am more than content and ride along on the dark Bridge with the barely communicative First Officer after Captain departs.

I sit in the Pilot's chair, ruminating about the maneuverability of this huge ship. As Captain earlier called the heading and Helmsman responded – one six oh – one six oh, surr - one six one – one six one, surr – my midships view showed the ship turning dramatically for only that one degree.

Now, there is only black sea through the massive Bridge windows, except for our three onboard cranes rising eerily above the boxes in the muted reflection of deck lights. Way ahead on the forward mast, the steering light that no one admits using is glowing. I feel the sea welcoming us – me – back. Tonight, she is calm, breathing a soft damp breeze. What she will do to us farther along in The Atlantic, I cannot say. Tonight, this moment, I wish to enjoy. And the glassy Med seems to be enjoying with me.

Chief Officer leaves the Chart Room light on and comes to sit in front of the radar, light falling across the floor behind him. Not a word.

He stands abruptly, and a small paperback book falls to the floor between our chairs. I lean over my chair side and pick it up, tilting it toward the light. *English Dictionary and a Compendium of American Phrases and Slang Expressions.*

"What's this?"

He moves to take the book, and I hold it away.

"First Officer, your English is very good, the little I've heard of it. Better, in fact, than most Americans and Canadians I know. You don't need this."

"Always room for improvement." And he smirks with satisfaction. "I find that I need much improvement." The smirk disappears, and he looks at me in disgust.

The little book has bold, shiny black letters emblazoned on a shrieking yellow background. "Where did you get this, um, *Compendium?*"

"A bookstore in Warsaw," he replies huffily and reaches for the book, which I release to him. He places the small book carefully in an inside pocket of his blouse, then strides across the Bridge to examine the GPS near the port bridgewing door, using his flashlight to examine the display. The surprisingly small, but sophisticated gadget is tacked up in what appears to be an afterthought. It might be mounted in a haphazard way, but as much as sailors depend on weather and, hopefully, accurate forecasts, afterthought or no, it is an important and integral part of a ship's operations.

"Have a good watch, First Officer," and I'm off to my cabin, quietly giggling down the inside stairs. *Compendium*, indeed.

MarkShip Mexico lulls along on calm waters, heaving just enough to remind that we are at sea. Below, the engine throbs, sending a magic vibration through muscle and bone. *Good night, Mediterranean, Good night, MarkShip Mexico. I love you both.*

Monday, October 30. The Mediterranean

Sunshine, glorious sunshine! Clear blue sky. Force 1: Calm, less than 1 knot winds, .25' ripples. Retard clock one hour. That makes two, I remind myself.

I exercise and scrub the bathroom yet again. Clothes-washing day coming up.

"Dryer is broken," says Alex, who arrives to clean my cabin. His narrow shoulders sag.

"How do you dry the sheets?" He makes a motion of throwing them over the dryer room clothesline. "What about the electrician? He can fix it."

"Too busy," and his sunny smile is replaced by a disgruntled frown. "Well, we have been in port, and they have been fixing a piston in the Engine Room," he hedges, but still he frowns.

I shrug, wondering how that could include the electrician. Primadonna electricians! What can you do? Yet, this is cute Roberto, who is so pleasant and charming, if somewhat vacant. Oh well, I make a mental note to chide him about the dryer. I'm sure he will respond.

My cabin is strung from stem to stern with wet laundry, so I'm off to walk the stairs in warm sun.

Coming from lunch, which I have taken alone, I meet 2nd Officer on the stairs. I am determined to chat with him, the vibes of which he must receive, because he stands in front of me without smile or greeting, but unmoving. After a few minutes, he relents and even volunteers information.

At twenty-eight, he already has his Chief Officer papers and must spend two years as Chief Officer before taking the test to become a Captain. No question in my mind that he will be a very young Captain. Boy, is he serious! Not many Filipinos are officers, most are deck crew. This can cause some difficulties, but he refuses to answer my "Like what?"

"Why don't you eat in the officers' Dining Room?"

"Well, I'm the only Filipino officer on board, and, well…" I wait. Nothing.

"Yes, OK, I'm the only woman - American! Woman! – aboard, and I eat there. You see, I have more strikes against me than you do. But I refuse to give in to stupidity."

He ducks his head. Point taken.

The crew is washing decks again as I make my third turn. Mr. Chief Officer sure likes to keep a clean ship. Seems there's always scrubbing going on inside and out. I look at my peeling and bleached fingers, wishing Mr. Clean had some magic elixir for the blasted toilet.

Vodka and grapefruit juice, accompanied by tinny classical music from my computer, go very well together on a late sunny afternoon just before my dinner, staring out the window past my drying shoes to the glorious sea.

Captain sits morosely alone in the Lounge, and I can't tell if he has a beer hiding out or not. After ten minutes at table, Stan storms out after requesting some small tinned delicacy and being told by an anxious, shaking Alex that there is none. So he orders a tin of sardines. "All ships have sardines."

"None. Um, for Captain only."

Stan glares at me as the culprit. I shrug, and he carefully pushes back his chair, stands very erect and marches out, banging the door behind him. *Ah, what a group!*

When 2nd Engineer comes in with a group of officers, we speak a bit of Spanish ("Everybody speaks some Spanish as we spend so much time in Spain."), and I present my e-mail joke disc to him.

"I don't know your name."

He stands formally and shakes my hand. "Florin."

"OK, 2nd Engineer, nice to know you.

"Florin, please."

"Why?"

"Because it is important to me."

"Why?"

He is very flustered, and a shocking pink rises from his throat, suffusing his sharp-featured face and shaved head. This is the young man who was the head of the bullying committee just a week ago, and his expression relays that he is well aware of it. Maybe something else, too. That's a lot of pink for some bullying.

"You are the first American woman I have ever met, in fact, the first American. I have been observing your easy friendliness with my boss, the Chief Engineer, and I hoped that I, too, could make the acquaintance of an American. Perhaps, also, I could improve my English."

"Trust me when I tell you, 2nd Engineer, your English needs no improvement. It is perfect."

"Florin, please. It would mean a great deal to me. If you could. I know your rule, but…"

Oh man, that rule isn't much of a rule anymore. Kaput! Oh well. "All right, Florin. Please call me Cari."

"Well, I doubt I can do that. It would be too presumptuous."

"Florin and Cari or 2nd Engineer and Mrs. Lindley. Take your pick."

"I thank you, Cari. If you ever need any help, call on me."

"Thank you, Florin. Now, look at the disc and decide what you want to distribute. I don't have any more blank discs, so you'll have to do the honors. And I'm still having computer problems, so hope this all turned out well. Frankly, it's that I don't understand the bloody thing."

"Do I have the video of the guy bashing his computer?" he asks excitedly, while everyone looks at the disc as if desiring to tear it from his hand.

"You sure do, plus a lot more. And Engine Room statistics of last year's cargo ship. I thought they might interest you guys in Engineering since the ship was a lot bigger."

"But," Roberto says in Spanish, "we thought this was your first cargo ship."

"No, no, last year I went once-and-a-half around the world, well, three-quarters around and back." I tell them the ports. They are impressed, and I am tickled with their awe. "I've been on lots of ships, but this is only my second cargo ship."

Half an hour later, I return to 'our' refrigerator to put my grapefruit juice back. Florin jumps up, runs into the Lounge and says he'll help me with my computer problems now, if it's all right.

And so he does. 2nd Officer appears at my open door with discs in hand to give to Florin (*now how did he know where to find him?*) and actually smiles at me. *My, my, computers – the great levelers.* Florin turns the computer over to 2nd Officer, saying he is the computer genius on board, and a marathon of computer stuff ensues, while we hang out over his shoulders, I ooohing and aaahing at his expertise. I can now listen to less tinny music and write at the same time, even if he can't fix the dumb cursor's jumping around. They leave, jabbering in computer-eze. If 2nd Officer were allowed to sit at a table other than Captain's, maybe he'd eat in the Dining Room since he seems to get on very well with Engineering.

Tuesday, October 31. The Med

Sunny with a chilly breeze that prompts me to shut the porthole as quickly as I open it. I gauge the rolling sea – maybe Force 6: Strong, 22-27 knot winds, 9-1/2-13' larger waves. Spray. White crests. *Wish we could find that Coast Guard book.* It's just past dawn, and the light show over The Med is mesmerizing.

Deck and stair-walking plus another go at that bloody bathroom take up the morning. Tenny-stompers reside in the window, hopefully to dry out in the breeze.

Captain is already at the lunch table when I arrive, alone, hunching over his Polish food, arms encircling the plate. Mine! Mine! *Don't worry, I wouldn't eat the damned stuff if you shoved it down my throat.*

Conversation is nearly non-existent as he pushes his goodies into his mouth, and I look away. Either he does not want to – or does not know how to – carry on a simple conversation. I wonder what drives him to occasionally sit at table with me with his sly, leering glances and remarks. *What is it with this guy?*

I mention the two boats we are carrying as cargo – one, an absolutely splendiferous yacht; the other, a huge sailboat that the crew refers to as a 'competition' boat. Both are very grand. Captain thinks I am talking about the rescue boats and says they are nothing. I think he is talking about the yacht and say, "Are you sure that is a rescue boat?"

"Am I sure?" he snorts nastily. When the whole thing gets sorted out, he is embarrassed and less communicative (is that possible?), and I laugh. But he, of the dark Eastern European type, has no humor unless it is at someone's expense, at least not to show Westerners, and cannot bring himself to find anything funny in the misunderstanding.

Since the Tom episode, he has not had a beer in his hand in my presence. Frankly, I wish he'd turn up plastered to the gills when he doesn't seem so edgy in my presence. *Why is he so uncomfortable when I twinkle away trying to spark a positive reaction? Aw well. Never mind.* He leaves abruptly and sits in the Lounge smoking, regarding me with sorrowful eyes as I wish him a good afternoon.

Halloween! As a kid and as an adult, until the moment my husband died and I never celebrated a holiday again, Halloween was my second favorite holiday. As a kid, popping corn and wrapping it plus sticky corn candies and jelly beans into orange, brown and black napkins sprinkled with hissing cats and witches and tying each with orange or black ribbon, I anticipated trick or treating in our small town, where one house even gave a WHOLE candy bar, for weeks as the North Dakota evenings got colder. One didn't need a costume; it would have been lost beneath our bundled jackets.

"I can smell Halloween, Mom." And she would smile her perfect French smile for me, and we would plan all that would go into the napkins. Weeks, and finally days, of anticipation.

As an adult, even before marriage, I carved pumpkins and decorated my apartments, later houses, with leaves and flying witches, savoring the smell of pumpkin burning from a too-close candle. My soon-to-be husband thought I was slightly mad, but entered into the fun. Had to start early. It was Halloween!

Halloween aboard MarkShip Mexico. Halloween! Although I have a hell of a time convincing anyone of it. Apparently Halloween is not celebrated in Romania and Poland. In fact, in those countries, it is already November 1.

But, in the Philippines, where it is also already November 1, Halloween is a two-day holiday, starting October 31, All Hallowed Eve, and culminating in the Biggie on November 1. It is a REAL holiday in the Philippines, and while I am on the Bridge, a call comes from Bosun, advising that fact. What will the ship do for its Filipino crew? Why do I believe deep in my heart that MarkShip Mexico has not a plan one for its Filipino crew?

But I have a plan for those chocolates in their fancy gold wrappers that were to be doled out on dreary Atlantic days. Tonight - Four each for the officers and for the crew two plus cookies. All right, discrimination, but I can't help it. If it were me as a crew member and I got fancy chocolates and cookies when I was used to one icky ice cream dessert in the whole week, I would be happy.

Thinking to ride along with Marius, I present myself on the Bridge to find grouchy First Officer still there. Marius is talking loudly and long-windedly, full of great glee, on his portable phone to a friend in Spain, which is riding just to starboard. He obviously is not going to end this marathon conversation within our lifetime, so I ask First Officer, "What is that over there?" The sea, you idiot, his disgusted gesture allows. "No, I mean the land."

Rrruuhrrrr.

"Spain?"

"Yes, Spain."

"Isn't this 2nd Officer's watch?"

"Yes, we are sitting in for him because he's…because…"

2nd Officer, I sing-song to myself, *you cannot be all that unhappy on this ship. Chief Officer and 3rd Officer appear to be your friends, plus 2nd Engineer, and who knows who else? Well, maybe not Old Spare Tire, and, as we all know so very well, he's The Master.*

Now comes full-of-life Marius from the bridgewing, brandishing his portable phone, pleased with his conversation, long hair flying, face full of pleasure. God, this man with rumpled T-shirt over his little round belly, wrinkled shorts and Jesus shoes, is absolutely brimming with life's greatness. If you met him on the street, you would say, "Yuck." But that would be before you were treated to Marius' own version of life – everything interesting or wonderful!

The three of us get into a conversation of all things – Halloween. "We don't celebrate it in Romania. Only in the United States. Not Europe either," First Officer sniffs haughtily.

"Wrong," shouts Marius. "They celebrate Halloween in Spain. My friend just told me they were getting prepared, and everyone is excited."

"Honest," I add, "I have seen Halloween things all over Spain, Portugal and Italy. Decorations, candies, lots of stuff."

Now's the time to get the chocolate thing taken care of, so I casually ask, "While we're talking about candy, is there any shipboard regulation against chocolates?"

"Chocolates!" Their eyes light up. "Chocolates."

"Well, I bought some chocolates in La Spezia, and today is Halloween, so I thought I'd do a Halloween treat thing."

"Chocolates!" Their faces glow as they smile with delight.

"First Officer, is there any problem with putting chocolates on the crew's and officers' tables? You know, any regulation against it?"

"Problems? Regulations? NONE!"

Now the three of us hang out over the half-wall of the Chart Room, ship on automatic on this glassy sea, and blab on about liquor and liqueurs, making home brew. I learn about Palinca, 90% alcohol, the most common drink of Romania, which one drinks by tossing off two fingers in one gulp – no sipping allowed. Of fruits, mostly plums, of gardens, the pleasures of eating real home cooking, Marius, of course, knowing how to cook, First Officer not. "Woman thing."

I snort and laugh in his face. "Sir, the world's best chefs are men."

He backs down, "I know, but I do other things well."

We see wind generators on the hills of Spain, examine them through binoculars, and I tell them of the millions in the U.S., many used as tax write-offs and in terrible disrepair. They grimace, understanding firsthand graft and corruption. Now we are talking about nuclear energy, hydro-electric dams, the many sources of power, storing energy and capacitors. I wow them with the capacitor Kraft Paper story (best from trees grown on the northern slopes of Norway), tightly wound and impregnated with castor oil, the dielectric combination to store energy.

"My company made them in all sizes for many uses, including when combined in series, lasing."

"Some as big as stadiums," First Officer adds and looks to me for confirmation, which I do (although I admit I have never seen ONE capacitor that size. Well, maybe there is one somewhere in the world, but odds are it's a capacitor bank, which is probably what he meant.)

I talk of power transmission and how, over long distances, 70% of the power is lost. "Not possible," snorts First Officer.

"It's true," says Marius.

I add, "My friend, Joe, is probably the U.S.'s leading authority on power transmission, and that is what he told me." I talk of collecting power from transmission lines, building collector boxes, which, if legal, could produce enough energy to power a small town. They stare at me. *Tell me, lads, would you be staring if it were a man talking about this stuff?* All pretense of male dominance is gone, their attitude toward women vanished.

First Officer says he has read of this, and I listen to his drivel carefully. Why not? It doesn't cost me anything. Besides, regardless of his faulty memory, I can tell he has read about this, and I encourage him to continue. He shows off before Marius.

They both talk at the same time, out-yelling each other, and my head swivels from one to the other, carefully stopping with first and then the other. They laugh and yell with wonderful exuberance. I say I must leave, and they follow me to the starboard bridgewing door. They're not done yet.

To think this all started with chocolates. Aren't chocolates amazing?

Arrangement of chocolates at each plate is next – four each for the officers, two each plus cookies for the crew, one small box for Cristori and Alex, and another small one for First Officer as he may not be joining us since it's his watch. Each table gets a Happy Halloween sign.

Cristori and I are in the galley when Captain enters, full of sneers, asks if we're having American food – since I'm in the galley, I must be cooking. "Hamburgers, I suppose," he sniffs.

"No, thick steak, baked potato, and maybe crab cocktail and lobster bisque." He looks abashed, and I can tell he loves all the foregoing foods, just can't help the Eastern European tendency of putting down anything American. *And screw you too, sir.*

I deliver the chocolates to First Officer on the Bridge, explaining that I couldn't trust him to be down for dinner, and he dances around with the small box in his hand.

"I have something for you, too," and he hands me a mini-Snickers bar. "Happy Halloween."

Touched by the thought of both gift and acquiescence to the Halloween he did not want to admit existed, I tell him it is my favorite candy bar. "It will ride in my cabin the entire voyage."

He grins widely. Then, "Will you sit a minute? I have something to ask you. It's, well, the thing is that I, you see…" He squirms in his chair, big body twitching, square face anxious. What he's about to ask is obviously causing him great consternation.

"I mean, you already call the Chief Engineer, Stan, the 3rd Officer, Marius, and the 2nd Engineer, Florin." He looks away toward Spain, fidgeting. "I know about your rule and all that." My eyebrows shoot upward. "But, I was wondering if you could, that is, if you would call me Ion." Whoosh, it's out, and he sags back in his chair, looking like he's gone ten rounds with the world's champ.

"Yes, I will, Ion. And you can call me Cari." I am amazed to realize that he has never actually called me by any name. "I want to make sure of the correct spelling and pronunciation. I–O–N, right? Pronounced "Yohn." He nods.

"Good, that's settled," he sighs, unwraps a chocolate, takes a small bite and closes his eyes, savoring it until it completely melts away, while we sit quietly watching Gibraltar come into view.

Ion smiles. "Now we don't have to bat that Chief Officer/First Officer thing around anymore. I was getting seasick." We both laugh.

"If I don't get up here in time after dinner, will you toot the horn when we enter the Atlantic?"

"Toot the horn? Toot? Oh. Probably not. Well, but maybe. Although we won't make Gibraltar on my watch."

Then I realize that tooting the horn for no reason whatsoever probably is not allowed on a ship. I'm sorry I brought it up, wondering what the consequences could be for a mad, errant horn-tooter.

We suddenly find ourselves in a heavy conversation regarding Romania, I not able to remember what got us there.

"Do you want the Russians back again?"

"No! Understand we were a democracy before Russia. They came with their tanks, and we were nothing. Stalin agreed at Yalta, but ended up showing the world that Russia's share was as far as his tanks could go."

"My God," I breathe.

"No, I don't want Russia. It would be best if someone like the Germans or the United States took us over. What we have now is a jungle. Then we could start from ground zero." My heart aches for these poor, downtrodden people who wish that someone would conquer them in order to save them.

I say, "Most people I know think Russia is dead, broken apart. I say Hah! Have you heard there is no more KGB? People say to me that I can go to Russia now. Why in hell would I want to? Just because my government wouldn't let me go in the past?"

"Why not?"

"Too many security clearances. I didn't want to go anyway. And I sure don't want to now. Although I knew then - know now - nothing top secret, NOTHING, they don't know that. And they still know me."

"Ahh." He regards me almost with sorrow. "Of course, you're right. They simply change the name of the KGB and other agencies. Russia is like a sleeping bear." He lays his head on his hands on the radar screen in front of him. "Believe me, we know. Sleeping only."

I nod. "And when he wakes up, he's hungry and mean." I stare out the forward panorama of Bridge windows, not seeing the placid Mediterranean.

"Yes," Ion breathes. "Hungry and mean." He opens chocolates and gulps them as if they are his last.

And I moan inside, wanting a different world. *Just how bubbly happy can you be when this beast faces you daily, with you never knowing, never knowing?* I change gears in my head and try once again to identify with these dark Eastern Europeans. *Would I not be dark too? I'll try harder. It's almost too much to bear. And I am the outsider, only listening to, not experiencing, the sorrows and horrors. I'll try harder.*

And I'd better not say Eastern European out loud. Just because the United Nations classifies Poland and Romania as Eastern Europe, maybe they don't consider themselves that – and everybody is very touchy about what they consider their correct classification. Maybe they like better the CIA's Central Europe for Poland and Southeastern Europe for Romania. All of it has more to do with culture, tradition and religion than geography. *Oh my.*

I trudge down to dinner, Stan in attendance. While the other tables are ecstatic as they munch chocolates before eating dinner, he scoffs at my chocolates, his intense brown eyes boring into mine.

"We don't celebrate Halloween."

"I know, but the Filipinos do. In fact, have a two-day holiday." I smile inwardly, hoping the crew is enjoying chocolates and cookies.

"That's because they follow the United States. Not everyone in the world follows the United States."

"Nor would I want them to, Chief." I think of Ion on the Bridge praying that his country would be conquered by the United States.

"We have things in Poland that are centuries old. In the United States, our houses would be museums. Halloween, what is that? What does it mean? Why should we act as if we care?" *What the hell is going on here – everybody is going nutsy over frigging Halloween.*

"Stan, I don't ask you to celebrate Halloween. I wouldn't presume to tell you or your country what to do. But, for information sake, Halloween is not a nice 'holiday,' it's made up of wretched souls and goblins. Yet, if memory serves, its origin is not from the United States. It's from the Druids. Do you know the Druids? I think they probably predated Poland."

Silence. *Wow, what a day!*

Captain never shows up, but Ion runs down, gulps dinner. Says Captain is relieving him on the Bridge – an amazement that makes Ion very jumpy and causes Stan's thick eyebrows to rise dramatically. Ion grabs the chocolates at his plate, looks longingly at the Captain's, but resists, then bolts. This guy is a chocoholic.

Now Stan turns into a pussycat, ashamed (as well he should be) in his aristocratic way, of his behavior. He changes the subject.

"If Eve and I travel to the United States, where should we visit?"

"Visit the United States! Now, why would you do that, Stan?" *Mean, MsSelf, mean!*

"Uh, Eve has always wanted to."

"What does your wife like to do?"

"Everything," meaning, by his tone, everything Stan likes to do. *Aw well, these Eastern European men, what can one do?*

Nonetheless, we get into a spirited and meaningful conversation of places for them to visit. "Do the West Coast, Stan, it is beautiful. I will get you a map, and we can look at places like Seattle, Portland, San Francisco, Las Vegas, snow-capped mountains, immense forests, empty, beautiful deserts, many cultures. We'll do that soon."

We end up forgetting about Halloween, obviously a good thing, and turn to the problems of the ship's performance.

"Ships are best when they are three to five years old. All the problems of a new ship are behind them." Then, imperiously, "A ship is like a woman. Must be taught so that she becomes just what you want."

I hoot, while he regards me with dismay. "Hah! Little do you know that you, the small-minded men, are the ones being taught and trained. You all are just too full of yourselves or too dumb to recognize it."

He laughs. "All right, all right," and we continue about MarkShip Mexico.

At Ion's request, I take my computer up to the Bridge, where we look for U.S. maps and just hang out. "I didn't hear the horn toot."

"That's because we haven't passed Gibraltar yet. Maybe midnight. I don't think 2nd Officer is going to toot for you."

"We're going kinda slowly, aren't we?"

"Yeah, they are trying to fix something in the Engine Room."

"Nice computer, Cari. A good one." He takes the gold wrap off a candy and looks at it forlornly. "Last one," and he pops the whole thing in his mouth, closing his eyes and smiling. *Geez, the power of computers.*

And, wow! the turnaround all in one day. *Those Amazing Chocolates.*

Wednesday, November 1. The Atlantic

Sun, glorious sun. Force 3-4 seas. Force 4: Moderate, 11-16 knot winds, 3-1/2-5 foot waves. We are pleasantly rolling along on gentle swells. Retard clock #3.

I walk around the decks and run up and down stairs, ending on the Bridge.

Marius is loving this day and full of energy and fun. We swap Suez stories.

"What do you know of that boring place, Marius?"

"Only that it's hotter than hell, the wind blows all the time and sand gets in your teeth and ears and makes you crazy. It's a very long ride at eight knots, 100 miles, I think, with swarms of tiny black flies biting."

"Wow! You've summed it up very well. Except now it's 120 miles long with the new expansion, even though it's still not much more than two American football fields wide. So it's a single-file, one-way deal on a canal flatter than a pancake.

"Capt. R. on The Other was a veritable storehouse of info. If I close my eyes, I can hear him telling it was ten years in the building, opened in 1869 – that stuck because we transited in 1999 and we commented on the 130 year history. Lots of back-stabbing and political skullduggery went on, changes of ownership and many closures due to wars. Somewhere in the 1950's, Israel, furious that Egypt wouldn't let them use the canal, invaded Egypt followed by France and Britain who were disgruntled because passage on the canal wasn't free. Now Egypt was mad, so they sank forty ships in the canal. Guess that stopped traffic, huh?

"Did you notice all those war memorials on both sides of the canal? They were practically the only signs of civilization on the east side. I just *loved* the highways and huge black-topped parking lots for the war memorials with, of course, nary an auto – nor human - in sight.

"Egypt used the fees from the Canal to finance the Aswan Dam. What did your ship pay to transit? We paid over to $200,000 for our twelve-hour boring ride, which should have been ten, but we had a goofy ship stuck ahead of us. That's versus $120,000 for Panama. Pretty spendy, huh? Sure, we were a big ship, and it's probably less for smaller ones. Still, at fifty or so ships transiting a day, that's a chunk of daily bread. Oh, plus a $25,000 or thereabouts fine if you don't make the cutoff time, 0300 I think, to one of the holding pens just outside the Canal in the Med or Red Sea.

"When we made our south-north run for Suez, engine pounding, the weather in the Red Sea was horrific – rougher than a cob, wind driving straight at us out of the north with blowing red dust that made visibility nearly zero. It stuck to the windows and made a hell of a mess. Surprised we made it on time.

"Plus the pirate problem in the Gulf of ... What is it? Aden? Anyway, it's before the Red Sea. We stood off fifty miles-plus from Somalia, running full speed, holding our breath. Times like that you wish you'd taken an airplane."

"My God, what are you, Cari, some kind of a canal nut? First Panama, now Suez."

"There are more canals, as you know, Marius, but those are the biggies. Might just as well collect a fact or two. Just remember that once through Suez is quite enough for a lifetime, but twice through in a month, like I did, is way too much to bear. The second time I saw what I didn't see the first time – poverty, squalor, men and boys cavorting in the canal waters while women and girls stood watching from the bank in the blazing heat, wind and sand blowing their layers of heavy long-sleeved jackets, long skirts and burkah-ed faces. Poor Capt. R, shaking his head in disgust and commiseration, bravely bore my wrath that day. I had always wanted to visit there, but after Suez, Egypt was promptly scratched.

"But, we're here to tell Suez stories. Seeing as how I'm all wound up, can I start?" He nods. "OK, here goes. The beat-up excuse for a ship in front of us pulls slightly out of the convoy, a loud, very irritating humming sound coming from it – making your teeth ache. 'Resonance,' says Capt. R. 'Under certain circumstances, the engine sets up a harmonic, a vibration throughout the entire ship, causing the steel to resonate, and everything shakes. A phenomenon barely understood.'

"Unable to pass in the narrow canal, in the sweltering heat and humidity, flies biting, we wait, moving back and forth between the air-conditioned Bridge and the torrid bridgewing, where the action can best be viewed. Small boats, carrying the Canal 'experts,' scurry to and around the affected ship, darting in and out, barely missing collision as everybody hollers and curses, arms waving on board and in the small boats. You'd think for $200,000 a pop, there would be radios or walkie-talkies. Nope. It's a comedy of error and mismanagement. Capt. R. mutters under his breath (far be it for him to actually curse out loud on the Bridge), but settles in, resigned and sweating, his sparkling, perfectly pressed white Captain's shirt with epaulets and crisp, black Bermuda shorts slightly wilting. In the meantime, on Hatchcover Deck, our Egyptians are doing a land-office business selling their junk.

"Marius, have you been in the Ballah Bypass, the place where south-bound ships in the dreaded Second Convoy wait hours, seems like days, for the northbound convoy, which has clear sailing from the Red Sea to The Med, to pass on the main canal? (The First Convoy, of course, is doing their waiting by bobbing happily in the middle of the canal on Great Bitter Lake.) A large sand dune separates canal and bypass, and if you stand on the Main Deck, there is the illusion of those mammoth ships sailing on sand, moving sedately, grandly on sand. It is breathtaking."

Marius nods. "I have never seen it, but I would like to. We did our waiting in Bitter Lake, part of the much-preferred First Convoy. What captains do to try to get in the First Convoy southbound - they all hate the Second Convoy."

Now, it is Marius' turn.

"You already understand, Cari, that all Egyptians working the canal want baksheesh, which is VERY illegal, but the norm, nonetheless, even with Suez Rules posted conspicuously on every wall: 'No presents,' repeated over and over, using other words for 'presents.' The canal work-ers get very testy if they don't get their presents – and presents mean cartons of Marlboro cigarettes. No other brand, only Marlboros.

"One time, in Suez, our bonded store was absolutely empty and when Pilot demanded cigarettes, Captain said, 'We don't have anything left. I can take you down and show you.'

"'Drop the anchor! Drop it now, there is something wrong with this ship, and it cannot transit Suez,' Pilot hollers.

"'What? This ship is in excellent condition. Besides, we're underway in the canal.'

"'Drop the anchor. We cannot proceed.'

"So we dropped anchor, holding up the entire convoy, while a run-about went from ship to ship trying to buy a couple cartons of Marlboros.

"So with that established, you can imagine that any Captain would not be surprised when, upon entering the canal, a Suez tug worker hollers up to the Bridge, 'Welcome to Marlboro Country, Captain.' They don't smoke them, you know, only sell them – at exorbitant prices."

"You know, Marius, Capt. R. on The Other Ship told me some interesting stories about the, um, Wonders of Suez. I asked him about a room on D Deck, which was always locked. 'For Suez electrician. It doesn't matter that we have our own electrician. We must hire an electrician and a boatman, although we have a full complement of sailors. Both electrician and boatman do nothing more than set up shop in the Hatchcover hallway to sell Egyptian trinkets they have brought onboard.' And sure enough, they had a whole array of junk displayed on tattered blankets. They used the D Deck room mostly for prayer – and to nap.

"I remember going out onto the bridgewing and seeing a huge, very sophisticated spotlight set up. 'What's that?'

"'Suez light, required in the canal. We cannot transit without it,' Capt. R. said.

"'But there is no transiting in the dark, only in daylight hours.'

"Capt. R. sighed, 'I know.' But, Marius, the Suez light wasn't a total waste. We set it up on the bridgewing in pirate waters, too. The better, I guess, to identify the thugs and murderers coming at you about which you can do nothing since merchant ships are not allowed guns on board." We both snort loudly at the stupidity of such a maritime rule.

Marius' last story is about the pilot who was whining for cigarettes (Marlboros, of course) when he suddenly asked Marius for a flag, any flag. "A flag? What do you want a flag for?"

"To pray."

"You are going to pray to a flag?" But, Marius finally gets Pilot a signal flag, Pilot spreads it out and drops to his knees, salaaming to the East. For the next half hour, the guy moans and prays atop the flag.

"'But what about the canal? We're in the middle of Suez! Aren't you supposed to be working? Hey, hey there, you are supposed to be guiding us.'" Moan, yummmmm.

Now Marius has this vision of all the pilots on all the ships in the convoy stretched out on flags and salaaming to the East. What if there is a problem? Will these $100 million ships all go crashing into each other like a freeway pileup? Crash. Yuuuuuum. Crash. Yuuuuuumm.

"'Hey you, Mr. Pilot, hey.'" Yuuuuummm.

We laugh and agree that Suez is fascinating and boring all at the same time.

"See you later. Good watch, Marius."

Around 1100, everyone, waving from atop boxes and grinning, is full of delight and enthusiasm for this lovely day in the Atlantic.

On my third deck round, I come upon Ion checking the very sophisticated lashing setups on the yacht and sailboat, hanging bow to stern, port.

"Do you want me to take your picture with them?" he asks.

"Fun idea, I'll meet you back here with my camera in a few minutes."

We climb up on the boxes, he takes my picture with boats in the background, and we hang out between the boxes, talking of ships, TEUs, FEUs, loading procedures, loading innovations and upcoming ports. He shows me the lashings and turnbuckles and tells me about semi- and automatic devices on the box corners.

"What about piracy, Ion? We won't be in pirate waters, will we?"

"Not really. The Dominican Republic, where piracy is rampant, will be as close as we get. But piracy is growing by leaps and bounds. (His eyes dart to me – more wonderful slang.) Right now, it's bad. Soon it will be the most dangerous thing at sea and won't be confined to certain areas. Sophisticated pirates are after big-money cargos. There is nothing funny about pirates, but you might find it interesting that fancy shoe designers send left shoes on one ship and right shoes on another."

"No kidding!"

"Somehow they get hold of ships' manifests and know exactly what's in each container. The big-time pirates are smart, dangerous and absolutely ruthless."

Sure glad I asked.

At 1630, I run up to the Bridge to ask about getting copies of the two empty discs I found in my computer bag, now loaded with my thankfully-saved-for-years-funniest e-mail jokes. And it all goes swimmingly.

"Look, Ion, let me wash and repair the poor old bedraggled flag that we hoist in every port. Even though it is only a Liberian flag (Liberian flag – flag of convenience – ship registrations one obtains by simply sending money to a Post Office box in New York), I hate to see any flags mistreated." Ion nods in agreement. "Is it all right if I wash, iron and repair the U.S., Mexican flags and, of course, Liberian flag? They are the ports we'll be in next. I will be very careful with them. They're, after all, flags for countries. And it's so tacky, if not irreverent, for us to fly tattered flags."

"Of course," and I see that look of how strange are American! Women! "But we have lots of flags, some new. As on any ship, at least two for each port we might touch, plus signal flags. You don't have to do this, Cari."

"Well, we weren't flying the Italian flag, or Dangerous Cargo either, in La Spezia and poor old Liberia looked like she was down for the count."

His mouth opens, closes, eyes narrowed. "You are sure?"

I nod. *Somebody's gonna get it,* I sing-song to myself. *Damn! Why did I mention it?*

He rushes to the flag cabinet, flings open the door, and we both stare at the nearly empty elongated pigeon-holes where flags should be nestled. I lean over and pull out one sadly misused United States and one Mexican flag, hanging onto them tightly. The larder is now empty.

Ion grips the tops of the cabinet doors, perhaps ready to slam shut the doors so we needn't stare at the empty holes. "Ooohhh noooo, even the flags." And he slams the doors. His face is bright red, and he trembles, fists clenching and unclenching.

"What is it? Are you all right?"

"What? Oh. Yes." He may say so, but he is in an enraged world of his own that does not include me.

"Goodnight, then (although it is only 1700.) Have a safe watch." And I rush away with flags under my arm. *MarkShip Mexico, what now?*

In my safe cabin, door locked, window open to the beautiful breeze, shoes drying in the window, computer volume turned to full blast, classical music soothing, I drink my two drinks, watching the rolling sea, blanking my mind, allowing not even a hint of the dark undercurrents of this ship to intrude.

This evening, I am going to dine in my cabin alone with tortilla chips and beans purchased in La Spezia. A raiding trip to the galley is in order to secure onions, yellow cheese and hot sauce. "I will not be down for dinner, Alex."

"And thank you too, Mum."

Drinking wine and chomping away, I find this just an OK experiment. Damned Italy makes everything sweet, including, if one can believe it, tortilla chips. Even the vodka with lemon, which I like and have sampled many brands in the past, is sweet.

I watch the fading light turn to black, the ship rolls with occasional quick jolts, causing me to brace and glasses to clink in the cupboard. I grab my shoes and slam the window. Suddenly, we are rocking and rolling, and I grip the desk. The few glasses in the cupboard are crashing wildly and loose objects on the coffee table, cupboards and desk fly. The deck tilts crazily, and I hold on with all my might, thankful that all the furniture is bolted to the deck against just such an event.

Unlike the time, while on one of our fancy cruises when we encountered a ferocious South Pacific typhoon, the grand piano came charging on its rollers across the sharply-tilted ballroom floor like a freight train, strings twanging in a cacophony of discordancy, bearing down with determination, sweeping everything in its path before it, sending us few still-healthy passengers scattering, luckily ending up with a humongous crash in a mountain of crushed tables and chairs. It had been set up grandly in the ballroom corner for visual pleasure, no doubt, by a landlubber who knew not the power of an angry sea and the need to safely secure everything.

We've hit a big one. MarkShip Mexico bucks and pitches for half an hour, noise ear-shattering, creaking and rending of steel terrifying, then it's over as quickly as it began. I continue my tortilla/bean repast, which I had jammed in a cabinet surrounded by towels, now rearranging everything on the paper plate. Only a few beans to be scraped up.

When I am sure everyone will be gone from the Dining Room, I run down to put my leftovers in the refrigerator. Who knows? With the miniscule portions on this ship, I might want a bit of sweet snacks again. Or give them to Cristori. Anyone who is not a Mexican food fanatic will happily eat them.

Captain and Stan sit in the Officers Lounge and look up in surprise. "We thought you were seasick." Captain covers three beer cans with a newspaper, while Stan takes a brief swig of his.

"Why? Do I look seasick?"

"No, but you didn't come down to dinner and..."

"You," I glare at Captain, "I rarely see for either lunch or dinner. And you," I spit at Stan, "I see only half the time. Do I ask if you two are seasick? When you don't appear, are you REEALLY seasick?"

"Of course not!" they snort.

"Well, I ask you again. Do I look seasick? Any more than either of you?" They look chagrined, and I laugh.

I cross to the refrigerator and put my stuff in, which causes Stan to sit up in surprise. "Refrigerator, Stan. For all officers' use, right Captain? Why, you can use it just any old time you want, Chief Engineer." Silence. Stan shoots Captain a murderous glance.

"By the way, Captain, 2nd Officer tells me I can't download my computer games for you, just one game is more megabytes than a disc can hold. Now if we had the cables, which we don't have on board, maybe we could transfer directly from my computer to yours." I look at the ceiling.

"When we are in Miami, we can buy those cables." I snigger inwardly. Exactly the answer I was seeking, since Ion had tentatively suggested it earlier, but he doubted the expenditure would be approved. *Hee, hee.*

"Why don't we get some cards and play real poker," Captain suggests. "Maybe undressing poker."

"Undressing poker? Oh, you mean strip poker." I roar with laughter. "Why would anyone want to play strip poker with you? You cheat. I bet you cheat at every game."

"I played it once on the Internet," finishing his beer in one gulp, ignoring the 'cheat.' "The lady kept taking things off. It was live video, you know." He leers at me, and, yet again, I experience the uncanny chill that he knows something about me, which causes him to grin like a satisfied satyr. I twitch my shoulders. *There's something very wrong here.*

"How much did *you* have to take off?"

"When it came my turn, I turned the video off so she couldn't see."

I turn to Stan. "See, I told you, this man cheats at cards, obviously everything." Stan giggles, but squirms uncomfortably in his chair, the conversation not to his liking - not undressing poker, not calling his Captain a cheat, or maybe the squirming comes from calling him a cheat hitting too close to home. *Well, folks, there will be no undressing poker while I'm on MarkShip Mexico.* Then I say it aloud, "You'll have to keep your undressing poker to yourself."

"I must leave now," says Captain, crestfallen. "So much work. So busy."

"You asked for this job, remember? We can only shed so many tears for you, you poor, poor man." He laughs. *Hope he doesn't stagger full of beer to the Engine Room and get entangled in something down there. On the other hand... MsSelf, behave!*

Stan and I talk about his maybe-someday trip to the U.S. If I give him an itinerary for the U.S., will he do the same for me for Poland? Yes, yes, he will tell me all and write it down in case I ever want to visit. Besides, we can exchange e-mails if we miss something here on board.

2100: I go up to the Bridge and ride along with Marius, looking at the moon's reflection streaming across the smooth water like a molten river of silver. It is so beautiful from this high vantage point on the blacked-out Bridge. And these guys are so inured.

The quarter moon turns bright orange and sinks over the horizon. "Wait!" hollers Marius, "She's coming back up again." The tip of the moon reappears, then sets again.

"Wow, that was something!" I marvel. Then, as if to *really* show us what she can do, she reappears again, tip rising right up over the inky water. We are awed, can't believe it. "All Hallowed Souls Day, no, All Saints Day," I whisper, and we both laugh uneasily.

"In fact I have seen this once before. My husband and I were dining in a seaside restaurant in Puerto Vallarta, Mexico, the entire clientele watching the moon set, sighing collectively when it slipped over the black sea. Suddenly, a guy a couple tables over, yelled, "Look, look, it's coming up again." And the moon did exactly what we just saw. Think it has something to do with atmospheric conditions. Like a Green Flash, which, by the way, I have seen twice. All conditions must be absolutely perfectly attuned to see these phenomena."

We talk of the Ghost Port in Rotterdam, turning from one spooky subject to another. Marius has never seen it and does not really believe me.

"The Ghost Port is a huge area, Marius, with cranes and trucks running here and there, just like normal. But not a human in sight. The whole shebang is computerized. It gave me goose bumps and the willies just going by it in the Rotterdam harbor. Ask Ion or Captain; they both know about it. Ion tells me their equipment can load seventy boxes to our twenty-five. Don't believe me, ask them."

He backs down, marveling, shaking his head at such a place. "It's not right, you know, robots taking the place of men."

"Have you ever heard about how the experiment with robot ships went?"

"Cannot be."

"Capt. R. told me that they were trying out robot ships, everything computerized. Needed only two officers and, I think, two crew members. Something like that. He said that it wasn't going too well. That even the smallest glitch with the computer brought on disaster. Makes sense to me."

I peer through the upper reaches of the Bridge forward window. "Look at the Milky Way. It's gorgeous. I want to see it from the bridgewing." We step outside.

"What did you just call it? The Milky Way? That is funny. Really funny. Crazy name. Cannot be." And he roars with laughter.

"That's the name of it in English. What is it in Romanian?" He gurgles something. "What does it mean in English?"

Meekly, "I do not know. Maybe Milky Way." We both howl, clutching our sides, on the black bridgewing with the stars so close we can touch them, the Milky Way a bright, creamy streak across the sky.

"You are a very funny man," I say before opening the inside Bridge door to go down to my cabin. His laughter follows me until the Bridge door clicks firmly shut. I chuckle loudly down the two flights, the jolly sound echoing in the inside stairwell.

Thursday, November 2. The Atlantic

Sunny with drifting clouds in a cerulean sky. Maybe Force 4 with 5 foot swells. This is the most pleasant sea of all, the ship moving gently from side to side, then topping a mild wave and bobbing forward and aft. God, I love it. No time retard today, thanks be.

I reluctantly exercise, walk a bit, not much for I am very tired today. Nap off and on for three hours. Can't seem to get out of bed, although I want to go up to Monkey Island and sunbathe. The sweats attack off and on, and I remember Coimbra in a fit of panic, so succumb to resting and fitful sleeping.

Flags, all mended, washed, ironed and folded (hopefully correctly), are returned to the Bridge, where I watch the sun slip into the sea in a blaze of glory, thinking, "Nothing like sunsets at sea."

The only folks for dinner are Ion (who is being relieved by whom?) and me. We idly talk about the ship and dreams.

"When I am Captain, I will be like the Germans. There is not much I admire about Germans, but their Captains don't bow and scrape to The Company. 'I am Captain, I know my vessel, and you guys are shit.' Not like him," and he waves disgustedly toward Captain's chair, "who grovels before The Company. But then, he doesn't really know his ship, either." He snorts. "I won't be like him, that's for sure."

"Are there many Romanian Captains?"

"No, but I will be one."

"Remember, Chief Officer, remember, Ion, you must have humor. It will make you a great, not just a good, Captain."

He smiles one of his rare smiles. "I will remember."

Stan appears, and we have a leisurely time, I nearly blurting out that I consider Captain a male Chauvinistic pig, but even with Captain's wine whaling away in my gut, I keep it to only innuendo. *Tut, tut, MsSelf, keep it under control.*

We are all regarding our plates with mild distaste when I start to giggle. "You know, this isn't so good, but Cook is a genius with what he starts with. On The Other Ship, we had a weekly menu and a drunken Estonian cook who turned perfectly good provisions into vile gruel, things like "Torero Slice (one slice of salami and cheese on heated bread), Power Slice (one slice of salami and cheese on heated bread – the same you say? Yup.), Italian Farmers Breakfast (omelette with tomato-less spaghetti inside and, of course, the ever-present hot dog chunks), Smashed Potatoes, Spaghetti with no tomatoes or sauce, just hot dog chunks, Soljanka (Russian soup with veggies, pork and hot dog chunks), Lens?, Pelmeni filled with meat?, Fish with Grated Hard-boiled Egg, Hamburger with fried Onions (that's it – nothing else on plate), Hoppel-poppel (fried eggs and potatoes together – not bad if it had been cooked sometime in this century), Green Cabbage with Knacker, Laubskow (what was it?) and the famous Horse Sniffles (a misunderstanding of the Estonian language by a none-too-bright passenger), which to this day, no one knows, or wants to know, its ingredients. No wonder the middle of the table was filled with condiments." I look at our table and clamp my mouth shut.

"But the capper was Pudding Soup. Capt. R. was in a vile mood and, uncharacteristically, greeted no one as he entered. 2nd Officer, a shy young Russian, finished his lunch and stood to leave. Capt. R. jumped up, one hand grabbing 2nd Officer's arm, with the other the dish of Pudding Soup the Estonian cook had served hot for breakfast this morning and now cold as a sort of lunch dessert. I saw surprise, then panic flit across 2nd Officer's face. Capt. R., pulling his Russian officer-cum-translator in tow, stormed into the kitchen shouting, 'Pudding Soup? Pudding Soup?' his thick German accent grating out the words like the most profane curse, walls shaking. 'What is this Pudding Soup? There is pudding, and there is soup. Pudding Soup? I don't know Pudding Soup!' And on he raved, barely giving his Russian officer a chance to translate. Capt. R. retraced his steps to table while 2nd Officer slid out the door. Nary a peep nor a stirring from the shocked galley.

"Pudding Soup never appeared on the menu again. But, to Capt. R's despair, neither did the food improve. So he would occasionally go into the galley and cook something for him and me – a special sausage, a delicious sandwich of thickly buttered black bread, marinated tomatoes, onions, salt and pepper, or a crisp weinerschnitzel. The ingredients were all there, but Cook made slop of all of it.

"'Only,' Capt. R growled as he rather rudely plopped the plate at my place, 'because you hate the food as much as I. And none of my exhortations can change the output of this, this Estonian cook.' Then he would turn on his heel and retreat to his own table, where his own cooking would provide a tasty meal. He was a good cook, too.

"After one chandlering port, a small table in the Dining Room was covered with European cheeses. 'You say you like cheese, Mrs. Lindley? Here!' said our Captain with a wide grin. And Mrs. Lindley, plus the other two passengers and all the officers, had a feast.

"There was lots of food if you asked. If you wanted ten Horse Sniffles or fifteen Pudding Soups, you could chow down. Plus as much fruit as you could eat. And the planet's most fabulous muesli in large glass jars. You guys know that, for the mostpart, food at sea sucks. It's some kind of code between cooks that the rest of us can't fathom."

We all laugh and finish our plates.

Ion says he must hurry back to the Bridge. "My watch, you know," he says for my benefit, and I roll my eyes to the ceiling before he rushes away.

But Stan is not done with our Captain – or his name.

"What is his name, Stan?"

"Romauld."

"Really? The first time I ever laid eyes on him, he shook my hand and asked me to call him Romick."

"Ah," says Stan. "How interesting. You see, Romick is the diminutive of Romauld. He would be called Romick as a small boy. Or his mother or wife would call him that. Why he asked you to call him that I cannot say."

"Perhaps it's my age. I'm fifteen years older than he. That must be it."

Stan smiles secretively. "I doubt it. And I also doubt you are fifteen years older. Perhaps five. Yes, I'm sure, five." *Now, how do you know that, Stan?*

"Dammit," I explode. "What do you mean? What the hell does any of this mean?"

Abashed, he replies, "I really do not know why he asked you to call him Romick, Cari."

I throw my hands in the air. "Lord, this is all so difficult. I don't understand you people at all." Then I'm ashamed and sit back, repentant, fiddling with my napkin. When I am finally able to meet Stan's eyes, I say, "I'm so sorry. It's just that the tension is..." *Unbearable. No! Don't say it, don't even think it. I will not give in to this.*

"Perhaps 'thick' is an appropriate word," Stan supplies. He looks away, and I can practically hear his brain whirring as he mentally thumbs through his English thesaurus. "Yes, thick."

"Thank you, Stan. 'Thick' is an excellent choice." He smiles gently, and I want nothing more than to immediately change the subject.

"Tell me about your wife, Stan." She is also 'a blondie,' my size, likes to garden, a wonderful cook, very kind and caring. He smiles lovingly, his aristocratic features softening, face glowing.

Mr. Speak-of-the-Devil comes into the Lounge, missing his footing and nearly falling onto the couch. A few too many brews, mi capitan? "Come in here. We can smoke." Stan shrugs, and I grimace, but we move to the Lounge.

We talk about Ruth Cris, a steakhouse in the US. "Very expensive, but worth it," Stan adds. "Oh, to eat one of those wonderful steaks! A filet mignon, thick, garlicky, charred on the outside and deep pink inside. I love American steaks," he says wistfully." I glance at him in astonishment – he actually likes something American.

"I wonder if there is a Ruth Cris in Miami. Stan and I will pay for dinner and you, Captain, will pay for the cab." *Whoops, MsSelf, there's another invitation, even if it's mostly to Stan. Better watch it!*

Stan snorts. "The agent will pay for the cab." But I can tell he loves the idea.

Out of the blue, Captain starts talking about Viagra, causing Stan and me to frown.

"Can't understand why anyone would need it," Captain says, leering at me again with that 'cat' look.

I burst out laughing, "What a hoot you are! You, sir, are really a very, very funny man." Suddenly, I don't feel like laughing, sick of his cunning face and attitude, and I hiss at him, "By the way, what's the story with you and your topics of conversation? Undressing poker and Viagra. Can't you talk about regular things like ships, ports, your wife, your dog, your garden, as the rest of us do?"

He glares first at Stan, then at me, his face a mask of meanness, then storms out.

Stan and I sit morosely, finally drifting into rambling conversation. I tell him about my life with my husband, my sorrow, my life alone.

"And there is no one at all for you?"

"Understand, Stan, the answer is no, not for nearly seven years. And I don't want anyone. Only to seize the small pleasures of life. I am not looking or wanting or expecting. Once you've had the best… Yet, what I miss the most is the beauty and tenderness of being held. Like Eve will hold you when you get home."

His face is so sad I wish I had never said it. Tears well up in his nearly black irises surrounded by astonishing pure white. The long hands of this young/old man twine and twist in his agony for me.

"It's all right, Stan, honestly, there are small pleasures. For instance, because my husband and I had so many happy cruises together, I haven't been able to get on a cruise ship without him. But, I love the sea and so have substituted freighters for cruise ships. And I've met many lovely people – like you." He brightens, and we move on to other things.

I decide to ride on the Bridge for a bit.

"Ion, want some cookies?"

"Cookies?" he asks brightly.

"Sure, I'll just go down and get them." He demurs. "Oh, for heaven's sakes, it's only two decks down."

I return in minutes. "Here," I hand a packet to Ion on the dark Bridge. "And here's one for Marius when he comes up. I'll just put them on the chart table." I push the curtains aside and walk to the chart table. Captain is working the computer across the aisle. "Hi, do you want some cookies?"

"No, only beer and Polish sausage," he grunts. I shrug and leave him to his computer, pulling the curtain closed as I leave. *Yeah, well, don't you have two suitcases full?*

While Ion munches cookies (which, I hasten to loudly explain, are ones I bought in Spain and Italy – don't want Mr. Captain, skulking behind the curtain, thinking I am giving away his cookies. Heh, heh.), we begin yet again to discuss Romania and its former and present place in the world. I swear when I get off this ship I will know the entire histories of both Poland and Romania, every war and who did what to whom – and how the United States screwed up at every turn. (Probably more truth than poetry, but it sure gets tiring hearing it.) Somewhere in there, Mr. Captain must have gum-shoed out, probably sneaking out the open starboard bridgewing door, since we heard no clicking sound from the inside door.

Change of watch, and I ride along with Marius for a while, getting into heavy stuff about friendships and the meaning of life. *Whew! And to think I wanted only to see the moon.*

In my cabin, I fix a goodnight toddy and sit by my window, watching the sea, deciding to make a Wish List for MarkShip Mexico. The moon is gone, but the calm Atlantic hisses by my window at maybe fourteen knots. The midship crane's gantry rides tucked in aport my window. The throb of engines is even, steady – the ship is without problems tonight, and the Engine Room officers and crew are hopefully, happily nestled in their beds.

I Wish, MarkShip Mexico, I Wish:

-That I didn't ask so many questions whose answers break my heart.

-That First Officer Hartmut from The Other Ship would appear, his long Yoga-enhanced body gracing the Bridge, his kindness and easy smile filling the corners and corridors. He, who pulled every string and trick to stay First Officer during all of his East German career (although The Powers demanded he be a Captain) so that he wouldn't have to sit in the nightly after-dinner meetings with the despised Communist Intelligence Officer.

-That I weren't surrounded by down-trodden Eastern European people, who can't fathom what has happened or will happen to their countries or to them personally.

-That there was laughter and pleasure wherever I looked.

-That Roberto had answered Captain's first ship-wide call to the Bridge (the only time I ever heard such an announcement), so that the entire ship hadn't heard the third call which bellowed, "ELECTRICIAN, this is the Captain, come to the Bridge NOW!" And the ensuing clatter of shoes scurrying up the inside stairwell, their echo full of angry panic.

-That we felt comfortable enough with each other to drink a few beers and laugh the evening away instead of hiding behind our individual closed doors, their fireproof slamming jarring the senses.

-That I had a refrigerator, TV set with VCR or even a radio and maybe a couple feet more cabin space, although I'm growing attached to my little nest on the sea.

-That my darling friend, David, one of three passengers on The Other, were on board to tell me witty stories, make pithy observations in his oh-so-English way, provide intelligent conversation and display his sweet caring for his fellow human beings.

-That Captain was seasoned, erudite and gracious, not a jumped-up peasant full of his accomplishment, full of leering and rudeness, saying ridiculous stuff, such as when I inquired if he would take just a second to show me the Rhumb Line on the charts, "That's what I have officers for."

"Excuse me?" I stared at him in distaste.

"Well, ha, ha," he giggled uncomfortably. "Here, let me…"

"Never mind." Holy shit, what a clod!

-That we would all speak the same language all the time, so I wouldn't be treated to guttural Polish or Romanian at table.

-In the same vein, that Polish and Romanian were the same language, so even the officers could understand each other, which they can't and don't seem to care..

-That the damned smell in the bathroom would stay GONE, rather than reappearing shortly after each day's bleaching.

-That Chief Officer Ion would often smile for the sheer pleasure of it as he did this morning when we met on deck, he in his orange work coveralls, I in shorts. As I approached, he pointed, his forefinger like a steel rod at the end of his comically stiff arm, to the sunlit blue sky, anticipating my gushing oohing and aahing at the fabulous day. I did not disappoint him, laughing and jigging around him with joy. And he, who once growled that he never noticed skies, sunsets and deep blue seas – not important, not important – smiled and smiled at the clear blue sky, fabulous day and me.

-That everyone in the Dining Room would stop screaming at Alex like he were an animal instead of a wanting-to-please young man.

-That Cook would have excellent provisions to start with so that officers wouldn't growl at Cristori when the meat is gristly, the fish boney. He is doing an incredible job with what is available to him from stores.

-That I wouldn't have seen that large lump of something on the galley counter.

"What is it, Cristori?"

"It's meat, Mum."

"Ugh!"

"It's what I have, Mum. Inferior, but better than nothing."

"Who would order such crap?"

"Not I, Mum. It was provisioned from Barcelona before I came onboard. I have secrets to make it taste better for the officers. Then, the scraps I put into the crew's food, because they don't have eno...because it will make it taste better."

"Scraps? The hardworking crew eats scraps?" I look at him inquiringly, and he looks away.

-And speaking of food, that the officers would stop their testy grumbling and accusatory looks at Alex when he tells them there is none of any small specialty item that they are obviously used to eating on occasion and are definitely not now receiving. Have they already eaten it all and just can't remember? Boy, they must eat fast since we're not that long out of Barcelona.

-That half of the No Liquor/No Drugs signs would be taken down. We get it, we get it! Whether we obey is a whole different ballgame.

It's 2300, and we've hit another of the Atlantic's bad spots. Are these called squalls or what? Must ask someone. We are 'arockin' and 'arollin', papers flying, glasses crashing, boxes on deck trumpeting their mistreatment. Capt. R. on The Other said the boxes sounded like 'ely-fawnts' in heavy seas, their screeching akin to an 'ely-fawnt's' roar. How true.

At 2400, we are calm. I release my grip on the bulkhead side of the bed and sleep.

Friday, November 3. The Atlantic
Calm and sunny from my open window. What would we call this? Force 2: Light breeze, 4-6 knot winds, ½-1 foot small wavelets, do not break. It is a most spectacular day. Retard clock #4. Lunch is now bumping into breakfast.

The day floats by hour by beautiful hour.

A quick dinner with Stan, who, surprisingly, talks about on-board barbeques he has attended and that maybe tomorrow we'll have one of our own.

"Yyeeesss!" I shoot my fist into the air in a victory salute. If anyone would know the real scoop, Stan would.

He shakes his head, smiling at me, eyes dancing. American! Woman!

I ride with Marius. He thinks my stories are hilarious of 'seasickness' and Florin asking "Were you scared?" when I told him I hung onto my bunk for dear life last night between 2300 and 2400.

"Scared? It never entered my mind. I was simply trying to keep from falling on the floor."

"Maybe they were trying to show male superiority," Marius chuckles. "Kind of dumb."

"Hmm, exactly what I was thinking."

"Well, Cari, machismo is like superstition. Stupid, but deeply ingrained to the point it cannot be cut from the human psyche. No amount of high-tech surgery is going to remove the problem. And no amount of social reform by do-gooders or do-badders is going to even touch the root." *Oh Marius, you darling, scruffy thing. You blow me away.*

"Which makes me think, Marius, you were going to tell me about seafarers' superstitions."

"This could take days. But, OK, here are a few. Remember that seafaring is one of the world's oldest occupations – right up there with prostitution." He smiles his deprecating Marius smile. "Going to sea in the old days – even now – was riskier than going to outer space today. It naturally follows in the old days when inexplicable events at sea occurred, superstitions were right up there leading the band as to WHY they occurred. The uncontrollable nature of the sea paves the way to nautical lore and unbridled superstition."

"Let us start with the very thing we were talking about. Machismo, stupidity. And the one closest to you right now, which has affected you here on this ship whether you allow its ridiculousness or not.

"No Women on Board. Women were/are said to bring bad luck because they cause sailors to think about things other than their duties, which angered the seas that would then take their revenge. Oddly enough, naked women onboard were completely welcome."

Marius stops suddenly, jolts upright in his chair and turns away, staring at the sea. His flaring anger is so intense that it flows from him in jagged red streaks flashing on the dark Bridge, and I shrink away.

"What is it? What's the matter? Marius?"

"Uh, nothing. I will tell you later." He sits back in his chair. "Later I must tell you. But now we are talking seafarers' superstitions.

"Anyway, naked women were supposed to calm the sea, which is why so many topless women figures adorn the bow of ships. It was said that her 'breasts shamed the stormy seas into calm and her open eyes guided the seamen to safety.' Figure that one out if you can.

"And then add this to the silliness: Male children born on a ship were called a 'son of a gun' because the most convenient place to give birth was on the gun deck. Now, you were not supposed to have women on board, yet having a male child onboard was a sign of good luck. You have to ask, WHAT?

"Strange sounds heard at sea are often blamed on mermaids or sirens, who sing enchanted songs, which can lure sailors into treacherous waters where their ships would be dashed against the rocks."

Marius regards me seriously in the dim light. "Do you not think, Cari, that with all of this writhing around in a sailor's belief system that you did not cause some dismay? Maybe two or more women would have been easier, but one woman? Particularly with men from highly superstitious backgrounds and countries, sheltered, no, repressed all these years, countries where women are not treated as equals, but sla... less than equal? Take Transylvania, for example, a part of Romania, where Florin's from, by the way. Do you not think that vampire believers are well beyond superstitious? Add sailors' superstitions to the mix, and we have a raging bonfire. It adds up to more fear than sense."

I regard him, equally seriously but wordless, and he nods, continues.

"Red Sky at Night, sailor's delight; red sky in the morning, sailors take warning. A red sunset indicates a beautiful day to come, a red sunrise indicates rain and bad weather.

"A jolly punch in the nose will reverse bad luck words – like 'goodbye', 'drowned' and even 'good luck' - and crew's safe return by drawing blood, a sure way to reverse the curse.

"No whistling or singing into the wind unless you are in becalmed waters. It will 'whistle up a storm.'

"Sharks following a ship are a sign of inevitable death, dolphins swimming with the ship are a good sign.

"And birds play a big part. Witness *Rime of The Ancient Mariner*. Seabirds are thought to carry the souls of dead sailors. Do not kill one! But, it is good luck to see one.

"Bananas are evil fellows. Bad luck, dating from the empire between Spain and the Caribbean in the 1700s, since most ships that disappeared were carrying bananas. Guess they never heard of the Bermuda Triangle.

"Whatever you do, do not sail on Thursdays, Fridays, the first Monday in April or the second Monday in August.

"Thursday is bad because it is Thor's Day, the god of thunder and storms.

"Friday is unlucky because Jesus Christ was crucified on Friday.

"First Monday in April – Cain slew Abel.

"Second Monday in August – the kingdoms of Sodom and Gomorrah were destroyed.

"The only good day to set sail is Sunday.

"Obviously, we do not adhere to that stuff anymore. We sail when the schedule dictates or else!

"An earring, let me see, is it in the left ear? was and still is a sign that a sailor has traveled around the world or crossed the equator. I see that you are not wearing an earring, Cari, although you are entitled to, more than one. A gold hoop brought good fortune because gold brought magic powers, including the protection that would prevent the wearer from drowning.

"Tattoos are lucky; cutting hair, fingernails or shaving are no-no's.

"Most sailors could not swim, so they had a healthy fear of drowning. Even bathing in the ocean was tempting fate, so stay out of the water. Nice smell, do you not think? Anyway, even if a poor soul fell overboard, probably a rope would not be thrown since his death was already preordained. 'What the sea wants, the sea will have.' And maybe a little sacrifice to the sea gods might satisfy them so other crew members would not follow.

"Flowers are not to be brought onboard. Having to do with funerals. Same with clergy. Keep those evil guys away, too.

"Bells were not good things for the same reason. Yet, ship's bells signaling time and change of watch were exempted.

"When you get on a ship, put your left foot on first.

"Do not throw an old pair of shoes overboard.

"A ring around the moon means rain is coming.

"Do not clap onboard, which will bring thunder.

"Ships are always referred to as 'she.' Just like Mom and Mother Earth, she will shelter and protect you, this time as a home and refuge from an angry ocean.

"And the last one for tonight, only added because it so rarely happens. Changing the name of a ship is bad luck. It was thought, still is, that ships develop a life and mind of their own once they are named and christened. If you are silly enough to interrupt this pattern and rename a ship, there must be a de-naming ceremony. This ceremony includes writing the ship's current name on a piece of paper, folding the paper and placing it in a wooden box. Burn the box, scoop up the ashes and throw them into the sea. And hope your feeble little ceremony has more power than the ship's personality.

"Know, Cari, that Superstitions of the Sea are rarely spoken on board. There are many of them and are written in stone in a sailor's soul. Indeed, even to talk about them is bad luck.

"I have only mentioned a few because you asked, and I promised to do so. I wouldn't think to scoff at the Superstitions, although I really do not believe 100% in those that cannot be scientifically proven. But, I understand the purpose of them – it is a code of living, so to speak, it was and is a means to try to secure oneself against the treacherous seas, against the unknown and unpredictable, a path to safety." He laughs, "After all, 3rd Officer is the Safety Officer on a ship. And that is I, Madam."

Oddly, I did not mention the barbeque.

CHAPTER NINE

The Peasant

Saturday, November 4. The Atlantic.

Calm and sunny with two-foot swells. Doesn't get any better than this. Force 2 again.

0700: I pop up to the Bridge, full of good cheer, coffee in hand, to see the sunrise. "Hi, First Officer, how goes it?"

"OK, nice day again." He clears his throat and jiggles his knee. "Ask Captain if we are having a barbeque today. He promised." The knee jiggles harder. Ion's been stewing about something.

"I'm not asking him anything. I'm sick to death of him. You ask him."

"He promised, and we probably won't have it. He complains that we eat too much, that it's too expensive."

In a mighty explosion of pent-up frustration, the First Officer spews his litany of anger. "He says we eat too much! Hah! The Company allots $6 a day per person, and he is only spending $4 to $4.50."

"Well, Ion, we can hardly be eating too much with these miniscule portions. But, he told me he spends $6 a day per person." (I don't mention that on The Other, $9/day/person was allotted - 33% more!)

"Hah! I have prepared lots of chandlering lists for other captains. He is putting the difference in his pocket. For $6 a day per person, we had very good food on other ships – salmon, cheeses and cold cuts. No, he may buy these things, but he sends boxes of food home to Poland. At Valencia, Barcelona, La Spezia, Miami, you can see him sending big boxes with the agent. And he has never been off board to make shopping. Where do you suppose it comes from? This ship, that's where. Money and food that are supposed to go to the crew go into his pocket or are sent home."

He stops and glares at me, although his eyes seem to divert around me, as if not really seeing me. "You've seen them. You've seen the boxes! The brown-wrapped boxes tied with string. They are the same every port, except more boxes after a chandlering port. You've seen them, Cari! First at Barcelona and then at La Spezia. What do you think the technicians were carrying off? They weren't here to carry things off; they were here to carry them on and make all repairs. And they did, bringing all machine parts and special items with them. If Tom and the others had known what was inside those boxes to Poland, they would have thrown them at Captain, maybe wrapped them around his neck. They were HERE! They knew about his kind, you could tell from their eyes, and how they tried to avoid him." *Yes, I know, Ion, Tom knew for sure.*

His fury is so great, he continues without a breath. "Nothing for the crew. Nothing! Believe me, I know." (Now I wonder about Cook who left us at Barcelona. Captain said lots of provisions were missing. *But who took them, Captain?)*

"I am Chief Officer. It is my duty – it says in every handbook, every school, in my papers and in my contract – to see after the welfare of the crew. I am responsible for them, for these people who work so hard on this ship."

He is wound tighter than a drum and shouts, "Often I personally buy presents for the agents and pilots, some beer or cigarettes. They say I am a rich man. I say no, but they should have a little present. He gives nothing and takes everything. There is plenty of money in the Slopshop to buy these things. No, no, he says he buys them, but he puts the money in his pocket. He received all sorts of Polish foods from home when the technicians left the ship. He keeps them all for himself. Nothing for anyone else. I wanted a couple pieces of special bread, which I also like. He said no, it was his. Only for him – me, me, me - nothing for the crew."

"Ask him about the barbeque. Ask him! When a passenger is on board, he acts differently in front of them. Also, in front of Chief Engineer, who has been with The Company for eight years. He is afraid of passenger and Chief Engineer, afraid they will complain. The Company will listen to them, and he knows it."

"Don't ever sail with a Polish captain. Sail with a German. They don't do such things. Believe me, I know." *I believe you, Ion, I believe you.*

I am astounded, bruised by his flaring anger, my own gorge rising in my throat. *So this is what it's come to – all of your Pollyanna determination is in the toilet. Well, Miss Goodie Two Shoes, the blinders won't stay in place any more. This Captain is a thief of the lowest caliber and a peasant – a boor, an oaf, a lout in every aspect of life. Damn this Peasant Captain all to hell.* I follow Ion to the Chart Room.

"Strictly between you and me, Ion, you can take the boy away from the peasants, but you can't take the peasant out of the boy. Do you understand what I mean?"

"Yes, I do." But, as he leans over the chart table, he is shaking with fury.

0800: I am white hot. What to do about it? First, do some rigorous exercises to burn off this rage streaming through my bloodstream - which doesn't really work since I continue stewing, cursing and muttering under my breath.

Alex knocks on my door, cleaning day, and is dancing a jig. "Maybe a party today," he glows, beaming.

"How do you know?"

"Chief Officer said."

"What time did he say it?"

"About 0800. Just awaiting orders from Captain. A party!"

In a flash, I'm out the door to confirm all this with Cristori and practically smack into Stan at a hallway corner. "Are we having a barbeque today?"

Stan grimaces. "No."

"No? Why not?"

"Captain's decision. No barbeque today."

"I'll go talk to him. Right now."

Stan looks alarmed. "Don't tell him I said anything about a barbeque last night."

I want to yell at him, "Why not, Stan? Ion says he will listen to you, is afraid of you. My God, can't you see why? You are an aristocrat, but more important, a person of substance, and he is shit."

I say instead, "Don't worry, your name won't enter the conversation. Besides, other people have mentioned it. And most of all, he promised me a barbeque and that's how I'll put it to him." Stan sighs and walks onward. *Why didn't I insist that he come with me? Because he's such a nice man, and I don't like to upset him? Bunk! I don't think he will help, and I want to punch him - A jolly punch in the nose to bring good luck.*

Up five decks to The Peasant's cabin. The door is closed, and a clipboard is stuffed with papers, obviously not at home. Or maybe he's not up yet, and I sure as hell do not want to see Old Spare Tire half-in or half-out of a state of undress. Definitely not if he's on or been on another binge. Never know. I walk the decks, dodging Saturday's cleaning hoses, telling myself to calm down, three times running up five decks to check on The Peasant's door, but it remains firmly closed, clipboard papers intact. Every ascent and descent brings on more fury, and I am drenched with sweat. If I stand in one place, water cascades down my legs, and puddles gather on the deck. *Oh, Coimbra, beautiful city of rivers, parks, charming winding streets, roasting chestnuts, your venom still lurks in my innards, surfacing with a vengeance when I'm stressed.*

Showering interminably in my newly-bleached bathroom, I distract my seething anger by thinking about the onboard evaporators that distill sea water to be stored in huge tanks for potable water – ingenious pieces of equipment. Thus, fresh water, water everywhere and many drops to drink.

I finally drag down to lunch. Stan and I discuss the Mexican peso, great Mexican beer and other things Mexicans like to drink.

The Peasant walks in and heads straight for the galley. I hold up my hand for Stan to stop talking, and we try to hear if he is ordering Cook to prepare a barbeque. Nothing intelligible. He returns with a plate of Filipino food and sits at table.

"I like to eat this stuff. I really like Filipino food every so often."

I regard his plate with distaste. *Remember, flies like honey, not vinegar, MsSelf, and you really want this barbeque.*

"Such beautiful weather," I begin.

"Yes, but only God knows how long it will last."

"Well, before the beautiful weather goes away, when are we having the barbeque you promised me?" The Dining Room is instantly quiet. Nary a clink, sip or chew.

"For you, anytime. Tonight?"

"Sure, tonight." I see Alex's beaming face floating before me.

"Can't tonight."

"Why did you mention it then? OK, tomorrow."

"No, Tuesday. But only for you."

"What does that mean?"

"We'll have barbeque here," he gestures to the grim Officers Lounge. "Just officers, here, inside."

"What? When you said barbeque, I thought you meant the entire ship, the entire crew."

"Can't. Too much work. Too much upset." Mumbling, "Too expensive."

"If this ship is so poor, then I'll pay for it. When I write to The Company about my voyage, I'll request they reimburse me." NOW we have his attention.

"Can't do it with the entire crew," he stubbornly insists. He sits up ramrod straight in his chair, belly pulled in, stern countenance. I am The Captain! is the demeanor, but panic flits across his face.

"In that case, if it's only for a few people, don't bother. You say it's my barbeque. I want everybody, officers and crew." Silence. "This poor, poor ship." I shake my head, wondering if he is interpreting my words as it is too financially poor to pay for a barbeque or that they are poor to be under the command of such a miserly master. I mean both and say, "This ship is poor in every way, Captain." No response.

Silverware clanks and the Dining Room resumes quietly, carefully. The Peasant pushes the Filipino food away and magically produces his special Polish bread from a sack hiding under his chair, with no offer to share with Stan or me, shoving half pieces into his mouth at one time. (Mine! Mine! *Why don't you eat this frigging stuff in your cabin?*) I turn disgustedly away from him.

"Back to our conversation about the peso, Stan," excluding The Peasant completely, shoulder turned away from the food-shoveler.

"Good fish," Stan says in a mollifying tone.

"Full of bones," I snap, pushing the boney mess around my plate in the ensuing silence.

Stan and I talk about computer controls in the Engine Room and on the Bridge, all backed up by manual controls. Stan really doesn't want to talk about this; his eyes keep sliding to observe his Captain, although he has moved his chair well away from The Peasant, leaving a noticeable gap between them. *What, Stan, would you rather continue talking about the non-existent barbeque?*

I suddenly remember that I have not yet seen the Engine Room and am about to request it, when Stan asks sternly, "Do you understand tons?" *Stan, why are you doing this dumb stuff?*

"Are we talking metric tonnes or U.S. tons?" I grate. "Let's see, I think the metric tonne is 1.2 times the U.S. ton." Stan is open-mouthed.

The Peasant jumps in, voice hearty and full of approval. "That's right, it is." I regard him stonily, silently, and he returns to shoveling.

Into the breach, I request a tour of the Engine Room and make a plan for tomorrow. Stan looks at the clock, his lunch always a race against the noon engine report to The Company, excuses himself, breathing a sigh of relief. Chief Engineer likes to battle with engines, not people.

I stand immediately with him and intone flatly to The Peasant, "Excuse me. Have a good afternoon." *Hope you choke on your Polish bread, you stupid bastard.* He grunts, eyes on his precious food.

I hand Stan my pear as I leave, watching delight cross his face. "Sure you don't want it, Cari?"

"I'm sure." Even the officers are on short rations while The Peasant stuffs his face from suitcases full of Polish goodies.

Still fuming, I walk the decks and end up on the Bridge with 2nd Officer. "Hi, haven't seen you for a while, so just stopped by the say hello."

"Hello." He leaves the Chart Room and sits in the officer's chair, gesturing with a smug little smile for me to sit in The Peasant's chair. Somehow, my sitting there tickles him.

"We're having a safety drill today at 1630." I look at him in dismay. *Well just jumped-up wonderful. 1630 should be about the time the anticipated barbeque was to begin. Also the time the crew would normally be off-duty since it is Saturday, so no rest today. God, Peasant, you are the world's asshole.*

My face must tell it all. He shrugs one shoulder, frowns and moves back to the Chart Room.

I want to scream, but at the same time, I want to lighten the leaden air to enjoy the rare event of riding with 2nd Officer, this most difficult man to know, the officer in charge of navigation on this and every ship. That's it!

"Seafaring magazines talk of the dangers of The New Millennium. Could ships really have the problems they gloomily forecasted? We're months past the event Year 2000. Could things still go goofy?"

"Perhaps, but doubtful, now or even at the outset of The Millennium. Even if GPS and other systems went, or now go, awry, we had and have this," and he sweeps his hand across the charts, "and the North Star. We sailed long before today's sophisticated communications. And if everything electronic breaks down, in a very short time, we will still be sailing. There will be huge problems, no doubt. But these charts will keep us delivering goods to ports, just as in days of old, even if we have to row." We laugh.

My, my, 2nd Officer. You are going to make a great Captain. And so I say it. "2nd Officer, you will make a great Captain. But you must add some humor."

He smiles, a very pleasant addition to his handsome face.

"Oh yes. But not on this ship."

Then he turns away, and I start to leave. "Thank you for joining me, Mrs. Lindley. It has been a pleasure."

"May I again?"

"Probably not wise." Then he adds softly, "For me. Although I would enjoy it very much."

Oh God, is it this ship, this world or this time in place? Why have we so miserably failed?

In my cabin, I try to turn my mind to Stan's itinerary, which has been falling by the wayside of late, but cannot keep from whirling back to what has just transpired. Still I persevere – must get this done. I can always edit it later. Travel, think travel. Forget what happened at lunch.

OK, Stan, so we head north and east out of Flagstaff, destination Jacob Lake and the North Rim of the Grand Canyon, probably a five-hour drive. The highway will take you through a small part of the Navajo Indian Reservation, its vastness and desolation impressive, although you can turn up your nose at the way Navajos live. Sometimes ramshackle and kind of messy. Nonetheless, interesting in that you get to view an ancient culture's way of life, complete with their traditional housing (intermixed with falling-apart trailer houses and conventional house construction), hogans. Hogans are octagonal, made of wood and clay. All doors face the east to greet Dawn Boy, their name for the rising sun.

If you ever read English books and want an entertaining way to learn about the Navajos, a very popular author named Tony Hillerman has written a series of novels about a tribal policeman on The Res (Navajo Reservation). The stories and characters are very good, but the background of Navajo culture, which he so easily works into his books, is clever and wonderful. If you read all his novels, you will end up with a very good education about the Navajos. In fact, although he is a white man, the Navajos have made him an honorary tribal member.

Understand, Stan, the cultures of the many Indian tribes in the US are as alien to most Americans as they are to you. Strange as it may seem in that "melting pot" called the United States, those of descents from all over the world who live in the USA have not taken the time to find out about the indigenous ones, the American Indians. And the white man's traditional treatment of the Indian has been abominable. For that reason, as well as their own sacred cultures, the American Indians have drawn in upon themselves and, in today's world, only let the white man know what they want him to know. It is disgraceful discrimination on both sides.

However, as I listen to idle chatter on this ship, I find that Romanian and Polish are every bit as discriminatory as Americans. Maybe more so, since both Poles and Romanians appear to only live among other white men. Aryans, I believe a famous housepainter loved to call himself and cronies he considered untainted. Do we find it strange that his 'Aryan' philosophy and its horrifying results continue to frighten the world some sixty years later? Americans, for better or worse, are of every color and religion. Much as we may not understand each other, we do live together. Not always in harmony, but we reside side-by-side.

We surely have not 'melted' together. Indeed, it is the new rage to search for your roots and take pride in ethnicity. Hey, I say, go ahead and do it. But how is this fabulous ethnicity of yours going to help you understand and live peacefully with your neighbor of a differing ethnicity? The world recalls with horror that runt who fashioned ethnicity into an Idol, who attempted to eradicate entire populations and religions he considered 'impure.' Will this stupidity never end? Probably not as long as there is more than one human being alive on earth. Never mind, never mind (English words which I have taken lightly all of my life until I have heard them pronounced with anger and despair aboard MarkShip Mexico. "Never mind, never mind" has taken on a new meaning for me.)

Discrimination, humankind's coverall word to mask its age-old intolerance of one to the other, creeps up, enters the soul and melds with a person until he doesn't even recognize it as a human failing.

However, as a recipient of discrimination, it can make a person see Bogeymen around every corner. For example: What if, I think to myself as I consider some attitudes aboard MarkShip Mexico, what if I were considered by the Male Titans (chuckle, chuckle) aboard as not 'merely a woman' (here I pause to laugh silently with great disdain, judging my life's accomplishments against theirs), what if I were Jewish or Black or Green? Would the Great White Males throw me to the fishes?

Discrimination, I know it well. Having spent a working lifetime as a female authority figure in a sea of male faces and posturing, I understand well the ebb and flow of discrimination, Planet Earth's fatal disease.

Hhrrmmpphh! That itinerary-writing went out the window, didn't it?

1610: To the Bridge to ask where to watch the safety drill since I am obviously not invited to attend. "Don't you think I should know what to do in case of disaster?"

Both Marius and Ion shrug. "This isn't really important information; it's mostly a training film that doesn't say much. Not a lot of doing real stuff." *Oh good, Peasant, you've taken the crew's badly needed off-duty and rest time for this.* "Watch it from your window. What little will happen will be to port."

And, then, at exactly 1614 on the radar screen, Ion again launches into a tirade about the barbeque, Marius leaning silently against the bulkhead.

I tell them Captain is not speaking to me, probably never will again, after our lunchtime conversation, and I fill them in. When I get to the words, "I'll pay for it," Ion jumps up and streaks across the deck, hollering, "You will NOT pay for it. The Charterer provides money for things like an occasional barbeque, for a couple cases of beer, a case of wine, soft drinks and a few kilos of extra fish and meat. It wouldn't cost more than $50. I know, I know. I've done it many times before."

Rushing on, words tumbling together, "You wouldn't believe what has gone missing from provisions. We took on cans and cans of smoked eels, many specialty things in Barcelona. There are NONE LEFT! I can take you down and show you. I can show you bills for what came on board and what is left. It all went to Poland. We already know that it went there with the Polish technicians when they left La Spezia. They had a driver. It was easy. Just give the boxes to the technicians and tell them to tell the driver to deliver it to Mrs. Captain. So easy, so easy."

I stare at him, swaying with the roll of the ship, wishing I was on another ship.

"When we get to Miami, I call the Big Boss. I will ask for guidance as to what to do here."

"Ion, be careful. You could and probably will lose your job. I'm sure companies don't like officers complaining about their captains."

"No, I won't lose my job," he says stubbornly.

"Oh yes you can. Depending on who has the most power with the Brass. And I'm willing to bet lots of money that it's not Chief Officer."

"I have witnesses. A few Filipinos are watching, and 3rd Officer said he saw more boxes leave with the agent after I had left the area." Marius squirms, but holds his tongue, wishing, I am sure, that he, too, were elsewhere.

"If I receive the authorization, I go into Captain's cabin, open the boxes, call the police, and, swoosh, he is gone, locked up. Like he should be – now."

"My God, are you serious? Are you nuts? It won't work that way. The Company will do the reprimanding. But of whom?"

Ion shouts, "Lots of things are missing – flags, many books, small replacement repair parts as well as the most important item, FOOD. Who knows what else? Every day it's something more, something new that can't be located. We will see what the Big Boss says. I have proof. Never mind, never mind. I have proof. Besides, the Filipinos will report when they return to Manila after their contract.

"I HAVE to do this. If it comes out later, The Company may think I didn't report it because I was doing it, too. In with Captain for the thefts. Besides, this is OUR food. It belongs to the crew, in their stomachs to keep them well and fit, not in Captain's house in Poland, where he's either to gorge himself on it or his wife will sell it. *He's* not hungry, he's got suitcases full of food."

I look at Marius and Ion, both twice my size, and ask softly: "Are you hungry?" Shrugs from both. They look at the floor.

Oh my sweet heavens. What a mess we have going on here.

The crew gathers below my window for the safety drill. I feel like What's-Her-Name in her ivory tower. We wave and laugh, one of them hollering, "Come on down."

"They don't want me down there."

Ion, surprisingly, is at table with Stan and me for dinner. No Peasant, as expected, although he calls to say he won't be down. Now, why would he do that? Do we care? Not one whit as we laugh and carry on like regular people. Very nice. Ion even gulps a glass of wine – a waste of wine, but what the hell?

At 2000, I am writing, fingers burning up the computer keys, when there is a timid knock at the door. "Alex! Hi. What's up?"

"Captain asks for you to join the party in the Lounge for 2nd Engineer's birthday, Mum."

I am so astounded at such an event that I blast out, "Really!" Then add, "Tell them I'll be right along. Thank you, Alex."

"Yes, Mum, Captain says. Yes, Mum, I'll do. And thank you too, Mum."

3rd Engineer, Florin, Roberto, Ion and The Peasant are drinking Palinca and Scotch. Stan is noticeably absent, although it is one of his crew having a birthday. After the briefest of hugs to Florin (nobody touches on this ship, even a handshake a scorching brevity of human contact, a mere touch – and I'm sure not the one who is going to encourage it), who blushes bright red and stammers, and a toast "To the Birthday Boy," I shoot back a Palinca as Ion and Marius had told me how to do when we talked about it days ago – or was it years. "You know how to do it!" they all grin, full of approval.

"Oh sure," as if I had been doing it all my life, giving a surreptitious glance of thanks to Ion. On the other hand, shooting a tequila in Mexico is no different.

Sitting on a couch between Florin and Ion, getting garlicked into next week by the special Polish sausage and garlic sandwiches they are eating, I light into the Scotch. So, The Peasant is finally sharing, maybe half a sausage by the looks of it, for the first time since those fateful suitcases arrived on board. A very thin slice of sausage with four or five pieces of garlic. Gadzooks!

The party is progressing nicely, all of us sidestepping The Peasant's leering jokes and innuendos, which cause each to twitch and exchange glances, when The Peasant, well into his cups, hollers,

"Who's God on this ship? Who's God? I am! The Captain! The Master! The Master of Everything! Everything and Everybody!" And he eyes his officers smugly, yellow teeth bared beneath the unruly bush of mustache.

The party stops short, and laughing faces turn anxious, heads dropping, eyes on floor, the birthday boy holding his head gently in his hands. The silence is breathtaking. *You nasty bastard!*

"No, you are NOT God," I say into the vacuum.

"WHAT? I AM GOD," and he beats his chest, surveying the drooped heads as if his officers' heads are bent in supplication to him. Why aren't they on their knees? I expect him to roar next.

"NO! *I* am God on this ship," I say loudly to match his tone. All heads jerk up, mouths hanging open.

He slams back against the couch, face chalky, mouth contorted, saliva slipping from one corner, fat legs and feet flailing in the air, rolling from side-to-side, as if he can't get a purchase on the couch he solely occupies.

"You are simply being PAID. I am PAYING. And paying passengers are God!"

He is so suddenly still I think he has died. "Passenger," he breathes as if praying.

"My ticket pays for nearly the whole crew's food on this voyage. I know it, and you know it," I snarl. All eyes turn to me in an amazed *Really?* Until this second, only First Officer knew facts like this.

The Peasant sprawls on the couch, as if punched, softly repeating, "Passenger." Color returns to his face as he giggles and struggles to sit upright. "Of course, passenger is God." Giggle, giggle. Then slyly, his drunken eyes narrowing, the resemblance to a pig uncanny, "Everything for the passenger. Which is why passenger gets barbeque."

Why, you sweet piece of crap, look what you've just done. And I smile hugely.

"Now, about the barbeque, Captain. You will remember that I told you I'd pay for it, since this ship is so poor, and request the Company to reimburse me." Another surprised swivel of heads, while The Peasant pales. Then, slowly, each word distinct, "And I Will Do Just That. Barbeque for the whole ship – officers AND crew - tomorrow night." We stare at each other.

"OK, OK," he mumbles.

Everyone leaps up and slaps hands in high-fives. Somebody hollers in the melee, "We're all witnesses." Then sing-songs, "Barbeque tomorrow night." Followed by excited talk about the time. The Peasant wants it at 1300 and everybody else at 1800. "I am the Captain, I say the time." Then he ducks his head and hunches into himself.

Screw his God complex, we're having a barbeque at last, so can I afford to be magnanimous. "OK, we'll compromise. 1745." Everybody howls.

While the excited talk of past barbeques on other ships and the expected one tomorrow roars on, The Peasant slugs down Scotch, slipping into a near comatose state, occasionally rousing himself to slur another lewd remark or anecdote. We all watch him with despair, the officers sending me apologetic looks. *Hey, you're not the ones doing it.* I shrug and smile at them.

The Peasant staggers off to tinkle, stumbling, slamming every piece of furniture with his round body. No one rises to help him. During his absence, one officer turns to me and says, "You should agree with him more, and let him be in authority. After all, he is Captain." I snort in his face. "Please," he begs. "You see, he can get very… And then we all… Please."

"OK, I will," I promise, wanting to slit The Peasant's throat.

But, by that time, it's too late to be more agreeable – or to slit his throat. When he finally falls back onto the couch, Scotch splashing in all directions, he sags and nods his head in semi-consciousness. All his wild laughing, leering jokes and ridiculousness are at an end for this evening.

Everybody but Florin files out, heads down, embarrassed eyes sliding to me with a good-night nod. Last in line, I turn at the door and ask Florin, "You'll be able to get him up the stairs?"

"Don't worry I'll take care of it."

"Why you? It's your birthday, after all. Why you?"

"Because I know how. I've done it many times before. Many."

I trudge up the stairs past the No Liquor/No Drugs posters.

CHAPTER TEN
Intrigue

Sunday, November 5. The Atlantic

Partly sunny, warm and hot, very humid wind. Force 6: Strong, 22—27 knot winds, 9-13 foot larger waves, spray. White crests. Ship rocking.

0800: I present myself on the Bridge to find out the time of the barbeque so that door-to-door invitations in The Peasant's name can be issued, as I agreed to do last night, mostly to satisfy his 'I am The Master' syndrome. Will Bosun let me go to the crew's doors or would he rather do it himself? Who cares? I'll find out. I dance a little jig. "Party tonight."

Ion doesn't know the party time. "Haven't spoken to him, probably won't until after 1200. He won't be awake until then."

He eyes me with a satisfied smirk. "Did you think Captain was dead a couple of times last night? He looked like he was dead to me. But that's normal for this Captain, his normal state." He stops abruptly and looks out the window. "Except since you, the passenger, has been on board, I do not see him so much. He sits in his cabin, plays computer games and drinks, sometimes lurching up here to bark ridiculous orders, which I have to straighten out. Sometimes, before you came, he was not even on the Bridge in port." He shakes his head. "Did poor Florin get to drag him to his cabin last night?"

"Guess so. Poor guy, it was his birthday. Let me know the barbeque time, and I'll knock on doors inviting. A silly idea really, since even the following dolphins will know the time by Jungle Drum once the hour is set. But I said I'd do it."

1030: Tour of the Engine Room. With Stan hollering garlicky explanations in my ear over the roar of the engine, I write notes as he closely watches. We end up in the blessedly cool and quiet control room, computers humming, dials and gadgets flashing, windows looking out onto the engine.

"Welcome," Florin grins. "We try to be good hosts on this ship. Cookies?" *Oh, these Cookie Monsters. From whence have they cadged them? They surely must be running out of their personal stashes by this time. Oh my God, Florin was in The Peasant's cabin last night. And if some of the brown boxes were open, not yet filled? Is that why he is so pleased with his cookie offering?*

"Thank you. You are good hosts." He smiles happily.

Many officers have gathered to see this spectacle of a woman running around their very impressive Engine Room, taking notes. They watch carefully as Stan and I go to the end of the control room to view yet another gadget, I scribbling, and all appear very satisfied with the whole scenario.

And their jobs? Who's covering? Even Ion is here, enjoying the curiosity.

"What time is the barbeque?" I ask between munches. "Have you talked to him yet?"

"Talked to him? Hah! A joke. It is only 1100. Way too early."

Stan laughs uncomfortably, and the others snicker.

This is a much smaller engine than The Other, but still very impressive with its ten-meter height and fifteen-meter length. The thirty-meter housing-to-propeller shaft is a half-meter in diameter, solid metal that will take 100 years to wear down. The area is commonly called 'Shaft Alley.' Average Engine Room temperature is 45 degrees C. The Engine Room itself is immaculate.

I hope I have asked intelligent questions, but can see by the forced patience in Stan's eyes that they are very mediocre. Oh well, I got to visit the Engine Room, anyway. And, as always, I loved it.

As I top the stairs, the ship rolls dramatically, and I hang on tightly to the railings in the staircases to my cabin. Amazing how smooth was the ride in the Engine Room compared to this. Good thing I left my window closed as gale force is pounding rain. A moment's glimpse through a rivulet shows heavy seas, very large swells.

Finally acclimated to the bouncing and pitching, I run up to the Bridge to get copies from my floppy since I promised Florin and Co. some funny thing on their table every day.

"No barbeque tonight. The Peasant has the luck of the Devil with him," I say sadly to Ion, who is briefly standing in for 2nd Officer.

"Sure, 1800."

"Nah, it's raining." I gesture disgustedly to the streaming Bridge windows.

"We have barbeques even if it snows."

"Believe me, no barbeque," and I point to the port windows. He runs out in the driving rain to the port bridgewing and peers over to see where the barbeque should be set up.

"Nothing! Dammit, nothing."

"You should know," I snap. "What did he say?"

"Say? I haven't seen him all day."

"What? Not all day?"

"Nobody's seen him."

"Well crapadoodle, do you think he's dead? Has anybody checked?" Then I laugh, "Does anybody care? People who don't keep their word disgust me. Even if he did keep his word this one time, he'd be so hung over he wouldn't enjoy it. That is, if he were happy giving it – which he is NOT. Double who cares." What a goofy situation. I would be panicked by lack of Captain if I didn't have complete confidence in Ion, Marius, the nearly-phantom 2nd and, of course, Stan. Who needs The Peasant?

"Chief Officer, I'm done with this barbeque business. Either it will happen or it won't. I have done my best and am frankly tired of the whole idea." Then it strikes me. "But, this whole thing really isn't just about a barbeque, is it?"

He looks at me so piercingly I feel my muscles tremble. "For the crew, yes. Some have been on board contract after contract. They need the money for their people at home. How fine it would be for them to have even the slightest amusement, a few hours of fun. Just once."

"For me and some others, no, it is not "just" about a barbeque."

`"I am very tired, Ion. So much is going on here that I don't know or understand. And nobody's going to tell me. It's ship's business, and I have no place in it. I don't think I really want to know, maybe I really shouldn't know."

He looks at me speculatively, opens his mouth, then clamps it shut.

"I need a drink, and I'm going to have one right now. See you." The inside door clicks behind me, and I clutch the handrails against the pitching sea and my violent thoughts, vowing to stay out of ship politics. I will listen to whoever wants to talk, but will remain disentangled. Big order, maybe too late.

How many hundred gallons of hot water would it take to deplete the ship's boilers? I am finding out under the steaming shower. At last, I am ready to face the world again.

I grab a bottle of the-oh-so-few-left wines and go down to dinner, sparkly, spiffed and full of vodka-bolstered good cheer. Stan and Ion, no Captain. "Think he's dead up there?" I laugh. Stan purses his lips and looks at me under his eyebrows, which causes The-Devil-Made-Me-Do-It remark, "Does anyone at this table care?"

Into the silence I pour wine. Little Miss Hostess. "If you gulp this, Ion, I will give you a jolly punch." He laughs, picks up his glass genteelly, small finger pointed to the ceiling, and sips. Even Stan laughs.

"Stan, I'm almost done with the USA itinerary I promised you," as I pour for him. "You'll have it soon." He gives me the softest smile, his eyes distant, and I know he's thinking of his Eve, and I picture them dancing at The Top of the Mark, which he doesn't yet know about, San Francisco glittering below them, Stan so straight and correct in his black silk suit looking down with that same softness to his Eve, graceful in her flowing emerald gown, her eyes glowing. Her trip to America.

I mentally jerk myself into the present, while Stan talks about Russian Engine Room officers he has worked with on other ships. "So intelligent, yet so stupid. In theory, they actually know more than the rest of us put together. Yet, there is a disconnect between the knowledge and the application, as if the school master will not yet release them to physically do what he has taught. It has been frightening at times. Their sense of the timing, the weather, the engine and its working don't seem to mesh. And engines, like ships, take on a life of their own, you know. You don't want to thwart them, but pamper them." He looks at me and grins a grin so unlike Stan. He is thinking about our previous conversation where he told me that one must teach an engine just like a woman, and how he got clobbered. (And I am thinking about my beloved motorhome, Skooter, in which I live when 'at home' and to which I talk as if she were a person. So, Skoot, we're not the only weird ones.) "We pet them, listen closely to their needs and wishes, play their little games until we are both satisfied." Stan smirks.

Ion's head swivels from Stan to me, his face questioning – What the hell is going on here?

Stan twitches his shoulders, steeples his hands in front of his chin, and says with serious sadness, "But Russians think you can brutalize an engine. The consequences are not nice."

We are intrigued and urge him for more, but he is done.

"OK, Russians," I say into the silence and have a sip of wine. "On last year's ship, we had East German lead officers – Captain, Chief Engineer and First Officer - and Russian second officers – 2nd Officer, 3rd Officer, 2nd Engineer, etc." Stan and Ion roll their eyes at me. Hello, we know who is who. "Had it not been for the finesse and humor of the Captain," I look at Ion sharply, "it could and probably would have been disastrous. It was never apparent on the glossy surface, but the undercurrents were incredible." Stan and Ion nod. Been there, done that. *Like maybe here and now.*

"Yet Capt. R., who rarely discussed politics, knew intimately the histories of the countries, the mentalities, the prejudices, the angers, the boiling recent backgrounds. He, after all, had lived through Communism and had observed with glee, he told me, its fall. I watched in awe as he threaded his way through the black water of it all. Everyone was treated the same, no deprecation ever, by his book of absolute Imperialism. My ship, my way. Yet, his kindness to his crew blew me away.

"Once I came upon him in South Korea, the mecca for pirated electronics, bending near a young deck crewman on the Hatchcover Deck, discussing the exact model number of the boom-box that lowly crew member wanted since Capt. R. was going ashore and the crewman's duties wouldn't allow. He jerked his head up sensing another person, but I had quickly stepped back into the hallway, leaving them to discuss his purchase for the crewman.

"Sorry, I got carried away. We were talking about Russians. I was riding with the 3rd Officer, a huge Russian kid, in pirate waters. He had been scarcely pleasant to me. '3rd Officer, why are you so stiff?' not really caring since he had been snidely rude.

"'We are in pirate waters.'

"'Well, no kidding. All the outside superstructure doors are locked - chained and padlocked on Hatchcover Deck. We're in here like a can of sardines. Only the bridgewing doors are unlocked, but look at what's out there.' I gesture to the bridgewings, bristling with the Suez lights and a special lookout with binoculars on each wing. He stiffens even more.

"Oh no! I have badly misjudged this situation. Softly I ask, '3rd Officer, have you ever been on a ship that pirates boarded?'

"'Yes.' He stands, arms hanging limply, legs apart, feet as if bolted to the floor, not a muscle moving in response to the tilting, pitching deck.

"'And?'

"'And,' he spits, 'and they lined us up like sheep on the Bridge, took everything we had, went to our cabins and stole everything there. Then,' his big body sags, and he puts his head in his hands, 'then, they returned to the Bridge...'

"To this day, I curse myself for asking, 'And?'

"'We were all lined in a row. No weapons, of course. Not allowed by the stupid people in charge. We are to face pirates with sub-machine guns and long, wicked knives on every part of their body, hand grenades in circles around their waists, rocket launchers on their boats. We are to stand defenseless. We are to...' He grabs his head and pulls his hair. 'We are to stand while they smile and circle us round and round, making a clicking noise, maybe a tribal sound.'

"'Which one?' they leer. 'Which one to show these stupid rats that we're not kidding.' They pad around us like lions, stopping here and there to jab one of us with a gun.

"'This one.' And they shoot 2nd Officer standing beside me, my workmate who'd told me all about his golden roses-his 5-year old daughter-his beautiful red-haired wife-his dreams to be a great Captain, my friend, blood spattering everywhere. I try to catch him as he falls, and they level their guns on me. 'Don't touch, Russian boy.' So, I, who should have screamed 'Fuck You!' stood straight again in the line. For all those dreams, all those nightmares, if I could only do it again, this time screaming, 'Fuck you!' And catching my friend in my arms, coddling his dead body, charge them like a raging bull, screaming, screaming. Why didn't I? Why?'

"3rd Officer on The Other and I stood silently together, while the ship tossed and the angry sea made itself known. '3rd Officer, you have been devastated by this, your life defined by it, but you are a man of substance, a man many will follow because of your overwhelming grief and your overcoming it to go on to great things.' Oh God, ooohhh nooo, I moaned to my shocked soul. 'Is there anything I can do for you?'

"He shook his head, and I touched his arm. 'Thank you, Mrs. Lindley.' He did not turn to me.

"'Have a safe watch, 3rd Officer.'

"This is the first I've spoken of it." Ion and Stan look at me aghast, tears standing out in Stan's eyes. "Well, we were talking about Russians…" I look down at my hands.

And the thought creeps so softly around the table. When the cat's paws come to each of us, claws extended, digging painfully in, the horrid truth pounces: We, too, are defenseless.

They sit for a few minutes, but there is nothing more to say. They must get back to their duties. I remain alone at table, riding yet again with that poor Russian boy.

Noises at the far table, which I had forgotten was there, make me realize that I am not alone. Florin, 3rd Engineer, and Roberto are trying to get my attention, yet not wanting to intrude on what they intuit is a bad moment for me.

I walk over and join them. They are in a dither about the book I'm writing (Obviously, somewhere in last night's melee, I mentioned my book.) "Can we get a copy?"

"Probably in a year or two."

"It takes that long?" And I briefly explain the slow, painful process of the publishing world.

"Will we be in it?"

"Of course, although you may not recognize yourselves. And other people on board will be in it, although nobody called by name."

They exchange glances. They know I'm talking about The Peasant, that I'm letting their Captain off the hook. The thought dances in the air between us.

"Look, gentlemen, although I travel around the world in odd places and ways," I shrug, "such as cargo vessels by myself, wherever I go, I like to surround myself with people of honor, integrity, character. I simply expect it. Do you know those English words?" I smile at them, and they smile back. They know and respect those words in any language. "Someone who doesn't keep their word is without honor."

They nod, knowing I'm not only talking about the barbeque or lack of it, as is the case tonight. They stare at me as if awaiting more.

"Honor, gentlemen. Good night."

The fireproof door to the Officers Mess bangs behind me, accentuating the total silence behind and ahead of me. I mount the stairs to Superstructure Deck 4, Cabin #403, thinking of honor and the ways I myself have transgressed it in my lifetime.

Ready to add to my daily record of shipboard activities, I sit in front of my computer, drinking slowly from my alarmingly dwindling supply of booze.

Honor, integrity and character really DO mean a lot to me. They are not words, they are actions, ways of life, that secret god that controls how you are inside, deep, deep inside, becoming one with you, shining outward. Out of control is one thing for an hour or a moment, but if you have them within your soul, honor, integrity and character cannot leave you. You are controlled by them. And although you may be lucky enough to find them by yourself in life's journey, in my case, they were taught in the most extraordinary ways at my father and mother's knees.

They wanted and expected of me, and I produced – all the time thinking smugly it was for me, but knowing, in my heart of hearts, it was for them. They had so little, yet provided me with the launching pad to do so much. It was so easy – and so painful it takes my breath away all these years later. But I could not disappoint them. And I did not. So easy, so easy, hiding the youthful pain of producing that ease behind smiles and accomplishment. Worth every moment.

Honor, Integrity, Character. I believe the words slid out of the womb with me tattooed to my forehead, sired by my father and dammed by my mother, each parent providing unique input. I am the product of very good breeding, although I have spent a lifetime denying it, always knowing it inside, only outwardly recognizing and giving merit in my latter life.

Yet my expectations of others tells me who I am, even when I disappoint myself. I shun the weak-minded and stupid and hold closely to the strong-minded and intelligent. I want to know what they know – and, to my amazement, they want to know what I know. To say "I do not suffer fools gladly" is an understatement. Produce, be of value. Otherwise, get the hell out of the way.

Even as I have mourned my beloved these last seven years, living in less than a half-life of grief and yearning, even within that cotton-brained time, I recognized those of value and those to throw away into the sea. It was so simple, so ingrained in my soul: Those with honor, integrity, character are 'keepers,' those without are garbage, unredeemable – fish food.

I sit, drink in hand, ruminating, feeling the waters shift beneath me, the welcome roll of the deck. Thoughts roil in my head. I am not done with this subject, I know it. Perhaps because the three words in question are so vividly shining in some cases and so abysmally absent in others on MarkShip Mexico. I turn off the light, stand at the window and watch the black sea, spume from the ship's running sparkling in the deck lights below.

Monday, November 6. The Atlantic

Sunny, deep blue sky. Warm and humid. Force 4: Moderate, 11-16 knot winds, 3-1/2-5 foot waves. Perfect!

0730: As I fill my coffee cup in the Dining Room, I smell frying bacon, the first time ever on this ship. I wonder where it came from, maybe spied as a leftover at the back of the freezer from the obviously dwindling provisions. Nothing will keep me from my favorite, and I eat four pieces on toast smeared with mayo, salt and pepper (ruing the lack of avocado. Avocado! Hah!), thereby sealing the doom of exercising today.

As I walk the decks round and round, flying fish leap everywhere, their iridescent bodies glistening in the sunshine, tails dancing on the water, causing tiny sparkling ripples that become a part of the boiling, shimmering sea. Sweat puddles around me, the humidity taking its toll. What did I expect? Flying fish only appear when it's hotter than the hinges of hell, air so full of moisture it could be raining in the blistering sun.

Lunch is Stan and me, him rushing away to make his noon report. The Peasant, the man who cannot keep his word even about a simple barbeque, appears. Huh! So he is alive, although looking like warmed-over crap. He opens his mouth to speak, and I glare at him, so he turns to his food. I speak five words to him, "Hello. Want Salad? Excuse me." Between this deluge of conversation, I try to chat with Roberto, two tables over, whose darting, nervous glances from me to The Peasant are so distracting, I finally give it up. *What's the scoop, Roberto? Why does this creep make you so jumpy?*

1300 finds me receiving safety instruction from 3rd Officer Marius, who, as all 3rd officers, is in charge of ship's safety. He advises that an abandon ship order will be verbally given over the loudspeaker. I am to go to the Bridge where Captain will instruct me. *Hope he's sober.* At which time, we will all go to the lifeboat. Marius shows me the inside, my seat and how to harness in, indicates the life rafts and the Safety Headquarters room.

Marius tells me, "The alerting system to other ships, satellite and radar emergency communications plus a manual and automatic communication to any ship within 200 miles would kick in. We would not be in the water long. They would come searching for us. There is so much communication equipment that half the world would know we are in the water. Signals bouncing off satellites, signals to other ships, signals to The Company."

And, I wonder to myself, *if the sinking ship's electronics are all damaged, then what?* But I don't utter a peep, just follow him meekly.

It is interesting, but I've seen it before. However, I'm glad to have this instruction for this particular ship so I know exactly what to do. Marius is friendly, but deadly serious about all he tells me and his role in it. "You may ask me questions at any time. I will be happy to answer. Any time."

My funny buddy on the Bridge is not funny now. We are talking ship's business, ship's safety. I feel safe in the middle of the Atlantic. Marius will look after me in a crisis. It is his business to look after the ship and its contents in crisis. I am a 'content.' Also a new-found friend. And if the ship founders, the first face I will see will be Marius'. There is no doubt in my mind as we now face each other across the sun-splashed lifeboat: Big, strong Marius, him of the laughing face and interesting mind, will take my hand and gently advise me exactly what to do.

1500: A knock on the door and it is Alex come to clean, presenting two more big boxes of cookies. "Thank whomever for me, Alex." And he looks at me in surprise. Who else could be sending cookies? *Where is The Peasant getting all this stuff?*

Alex waits expectantly, a big secretive grin on his face. He and I, plus the deck crew and half of the officers, know that the cookies get distributed as I walk the decks. "Take two," and just the grubby tips of deckhand fingers carefully touch the two selected cookies as brown eyes dance with delight, faces alight. "Just between us, yes?" I normally meet up with only a few crew members at a time, but over time, it evens out. I feel like the Fairy Godmother.

"Okay, Alex, take two." We peer into the box while he dithers between the biggest ones or the chocolate-dabbed ones.

"Oh, and about my order from the slopshop?" Alex looks at his feet and mumbles something about Captain. I don't pursue it; it not the poor kid's fault.

Three days ago, I filled out a requisition for three bottles of Johnny Walker, three cartons of L&M cigarettes (obviously this ship doesn't go through Suez – no Marlboros) and one can of peanuts, expecting them to be delivered within the day. On The Other, we, passengers and crew (who were allowed to buy beer, but no liquor) went down to the slopshop on Tuesdays between 1800 and 2000, drooled over the array of goodies from behind the half-door, picked out what we wanted or could afford, paid and tripped away with our purchases. I don't even know where the slopshop is on this ship.

To my amazement and anger, during 2nd Engineer's party, The Peasant pulled my requisition from his pocket and drunkenly waved it in the air, demanding slyly to know what I was going to do with three bottles of Johnny Walker. As a favor to the officers, I bit back the retort, *What business is it of yours?* "Drink one and take the other two off board with me in Mexico."

"Or maybe have a party," Florin laughed.

"Oh," slurred The Peasant and put the slip back in his pocket.

As yet, I have received neither booze nor cigarettes, but I refuse to discuss it with him these three days later, even though he appears to have sobered up. It has occurred to me that perhaps three bottles of Johnny Walker do not reside in the slopshop, that maybe they, amongst others, are at this moment reposing in Poland on The Peasant's very own shelf, that he may have to reorder in Miami to fill my requisition.

Yi, yi, yi, what a mess.

Well, bite my li'l ol' tongue. The Peasant and I sit silently at the dinner table, the only ones in attendance. The few words exchanged were as I entered. "Where is everyone? Thank you for the cookies." *Oh God, if he only knew where his cookies were going, what kind of fit would he throw?*

Halfway through our soundless dinner, he says, "We don't have peanuts in a can."

"Fine, I'll just take the other stuff on my order."

He scurries away into the galley, an odd place to retrieve anything from the bonded store (aka, slopshop), which, I just found out from Roberto in the hallway on the way to dinner, is one deck down.

Stan and Ion come in, and Alex hurries from the galley with a bottle of wine, my booze and cigarettes (So it's not all in Poland yet - probably had to raid one of his boxes), but no Captain. I pour wine and grin evilly, "Compliments of Captain."

"I will deliver your purchases to your cabin, Mum."

"Thanks, Alex, I'll take them when I go up."

"And thank you too, Mum."

Alex smiles at me mischievously, then returns to the butler's pantry. I turn to see both Cristori and Alex peering around the galley door, smiling. I regard them quizzically, realizing this is the second time they have done the same thing within fifteen minutes, the first time when I entered the Dining Room to be confronted by The Peasant sitting alone at table. After a moment, both heads appeared around the door stead, smiling like ninnies.

"Oh Ion, who did you tell that I refused a barbeque unless the crew was invited?"

"What? Who? Uh, Bosun and a couple of deck hands." He tackles the quite tasty spaghetti.

That explains the waving and minor hullabaloo on deck today while I was walking. One Filipino stopped his work, saluted and said, "Here is the First Lady." I laughed. Another joined him, and they both bobbed their heads.

"Thank you, kind sirs."

His joking smile disappeared, and he looked straight at me. "You are."

I didn't give it much thought at the time except for the pleasure of seeing all those smiling faces, but now it seems to be congealing into a strange pattern of light and shadows out of my control.

Damn you, Chief Officer.

The Dining Room fills, and everybody's talking at once. Haven't a clue what happened to The Peasant. Maybe he wriggled away into a hole. But, no. Somehow he got into the Lounge unseen and sits alone smoking. As I pass to the door, he starts a bout of nasty coughing.

"You shouldn't smoke so much, Captain."

"I know," comes the soft reply.

A hot flash of self-anger suffuses me, perspiration standing out on my face. Dammit all to hell, I want to go over, put my hand on his arm and say to The Bastard, *"Captain, keep your word to us. It's a point of honor, Captain, which is what raises us above the vermin. Just keep your word. Be honorable. And we will forgive you."*

Instead, I step through the door, furious with myself for such a sentiment, well aware he wouldn't have a clue what I was talking about and knowing in my heart it is too late for forgiveness by anyone on this ship, except maybe me and, perhaps, a couple of youngsters who want to believe in their Captain regardless of what he does. Want to believe, must believe. It's the Law of the Sea. *Please, please, Captain… Oh, it's all so hopeless.*

And now I come from the Bridge some hours later and am again filled up with hope for mankind. Marius, that disheveled one with the long hair and fascinating turn of thoughts and English words issuing from his tongue with gargling Romanian accent, amazes me. I had gone to the Bridge to calm myself and see the moon:

Marius and I look out over the moon-brightened boxes, watching the cranes tower over them, dipping and rising with the black sea, waves peaking silver in the moonlight. Large dark clouds with bright edges scud effortlessly over the sky. So serene, so tranquil, absolutely breathtaking.

"I think I might take a walk on deck. It is so beautiful."

"I wouldn't." The words come out "Aiii woo dent."

I laugh. "The only one who wants to throw me overboard is Captain."

Silence. Then, slowly, words echoing eerily on the dark Bridge. "People disappear from ships at night."

"Oh come on. We're looking at the radar, and there is not another ship within 240 miles. Are you telling me that someone on this ship is going to do me in as I walk the deck? This is probably one of the safest places in the world to walk."

"I don't want to scare you, but I don't want you to walk on deck at night. No one knows how crazy people can be. If you've been on board for ten months on top of a previous ten-month contract, etc., who knows what the sea will do to you?"

I stare at him in the darkness, green light reflecting from the radar screens. He and I have already discussed how overlong periods at sea can and do drive people to drugs, alcohol, insanity and suicide. And that no one understands the phenomenon.

His serious voice continues, "And suppose there are stowaways that we haven't found (and I think immediately of well-documented reports of stowaways discovered who have been onboard vessels for months and years). They would come out at night when nobody is around. And if they thought that you, an innocent person walking by, would report them, well… They don't come out in the daytime. Too many people moving around the ship. But, at night…"

The Bogey Man is out there. I can feel his hot breath. And then the unbidden thought: *Marius, do you know such stowaways are on board? I could believe it of almost anyone but you. Why are you telling me this?*

The boxes, cranes and sea rise and fall ahead of me. I can feel Marius some fifteen feet away turning toward me, anxiety tingeing his voice. "Please don't walk the deck at night. People disappear. When I worked on fishing boats…" and he tells me stories of people found in freezer holds or never found, simply gone. No clues, even when those found were obviously murdered. *Marius, do you know something that you should be telling me? This Captain thing has turned me loco.* "Please, don't walk alone at night." We ride in silence.

To brighten the mood, I tell him I want to see the interior of the yacht. Doesn't he want to see it, too?

"It is forbidden," he answers.

"Forbidden? You mean ship personnel aren't allowed?"

"No. It is not my property. I am forbidden to look at it. What if someone wanted to look at my property without my knowledge?"

"That's an interesting philosophy. Or is it religion? Why do you feel that way? You are simply looking at the yacht, not touching anything."

He laughs. "Philosophy? Religion? It is none of those things. Simply one should be forbidden to intrude on other people's property. I cannot."

"You mean you wouldn't look at, say, someone else's book in order to read it?" I think of the thousands of used books I've read.

"I could NOT. Suppose they had made notes of value to them in the margins. Or that there was a letter inside the book. If I simply were looking at their book, then I could simply look at their letter, couldn't I?"

"Regardless of what you say, Marius, this is philosophy. And now I'm going to go downstairs and ponder why we shouldn't look inside the yacht. You've given me something to think about."

Looking out my window at the glorious clouds, each edged in silver, each distinct and pristine, the evil face of a totalitarian society leers at me once again. Marius is forbidden to view the yacht or pick a book off someone else's bookshelf to read on a rainy afternoon or curl up with in the rose arbor seat because he has grown up with the idea that what is one person's belongs to all. And, much as he might deny it, he coveted a few possessions for his very own. But it was not allowed. It was forbidden. Therefore, because he wanted only a little for himself, some precious things that no one else could touch, under Communism's guidelines of what is yours is mine, the boy had nothing for only himself. Except in his mind. In the secret innards of his mind and soul, he kept a few things for himself that no one else could view, hopefully also a few beloved material things, but if not, then thoughts, feelings, sensitivities, never to be revealed. The boy would cry in his mind: You may not look! I forbid it! Ergo, it is not allowed that he look at that which is not his. It is forbidden.

Oh 3rd Officer Marius of MarkShip Mexico. Oh 1st Officer of The Other. Oh people everywhere who could not accept, cannot now accept, the steel boot that stamps out individuality, the need within every soul to keep only small unimportant to anyone but the holder, THINGS, ideas, thoughts, hopes, dreams. We can dispense with 'things' we have found at great emotional cost, but ideas, hopes and dreams are our sustenance. We shall perish without them. We clutch them closely to our breasts and, under despots, cleverly hide them in cloaks in our minds, breathe not a word of them. You may NOT look! I FORBID it! It is forbidden. My heart breaks with the years of yearning that produce those words.

Tuesday, November 7. The Atlantic

Sunny with two rain squalls. Force 6: Strong, 22-27 knot winds, 9-1/2-13 foot larger waves. Spray. White crests. Election day in the United States. I wonder who the new president is. Not that it'll make any difference. Sure hasn't in the past.

Sunshine streams in my window. First action of the day is the decision not to let barbeques, peasants or anything else ruin my voyage. *Today I shall be friendly to everyone - yes, I mean everyone - laugh and toss off all that has happened. The bloody hell with it. I'm going to enjoy my trip, and that is final.*

I walk to port, sun warming me, staying away from the bow where the spray is immense today. I time my walks on the Main Deck before 0800, between 1000 and 1030 (crew coffee time) or between 1200 and 1300 (crew lunch) since they are welding and painting on deck.

The wind is blowing like crazy, sea tossing us around like a cork. Dried salt crystals in lacy patterns glisten white against the newly-painted blue deck. The forward deck railings grate my hands, and salt adheres in shining glue globs. I wipe my hands together to rid them of sea salt, but the heavy fuel residue clings to every pore. It's OK, I know about this stuff and expect it. It's better than OK, it is part of this ship and my voyage.

Lunch is pleasant with my new-found attitude, if a bit forced. I talk to The Peasant as if nothing has happened. Surprisingly, he talks back, pleased with this new situation, actually smiling and joking. Lurking in his eyes is a triumphant, Hah! I beat her. I shrug.

He tells me this is his sixth contract with The Company. We chat about contracts. "Six- month contracts are too long – too long to be at sea. Although, some seamen's contracts are twelve to fourteen months, ten to twelve-hour days, a normal work week fifty-six hours. Too long." He looks to me for understanding, albeit a bit slyly, as if he knows that I know the disharmony aboard this vessel.

"But I only have a four-month contract this time. A Captain who works directly for The Company normally works three months with six weeks off. That is what I will do soon." He rubs his hands together with supreme satisfaction.

He scampers to the galley. His gait across the Dining Room when he is about to fix himself something special never ceases to amuse me. Bending his squat body forward at the waist, his short legs pump a hopping trot, face full of anticipation, but also fear that someone might have stolen HIS food. And, of course, he never looks to either side, which might entail an explanation of what he's up to. He never acknowledges or speaks to anyone when he's in the Dining Room or sitting alone in the Lounge, except for Stan, Ion or me. The officers keep a sharp ear on the head table, but do not acknowledge or speak to their Captain either. It seems an odd arrangement for men whose teamwork is paramount.

Never have I seen such a preoccupation with food. The officers hunger for it, talk about it and boast about their country's wonderful food, swallowing saliva as their Captain passes them with a plate for only himself – some concoction their mouths water for, but which he hunches over (Mine! Mine!). Stan often looks on unhappily, eyeing his tablemate's Polish food. As it turns out, nearly everything is covered with sliced onions and tons of garlic. Hard to taste the product in there.

Today, before Stan came in, The Peasant told me he had made Vigos, a combination of sliced cabbage, where he said he works the knife very carefully so each slice is exactly the same, ham and other meat.

Now as he arrives from the galley with his plateful of Vigos, he also has a small dish of pickled herring covered with onions and garlic and actually shares a few pieces with Stan, whose eyes light like a child's. Maybe this lapse to common courtesy is in celebration of my talking to him again. Maybe he just fixed too big a plateful.

"Would you like to try the Vigos?" I am asked.

"Only a small bite."

"Also for me," says Stan in his fastidious way, bringing a quick jerk of head, which Stan ignores.

"Aalleexx! Vigos for the passenger and, uh, Chief Engineer."

Both Stan and I jump. And I shake my head, growling to myself, *I tell you, Stan, I will put up with your Captain for you and the other officers because I happen to like them, you best of all. But if I hear Aalleexx many more times, blows will fly.*

Vigos, the darkened cabbage and meat, are very good. "Very good, Captain, you are a good cook. Oh, do we have any maritime magazines onboard, like maybe a Lloyds List? Yes? May I see them?"

"In your cabin in half an hour."

"Not necessary, I'll just pick them up at dinner." *And how come they're not set out where everybody can have a look at them. Like maybe in the Officers Lounge, but that wouldn't do any good since you're the only one who lounges in there. Tut tut, remember your resolution, MsSelf.*

In the stairwell on the way to my cabin, I smell something burning, like leaves. My unaccustomed senses shout, "*Whoops, someone is smoking marijuana. Superstructure Deck 2, you guys had better watch it!*" Then the smell of Bengay from some poor soul with stretched back or limbs follows me up to Superstructure Deck 4.

1630: To the Bridge to request that Ion print out Stan's itinerary. "You see," I plead as I watch him remove a ship's business program, "it's Stan's U.S. itinerary."

"I know," he smiles. Suddenly, like one of those crazed men at sea for too long, I want to scream, "How do you know? What do you know?" But I smile and watch the printed sheets fall into the basket. *Is that what makes people go crazy – that everyone knows everything about everyone?*

I leave the itinerary at Stan's open door, hallooing and receiving no answer, so tossing it on his carpet. When I go down to dinner, I peer down the hallway to see if he has picked it up. It is gone and, for the first time ever, all the lights in his cabin are on.

The Peasant and Ion are seated silently, staring at spots on the wall.

Lloyds List newspapers are on my chair. As I set them on the floor, I note Ion's hungry eyes following the newspapers. Oh my, it is obvious that Chief Officer has not seen any of these papers.

"I will share them, First Officer," I say brightly, then dart a black look at The Peasant.

"No, thank you, I will not have time to read them."

"Where's Chief Engineer?" I ask.

"Lots of paperwork," Ion volunteers, eating quickly, passing but never touching what he considers "the Captain's food," which miraculously appears yet again, this time a hunter's sausage never seen before.

In fact, I DO know where Chief Engineer is. He, who is rarely late for meals, is sitting in his lights-ablaze cabin and reading his USA itinerary.

An astounding twenty minutes late, Stan presents himself at table, hair wet and slicked, face red and blushing. I know immediately he has read the last couple paragraphs of his U.S. itinerary, which said nothing more than I look forward to meeting his wife and perhaps guiding them for a couple days through the USA. Also I teased that would give me the opportunity to tell her what a gentleman he is at table. "Stop blushing, Stan," I wrote, "I'm only kidding."

The Dining Room conversations cease, and all eyes are on Stan.

He is blushing furiously as he bows formally and thanks me for the itinerary. "I can't even be close to doing for you what you have done for me."

"I enjoyed doing it, Stan, it's my area. If you have questions, ask me. Now sit."

"I have e-mail also, and I will give it to you."

Ahah! He went directly to the end where I mentioned my e-mail address. *Charming, articulate, shy, aristocratic Stanislov, it was my very great pleasure,* I want to say to him. But, in view of The Peasant's glare and Ion's lop-sided grin lighting up his face while he ducks his head in a sort of salute, I simply smile at Stan who wriggles with pleasure.

"I must read it over and over," he breathes.

"Sit, Stan."

"Thank you, Cari."

All those hours of wondering why I ever got myself into this, if the damned itinerary would ever be finished, vanish like raindrops on hot pavement. "You are ever so welcome, Stan."

"I want a copy," The Peasant fixes me with a stare. "There is a copy for me." A statement, not a request.

Startled, I answer in a tiny voice, "Ah, well..." Then glance at Stan, whose happy face has fallen, crushed. Damnation! The Peasant is supremely smug, assured of a positive answer. I take a bite and chew in the silence.

"You know, Captain, the itinerary isn't mine anymore to give. I made it as a gift to Stan. And it's actually his now. I can't give something away that isn't mine. You're going to have to ask him."

Angry silence, then he turns and stares at Stan, who has just cut a piece of meat and is regarding it carefully on the end of his fork. Stan finally puts it in his mouth and chews thoroughly, then, in his finicky manner, slowly cuts another piece, examines it on his fork end and pops it in his mouth. His concentration is totally on his food, and his head never turns toward his Captain. There will be no copy for The Peasant.

The Peasant rises abruptly and stalks fuming to the Lounge, sitting alone in the dark while Stan, Ion and I blab happily away for a very pleasant half hour about interesting places we have visited. *You reap what you sow, Mr. Man in the Dark.* Ion leaves for the Bridge, giving me one more of those very pleased grins. That's why he came down to dinner – Ion couldn't stand not seeing Stan's reaction, although he himself has not a clue what is in the itinerary.

The Peasant decides to resume his seat at table just as Stan innocently asks me what I think of Bill Clinton. For the second time, the room is absolutely hushed. All eyes are glued on me, the prickly stillness banging against my ears making me light-headed and dizzy.

I can feel a sort of maniacal glee circulating, a mob mindset where all sense flees. Here's the opportunity to see a pompous American - one of those, we have been told, who runs around the world lording their glitzy possessions and imposing their ridiculous precious form of government and telling everybody what to do - our way or no way – the same as Communism - hollering about freedom as if they aren't shackled like everybody else with rules and taxes, stomping with steel boots sheathed in reindeer skin, grasping with leaden fingers hidden in calfskin their dollars that they think can buy every soul on Earth, kicking everybody around - humiliated by her own President, who may be an asshole and idiot, just like ours, but still... Even if this one is the first American ever met, who really isn't too bad, after all, who can resist witnessing with relish an embarrassment of this magnitude.

In an instant, I am no longer the Cari who traipses all over the ship, laughing and secretly giving away the Captain's cookies, but have become the American! Woman! again. The hated American, whose image imbedded for a lifetime can't be erased in the short time on MarkShip Mexico.

Let's see her try to get out of this one.

The Peasant's eyes gleam with malevolence and anticipation of my come-uppance. A pale imitation of this scorn is reflected around the Dining Room, and there is almost a smell of blood on the air. Heh! Heh! This should be good.

All my careful work for the last month is suspended, hanging on a simple question. I am so terribly sad that we always seem to be reduced to our basest denominator, even as I understand the reasons, or at least the mentality, the why of it, much more now than before my many interactions and conversations during the past month.

Mr. Clinton, you of the poofed hair and the oh-so-public dick obsession, how often in the last years of my traveling around the world have your ugly actions and filth been imposed upon me by a world population that finds us offensive and overbearing and who can't wait to tear down anything American? To get a good sneer and laugh at an American, who is sure to defend her President? What better target than a ridiculous common clown like you? But why me for the defense when I join their disgust?

So here we are again, MsSelf. Was it just last night or the night before when you told yourself that this subject, about to be trotted out again, wasn't closed, that you would be revisiting it again soon? Well, here you are, as advertised.

I sit back in my chair and address Stan's kind face, who realizes he's opened a can of worms but doesn't know how to get out of it, my eyes never leaving his.

"Well, Stan, I don't care how many women Mr. Clinton goes to bed with, if that's what you're referring to." I laugh. "And I assume it is since that's all the whole world has been laughing at and sneering at for quite some time now." Stan opens his mouth to protest – no, this is not what he was asking about – but it's too late. "He can screw all the women who are willing in the United States and Poland for all I care. What I do care about is that the man is a liar. Every time he opens his mouth, he lies. He obviously does not, cannot keep his word, which, in my book, makes him despicable."

I now transfer my gaze to The Peasant and look straight into his malicious eyes, enunciating each word with precision. "He lies, he cheats and he steals. He is without Honor, Character, Integrity. Is that what we want from the leader of the Free World? Is That What We Want From Any Leader?"

Everyone in the Dining Room knows I am talking about more than Bill Clinton.

Shock waves fill the room. Not a muscle moves. Stan sits like a marble statue in his chair, stunned. Only The Peasant sways from side-to-side, then carefully places his hands on the table as if to steady himself and looks down at them. The silence is deafening. We rock, hear the creaking of the ship, the spume-edged wake rushing by.

Stan, the gentle man who fastidiously avoids conflict, casts his wide, sad eyes around in near panic, not believing what he has unleashed, then clears his throat. "The economy is very good," he says weakly, in a master stroke steering us back to Clinton.

"No thanks to Billy boy who has been too preoccupied with his women – and explaining what he deems is or is not sex - to even run our nation. It shows that government rolls on very well without a President. We get to thank a man called Alan Greenspan, Chairman of the Federal Reserve Board, an excellent economist. Actually, he controls more than just the U.S. economy. The world is so intertwined today that in reality his policies to some extent control the entire world."

Now Stan says with relief that he knows something about the Federal Reserve Board and although he doesn't agree precisely about the man, he does agree…blah, blah, blah. I have never heard Stan blather before, but he keeps up a running patter.

The moment is past, eating resumes, embarrassment hovering like a panther ready to consume us all. Embarrassment for whom? For me or for them? The Peasant does not move. There is no doubt in my mind that he is plotting his revenge – and I'd better be ready.

I ride with Ion to see the sunset spectacularly reflecting on the tips of the high, white-crested waves.

"Stan was very happy. Really excited. I've never seen him like that."

"Oh, you mean about the itinerary." Ion will get an in-depth report of the later events, I am sure, before the evening is out. "Yes, he was."

"That was nice, Cari. I hope I'll get to read it."

"Maybe he'll give you a peek at it when he's done poring over it."

"Maybe. He's a very private man, very strait-laced. But a good man. He's an incredible engineer, who knows more about ships' engines than the manufacturers. A real whiz," and he sneaks a delighted glance at me. *My, my, Mr. Chief Officer has been looking up English words.* "You should have seen him when the shipbuilder's technicians were here. Stan was, was, spectacular. Captain kept interfering, when he obviously didn't know anything, and Stan kept pulling his bacon out of the fire." Another glance of satisfaction. *Not only words, but phrases too. He's getting to trot out all his new stuff today.*

"Have you sailed with a lot of good Chief Engineers?"

"Some, but nothing like Stan." Ion talks about ships he's been on, the year he will have to take off with no pay to go to school for his Captain's papers, and the fact he would really rather find a job on shore. "I worry about my three-year-old son. He is growing and growing, and I'm not there. Six months at sea, three months at home. It's not enough. I need to be with him and my wife."

I'll cheer him up, I think, *I'll talk about the Seaman's Missions,* those fabulous places run by clergy of every denomination from all over the world, who turn into bartenders, sweepers, confessors – whatever is required. Most Missions are inside port gates, but some are outside, as near as they can get to ports. The Missions have all manner of names – Apostolic Brotherhood of the Sea, Apostles Mission, Mariners' Club, etc., including plain old Seaman's Mission, which everybody calls them.

Inside the Mission, a seaman finds TVs, music from all over the world, newspapers and magazines in maybe twenty different languages, paper, pens, envelopes, stamps, banks of telephones, pool tables, dart boards, checkers, chess sets, snacks, whatever a guy could want for a few hours fun. And, always, a great bar with really cheap beer and very friendly bartenders (preachers, rabbis, priests, you name it) in jeans, speaking a myriad of languages, most of them smoking like steam engines. Somewhere, hidden away, is a chapel. In Hong Kong, there are even rooms for families of sick seaman stuck there. Nearly all the Missions have vans and offer free rides from ship to Mission for seamen who can get off board for a short time.

They are magical places where a hard-working seaman can relax for a few hours away from his ship, which might be the first time in a month, maybe more.

"Ion, I haven't been in a Seaman's Mission this trip. Last trip, I think I hit them in every port. I often think if I ever get rich I'll leave a pile of money to them. That piddly change the guys can afford to leave can hardly make a dent in the costs to run such places, although I know their churches help." I grin widely. "I stuffed their silly little money receptacles with bunches of bucks. I was one impressed lady."

Rather than cheer him up, Ion stands rigid as a statue. *OK, he'll like this a lot. It'll make him smile.*

"One stop in Hong Kong, I was coming back from town rather late, but decided to have a beer before getting back on board. Nearly all of our Tuvaluan deck crew was in there, whooping it up.

"'What's everybody doing here?' I asked one of our guys.

"'Crane's late, won't be at our ship until 0500. Master heard there was another ship in port with a Tuvaluan crew, so he let almost all of us off to come here. We're practically all related, you know. Tuvalu is a very small country. Only two beers, though, which is OK. We're just really happy to be here. We thank the Master,' and he raised his beer.

"I remember thinking, 'Wow, Captain, you are something special.' When I got back to the ship, officers were standing watch duty for the deck crew whooping it up at the Seaman's Mission. Don't you just love it, Ion?"

Ion covers his face with his hands. "Yes."

"Then what's the matter?"

"This Captain won't allow our crew to go to Seaman's Missions."

"Whaaat?" I am stunned. "Come on, Ion. Captains, COs and Bosuns make up a revolving list so everybody can get off once in a while. All sailors on all ships go to the…"

"He doesn't want anyone off board. Says it makes them crazy. What really makes them crazy is knowing he won't let them off, even to go to the Seaman's Mission. La Spezia was…Let's just say Bosun and I forced him to let the crew off for a few hours before a month at sea. It took a lot of threatening. He was furious and made life miserable for us."

"Oh, Ion. My God, can he know what he's doing?"

"Oh yes, he knows – very well. That's what makes it – him –so sick. Bosun and I sneak guys off, a couple at a time. We hope he'll be drunk and won't know. Everybody knows to not breathe a word of it. He's mean, Cari, he's cruel and wants complete control without a thought how his actions are causing disaster. And he has done this, plus lots of other horrible things, on all the ships he has mastered."

"He told me this was his sixth contract with The Company," I say.

"Sixth!" he snorts. "No, fourth." He rattles off the names of ships Captain has been on. "I know this Captain very well. I make it my business to know his background."

"Why would he tell me six?"

"Why does he send the crew's food home to Poland?" It hangs between us, neither breathing the words aloud: The man is a liar, cheat and thief. And I shudder when I think of how close I came less than an hour ago to directly calling him that to his face, although I was only a hair's breadth away from doing so.

"What really worries me," Ion speaks softly into the falling darkness, his thirty-six-year- old voice echoing as a child's, "is that I will be around someone like him for so long I won't remember how I should be when I am Captain."

From the officer's chair by the starboard window, staring into the radar screen blinking green, I say, "Ion, you will learn from this – learn everything you don't want to be."

He sighs from six feet away, rolling with the ship, legs apart for stability, hands clasped as though shackled behind his back.

"Sometimes, Ion, knowing what you DON'T want to be is every bit as important as knowing what you DO want to be." Silence.

Great anguish buzzes like a saw. "I want to sail with good Captains. *I* want to be a good Captain."

"You will be." The subject has been exhausted, and we ride along, he like a statue, I relaxed in the chair.

Finally he moves off to the Chart Room and calls to me, "I once had a friend who was just starting out on the sea. I asked him, 'Do you have a dog?' He said, 'Sure, why?' 'Because after six months at sea, your wife will ask you where the money is and your child will look at you as a stranger. Only the dog will remember you.'"

"Goodnight, Ion," I laugh. "Put a picture of your dog next to the computer." He waves without looking up. I carefully let myself out the heavy inside Bridge door, tears prickling behind my eyes. Life can be so unfair.

In my cabin with nothing to do now that the itinerary is complete, I stare out the window. I'll fix a drink, I'll finish my journal for the day, I'll… But I can't rid myself of the Dining Room scene and fall into deep introspection.

It's odd how the sea affects me. It's daunting power, split-second change-ability from soft to raging, incredible beauty, unending vastness reduces me to minute fragments of humanity. It humbles and forces me to view things, people and events from angles never before considered. The sea evokes my best and my worst, drawing response from my deepest corners.

Soft illumination from the ship's running lights below and glow from the bridgewing lights above fill the cabin with strange shadows. I slowly pour a drink, sit, put my feet up on the desk and roll with the ship, occasionally grabbing the desk edge for support, hearing in my soul the screeching of boxes, the rush of wake as the ship fights through the night on heavy seas. I feel drained, exhausted, yet so comfortable that I can barely move my arm to pick up the half- glass of Scotch.

You've done it again after making a pact with yourself that you wouldn't. You cannot get involved. Equally important, to what type of retaliation for your words will you be subjected?

Well, you didn't exactly say it out loud, just like that. You didn't say, "Captain Peasant, you are without Honor, Character, Integrity." Get serious, MsSelf, what you did say brought the evening meal to shocked silence, the officers frozen, The Peasant moving side-to-side in his chair and looking at his square, rough hands on the table, dirty nails bitten (the first time you've noticed). As your measured, conversationally-toned words continued, a gathering brackish cloud of black anger and disrespect toward this man from his officers seemed to dim the light, honing each of your barbed words distinctly, which you continued in a near-monotone.

When I finally pushed back my chair suddenly, noisily and said, "Good Evening, Gentlemen," everyone jerked. As I opened the door, telling myself not to look back, I turned to view the room. All officers' eyes were on me. Only one met my eyes and smiled surreptitiously, the rest were sober, calculating, maybe worried – for whom? Themselves or me? The Peasant sat unmoving, his eyes on the table, his coarse features hidden in the droop of forward flesh as he regarded his hands, his pudgy, powerful body leaning forward. My God, how could such a vile, disreputable man know of the words I had pushed across the table at him like chess pieces?

Honor, Character, Integrity are umbrella words, under each a whole bevy of words defining the blessed word more closely. These are not just words; they are a way of life. One does not have to ask what is right or wrong – one just knows – one already knows before the question is put. If you are one of the lucky ones, your choices on how to live your life are nearly non-existent – you do what is required – DEMANDED by Honor, Character, Integrity.

To some the words are a blessing; to others, a curse. To some a denial, to some a blatant reality to fearfully shun and run from, to others a soft featherbed to sink into, with thanks, that one simply acknowledges and embraces. Even when they come emblazoned on your forehead, they require more work and sometimes sacrifice than many care to invest. We can know they are there - tough, meaningful, in-your-face - and stomp on them to blot out their existence, never really ridding ourselves of their residual clinging. Or we can examine them, lay claim to the best of each and find a home in our very soul where each can nestle and grow.

Does it actually make a difference how we react to these disembodied words? They are simply words. It is what they stand for that makes the difference. Can we say to ourselves: I have Honor; I have Integrity; I have Character? Do we even want to? Or, with some, do we have a choice? Do I have them? Is this the way I actually live? The answer is so deep inside, yet so obvious, that one really doesn't need to answer. We know - either way – hoping for a positive answer.

My father made sure, tick-tock-double-lock, that my sisters and I understood every nuance of each word, not by bluster or long lectures, but by example and repeated snippets.

I don't need to close my eyes or be in a state of reminiscence to hear, "Your word is your bond. Your bond is your word. Your credit is your name. Your name is your credit. A handshake is a contract. Your hand-shake is a contract. Girls, you must be true to the best parts of yourself, and it will naturally follow that you are true to others." They sing in my ear, and I smile.

Yet, even this man, my idealistic father, was brought to his intel-lectual hell by his own shortcoming. At his German ancestors' knees, he had been imbued with contempt for Jews. He grumbled about Jews, because it was expected, just as he grumbled about bad weather. He seemed not to even know it – until he met Mr. Grossman, the Jew who owned the house my father was buying.

There came times in those hard days when one couldn't make the payment on time. Many were simply not paying their contracts, as if the debt were not owed. In perfect accord with the bigoted attitude of the era and area, my father was advised not to bother to pay either. After all, 'that man' was only a Jew, how could it matter? Still, against all advice and denigration of Mr. Grossman, my father had to talk to him, explain why he couldn't make the payment that month, hopefully negotiate a 'bye' to be made up when my father had the money. He would find yet another job, do anything to keep the house that his wife and three daughters called home. My German Jew-despising father had to try to make 'that man' understand, make it right. It was simply my father's way.

I, maybe four years old, remember standing in the front seat of the car, bundled layer-upon-layer by my father's hand since mother was work-ing the swing-shift at the potato warehouse, snow banks piled like sooty mountains around the parking area, their height attesting to the ferocity of North Dakota winters. The steamed windows of Mr. Grossman's dry cleaners, hard on the railroad tracks, streamed rivulets of water down the plate glass, allowing me a distorted view of the brightly-lit interior that frozen January eve.

Inside, Mr. Grossman bustled to the front of the dry cleaner counter to meet my father, stopping far short so that each man stood away from the other. My father, never a hat-in-hand person, stated his case, his body stiff, unsmiling, resisting both his need to be there as well as The Jew. Mr. Grossman replied. There was more conversation, a relaxation of bodies, brief smiles, each man taking a step toward the other, heads inclined. Now they were close enough to shake hands, each smiling and touching the other's shoulder. A satisfactory agreement had been reached, and each was happy.

"Well," my father said to me gravely when he returned to the car, "I guess there are Jews, and then there's Mr. Grossman." There was a tone in his voice as he pronounced the name that has stayed with me these many years, a tone I didn't understand, but which made a deep impression. I know that tone now, rarely heard in today's world: Respect.

Years later, my father told me that he never knew a man he admired more, that his firm handshake (a bond, a contract), his steady look into your eyes (which your forbearers said a Jew would never do), and his innate kindness cut through all the other crap one had been so carefully taught, causing hours upon hours of self-introspection, plus unspoken misery of embarrassment and shame. Because of him, something odd happened to that scorn you had for Jews. That you yourself were forced by your own conscience to publicly stand for Mr. Grossman when his name was impugned by the unknowing and unwashed, as uncomfortable as it might be and regardless of the consequences, only made your personal shame at your stupidity more unbearable. It could be no other way – for here was a man of Honor, Integrity and Character.

Mr. Grossman, unbeknownst to most, owned a large part of our small town. He worked like a slave at his known, insignificant businesses and was the unsung hero behind almost every civic and often personal progression, of every improvement in our town, regardless of how his community regarded him. Decades later, after his death, his silent contribution to the town was revealed, the legacy staggering. I wish my father had known. Or did he?

What did they say to each other that frosty North Dakota night in the steamy cleaners? Did 'that man' change my father's generations-upon-generations hatred of Jews? Well, maybe not. I grew up knowing my father had a bias toward Jews, except, of course, for Mr. Grossman. But, when I got old enough to be happily past the era's rigid prejudices, I didn't know who was a Jew, a Protestant or a Catholic. Looking back on it, I was, surprisingly, never taught to hate Jews. That step in itself was gigantic. My father did not allow his prejudice, as ingrained as it may have been, to be instilled in his children.

Well, Mr. Grossman, you had some kind of effect, Mister. My father knowing you sure made my entire life sweeter.

I, MsSelf, wish I could shake your hand.

Wednesday, November 8. The Atlantic
Sun. Force 7: Near gale, 28-33 knot winds, 12-1/2 – 19 foot waves. Sea heaps up. White foam blown in streaks.

Last night we were rocking, with only a few rough spots, and sleeping like babies. Today, the sun makes rainbows in the high spray that follows from the bulbous bow, hits the bow of the ship and caroms in spuming waves alongside, leaving spidery sea-foam green and aqua patterns upon the deep blue sea. We are moving around, and I picture my 'smart' ship sighing in vexation as she tries to avoid a thrall of oncoming waves.

I walk the sunny decks to port, dressed warmly, holding on for dear life, marveling at the crew jumping from box to box in the pitching sea, waving to me, then bending to the errant turnbuckle. Inside stairwells resound with my pounding shoes.

A day for catching up with my cabin and belongings, a day for regrouping body and soul, a day to renew promises yet again with myself about NO INVOLVEMENT, a day of rest, shoes riding in the window.

I idly thumb the pages of Lloyd's List, as always fascinated by the odd events of the maniacal world that this mariners' newspaper has been publishing along with its real purpose, shipping news and movements of ocean-going vessels, since 1734, the oldest continuously published newspaper in the world. Copies of Lloyd's List from the mid-1700s are available to study and in 1752 crosses the change of calendars from Old

Style Julian Calendar (when the New Year commenced on 25 March) to the New Style Gregorian Calendar (New Year commencing on January 1). Once published weekly, now it is published daily and incorporates fascinating snippets of world news:

"The Malaysian military is to step up patrols in the busy Malacca Strait in an effort to combat piracy... In the first quarter of the year, seven attacks on ships in the Malacca Strait were reported. These included the hijacking of the Japanese owned tanker Global Mars by 20 pirates armed with guns and knives shortly after leaving Port Klang on February 22. Although the 17 crew were freed after a 13-day ordeal, the ship and her cargo of 6,000 tonnes of palm oil products are still missing." *Ye gods! I was just in Port Klang on The Other.*

"Filipino burden of guilt. (A picture shows a man pulling a cross.) A Filipino penitent carries a wooden cross on his shoulder while being whipped along a Manila street. Every year hundreds of penitents in the largely Roman Catholic country take on some form of bodily penance to atone for their sins and this year 10 penitents will be nailed to crosses in the northern Philippines."

"Colombia is now producing 70% of the world's coca, last year producing 520 tonnes of cocaine. U.S. drug consumption problem is going down...Latin American's is on the rise."

"Avondale Industries is one of the few giants of the U.S. shipbuilding business to have survived the cull of the past 20 years...And it remains the largest employer in Louisiana, with a work force of 6,400."

"Blood of Bangladesh believers. (Picture shows two men covered with blood.) Bangladeshi Shi'ite Moslems bloody themselves in an act of self-flagellation during a mourning procession celebrating Ashoura in Dhaka. The day marks the death of Imam Hussein, grandson of the prophet Mohammad, 13 centuries ago in a battle for justice."

"With water in the Great Lakes at its lowest level in 30 years...Only a few years ago, the Great Lakes, which contain 20% of the world's supply of fresh surface water, had risen to record high levels...Concerns over the withdrawal of water have mounted as schemes to export the water to Asia have risen."

"Indonesia, Jakarta. Violent communical (sic) clashes have erupted in Indonesia's bloodied eastern spice islands...All victims were killed by home-made bombs and guns and other weapons such as arrows."

I lunch in a completely empty Dining Room, Stan having sent word via Alex that there were problems in the Engine Room requiring non-stop attention, no Peasant, as expected, and who knows where Ion and the rest of them are. Maybe last night was too much for all of us.

Cristori says he has time today for vegetable flower-making, and we set a 1400 meeting in the galley. A perfectly benign past-time for this day. I am a wash-out at the delicate art of fashioning vegetable flowers, although Cristori is patient and astonishingly adept, smiling hugely at my continuous oohhs and aahhs.

Wandering around the galley, I view all the equipment with a restaurateur's eye. The Estonian cook on The Other had a veritable restaurant supply house of equipment, plus excellent provisions to start with, and still he managed to put out barely edible food. Once Capt. R. told me when I was delirious that we were going to have pizza, "Don't let your expectations fly, Mrs. Lindley. This is Estonian pizza." Right he was.

"You are already cooking for this evening, Cristori."

"Yes, Mum. I must start early because only three of the six burners work. The grill doesn't heat. And the oven sometimes works, sometimes not.' He laughs humorlessly. "It's the controls -they take special parts. I was told we had them, but now..."

"What? How can you cook three meals a day for twenty-three people on three burners? No oven? No grill?" I think back to my restaurant days when, at peak dining hours, there never seemed to be enough equip-ment, no matter how sophisticated your kitchen..

He spreads his hands. "It takes all my time, Mum, because I have to juggle all the pots. No time for rest."

"Why not just ask the electrician to fix it? I'm sure he would. I mean, he eats here, too. Besides, it's his job." Now we know why Cook can't bake bread. *He* can; the oven can't.

"No, Mum, he won't. Ah, you see, ah, I…that is, he and Captain, well, Captain he…I'm not sure he likes me, Mum, although I am very thrifty with the food. I mean, I have to be since…ah, you see, I report to Captain, not to Chief Officer who can't really do all he would like to help me." He looks at the floor and shuffles his feet in tiny little shooshes. "It's quite difficult, Mum. But I manage."

"Cristori, let me see what can be done. Surely something. This is insane."

"Yes, um, thank you, Mum. But," and he looks at me pleadingly, "you won't complain directly to Captain, will you? It's that, he can be, um… can you not talk to him? Maybe find a way around?"

"Don't worry. I just hope we can get this equipment fixed. In the meantime, you are a saint and a magician."

I go hunting for Roberto, that familiar hot white heat encompassing my body and, as luck would have it, he is descending the stairwell on Superstructure Deck 3, where I seem to meet him on a fairly regular basis. *Is there some kind of special electrical box up there?*

"Hi," Roberto says shyly, his blue eyes lifting upward edgily as if an apparition will appear on the upper landing.

I take two steps toward him in the narrow passageway. "Hi? Is that what you have to say to me? HI? HI?"

He backs up against the bulkhead until he has nowhere else to go. Now I am nearly touching him, my anger leaping at him like a tiger

"DO-YOU-KNOW-THAT-THE-STOVE-IN-THE-GALLEY-DOES-NOT-WORK? DO-YOU-KNOW-THAT-COOK-IS-TRYING-TO-COOK-FOR-TWENTY-THREE-PEOPLE-WITH-THREE-BURNERS-NO-GRILL-AND-AN-OVEN-THAT-IS-INTERMITTENT? DO YOU?"

"Ah, well, ah, yes."

"You KNOW? You KNOW? FIX IT!" the words hissing up the stairwells. "FIX IT NOW!"

"I can't. Cook said something to Captain, and Captain is angry with him."

"What? Are you mad? Cook is trying to feed the people on this boat three meals a day. All twenty-three of us. You included, dumb ass."

I have him pinned, and my anger is so great that he literally tries to disappear into the bulkhead. Still, he wants to save face. "I can't." His complexion is changing from white to red to a dirty purple in front of my very eyes.

He is taller by a head than me, and as I glare up into his young face, I am almost sorry for him, his life, his choices on how to live it, for my overwhelming anger, for the need to be in this small space in this narrow passageway.

"Fix the stove, young man!"

"I can't. The parts are missing."

"Missing?"

"The Polish crew brought the parts to repair the stove, but they're missing."

"What do you mean – missing? Tom told me that they had supplied everything needed for the next year. Missing?" I hiss in his fearful face. "Missing? How many parts are missing?"

He stares at me, and I return his stare with a contempt that withers his tall, spare body.

And then I back away from him and begin to turn in small circles, my hands raised above my head, body responding to a childish dance, voice sing-songy like in a playground.

"And I know where they aarree…..I knooww where they aarree……"

He barely breathes, "Where?"

"Iinn aa booxx. They are innn aa booxx."

"A box?"

"Onn its waayy ttoo Polaaand."

He jerks back, face white, eyes wide and round, mouth working like blowing bubbles. My God, she knows!

Immediately I regain my senses. *What have I done? Will he tell The Peasant? What further jeopardy have I put myself into? Or Cristori?*

I pin him against the wall, spitting, "Not a word, do you hear me? Not a word! I will know, Mr. Young Electrician, if you betray me, and I'll make your life hell. I will know!"

He sags, an odd relief seeming to shake him, as if "Thank God, somebody else knows, I don't have to carry this by myself." Oh, young man, puulleezzee (Alisha's face flashes in my mind), take responsibility for your own actions.

I start up the stairwell. "Fix the stove, young man! Now!"

He remains pasted against the wall like the effigy of the donkey on which we, the diners on this ship, will pin the tail.

I run down to the Lounge to get my drink fixings, something cold tonight, and come upon three officers actually sitting in the dingy Lounge. I thought only The Peasant sat there. One points to the ceiling and mimics drunk, his eyes crossing and tongue hanging out, then sleeping. I guess it's OK to sit in there as long as you don't have to sit with *him*.

Ion enters with a small handful of newspapers, which he extends to them. They fall upon them like famished dogs on a bone. "From Captain?" and they are all smiles, turning pages as fast as they can, hungry for news, even weeks old. The Peasant has thrown scraps to the peons. On The Other, the Officers Lounge had two neat stacks of old mariner magazines and newspapers. But, then, the Lounge was a big room with windows, TV, VCR, a wall of books, games…*Stop it!*

I remind myself that these guys cannot get off the ship in ports to run down to the nearest newsstand. Port privileges are just that – privileges – and far between. And they certainly wouldn't presume to try to arrange with The Peasant to bring them newspapers, not that, as Ion pointed out earlier, he ever leaves the ship. Maybe they'd sail without him?

I glance at the television set, then remember that The Peasant has the only connection on the entire ship, the slender white cable snaking across the bridgewing and over the side to his window, thence inside to his TV set. He could splice it so others could receive it, even here in the Lounge, but refuses to do so. *Bastard! How can I be civil to this Cretin?*

Yet they are so pleased to receive anything from their Captain, who has kept maybe eight thin newspapers in his cabin for how long? – certainly the weeks since we left La Spezia – leisurely hoarding them (Mine! Mine!), then dispensing his castoffs to the animals who practically kiss them and clutch them to their breasts.

Wonderful, Peasant! Dear God, I despise you. Much as I love the sea, I can barely stand to be in your presence, and you taint my enjoyment. Does this ever stop? Veracruz, come quickly! Get me away from this horror of a man called Captain.

As I leave, I ask, "Do you guys want some English newspapers or magazines? I'm getting off in Miami and can bring you some."

They look at me as if I have blasphemed. "Yes! Yes!" Like I was offering water to parched souls.

I close the door and tromp up the steps, my anger hot, my disgust rampant. *Bastard! Bloody bastard! Captain, my ass. You are The Devil Incarnate! If I could ordain it, you would roast in the hottest part of hell.*

I continue to stew through dinner by myself, glad to be alone with my wild and uncontrollable thoughts. (Another Stan emergency in the Engine Room, which I know to be an emergency of conscience about last night, the Peasant drunk in his cabin, the First Officer controlling the Bridge, eating there, I know, since Alex runs up with a plate.) Best to be alone right now, for sure. I barely acknowledge the few officers who enter and they, seemingly abashed at last night's behavior, talk quietly amongst themselves, eyes darting in my direction.

In #403, my fingers pound the computer keys as if they were my mortal enemies, wishing I could hear a real clicking sound from a typewriter as my fingers fly.

Suddenly, I must hear Marius' kind, lucid voice, his clear otherworldly thoughts. I need to hear his gargling English. I require order in chaos. I crave respite from my consuming anger, peace with the sea. I will climb the two flights to the Bridge and look out upon the sea through the panoramic Bridge windows. And when I return, the sea and Marius' odd look at life will have revived me. Quickly, quickly, before my body and mind turn to ashes, before my abhorrence of The Peasant transforms me into dust.

"I am a very angry person tonight, Marius." In true Marius style, he does not ask why. "Help me forget this anger. Tell me about your life. Did you have a nice childhood? Do you have brothers and sisters?"

"My childhood was all right. Remember, I lived under the Communists. Yes, all right. And I have three brothers. One I do not talk to. He did something very bad. Very bad. So I cannot talk to him. Have not for a long time." I cannot help but wonder what it was, but do not ask.

"Oh dear. Well, do you talk to your other two brothers?"

"I would if I could. But they have died, one from cancer and one in a car crash. Yes, to them I would talk. I wish I could."

"Oh Marius…"

We ride in long, sad silence, watching my 'smart' ship turn her bow a couple degrees into the rolling northwest waves, then turn back to her course. "It's so cool," I have crowed many times to the officers' great amusement. "She is so smart, knowing exactly which waves to avoid." I never tire of watching it, saying it – and they never tire of smiling at me with amused condescension, eyes full of delighted laughter at this goofy novice on the sea. So I say into the silence, "It's so cool." And Marius chuckles, knowing the routine, sadness lifted.

We ride forever, he twisting and punching knobs and dials and going to and fro on his duty errands, I riding. I am so pleasantly relaxed, mesmerized by the sea, that I hardly hear him click on the Chart Room light, then come over and sit in the officer's chair.

"I must tell you, Cari. You must know…" His voice is very soft.

I am jolted from my reverie.

"He did WHAT?!!" I shout. "He did WHAT?"

My horror of the man is complete. I have just been told that the Master of MarkShip Mexico rigged up a sophisticated mirror system on the bridgewing to look into my cabin shortly after Valencia, using binoculars as a backup. Yes, I sleep in the nude, have since I was twenty years old, and yes, because my cabin windows are secluded from sight, yes, I occasionally putter around my cabin in a state of partial undress, a perfectly natural occurrence in my entire life, making sure the door is locked so no one can enter. After all, no one can see me because I've checked and know my cabin is out of view of any place on the ship. Plus the sea reflects from the windows in daylight, and at night, *all lights are off*, making sure no one can see me, **except in the unlikely event that a sophisticated series of mirrors is set up to see around corners.**

"He did WHAT?!!" I shout again, then sputter, the enormity of such an action and possible result, with twenty-two men on board and the

Jungle Drums beating, horrifying me. To maliciously stir up such potential danger to my person is astounding. Now comes the explanation as to why Mr. Captain always regards me slyly, like the sexy fat-cat contemplating the unsuspecting canary.

"That sneaky, low-life son-of-a-bitch!" I spit.

Marius must have been anticipating such anger and disgust. Still, he jerks back in his chair as if shot by a cannon. "Well, he… They are such children. I don't understand my people. Children!" My God, Marius is going to cry, holding his head in his hands.

"Children! Children? Have you considered the danger in which his stupidity put me? Is that why you didn't want me walking the decks at night? Too damned dangerous because that idiot purposefully riled up the sexually-deprived troops, so that even an old lady would look good to them?"

I stare at him accusingly. Another of the ridiculous men I have encountered all my life, East or West, concentrating on their peckers rather than the problem to be solved. The finesse and extreme effort it took to get their hands and minds off their penises and to participate in the business problem-solving saved my career, my marriage and my self-esteem. How my perfectly tailored Lily Ann suits (still one size too large to discourage the gawkers) could be of more importance than the business crisis at hand never ceased to amaze me. What piece of crap *they* were wearing never registered with me. The word passed like the ship's Jungle Drums between those powerful, famous physicists from literally all over the world: Don't try to screw with Cari. She's very married, she absolutely will wither your bones if you try to entice her to play – and her two bosses, whom we all know very well, will crunch you into nuclear particles if they hear of any nonsense

Suddenly, I begin to laugh - and laugh, tears flowing from my eyes. The comparison of those hotshot physicists to whom the world kowtowed and these poor guys trying to make a living on this ship simply blows me away. I cannot stop laughing.

"You think this is FUNNY! You think this is funny?" Marius is aghast.

"Who looked in the mirror?"

"Almost everybody. The Captain thought it was some kind of treat for the crew. He said you deserved it for being so dumb to be on this ship. He looked for you all the time, even though you weren't often in your cabin and rarely, um, undressed, he said. The others, well, they wanted to make you less, what they thought an American woman should be, what they'd always been told you would be. Then, then, they watched you for a few days, not in the mirrors, but in other places on the ship, and then, well, they didn't want to look at the mirrors any more.

"And did you look?"

I can barely see him, but I know his face is beet red. "No." And I meanly wonder if he is being truthful, then instantly regret the thought.

"Why not?" I'm sure he is going say "It is not permitted."

Instead he says, "You and I became nice companions early in the voyage. I didn't want to ruin the thought of you sitting here in the Captain's chair, your feet up on the radar rail, talking about volcanoes, heavy fuel and Romania. My mind simply could not put together the image of me spying on a naked Cari and the Cari often sitting here as the night hours wore on, us sitting side-by-side and enjoying our conversations, debates and laughter. It wasn't worth…" He shook his head – he had wanted to look. But he made his choice and did not permit himself. *Aw, Marius, you incredible soul.*

I regard him sorrowfully. "Please don't mention this conversation to anyone. I want to deal with this in my own way. Promise?"

"I promise, although I should tell Ion and Florin. They have been having what the philosophers call a 'crisis of morality' or is it 'conscience?' and have been urging me to tell you for some time. They really should know."

"Why you? Because you didn't peek at a sixty-one-year-old lady, well past her prime and over the hill?"

"Yes." And I can feel his gaze in the dim light, making his own judgment of the over-the-hill, sixty-one-year-old lady.

"All right, only them. Although I think they should stew in their own crises. Promise?" And I wonder how he can possibly keep such a promise when the very bulkheads have ears.

I start for the door.

"Cari." I'm always surprised when people on this ship call me by name, as if without it, I am not a real person in their midst. Marius is the only exception.

"About last night." Marius had been one in attendance, whose eyes for a brief moment registered that glee of oncoming humiliation during the Clinton fiasco. My disappointment had been rampant, but I have forgiven that momentary lapse.

"Mmm?"

"I'm…"

"It's all right, Marius. There are probably a lot of unhappy men today. Whether they are unhappy for me, their Captain, themselves or because the result wasn't more, uh, satisfying, only time will tell."

He shuffles his feet. "He is a vengeful man, Cari. Very clever and very vengeful. We all know." He pauses, turns away, then adds, "We know very well. Be careful. We're all watching, but we can't be with you every moment. Be careful."

Damn, why didn't I just randomly pick another ship. Because this was the right one for the time and place.

"Thank you. Have a safe watch, 3rd Officer."

I hear him barely breathe, "Marius."

Thursday, November 9. The Atlantic
Sunny and warm. Force 6: Strong, 22-27 knot winds, 9-1/2 – 13 foot waves, spray, white crests Large but gentle rollers from the Northwest. Last night's sleeping wonderful as the ship rocked up over one wave and into the next trough.

He's going to do it! Chief Officer is definitely going to call The Big Boss at Asteroid Ship Management Company on the Isle of Man when we get to Miami, he tells me as he finishes his breakfast and I drink coffee, the two of us alone in the Dining Room. I note, but do not mention, that the Ship Management Company is a downgrade from The Company, although since it is the employer of nearly all ship's person-nel, it should carry tons of weight. Did I hear or just dream that The Peasant was on the verge of breaking through from the Management

Company to The Company itself, a coveted quantum leap for continued and 'perked' employment.

The lead-in to this bombshell was when I innocently inquired if they decorated a tree for Christmas.

"With other companies, yes. Sometimes a $50 bonus for everyone. With this company, no. Nothing. But I will ask the crew if they want to buy a tree, not a real one, just a plastic one. They may not want to since they will have to chip in money. I may buy it out of my own pocket. The Crew Fund is almost empty since Captain used the money to buy a TV satellite dish, which only he is allowed to use to watch TV. You've seen it. So tell me, do you see the cable going anywhere but to his cabin?"

Oh God, I moan to myself, thinking of that snaking white cable over the Bridge edge to Captain's cabin window. The Crew Fund!

"Alex," he hollers, and I glare at him as a smiling Alex appears, although I admit Ion's voice does not carry that insulting rasp. "Take this to the Bridge, please," and he hands Alex an envelope. "Then stop by my cabin and take the little green box on my table to the Engine Room." Ion nods with satisfaction as Alex hurries out – good, rid of him for a few minutes. *Because?*

"I'm definitely going to call The Big Boss and tell him what is going on. As I said before, if they find out I know and don't tell them, they will think I'm in on it."

"Ion, I tell you again, your job is on the line."

"Never mind, never mind, don't worry. I can always get another job, maybe go back to tankers with not so nice conditions but more salary. I will tell The Big Boss that if he doesn't do something about Captain, I will put my bags on the dock in the next European port or maybe Miami." He pauses. "Although my friend tells me there are better connections from Houston, the port after you sign off." *Wow. He's really been thinking on this.*

He springs up, a veritable jack-in-the-box, pulling papers from his pocket and moves around my chair with his back to the galley, pausing a moment to look over his shoulder, hears the banging pots of a disgruntled Cristori, then plunks papers on the table. "Here, I have proof. You will see." Three sheets of formal ship requisitions and payment are carefully unfolded. Veracruz: $220. Provisions for ship ordered and received. Barcelona: $220. Provisions for ship ordered and received. *How odd they are the same denomination, Captain.* La Spezia: $96.33. Provisions: Polish sausage. Delivered by technician's driver.

"I have witnesses and proof that very few provisions were received on board in Veracruz or Barcelona. Even the last delivery in La Spezia where the suitcases were delivered directly to his cabin was also witnessed." He snorts, anger filling the room. "This is what he says his wife sent him, this is what he won't share with anyone, this is what he says is his very own food, paid for by him. You see it? You see it? You've also seen him, only him, eating the food. It was paid for by the ship."

I stare at the proof.

"Again he lied and stole – all for $500 when he has a salary of more than $4,000 a month, a fortune in Poland. I have much more proof of many more irregularities, but these are the easiest to understand. He is buying from chandlers that the ship normally doesn't use. A special arrangement with them, do you think? I know everything, it is my job to know everything about this ship. Bosun and two of his men have seen him carrying loaded boxes of tinned food up the stairs from stores in the middle of the night. Don't believe me, Bosun will tell you himself. Does Captain think *he* can get away with this?"

"There's more, like Pilot having to wake him up on the Bridge. Once he smelled so strongly of liquor that I asked him to stand down. It was a U.S. port, and the Coast Guard would have relieved him right away. Why was I stupid enough to send him down? I should have let them catch him. They are very strict," he adds with awe. (Ion, who pooh-poohs everything American, is very impressed by the U.S. Coast Guard, as were the officers on The Other. Regardless of how they dislike and fear them for their strict standards, ships sparkle, and all safety equipment is in working order the moment they enter U.S. waters.)

"How can The Company keep on a man like this?" He slaps the offending papers with his hand.

"Who knows about this, Ion?"

"Only us, 3rd Officer and 2nd Engineer plus Bosun and a couple of Filipinos. About this," and he touches the papers, "but everybody on this ship knows this Captain is a cruel, devious and secretive tyrant, who skews everything to his distorted way of thinking and makes even the best worker look foolish and inept. Too many years with the Communists. But everybody is afraid for his job, everybody. And I don't blame them." He sighs raspily.

"I run a very tight crew, and all members do their jobs and then some. Yet, this Captain tries to break them, break them apart, going to the crew's quarters in the middle of the night and issuing drunken orders, which I get to clean up, threatening them with his meanness. He knows quite a bit about Filipino culture, and he uses the occult side of it to scare them. As if there isn't enough to be afraid of at sea, that MAN uses voodoo-like intimidation. He's mumbled words like Kulam and Barang. I don't know what they really mean, but from the gleam in his eye and perspiration on his face when he smugly says those words, he sure as hell does. The use of such menace is probably why he learned about The Philippines in the first place since, as you know, Filipinos make up the world's majority of ship workers, hence, putting many under his control. His drunken sorties are causing huge problems.

"But when he is sober, he is never seen anywhere except the halls and stairways between his cabin, the Bridge or Dining Room. When he is sober, he is the scared one. I'm sure you've noticed he rarely speaks to anyone but us, never mingles unless he's drunk. Bosun says he has never been seen on deck, ever. Probably doesn't want a worker to get close enough to relieve him of a hair or something personal, so they can use black magic on him. Now, wouldn't that be a nice turn of events?

"Certainly you have felt the mood of this ship. Scared, angry, rebellious. Bosun and I use all our talents and wits, and he's got lots of both – a very good man - to keep this ship on an even keel." He can't help a quick smile at his own witticism.

"Chief Engineer is on short contract, as he probably told you, and wants nothing more than to go home. His wife needs him. She is…well, she needs him. He only took this contract for the money for something big. He could do lots to help here on board, but doesn't want any conflict as he's about to leave. He is determined to stay out of it. *"Me too,"* I wail to myself.

I hope the 'something big' is the U.S. trip, but from Ion's dire tone of voice, it surely isn't. Oh Stan… "And 2nd Officer?"

"2nd Officer wants only to complete his time toward his Chief Officer papers and does not say a word, as I'm sure you've noticed. He is a very angry man, who wishes he had never taken this contract. But he is determined to be a Captain, and I help him all I can. It's very difficult when the boss is a racist and debases him all the time. Also, 2nd Officer helps me try to keep peace with the crew. He is a very intelligent guy, educated far beyond the rest of us and certainly beyond the crew. He knows his countrymen, but sometimes I think they believe he is so far superior that he has forgotten the roots of the culture and the dark, evil stuff, which Captain uses as a stranglehold on them. He hasn't forgotten anything and is smart enough to use his intelligence and education as a balm on troubled waters. He does not preach and he does not strut. I would be pleased to sail with him, be he an officer or a Captain, anytime..

"The rest of them are hoping to get off this ship as soon as possible, always stinging from Captain's barbs, jabs and unjustness, their attitudes now changing to disgust, resentment and wrath. This man is dangerous in all ways to a working seaman. It's impossible to trust him or know where you stand from minute to minute – whether you're excellent at your job or not. You've seen the way he operates. A ship's Captain has absolute power, absolute rule, and all seamen know it. A seaman may not like his Captain, but to distrust him is terrifying. Most are really scared of this Captain, but mostly for the lack of trust and this job and future jobs, which he can definitely wreck."

"You should be too, Ion. I'm afraid for you."

A smile lights his face, and he looks like a little boy. "Thank you."

Oh my, what will happen in Miami? Will he really and truly call? Will we have a new Captain or Chief Officer? Call, Ion, or you will never be able to live with yourself again. But, with all the Chief Officer has to do on board during loading and unloading, when will he be able to get off and make that call? Will I hear after Miami that he was not able to leave the ship, that all of this was in vain, at least for the moment?

He starts for the door, then turns around and stands over me.

"Cari, about the mirrors..." The man-in-charge has been transformed into a nervous pulp.

I wait.

"I, uh, that is, we didn't know you and… but that does not excuse what we did. There is so much shame to bear, for all of us. I, of all people, should have known better, should have recognized the danger, should have somehow stopped it, although he was like a man possessed." The Polish gargling of the English words is rampant, and I strain to understand. "Marius is right, we acted like children. More like beasts, snakes," he searches for a more despicable word and sighs, "yes, snakes." Will you accept my sorry?"

I wonder if he has ever said those words before. I purse my lips and frown, looking at the anxious young face of this boy made old by the unrest and responsibility on MarkShip Mexico, harsh decisions ahead, conflicted and unhappy past. How incensed I had been that he had been a part of this demented scheme, having thought better of him. Should I add even one iota more worry to this wracked young man?

Then my mind abruptly switches gears, and I smile inwardly. Mr. Chief Officer has been studying his English dictionary and *Compendium*, because such speeches as the foregoing included words that were pronounced and used correctly, but often with a slight hesitation or faintness that belied frequent usage. Only the "sorry" sticks out like a sore thumb, but is nonetheless endearing.

"Yes. I accept your sorry." Were it possible, I believe he would have hugged me. But not possible.

"Again, thank you."

"You're welcome, Chief Officer." His face is so sad, I add, "Ion."

Exactly forty-five minutes from the moment I left my cabin to go down to breakfast, I stand at my window and stare at the dark blue Atlantic, white caps sparkling in the sun. *Exercise, MsSelf, until blood rather than sweat runs out of your pores.*

An hour later, on the salt-encrusted deck in glorious sunshine, I stand on the bow, lungs filling with clean ocean air, wind blowing my hair as the ship rises and falls in the familiar, ever- exciting pattern of the sea. My mind turns the problems over and over as I pound the outside stairs – up 100, down 100, up 100… *Boy oh boy oh boy!*

A strange occurrence with the TV satellite the crew paid for. The connector to extend the cable is disconnected, each cable end tied around a separate post on the outside passageway behind the Bridge, although the disconnected, useless slender white cable continues from the tied end onward to the Master's window. Somebody we know is not receiving TV reception as we near Miami. I wish I had thought of that.

I stop in to ride with Marius for a bit, and we talk about traditional foods for holidays.

More food conversation. It's overwhelming. And Stan and The Peasant eat in the most unusual manner. Whatever is served for dinner is consumed first, then, the few times The Peasant is in a sharing mood from his suitcase stash (since Stan can't order his own specialty tinned items from the empty pantry – to his constant dismay and anger), the special sausage or fish is served with bread and garlic. It is like two meals. I'm positive Cristori is delighted when The Peasant produces and shares his special stuff as there will be less complaining about miniscule portions, about which Cristori can do nothing. It's simply not there to cook.

As it turns out, Romanian, Polish and American holiday meals are very similar, with some specialty dishes for each. In fact, we eat pretty much the same way, Americans sans tons of garlic and sliced onion. They kill a pig, smoke part of it, sausage part of it and partially cook part of it in slices, then cover with melted pork lard and store in a wooden barrel. No refrigeration required. It's delicious, Marius says, kind of like Iberica ham in Spain but better (of course).

I am just arranging myself at table when Stan hurries in for lunch. He seats himself carefully, as always, fussing with his chair and napkin, then turns to me, head inclining in a half bow, face alive with happiness.

"I've read the whole itinerary you prepared. I am astounded, cannot really believe it, really surprised."

"By what?" thinking he may mean my discrimination spiel.

"Everything. You really know your country well. And such a big country. So much detail with so much heart offered in such a friendly way. So much fascinating information on so many subjects. I simply cannot believe you would do something like that for me." His whole long lean body smiles, even, I'm sure if I could see them, his kneecaps.

"It was my great pleasure to do it, Stan. It is my gift to you."

"I am truly honored. I don't have words to thank you."

"You're very welcome."

I think for the hundredth time of the incongruity that this elegant, fastidious, almost frail man's profession takes him into the heat, noise and grease of the Engine Room (although his is immaculate, but of course). Such an unlikely duo.

Then he drops the bombshell that he can't compete with such a document, so hopes I will understand he won't be giving me Polish information. I don't understand and say so, as he winces.

"Please, Cari, just let me give you my e-mail, and when you decide to come to Poland, I will assist you or your travel agent in every way. When you get there we will meet, as you suggest when Eve and I come to the U.S. I am taking shorter and shorter contracts on the sea, this one is only two months, so will have more time at home. If I am there, which I will definitely try to arrange, I will guide you. I don't know my country as well as you know yours, but I will try. Please, please understand."

I want to throttle him, but say, "OK, Stan, that's what we'll do."

He smiles and sighs relief, adding, "Chief Officer was looking for you. He wants to talk about the pool."

"I saw him on the stairs, and we talked about the pool and…" A tour of the yacht which Chief Officer suggested, I almost add, then decide against it. Each thing that happens to Stan is so special that he holds it close to his heart. Ion has already given him a tour of the yacht, and I don't want to ruin Stan's pleasure that he might be the only one to see it. It's that Eastern European thing again – please let me have something just for me.

And I probably won't tell Marius myself either, although he will surely know. Everybody knows everything on this ship. Perhaps if I don't actually say the words, it will be more palatable, It may be forbidden for him, but it is not for me.

On the way to my cabin, in the midst of the barrage of No Liquor/ No Drugs signs, I finally locate the roster of ship's personnel, which I know by sea law has to be posted somewhere, in this case on Deck 3. Kieleszczuk, Ciuglea, Drebiennik, Madulescu, Kiobanovschi. Whew!

The afternoon is spent reading, writing and thinking – and there's plenty of that to do. I finally shower, don blue slacks with a bold blue and white striped jersey shirt topped with a white long-sleeved linen blouse for the dinner hour.

Again, it is only Chief Officer at table. I met Stan on the stairs earlier, and he apologized that he would not be at dinner, another small crisis in the Engine Room. He grimaced. Stan loves to be at table, where he manages to make the meal seem a formal occasion, although I have been told by one and all that he rarely took meals in the Dining Room before Valencia.

The Peasant hasn't appeared for breakfast, lunch or dinner, on the Bridge or in the hallways. *Who do we think is stumbling around with bottle in hand behind closed doors on Deck 5? Or maybe it's a touch of Clinton message received?*

I'm in a good mood since Alex has just informed me that Cook sends his thanks. Two more stove burners are working and the oven – kind of. "Some of the parts were found," Alex says slyly, "but Electrician didn't hook up the oven correctly. But it works better than before, Mum. Not the grill, though, the parts are still missing. Thank you too, Mum." *And from which brown box, Mr. Electrician, did you filch the parts? Perhaps while Mr. Captain was away?*

Roberto, at the next table (the filcher in question, who seems to have forgotten our shouting match on the stairs about the galley), brings up the barbeque, and we go into a crazy routine, masking our discontent with humor. Is barbeque a new word? Barbeque, what does it really mean? Barbeque comes from the Hindu… We go around the room, each person more outrageous than the previous. *Will this frigging barbeque never go away? It is an albatross, but a definite focal point to vent, what shall we call it, frustration?* I am surprised that Roberto gets into the action so deeply, since he and The Peasant are friends.

Ion leaves for the Bridge, and other officers appear. We talk about Disneyland, where everyone wants to take their kids. Wait until they are ten or twelve so they can really enjoy it. But you'll enjoy it more than they will. "Yeah?" they regard me incredulously.

"Yeah, just you wait. It's the greatest."

Next is Las Vegas, which everybody wants to see. "In front of your very eyes, from the sidewalk, you don't have to pay, pirate ships sink, volcanoes explode, miraculous fountains dance. You have to pay for them, but there's great food, unbelievable shows and, of course, gambling."

Everybody gabs at high speed. *Hello, gentlemen, what happened to the 'I Hate America' syndrome?* They want to see and do America. And I want them to. Last night could have happened a year ago, maybe a century.

I want to ride on the Bridge, but think I'll just write a tad and go to bed. I'd go for a walk, but can't bear the scenario of Marius puffing behind me, waving his arms, stringy hair flying, Jesus shoes beating on the deck: I TOLD YOU NOT TO DO THIS! I check my locked door.

Just before sleep, I think of the sea - huge, empty, where seeing another ship is cause for jubilation, endless, sky and sea melding together in a vast blue sphere. The sea could swallow up one small body and continue its rolling rhythm into eternity without so much as a burp. My beloved sea - welcoming, infinitely powerful, beautiful, menacing, peaceful, frightening.

Friday, November 10. The Atlantic

Sea calm, sunny and warm. Maybe Force 1: Light air, 1-3 knot winds, .25-foot ripples. Sea deep, deep blue. Boy, is it beautiful! Retard clock #7.

0600: Jump out of bed in time to view the incredible sunrise. Too early to get coffee below, and the yellow thermos stopped weeks ago, so I climb the two flights to the Bridge. Now how could I have forgotten there would always be coffee on the Bridge? The sunrise paints the clouds peach and yellow over the perfectly deep blue sea.

Ion reminds me that we have an appointment to see the yacht's interior, so I meet him at 0900 sharp to climb onto the hatchcover and up the ladder to this glorious contraption. We remove our shoes even before stepping on the aft deck and tiptoe into the salon graced with ecru Italian leather sofas and chairs. Even the walls are covered with it. Beautiful wood, which I want identified but don't ask, gleams everywhere. Absolutely first class equipment. The yacht has navigational equipment that even MarkShip Mexico does not. Three bedrooms plus crew's quarters, four bathrooms, magnificent galley, which is really a luxury home kitchen, upper and lower salons and upper and lower decks for sunning and cocktails. *Yeeiikkes! What a boat!*

After the guided tour, where we put no fingers on anything, Ion returns to the galley and picks up a thick clipboard from the counter.

"What are you doing?"

"Checking off the interior inventory. When the yacht was loaded, I insisted the owner's transporter go through the yacht room-by-room and make an inventory list. He wasn't happy because it took a lot of time, but we inventoried every item on this craft, including a piece of blank paper in a drawer." He opens the drawer to show me. "We both signed off. I check it every week." He looks at me meaningfully.

"And?"

"It's all still here." He makes a notation. "But then the Italian owner is a *very* important man." He puts down the clipboard and looks around at the magnificence.

"This is what I want," he breathes.

"Me, too."

"You look very much at home sitting there. This craft suits you."

We laugh, and he leads me to the Bridge, where he portrays himself as Master of the yacht, his muscular, fit body needing only Tommy Bahama shorts and insigniaed Captain's hat to make it true. More than $3 million, he boasts. It gives him such pleasure I wish it were his. Or mine, and we could all pile aboard and go for a ride on this beautiful day, drinking aperitifs and margaritas, laughing and chatting. I picture the Bosun in the Master's glove leather chair, sipping a martini. I burst out laughing and continue to do so down the sturdy aluminum ladder to MarkShip Mexico's hatchcover, Ion eyeing me as if demented.

As I enter my cabin, trying not to compare my drab, gray cubicle to the yacht's luxuriousness, I hear pounding on the steps. It is Ion wanting to know if I wish the pool to be filled. "I haven't used it yet and probably won't, so no, don't bother."

"Listen, Ion, I want to ask you something. When I'm off tomorrow in Miami, I want to buy steaks and have a real American steak dinner for the officers. I don't want to step on anybody's toe. Should I ask *him* (and I point above). Do you think they'd like it? Is it all right?"

His eyes light up like Christmas tree bulbs. "Yes, they would like it. Yes, it's all right. No, you don't have to ask him." Then, smiling quizzically, "Why do you do this?"

"As a thanks to everybody for being so nice to me." He blanches, and both of our minds zing to the mirrors, about what happened in the Dining Room before the Bill Clinton speech, the American! Woman! syndrome and its nasty accoutrements. Then his smile softens, and he looks very unhappy. So I hurry to say I will talk to Cristori and arrange things with him. He rushes away. The entire ship will know about a steak dinner within fifteen minutes.

I close the door and look across my cabin through the open window to the sea. *Whatever made me to decide on the spur of the moment to do it, after the number of times I had thought about and rejected the idea? The luxury of the yacht? Its half-hour of returning to a sort of normalcy, albeit far above my standard, still a normalcy of life that did not recognize the inadequate conditions or rampant hostilities on MarkShip Mexico? Could a good old-fashioned American steak dinner conjure up any form of 'normalcy'? What craziness have I gotten myself into now?*

It is a forty-five minute walk into Miami, but maybe he can arrange a ride with the agent tomorrow, a bleary-eyed, blotchy-faced, but relatively clean Peasant tells me at lunch.

I might just as well tell him. "I don't really care about going into downtown or seeing the sights. I've seen Miami before. I just want a shopping center with a supermarket. I'm having a steak dinner for all the officers, and I need to buy the stuff."

His red-rimmed eyes regard me unimpressed, grumping a few seconds into his plate, then laughs when I say I will definitely be back on board by sailing time since I don't want to be left at the dock with all that food spoiling in bags. (He may disdainfully absent himself from the steak feed put on by this unruly passenger, but I can feel his mouth watering. American steak! Bet he'll be there. He will get an invitation just like everybody else. Besides, I suppose I should ask him about cocktails. He IS the Master. Damn it all to bloody hell!) Not a peep from him about not obtaining his authorization, etc. I don't mention that Chief Officer has cleared this dinner. No sense in fanning the flames, although he surely must know I got clearance from somebody and that somebody could only be Chief Officer.

Then it strikes me: Maybe he won't be or maybe Ion won't be on board if Ion makes his call and is successful. Nah. These things take time. Everybody will sail from Miami together, albeit not happily. I can only hope we stay together until Veracruz.

"Miami Pilot at 0500. Hah! Just watch, it will never happen. Probably more like 0730. Oh, we're supposed to sail from Miami at 1700." Great! Through those foggy eyes that droop and snap open in a most disconcerting way, like a frog on a lily pad, at least he remembers that his passenger likes to be on the Bridge for berthing.

1335: Engine stopped, and we are drifting some 100 miles out of Miami. Silence rushes at me.

A safety drill is announced for 1630 to test that nasty lifeboat suspended at a ninety-degree angle on a slide two decks up with nose pointed into the water. It is rumored that if the wind calms, they (maybe me, too) are going over the side, zooming into the water.

This is a drill carried out only every six months because it takes so much work to replace the lifeboat back onto the ship. Is this for my benefit, Mr. Peasant, just in case anyone ever inquires – like The Big Boss? Or do you, like every other Captain, want to have all safety logs in order before the U.S. Coast Guard comes aboard. I remember all the wild preparation aboard The Other for docking at Long Beach. Man oh man, I bet every ship in the world hates the U.S. Coast Guard. For my part, I say yayy. Who else will keep them honest with regard to safety? Although, I do read in Lloyds List that many ports the world over detain ships with inferior standards.

Lloyds List articles remind me that the officers on this ship, even in idle chatter, use the words "Ship's Safety" often. Answers to my questions revolve around Ship's Safety. Equipment, The Company, human action, even job-related attitudes start out with or end up with, "We must consider the ship's safety. Or, we do this for the ship's safety." The concern is very real, as well it should be, as we are riding around on this hollow piece of steel very alone in the middle of thousands of miles of desolate water. Intramural grievances and battles take a distant second place to ship's safety.

The feeling of no movement is so strange. Awesome silence stretches to the horizon. As I walk the decks and stairs, water laps peacefully against the ship, and the metallic echo of my own footsteps resounds. It gives me the willies.

I stop on the Bridge, where Ion and Marius are in deep conversation, papers and charts spread around them. The Peasant stands alone across the Bridge, smoking and staring at the sea.

"Captain, should I run up here when I hear the alarm?"

He turns to me in a cloud of smoke and mumbles, "Sure, Chief Officer will tell you what to do."

I bite back, *"But the Safety Officer says the Master says what to do - or don't you know what to do?" Easy, MsSelf, easy. In the case of emergency, everybody's got a job but me and they'll all be very busy. Who is the guy who tells me to stand in the corner or jump over the edge or whatever? I can only take a wild guess that it won't be you. I'm not going to get the answer here, I can tell.*

My lifejacket is poised for action on the bed, awaiting the terrifying emergency klaxon. Although I've wangled a seat on the lifeboat, I'm trying to stay out of the way since the ship is a veritable anthill of orange-clad bodies zooming in all directions.

1525: Wait, what's happening? An alarm just sounded, the engine has started, smoke is pouring from the funnel and we are moving, wake churning. We are turning rapidly, engine throbbing, setting up a harmonious vibration which rattles teeth. Maybe we are just repositioning.

1540: Engine stopped. We have turned 240 degrees, now facing south. We probably repositioned to put the lifeboat in the lee of the slight breeze. I'm glad that what looked like a fishing line off the stern didn't get caught in the propeller.

1630: Head clamped within the iridescent yellow helmet, orange lifejacket in hand, I approach the lifeboat. Don't put the lifejacket on until you get in – it's hard to maneuver in the cramped space inside. Some bodies are already sitting inside, the afternoon heat stifling, sending noxious waves out the door. One foot in, left foot for luck, two feet – nope. My claustrophobia, of the variety that precludes me from riding elevators, forbids. "Can't," I say to the guy at the door assisting me. "Only if I had to."

He smiles and hands me back out. "Not required." He looks very relieved.

The group filing into the lifeboat waves and hollers to me from my new position on Deck 3 aft. In fact, I'm standing right over them as officers and Filipinos alike holler, "Come on, come with us." They're laughing with a forced machismo that tells me they are a more than a tad scared. Looking down that chute into the sea is very daunting, in fact, heart-stopping. When trying to talk me out of my persistence in going, I had been told "I can guarantee you, it is not a pleasant experience."

"Can't, I've got claustrophobia." They don't know what c.... is, but they look back and up one by one, smiling at me, like the ship's good luck charm, as they enter the terrifying boat in the order ordained by the seating chart, looking ever so much like victims entering the gas chamber. I swallow hard and wave and smile at each of the fifteen: Good luck, good journey. I can see into the lifeboat and watch them curl into their seats, strap themselves in.

Everyone not required in the lifeboat is assembled on deck to watch. The deck people all look up and wave, and I wave back. I have my camera in hand, and they think I'm taking pictures of them. I'm not, but they won't know it. Captain is actually performing like a leader, swooshing here and there with radio in hand, white helmet squashed on his frizzy hair, making him look ever so much like a garden gnome gone berserk.

Marius gives me a thumbs-up sign, enters the lifeboat and locks the door. In a second they are catapulting down the sled and submerge with a spectacular splash, sparkling in the afternoon sun. The force of impact for those inside must be horrifying.

Three seconds submersion, I was told, a paralyzing nightmare as I wait for a sign of success. And up she pops, like a rubber ducky held under, then released by a child's hand. Boomp! Hi there!

In seconds, the door flies open, and bodies scramble to get out onto the craft's tiny aft deck. Windows crank open. I hope someone thought to record the temperature inside – Hell times two. Great whoops of laughter and back-pounding, waving and hollering as the tiny boat begins to circle MarkShip Mexico. Struggling to catch my breath, I sag against the railing.

The entire drill from start to finish takes one hour and is very thrilling. After the first terrifying plunge, the lifeboat steadies in the sea. At the completion of the second circle, all but three passengers are discharged via the Pilot ladder. Then, with great difficulty as it bobs in the sea, the lifeboat is finally grabbed by the crane hooks and repositioned with much skill and care in its sled. A real performance. As the three remaining passengers emerge, I clap and hoot from the deck above. I turn to Bosun, who is operating the crane, and whistle, clap and hoot. Everyone is happy with his own performance and laughs and bows to me. Damn, I'm glad they're back on board safely.

A perfect production, marred only by a few strange incidents:

Once the lifeboat bobs up, The Peasant leaves the Main Deck and disappears. He next appears with a very sophisticated computer camera in hand, snapping pictures of – me.

"Stop it! I don't want pictures. Stop it right now!" He grins slyly and turns away.

I move to a different deck and position myself to get a great shot of the lifeboat coming around the ship's bow when I hear a noise behind me. The Peasant is standing two feet behind me, my quick turn startling him to a standstill position.

"What are you doing? You scared the hell out of me. It's those damned shoes, they are so quiet." I laugh at his thick Jesus shoes worn over heavy socks, all enclosing his fat little feet.

"So I don't wake up sleeping passengers," he replies.

"Yeah, right. Who's the one doing all the sleeping on this ship? It ain't the passenger, Mister." He chuckles and moves away.

I change decks again to get a better angle of the lifeboat below and also to escape his creepiness, which is making me twitch. The preponderance of people on this ship are either in the lifeboat or attending to safety drill duties while I stand alone on the upper decks. *Got the heebie-jeebies, MsSelf?*

Then, lo and behold, here he is again, skulking up behind me, very close.

"I asked you before, and I ask you again! What the hell are you doing?" I scream in his face.

He jumps back, hands in the air like a Western movie holdup victim. "I didn't touch you, I didn't touch you!"

I glare at him and spit, "Yeah, and you better damn well NOT try it!" He scurries away, his gummy Jesus shoes slapping on the deck.

What do we make of that, MsSelf? Was he going to throw you over? In broad daylight?

Dinner is a huge success, with me congratulating everyone in the full Dining Room. The Peasant sits preening like a huge toad, and I avoid eye contact or speaking.

Lucky there is a lot of commotion because I can't eat my food, except the small piece of cauliflower and two tiny potatoes. I saw at the meat, then give it up.

"Just like American steak, yes?" says The Peasant, grinning craftily.

"Yeah, sure." I grimace, and Ion and Stan, who are managing to chomp on theirs and somehow swallow it, laugh. Good teeth. Young men, at least lots younger than me.

"You know, Captain (I have an agenda here and want to butter him up, but still can't quite do it regardless of how hard I try, and in view of his weirdness earlier, so I finally give it up and say what I want to), you can't prepare really good food unless you start out with really good provisions. Or have good equipment." I pause and saw at my meat. "I don't know how my steak dinner will turn out. It all has to be done in one pan since half the galley equipment doesn't work. Cook is a genius and magician as he finds a way to prepare food for twenty-three people without equipment and crap for provisions." Well, speak about talking to the wall. But, there *is* an embarrassed silence. Stan is horrified (at my directness or that the equipment doesn't work?), and Ion smirks.

I turn to Stan, whose sad eyes are staring at his Captain and his mouth is slightly ajar, about to say something or swallow it? "Stan, we can't go to Ruth Cris's tomorrow for lunch. I have to go to the supermarket and get all the stuff for the filet mignon dinner party." Stan portrays not an iota of surprise at such a party; but, of course not, he must have heard hours ago. He wriggles happily in real or feigned surprise and anticipation of the party. He shows no disappointment that our Ruth Cris luncheon is off.

Still looking at Stan, I sigh mightily and say, "I guess I should ask the Master, the one in control, right? if we could have a cocktail hour. I'm thinking of cocktails at 1730 and dinner at 1800. What do you think, Captain?" I nearly gag on my words, but remember the agenda I seemed to have forgotten earlier. *You can catch more flies with honey…*

Well, he thinks that would be wonderful. Ion and I exchange secret smiles, his congratulatory. *Heh, heh.*

Stan is just overwhelmed with the whole idea. "You are a very special lady." The Peasant jerks a frown at Stan, who either doesn't see it or doesn't care.

"Naw. Just something I want to do."

The Peasant suddenly smiles. *Man, this guy is a chameleon.* "Will the invitations be from the computer?"

"No. Hand-written or an invitation I will buy." This pleases him greatly. *Yup, he's coming to eat steak.* I consider his question and response absolutely astounding in view of my opinion of his lowly standing. *What does he know of written invitations? Who would want him in their house?*

Dinner breaks up pleasantly, and I go to the next table to invite the officers. They gape at me. *You mean you haven't heard? Ion, you little devil, you can keep a closed mouth if you want.* "I am inviting you now, but you will have an invitation at your plate."

"A *real* invitation?"

"Yes. Now, I would like to talk to you about what you like to drink. We are going to do this in the American style. Cocktails and cheese and crackers, maybe a few other hors d'oeuvres, then salad, then dinner, then dessert." A huge discussion ensues of different ways of serving: Salad after entrée, cheese and fruit after desserts, etc. They stare.

"Do we wear, you know…" 3rd Engineer makes a motion of tightening a tie.

"Only if you want. But I bet you don't."

Florin juts his ever-pugnacious face into the laughter. "I want to talk to you about how you prepare this steak. It is very black, yes?"

"Normally, yes. But you must remember, I am working with very limited equipment in the galley, thanks to him." I gesture at Roberto. He sits back, horrified while all heads swivel to him and glare. *Oh, oh, what have I started here? They obviously didn't know he was the galley culprit.* "I'll do it in brown butter, and I think you'll like it. Have you ever tasted an American steak?"

"Once."

Someone asks importantly and somewhat sarcastically, "Will it be filet mignon?"

"Yes." Their mouths drop open. It's obvious they have heard of, but never tasted, it. Filet mignon – joyful saliva fills my mouth. They are going to be happy campers. *Oh Lordy, what kind of pickle have I put myself into?*

I consult with Cristori. A filet for him and Alex, too. They dance.

"Cristori, about the crew…"

"They know, Mum."

"Cari."

"Yes," he ducks his head, "Cari. They know, Mu..ah, Cari, what you tried to do with the barbeque."

We look at each other sorrowfully.

"They come into the galley often. They know how hard it is to cook just basic meals with this…" and he throws his arm toward the malfunctioning equipment. "They know."

"What should I do for them since I can't cook for everybody on this." And I too throw my arm, thinking: *Damn you, you could too, you just don't want to buy filet for twenty-three people.* "I was thinking maybe a huge cake that they really couldn't eat all at once, so they'd have some for the next day."

"Dessert?" His eyes glisten. "Cake? Oh yes, Mu…Cari. With maybe little fruits on top, like on cruise ships. I would tell them it was like that.

They would like that very much, Mu…" Then, "Filet mignon wrapped in bacon?"

"Yes, Cristori. Day after tomorrow. Remember, you will not have to prepare dinner for the officers. I will do it, all of it."

He grins from ear to ear, and I feel like a heel about the crew.

"Can I bring you anything from shore?"

"Only, Mu…, if you would post a letter to my family for me, but I do not have a stamp."

"No problem. Give it to me, and I will take care of it."

"Alex, what can I bring you?"

"If you could, Mum, rubber gloves."

"What?" "Rubber gloves, Mum."

"Rubber gloves! What do you mean, rubber gloves!"

He open his hands, palms and fingers cracked and raw. He looks at them sheepishly. "From the water and detergents, Mum."

My temperature rises dramatically and it is all I can do to not scream. *Control, MsSelf, control*

"OK, Alex, rubber gloves."

I walk into the Dining Room, cursing.

"What's the matter?"

"Rubber gloves." I tell them about Alex's hands. "I can't believe this ship!"

"Did you say ship or shit?"

"Both."

Roberto says, "I would give him rubber gloves if he would clean my cabin twice a week."

"Really!" I spit. "You big piece of shi…" I don't have to finish since heads swivel once again, glares and grunts of disgust pinning him against his chair. *Well, honey, are you having a good evening? You creep! Wonder what tomorrow is going to bring for you in light of all this, um, enlightenment by your fellow shipmates.*

I stomp the five decks to the Bridge, thinking of smiling, eager-to-please Alex and his bleeding hands. I am so mad, so mad, my head buzzes. Whoever is on the Bridge is going to get it. And I hope it's that fucking Peasant.

It's Ion. He listens silently as I use many bad words, spouting my anger, telling the story. "How the hell is anyone supposed to do their job properly when they don't have equipment or things as basic as god-damned rubber gloves?"

"I didn't know about his hands. If he had told me… I put in requisitions for supplies. I ask at each requisitioning port. Although cook and steward report to Captain - *he* is supposed to direct them – they often come to me." Ion tells, as an example, about the washing machine that was broken for two days until Cook, in despair for clean towels, told Ion, who commanded Roberto to fix it NOW. I already knew about that and simply nodded. This tiny island afloat on the Atlantic…

"Ion, they're at the bottom of the ladder. They are scared. Weren't you ever at the bottom of the ladder? I was and know how it feels. So when I was in a position to direct what happened in a company or businesses of my own, I listened to all those small things. You CANNOT DO A JOB WHEN YOU DON'T HAVE THE PROPER SUPPLIES OR EQUIPMENT. Even frigging rubber gloves when your hands are so raw they won't work. You know it yourself."

"The hands…" Ion shudders. "I will get him rubber gloves tomorrow."

Pacing across the Bridge, each footfall an explosion, "Oh no you won't, I WILL. He turned to the goddamned passenger for a simple pair of rubber gloves, and the goddamned passenger is going to supply them. Don't you dare. I will be back on board by 1500 with gloves and soothing creams for him."

And then I relent. "Oh God, Ion, between those raw hands and that silly piece of shit of an electrician, who it's hard to imagine is really all there…" I stop ten feet away, holding my head in the green glow of the radar screens and moon streaming through the Bridge panoramic windows, bracing only slightly to the gentle roll of the ship.

Ion moves across the deck to the Chart Room and snaps on a low light as I stand halfway across the Bridge. "This electrician is very hard to direct. He works, of course, for Chief Engineer, but Stan has mostly washed his hands of him, because…But I really am in charge, as if Stan has handed him over to me because he cannot, does not want to, deal with the reality of… Electrician and Captain are very friendly, very friendly."

Hello beautiful full moon. Moon over Miami. Hello beautiful sea shining and dancing only for me like a picture book. The perfect moment as to why I so love the sea. I close my eyes.

I know what's coming. Nothing of real importance on land, but on the sea, on these floating islands, where centuries of brawny men come to work to provide for their doe-eyed wives and laughing children, where the danger and Superstitions of the Sea can consume you, where you keep your own counsel and defend against the hours and months of working so closely together, where discipline both from Captain and self is king, where the need to know yourself is paramount.

Harshly from Ion, "They're queer."

No they are not really queer - homosexuals. The blustering, overbearing Peasant is using pale, effeminate Roberto like a blow-up sex doll, albeit a live one. Roberto is finding what he considers the easy way out and lording his relationship with the Master and the privilege it provides over his lesser shipmates. It's very doubtful that his peers, who are sure to take a very dim view, know his real relationship with The Peasant. Roberto is a small persona with nowhere to go, with a mentality so small that being buggered means nothing more than me screaming at him in the hallway. And your orders, Chief Officer? Hah. He has Mr. Asshole, literally, to back him up with his many devious ways. And Mr. Asshole? He wishes only complete control. Those superstitious Filipinos only provide so much entertainment. Why not take a little turd like Roberto and bend him completely to your will, have at least one person abjectly at your total mercy. Mr. Electrician will provide it all.

Instead, I say, "What? You never told me anything like that."

"I did." He puts his index and middle fingers together. "I told you," glancing at his fingers.

"I thought you meant they made business together. It's your phrase, that is, understood by every seaman, 'making business' behind someone's back or illegally, like pilots demanding Marlboros in Suez or Captain buying a satellite from the Crew's Fund. I sure as hell didn't think you meant gay."

A blast of the alarm, the engine starts, and we idle forward. We have been floating 100 miles from Miami, too far from port, I would think, to be waiting in the roads. Besides, I don't see the bevy of normal sitting duck ships if we were waiting in the roads.

From far out on the horizon, a gaudily-lit cruise ship moves slowly toward us, setting the water afire in a blaze of reflected color. Ion asks me about them, since he knows I've been aboard many. "For me, it would be like nothing. But my wife would like it."

"Yes, Ion, your wife would like it very much, and so would you." And I tell him about cruise ships, the amenities, being pampered, prices. "It's different being a passenger." He nods.

"Alex said MarkShip Mexico only had two passengers – two men."

"Yeah, they were boring. Each was only on board for a week or so. Signed on at Valencia, rode to Barcelona, La Spezia and back again. We had some special contract that had us stopping in Valencia again before leaving The Med, so they just went for a little cargo ship ride, maybe to get away from their businesses, lives, wives, kids. Who knows?"

"You didn't see much of them?"

"No. They brought on lots of liquor and mostly sat in their cabins drinking and smoking. They'd come for dinner. Captain always saw to it that we had fairly decent food to eat." He pauses. "Not like the slop we're getting now. Maybe he doesn't want to impress you. Or maybe it was before he had perfected his theft schemes. Anyway, they'd sit at dinner and talk about Spain."

He looks at me with dancing eyes. "They sure weren't running around the ship with innocent smiles asking thousands of questions, like 'Does heating heavy fuel cause instability of the product? How much paint does it take per voyage to keep the ship in tiptop shape? How many boxes are carried in the hold? Why do you have all those posters about booze and drugs and none about hygiene and personal cleanliness? Is there a limit to the number of people who can be on the Bridge at one time? Why doesn't someone with decorator talent paint the public rooms a color easy to live with? Why doesn't a new ship like this have a bowthruster? Exactly where is the Bermuda Triangle? Have you ever sailed in pirate waters? Do the scuppers often get clogged up?' You're going to have these poor guys running around with a library of reference books on their backs. If only we had them," he adds ruefully.

He bursts out laughing. "I hear all these things, you know. Where do you get all those questions? And why do you ask questions when you obviously already know the answers? And where did you get all those answers?"

In a huff, I spit, "Well, Mr. Question-Man-Yourself, I like to know stuff. I got the answers I already know from the officers and deck crew on The Other, who made me their little project. They taught, and I learned. Capt. R., for example, loved to test me on passing ships.

"'What kind of a ship is that?'

"'A RO-RO.' And he'd grin with pleasure. If he were a drinking man, he would have clinked glasses.

"'Because?'

"'It's flat on both ends with doors that open like loading ramps for things to Roll On-Roll Off. Looks like a ferry.' I'd grab the binoculars and scan the shipping lane. 'That's a Liquified Natural Gas carrier with those big round domes on deck. Of course,' I'd look at him slyly, 'a dead giveaway are the huge letters LNG on the side.'

"He'd load me down with seafaring and merchant shipping magazines to keep me company. After all, I was on that ship for three months. You can learn a lot in that period of time.

"It was like a game for them, which both sides entered gleefully. Unlike what I've encountered on MarkShip Mexico where every question has been an insult and every answer like pulling teeth. Sometimes," I add spitefully, rolling my eyes, "I wonder if these people really know the answers. Maybe they're not reluctant, but simply, um, unknowing." *Mean brat!*

"Like pulling teeth," Ion breathes, head cocked, and I foresee a future consultation with the *Compendium*.

Change of watch, and Marius plods onto the Bridge, rubbing his head. All duties accomplished, we go out onto the bridgewing into the very warm, humid air and talk about crazy things, ending up in a boisterous argument about painting rollers. I noticed that ships use very small rollers. If they used larger rollers, the work could be done in half the time.

"Big ones can only be used once," he says with authority.

"Not if you buy good quality rollers. I know; I really like to paint."

"No, no, the big ones fall apart always."

We walk back inside. He sits, holding his head.

"What's the matter?"

"Nothing. Nothing. Just a little headache. It's been getting worse every day, but it'll go away."

"Take care of yourself, kid. Good night, Marius. You're not well, and I can't think of anything I want to talk about less on this beautiful night than painting rollers. It's so beautiful that I think I'll go for a walk on deck."

"Well, all right, do it!" he challenges.

"I can't. I'll be thinking of you running after me screaming I TOLD YOU NOT TO DO THIS." He roars with laughter, ending up holding his head.

There, I managed the whole evening without mentioning the weird antics of The Peasant sneaking around this afternoon. My gut tells me that these poor guys just can't take anymore right now. Maybe later.

As I descend the inside stairway to Deck 4, I see Florin standing on the stairs three-quarters of the way up between Deck 3 and 4.

"Florin. Good evening. What are you doing here?" I ask in surprise.

He puts his index finger to his lips, looks up the next stairwell, eyes raised as a signal, and moves halfway down the hallway toward my cabin. Whatever it is, he doesn't want anyone, that 'anyone' probably being The Peasant on Superstructure Deck 5, to hear. He faces me in the middle of the hallway, back to the staircase, his shaved head reflecting the harsh hallway lamp, short, powerful body taut.

Florin, of the perfect, succinct English, pulls out all the stops in a low, steady voice. "Marius indicated that he had spoken with you about...about the mirrors." I nod. "I do not believe that a simple apology is enough to convey my deepest regrets. It began as a sop of camaraderie with the Captain, of which, I am sure you have noted there is none, zero, on this ship. The mere idea of what he was doing was repugnant to nearly all of us, but he was so enthusiastic and, for once, actually friendly, and I guess we were attempting to form some bridge, any bridge, with him. And, and... Well, most of us had never met an

American woman before, and from all we had been told throughout our lifetimes...

"That bridge we hoped to form turned out very badly. The Captain would jab, slyly taunt us, accuse us of being pussies when we quickly found we didn't want to watch his 'best show on the planet,' in fact, to actually participate in anything with him.

"There is no excuse. We acted like pigs, worse. I do not deny that I have admired your neat little form from afar. You remind me of my mother, an attractive, convivial woman, who would be greatly disappointed in me for what I've done. No more than I am myself. But I want you to know that I never saw you in a state of undress, I really doubt anyone did, although I did try to look. A case of total immorality."

He sags and puts a hand on the bulkhead. Under the Communist upbringing beats the heart of an altar boy, who may very well have often been secretly on his knees in a dark closet of his home, his mother demonstrating the mea culpas and rosary.

"Will you forgive me for acting as a stupid boy and a great deal less than a man? My heart is not one right now, and I fear..."

"Yes, Florin, I forgive you."

"Thank you very much. I do not want to disappoint you." He regards me sadly, turns and marches erectly down the hallway and onto the staircase, his ever-present pugnaciousness gone.

2232: The engine is going full blast, my cabin floor vibrating with its intensity. Are we headed for Miami? Will anyone wake me for Pilot? Doubtful. I'll wait an hour and, if we don't stop, go up on the Bridge and find out what's happening. We're six hours or more to Miami at slow speed. The Peasant might be up there, strutting and posturing, but so will Marius. Maybe we can renew our paint roller discussion. I see him pushing that mop of black hair out of his face, eyes dancing, belly shaking, ready to do battle for small paint rollers. He won't take a stand on even the smallest item regarding this ship. But paint rollers? Get ready world!

Suddenly, I remember that we were to be officially underway at slow speed at 2230. Good on ya', Stan, for being Mr. Prompt. OK, I'll go to bed.

Saturday, November 11. Miami, Florida, USA

Clear, windy, cold. Force 6: Strong, 22-27 knot winds, 9-1/2-13 foot waves, spray, white crests.

At 0500 the moon is round and orange over Miami, and we float in a sea of dancing reflected tangerine. Pilot at 0600. We advance slowly into port, turn around and are shoved into berth by two tugs. Berthing at 0700 as the sun peeks over the cranes, shimmering the waving palm fronds, and the sunrise is spectacular, although with little warmth as we shiver on the Bridge. Miami is a lovely port, the nicest I have seen in all the world.

Pilot, dressed in sparkling whites, stares at me in amazement when he first glimpses me on the Bridge. The Peasant, dressed for the first time in clean khakis, is oh so friendly to his American passenger as he introduces the startled pilot. See, Mr. American Pilot, how courteously I treat your countrywoman?

As I look around the Bridge, I note that every soul is dressed in pressed khakis, including Helmsman. Gone are the advertising T-shirts and worn jeans. Geez, these boys clean up pretty well. Yet I can't help but smile that on The Other, all officers would have been in formal black pants and dazzling white shirts with epaulets or insignias.

After we've all hung over the bridgewing and directed MarkShip Mexico to berth, radios blaring, Helmsman erect, Peasant's sausage legs pumping importantly from port to starboard and return, Pilot screws up his courage to talk to this blond female apparition on the Bridge. I ask about the new President, which sets him into a wild rampage of the political happenings in the U.S. over the last few days. I am dumbstruck and Pilot is shaking with anger at the mess we have in the USA with no President and a political war being fought.

When the agent comes on board, a young man very full of himself and his 'exalted' position (Ugly American pops into my mind unbidden although he is obviously Cuban), I ask him his take on the election. He's not interested and rudely turns his back.

The Peasant comes into the Dining Room where I'm having coffee and toast. "The agent had to leave but will be back to pick you up to go to town." All jolly and full of smiles. *Make sure you get to that steak store, Mrs. Lindley.*

Ion is all smiley, too. Will he do it?

0830: *Oh dear me. I'm up to my neck in boiling soup now.* I am in Chief Officer's office, glimpsing Miami through the open Hatchcover door, the squeal of cranes and roar of trucks bursting through the opening.

"Captain says the agent will take me to town. Do I need a shore pass?"

"No, but I'll give you your passport." He unlocks and opens the top drawer, handing me the passport. "Maybe you'd like to see another of the Captain's brown boxes. It's all nicely tied and ready to be sent to Poland."

He sees my hesitation at getting involved. "You could help us a great deal if you saw it. Maybe I could give your e-mail address to The Big Boss, Belson, and I could give you his, just in case he needed verification that you saw it."

"I don't know. This is ship's business, and I'm just a..."

"Just look at it. Maybe use your photo-camera for only one picture. It would be proof that you saw it, just saw it. You've seen the boxes before."

So I run up five decks to get my photo-camera, very uneasy about the whole thing. But I have already heard, seen and experienced so much, I start to get angry again.

We walk to the Visitors' Lounge, a nasty little cubicle, door mechanism squealing loudly (a problem throughout the ship, which I promptly cured on my own door by applying a little Vitamin E oil. Just think what a spritz of WD-40 would do.)

Sure enough, to my dismay, there is a brown paper-wrapped, string-tied box addressed to Hannah K. in Poland. I recognize the address from the brief previous glimpses, although I haven't a clue as to what is inside the box. But The Peasant was only offboard in La Spezia, and I saw him coming back empty-handed. What, I ask myself, could he be sending to his wife? Idly, I pick it up. Very heavy.

"Maybe three to four kilos?" asks Ion.

"Much more," I whisper.

"Your photo-camera?" He takes it from me, asks me to stand by the box and takes a close-up of the address with my hand on the box and partial body beside it. *Shit oh dear, I'm sinking in this mess and beginning to drown.*

"More proof," he exhales in satisfaction. I say we don't know what's inside the box, only guessing. Guessing it must be something from provisions, at least, since Cook says we have no more of whatever is requested, anchovies, tinned fish, olives, spiced garlic. The response from Alex is always, "Only for the Captain" or "No more." And, of course, my nimble brain adds to the list, stove parts. By next port, will we be eating the sparse food dumped on the bare table with our fingers, drinking from cupped hands under the faucets?

3rd Engineer and Marius, both very sick, en route to doctor appointments and getting more nervous by the minute, and I wait by the gangway an hour for the agent, who is well aware of their appointments. When he arrives, he is haughty and surly, holding up two fingers from the driver's window, like he will only take two passengers.

I lean across the seat. "Why did you hold up two fingers? What did you mean by that?" I demand of his handsome, sullen face.

"Get in, we're under the crane," he answers with disgust.

"That crane is not moving and is seventy-five meters away, can't you see? He's in the midst of unloading a box." I get in and regard him with curled lip. He glares at the lowly woman, and I glare back. He starts the car with a jerk.

"Can you tell me where the nearest supermarket is?"

"I'm not going in the direction of any supermarket," he growls.

"That's not what I asked you," I snap. "I asked where the nearest supermarket is. Didn't you understand my English, or don't you know?" So I give it right back to him, and by the time we get to the gate, he is feebly trying to be friendly to my glacial stare. The two silent sickies in the back are nada to this guy, only a pain to be dealt with. I've ridden with agents in all parts of the world, and they have been unfailingly friendly and helpful. This made-good refugee bastard in the United States is above all us peons. We'll see about that. Agents are rated by Captains of ships and contracted and discharged on their recommendations. The Peasant will be good for something constructive.

"Bye, guys. Get a good shot and come back healthy." They smile weakly.

I grab a cab at the gate, a laid-back black guy who doesn't seem to care if he has a fare or not. As it turns out, we get into a conversation and he, from Haiti, is very nice. Fifteen dollars plus a fat tip later, he deposits me at the nearest supermarket, which is in dire need of a facelift. Well, at least I got to see a part of Miami.

I buy stamps and post Cristori's letter, guessing at the postage since this is a U.S. holiday. Put plenty on.

Miami is as foreign as any foreign country I've been in. Standing at the deli counter inside the supermarket, I overhear a conversation in Spanish between a black woman and a brown man and laugh with them. They jerk at my laughter, then regard me with interest. I listen as I walk and maybe, maybe not, hear English. Hard to tell. I quickly call my sister in Arizona and find out I may relax – everything is under control, everybody is well. Are you ever coming home? Not for months and months.

The supermarket is every bit as nasty inside as it is out. I grit my teeth and head for the meat market, praying.

"I need twelve of your best filets, two inches thick, minimum of ten ounces. Do you have premium meat?" The butcher looks at me like I'm an escaped lunatic. "I mean it. I want your very best." I tell him what I'm doing.

"A freighter?" he hollers. "You're serving two-inch filets to officers on a freighter?!" Half of the store's customers are running around end-caps to the meat counter, all of them joining the butcher in ogling me like an insane asylum inmate.

"Well, you see, I'm cooking them an American steak dinner. They've never tasted filet mignon before and…"

The small crowd of twenty rather scruffy souls relaxes, nods happily and looks very pleased with the whole idea. I field a few questions: "Whatcha doin' on a freigtah? Ain't cha' skeered, honey?" *Where is the perfect English spoken on MarkShip Mexico?*

The butcher tells me two inches is too thick, I insist, and we settle on 1-3/4 inches, at least ten ounces each, wrapped in bacon.

"Too big," he says, "nobody can eat all that."

I say "You don't know these guys. They can really eat, like horses." *If only it were available to them.* "Now, do you need my credit card before you start cutting?"

"Hell no. I'm going to sell this story to a local newspaper and make a small fortune."

Thus ensues nearly two hours of hectic shopping, where I ask at every turn, where is this, where is that, since they don't seem to have anything I want. Huh? They reply. Fresh strawberries? Chives? Angel food cake? Rosemary or jalapeno bread? On and on. Huh? Huh? Huh? You know, folks, stuff Americans eat. Huh? Just who the hell are you people? What country am I in? Isn't Florida a state of the USA?

I'm beginning to worry about time since I don't want to be the butt of my own joke, standing on the dock with sacks of melting groceries, waving goodbye to MarkShip Mexico on which I should have been aboard at 1700. At the rate this is going, I'll still be looking for crap at 1900.

With a heaping cart of fresh asparagus, Idaho bakers, fresh mushrooms, a big bag of garlic, to which I go back and add more, two hunks of Jarlsberg Swiss and Vermont cheddar, shredded Parmesan, specialty crackers plus three large tins of dusty pate (I check the dates), 10 bottles of Petite Syrah, two pounds of butter, four loaves of French bread plus salad goodies, three cheesecakes and, for the crew, two humongous sheet cakes, for which I pay $8 extra to add fruit on top, I finally present myself at the meat counter.

The beaming butcher opens the insulated box with a flourish. My oh my, does he have reason to beam: Before me is the most dazzling array of filet mignons I've ever seen, including in pictures. I thank him profusely and blow his glowing face kisses on the way to the checkout stand, where my heart can barely stand the strain of the bill. I then remember Alex's gloves and medicated creams and newspapers and magazines, so need to plunk down that depleted debit card another time.

Florida doesn't sell booze in supermarkets, and I'm too panicked for time to find a liquor store, so I hope I've got enough booze onboard.

Returning without enough booze is one thing, but if I had returned without the American Steak, eight officers, Cook and Steward would surely jump overboard. Their mouths are watering, and my (forgotten) cooking skills are on the line. *More hot soup to swim around in, MsSelf.*

A bonus for me, however, is that their Eastern European palates will probably reject every American thing I set before them. Screw it! Everything, including the very spendy cheesecake, I will cover with garlic.

The cab is loaded to the gills as we drive up to the gangway, the driver looking fearfully at the cranes. He deposits sacks and sacks, which he has extracted from both the trunk and back seat, on the dock, being extra careful with the huge sheet cakes. I feel like one of those how-many-people-can-you-get-into-a-phone-booth jokes. The driver, from Cuba, has been so nice and we have had such a friendly conversation that I tip him very well.

One of the crew bolts down the gangway to help me. Well, bless you Filipinos. No Tuvaluans ever did that on The Other.

My young man is so engrossed by the sheet cakes smiling at him through their clear plastic covers that I'm afraid he will miss a step and we'll all go tumbling into the dirty water between ship and dock. But we make it.

The mountain of sacks onboard causes a wildfire of discussion, although I have arrived at a very slack time. Most of the perishables I put in the lounge refrigerator. Cristori comes to help, and I tell him I will do it, but his curiosity is too great, and he watches carefully as I jam things into the refrigerator. He asks to see the meat and opens the box, oohs and aahs, sees the price tag on the box and nearly faints. *I can identify, Cristori.* He helps me carry items we agree do not need refrigeration for one day into the galley and deposit them on a side table out of his way.

Later I hear from the galley the words 'filet mignon' mixed with the Filipino. Oh hell, he is spreading the word, although I don't want him to blab. Filet for the officers and sheet cake drives another wedge, which I myself am providing. Face up to it: You are perpetuating discrimination with this filet/cake double standard. But I've tasted what Filipinos like best, and I don't like it. Ergo, would they not like filet mignon? Will the Polish and Romanians? Cristori, the cruise ship chef, knows about this

American stuff. Therefore, a filet for him and one for Alex because they will see it and I don't want them to feel left out. Will the others like it? Am I wasting my time? Why didn't I just ride quietly, shut up in my cabin like other passengers with my cigarettes, computer and booze?

Sitting in the Dining Room, hand-writing invitations on the thick creamy notecards I found in the supermarket, Ion joins me. Now he has second thoughts about the telephone call, and, frankly, I commiserate. So would I if I had a wife and three-year-old son AND a career about to blossom – a fact I keep reminding him of often. He wants all proof in hand, including that from my photo-camera. I do not remind him that getting the film developed in Veracuz during the short time the ship will be in port will be tricky at best. I can tell the call will not be made from Miami.

"Ion, it comes down to whether you can live with yourself if you don't do it."

"I'm telling you, he is not only cruel and unfair to the people on the ships he masters, but is an agitator, disruptor – that is, when he chooses to become part of the ship's business - and so often, just evil. Should he be allowed to go on and on?" All of this in an ominously quiet, distraught tone.

"There you are, kid. It's called a moral dilemma. You must do what you can or what you think is right, being reasonable and understanding the benefits of your actions to those you command, but also the consequences to yourself." *All those nights riding on the Bridge. Have I overdone it in my anger at this Captain? Have I instilled thoughts of morality, infused new ideas into their heads that they had not wanted to discover – or perhaps rediscover? And who am I do do these things?*

Marius said one sunny morning, riding in high swells, "I do not want to, would never want to, lie to you." In the odd way he presents himself, it was like a prayer. He was in attendance at the "Clinton speech" dinner and he, more than anyone, would take it to heart. *What have I done?*

Because we are sailing at 1700, I will not have my coveted afternoon cocktails. Can't be staggering around on the Bridge with Pilot and who knows who else in attendance. I hear the engine start and run up to the bridgewing.

Ion is there, playing with his new state-of-the-art Fuji computer-compatible camera, just like The Peasant's. He "made shopping" off board after I heard him request permission from The Peasant by telephone from the Dining Room earlier. And…

"My God, what have you done to yourself?"

"Like it?" and he puts the camera above and flashes his new SHAVED head. He smiles delightedly, resembling a very large pixie.

"It takes some getting used to. Well, OK, I do like it."

"I called."

"And?" I hold my breath.

"Mr. Belson will be back from vacation in Ireland in a week. They wouldn't let me talk to anybody else. Frankly, I just don't think they are going to be interested, but I will do it again from Houston. But, it was very hard. I saw my whole life dancing before my eyes. Like dying." He looks at the floor, camera dangling.

A mammoth cruise ship inches past, dwarfing MarkShip Mexico, decks jammed with happy people, bands playing, lights glittering in the gathering dusk.

"Probably has 5,000 or maybe 100,000 people onboard. Such monster ships take all the fun out of cruising. Now they are chock-a-block with amenities, where there used to be camaraderie and friendship." I curl my lip.

"So," he continues, "when they said only Mr. Belson could discuss ship's business, I decided if I was going to possibly change my whole life with one phone call, I might just as well change the way I look, too. I went into a barber shop and said 'Shave it,' as drastic an action as the phone call."

Roberto comes boiling onto the Bridge, looking from port where I am standing to mid-ships where Ion is holding his camera. If he sees our sour looks at him, he doesn't show it. *I told you, MsSelf, he isn't all there.* But, he is full of bubbles and exclaims approvingly of Ion's shiny head and can't wait to be shown the new camera, so I tell myself to set aside my personal disgust for the moment. Ion, who knows every bit, probably more, than I about Roberto, seems willing to let it all pass for the moment and takes photo-camera shots of us, of the bulkhead, his shiny shoes, coveralled butt. Flash, flash, flash in the near darkness. I am convulsed with laughter.

"You are so funny," I hoot as he flashes and flashes.

"Just like my son with a new toy, he plays with it." Good point.

"What time is Pilot?"

"Thirty minutes." Flash, flash.

The Peasant slips onto the Bridge, his face peevish as he glimpses Ion's new camera, probably angry that his minion has a camera like his, and watches our craziness. Ion and Roberto have their backs to the Bridge and don't realize he's there, and we continue our antics with the camera on the bridgewing – flash, flash – laughing and cavorting like kids. Finally, I tilt my head, they look around, and we all walk inside, still giggling and hooting.

I stay across the Bridge as The Peasant beckons Ion and Roberto to starboard, where he thinks I'm out of earshot. "You love that camera so much you'll probably take it to bed with you. Maybe you can fuck it." Ion answers something I cannot hear, but the joy is gone. And I, who had been having so much fun, am angry again. Condemning words fill my throat and nearly choke me. I walk out onto the bridgewing and watch three incredible cruise ships leave port, thinking of my husband's and my great times – the loving, the caring, the fun - on them, giving me respite from MarkShip Mexico.

Pilot is due, but the gangway is still down, so he's not onboard. We are all standing around, staring out the dark windows. The Peasant has decided he wants his waiting time to be on the side of the Bridge where I'm standing, so we wait ten feet from each other in total silence.

Finally, I speak. "Why do you hate the United States so much, Captain?"

"I have had many customs problems here. They don't want me on their shore. I am Captain of a ship, and they think I want to work in the U.S., those black bastards? I am Master. I am Polish. They say I don't have the right papers, can't bring this or that on board my own ship, many problems, many. They don't want me here?" He shouts. "They don't want ME here?" And he rages on, every second sentence containing 'black bastards.'

Well, I think, maybe they could see in you at first glance what it has taken me weeks to discover. Those 'black bastards' probably had better antennae than I. And I smile at him, eyes narrowed, thinking, *You're right, we don't want you here. In fact, nobody wants you once they get to know you.*"

Now that he's complained wildly, it should be my turn. I tell him about the agent.

The Peasant is incensed. "I told you, he is Cuban."

"Captain, understand that is not the point. He was arrogant and very rude, wouldn't even answer simple questions about the port, acted as if the sickies were too loathsome to address. I have ridden with lots of agents of all colors, and they were friendly and very accommodating. I didn't request and didn't expect that this agent would take me specific places, like a supermarket."

"Well, I do. You are a paying passenger." And I dream I was back in Valencia giving the Spanish agent an earful of practically the same words. "You are like one of the containers. Can he say that he does not like a box so it cannot be unloaded? No, all boxes will be unloaded, whether he likes the container or not. It is his job to take care of the cargo in port. You, because you are a paying passenger, are part of the cargo, and I expect that you will be taken care of in port. Captain's reports are taken seriously with regard to agents. I will report this and add a few comments of my own."

I am so shocked that my mouth literally falls open. *Well, well, well. Within The Peasant hides an iota of soul,* although I wonder at how his passion for passenger care failed in Barcelona, Gio Tauro and La Spezia."

But his reply sets me rethinking my role on this ship – lowly passenger, never bother Captain, never bother the agent, never bother anybody. I keep forgetting that I am cargo, but, now reintroduced, I like the idea very much. That's what ships are all about - shipping cargo for money. Paying cargo, that is what I am, paying for the crew's daily food, paying lots more than a box. Take care of your cargo, please Captain, Officers and Crew of MarkShip Mexico. How absolutely delicious! (I wonder if he remembers through his drunken haze the 2nd Engineer's party where

I announced, "No, I am God on this ship. I am paying." Probably not or he sure wouldn't bring it up again.)

Pilot finally appears, dressed in dazzling whites as opposed to our slobs, who have returned to shorts and T-shirts, and gives me the normal shocked expression, that always includes glazed eyes and open mouth. Pilots the world over must take identical "shocked" lessons. He says good evening, and I reply in perfect English, which makes his mouth drop farther. Normally, I like to wait half an hour or so before speaking, so they can do their wild speculations of what a blond woman, in this case, dressed in shorts and T-shirt, is doing on the Bridge, riding easily with obvious full consent of officers.

Capt. R. on The Other took particular pleasure in these moments. If Pilot spotted me standing to one side, good. If not, he would then carefully guide Pilot to me for introductions, closely watching the sputtering Pilot, Capt.'s eyes dancing behind glinting glasses, lips twitching with great glee. He loved it and made sure it happened regardless of the hour or weather, once telling me it was the highlight for entertainment of Pilot-on. When The Other touched some fairly exotic ports, Capt. R.'s delight intensified, and I often thought he rued not having film of the short event.

But then, Capt. R. also reveled in pointing out interesting sights on the approach to harbors, my favorites being the Ghost Port in Rotterdam and Dragon Holes in Hong Kong and Tokyo.

Dragon holes, he imparted, were large open spaces, seven-stories high, rimmed in gold paint, in the center of thirty-story high-rises, put there by the owners so that dragons, if any were trapped and confused, would always have light and be able to find their way out. The Chinese and Japanese are very superstitious, you know. True or false? Who cared? I adored the story, thinking of the immense lost revenue, at Hong Kong prices, such Dragon Holes entailed.

No such story-telling on MarkShip Mexico, but I am riding on the Bridge exactly where I want to be, so I do not complain. Besides, as no one talks to each other, it'd probably be a monumental chore to get them to talk to me.

This Pilot is Mr. Chatty, after the most important chores are accomplished. One eye on the water and ears open to the called headings, he still has time to tell me about Miami.

"It is a beautiful port," I say, and he wriggles with pleasure.

Suddenly he calls for a blast of the horn, rarely used. In the dark waters illuminated only by the port lights some distance away, we cannot see exactly what type of blacked-out boat is running with us at a ninety-degree angle into our path, continuing even after we blast. We are running full-speed as we clear the harbor entrance, full lights, and have blasted the horn. Still, he veers just ahead of us, crossing our bow so closely we cannot see him from the Bridge.

Pilot spits in awe and anger, "Unbelievable! Unbelievable! We cannot stop and will have to ram him." *Hello, Mr. Pilot, of course we can't stop; ships don't have brakes.* Just then, the boat pops up on starboard, fully unscathed, and the idiot runs his $4 million yacht, now brightly lit and "full of women, young women," Ion breathes, down our starboard side, everybody hooting and clapping. "Neaahh, neaahh, neaahh, we played chicken and survived." Driver has to be drunk. But we sure held our breath when he disappeared in front of our boxes, out of our sight for what seemed like forever, so close we could have splintered that teak wood and expensive leather into matchsticks and wouldn't even have felt it.

"Get his number, Mr. Pilot," I urge.

"Wouldn't do any good. The small boat lobby in Florida is very powerful."

"What? Lots of people were almost killed."

"Very powerful," he reiterates and calls for a new heading. A spectacular full moon floats over Miami, which Pilot says indicates very strong tides.

Moon gone, delicious warm breeze through my window, pounding pistons, rattling cupboards and doors, sounds I do not consciously hear any more, I pop into bed early.

I wonder how Marius, whose headaches are intensifying, is doing on the Bridge. The doctor could do little for him without time-consuming tests – and Marius had no time. And how the 3rd Engineer, pale and shaking, is doing in the hot Engine Room. And how the Captain – or I - is going to place 2nd Officer, who always eats with the crew, for dinner tomorrow night. Better make sure 2nd Officer is coming first.

Why in hell do I get so mixed up in all of this? It is not mine to solve.

Sunday, November 12. Gulf of Mexico

Sunny and beautiful. Force 2: Light breeze, 4-6 knot winds, ½ - 1 foot small wavelets. Do not break. Beautiful with the waves rolling gently. Retard Clock #8.

The hand-written invitation reads:

YOU ARE INVITED

Please join me for an American Steak Dinner to thank you for a very interesting voyage. (I ruminated long and hard, but ended up with "interesting" from a long list of not so passive words.)

Cocktails at 1730

Dinner at 1800

Sunday, November 12, 2000

Officers Dining Room

Casual dress.

See you there.

Cari

I receive directions from Alex to each cabin and slide the invitation under the door. At 1215 sharp, breaking my self-imposed galley slavery, I arrive on the Bridge, invitation in hand.

"2nd Officer, here is my invitation to join me for dinner this evening. I hand-deliver it to you because I want you to personally know that I would be very pleased if you could come. Can you? Will you?"

His face lights with the most beatific smile as he looks at the invitation, and I swallow a gasp. God, this guy is beautiful inside and out.

"Yes, Cari, I will be there. Thank you."

"Where would you like your place card?"

"Place card," he says as a statement. "Place card. How long it's been." He chuckles. "If you don't mind, I prefer sitting with the engineers." He looks at me sharply. "Everyone will be moving around and probably won't even notice. Do you mind?" *Oh yes, 2nd Officer, everybody will notice, but I don't care.*

"No, I'm just ecstatic that you'll be there."

"Well, I'll just run up a couple of times to relieve Ion first and then Marius so they can enjoy it, too. But I definitely will be there at 1730."

The day is a blur of preparation, remembered well from all my restaurant years, chained to the galley with little time to enjoy the gorgeous day outside.

Cheeses sliced, pate in bowl, crackers arranged on plates, assorted chips in bowls, wine, beer (compliments of Ion), Scotch, Sambucca and grappa for cocktails – an odd assortment, but everything I have in the way of booze. Olive oil, garlic, fresh lemon, Worchestershire, a tad of mayo, chopped anchovies and grated parmesan mixed for dressing; romaine washed and torn for the Caesar salad in two huge bowls in the refer (I wanted bleu cheese dressing on a garden salad, but Miami's finest didn't have any bleu cheese!); and sourdough bread sliced, buttered, lots of garlic slices and topped with parmesan for the toast placed on baking sheets. Filet mignon ready for the brown butter pan, potatoes washed and pricked ready for the oven; sour cream, chives and bacon bits in separate bowls for each table; asparagus snapped and ends pared in a large pan of ice water; lemons juiced and butter ready to melt; mushrooms cleaned and thickly sliced ready for sautéing with butter, garlic and Sherry; cheesecakes cut (alas, no fresh strawberries).

Every officer finds time to walk at least once through the galley to see what I am doing. Even 2nd Officer makes a pass through, stopping to chat with Cristori and grin at me.

"What's so funny? You think I don't know what I'm doing? I made a small fortune cooking for people in my restaurants."

They sober, and 2nd Officer vanishes. But the peering over my shoulder and anticipating glances at finished items make me hoot with laughter. Even the deck crew appears one by one to peer around the door and smile, some stepping into the galley to stand with Mother Hen Cristori.

Cristori wants to help, but I won't let him, even peeling and smashing that big bag of damned garlic myself. But he hovers. I'm catching The Peasant's disease: MY dinner. MINE-MINE.

We walk out onto the stern for a cigarette. "Are you fishing, Cristori? Lordy, you've got two lines out there."

"Yes," he answers proudly. "I get four or five fish every day. Sometimes more," and he jiggles the line.

"I love to fish. And sometimes I've caught some goodies."

"Good. I hope every day for at least enough… I hope to catch a lot," leaving me to wonder why we've never had fresh fish, but I don't mention it.

"Well, good luck. Fishing is lots of fun."

"Yes," he says flatly, stubs out his cigarette and looks toward the door. We go back inside to the drudgery.

I run upstairs to shower and change, donning black silk slacks and a Malaysian olive green scarf shot with gold and black, which I have fashioned into a sort of short caftan, belted tightly with a wide gold belt, gold chains, hoop earrings and silk shoes. *No heels, my dear, who knows what rocking and rolling will be happening in four or five hours?* I survey myself in the mirror: *Very nice, you old broad.*

I make it back just in time to carry the cakes into the crew's Dining Room and set up the cocktail table in Officers Mess. Alex has found some cloth napkins, which are fancily folded at each dinner place. I see the fine hand of Cristori here. Wine glasses for everybody. I had inquired about both and had received doubting headshakes. All center table condiments (that daily army of bottles) removed. Only salt, pepper, butter and dishes for sour cream, bacon and chives grace the tables. Very fancy in this drab gray room, very festive. I wish I had candles, but wouldn't be allowed to use them anyway. Fire hazard. And fire on board a ship is no small matter – in fact, that occurrence most dreaded.

Salad and heaps of garlic bread have been served. Cristori and I stand over the badly-behaving stove to finish off the steaks, then after a show-and-tell of arrangement, Alex, Cristori and I dish up the plates. I personally serve each person and run back to ensure nothing has been forgotten. Alex and Cristori are chowing down.

"Who's that steak for?" Cristori asks pointing to the pan.

We regard each other over the lone steak left in the pan. "A tiny bite of filet for each," and I wave toward the crew's Dining Room. "Just to taste. Oh Cristori, I'm so sorry." The world's, his, and, particularly, my inadequacies and failings are swept up in those three words.

He beams at me. "We appreciate everything, Mum, more than you can know."

"I wish..."

He starts to cry, tears rolling gently down his cherub cheeks. I hug him quickly and flee to the Officers Dining Room, where everyone, on their best behavior, is awaiting me.

"Begin, please. The hostess has lifted her fork. Begin." I smile through tears as forks and knives clink, and I wend my way to the head table.

To state that the dinner is a smashing success would be grossly understating. They gobble up everything, uumming and aahhing. Most, having never eaten tenderloin before, are beside themselves with delight. Baked potato with gobs of butter, sour cream, bacon bits and chives is second favorite.

That wonderful butcher in Miami's crappy supermarket really outdid himself – the steaks are heavenly and big! So tender that I show off a bit and cut the two-inch steak with a fork to show it can be done. Of course, I forgot to cook the garlic, so I rush to the galley, slam the steak pan (noting the lone steak is gone) on high heat, dump my tons of cut garlic into half a pound of butter and reappear like magic with pan in hand to slather what is left of steak with garlic.

Florin, the recipient of the remainder of my barely touched steak, totaling nearly twenty ounces of filet in his tummy, makes me promise "with an oath of blood" that I will write down every detail, "I mean every detail," on how I did it, and I promise.

After dinner, the serious drinking begins, and I know I am in trouble for booze. The Cookie Monsters are also Booze Monsters. But not to worry, people keep disappearing and reappearing with a half bottle of this, a third bottle of that.

To my amazement, they all tell me they are going to miss me when I sign off in Veracruz. I nearly drop my teeth. Well, The Peasant doesn't utter words like that. In fact, he utters no words. Not even Stan, sitting well removed from his Captain, is talking to him.

Ion appears and disappears before 2000 for only a sip of wine, then reappears after watch to mingle and drink and have fun. We toast over and over and are all very happy folks.

We're in full swing, bellies full of American filet mignon and GARLIC, baked potato and cheesecake, noise level rising dramatically as with any good party. I am at the farthest end of the room, the consummate hostess, laughing and kibitzing with everyone, when The Peasant hollers into the din, voice ragged-edged, raising to a high crescendo,

"You don't know, do you, that we have been watching you in your cabin. Naked. Through binoculars. We saw you. We watched you." He giggles loudly, nearly screeching. Then he adds, as if a clincher, "We saw your shoes. Why do you put your shoes in the window? They obstructed our view."

There are gasps, and the room is deathly quiet. All eyes stare at The Peasant in disbelief for what must be only a brief instant, but suspends forever, then swivel to me, horrified.

I am bending between Florin and the recovered 3rd Engineer, discussing, yet again, the favorite topic, whether it's really the right time to take their four-year-old kids to Disneyland, a hand on each chairback as we discuss the merits of waiting just a few years when both kids and parents could enjoy it more together. I feel like a broken record, but they receive the beleaguered information with excitement. Works for me – we're talking about Disneyland here!

I release their chairs and stand straight. Into the hush, I simper in my best Scarlett O'Hara imitation, "Why, Captain, are you tryin'to ruin mah li'l ol' pahty?" I incline my head coquettishly.

He leans back in his chair, nearly toppling backward, regarding me with a hostility that nearly frazzles. "Naked, I said!" He sweeps his hand around the room, stopping to frown at 3rd Officer. "Almost all of us have seen you with no clothes, naked." He begins a high cackle as Stan, face full of disbelief and shock, shoves his chair forcefully away from his Captain, the screech deafening in the stillness.

Each slow footfall clatters loudly as I thread my way through tables across the tile floor amongst the frozen tableau, approaching the head table with purpose. I skirt Stan's chair, which is lopsided in the aisle with a paralyzed Stan aboard, walk slowly to The Peasant, bend over his chair and laugh heartily in his face, hoping I am spewing spittle and garlic on him. He teeters in the back edge of the chair.

Then spitting, loudly, loudly, I want all to hear, "Have YOU wondered why the naked show stopped so abruptly? Would you think that the officers and selected deck crew would put up with your idiocy for any period of time? Do you not think that somebody or lots of somebodies would have told me? Do you really think that my time on this ship has been spent without making lovely acquaintances? Do you think, Romick," and another loud gasp erupts from the assemblage, "do you really think that we are all so stupid?"

And because I'm on a roll, am really angry, and am right in this bastard's face, and because I want these frozen men to understand just one time, I holler into his face, so all can hear, "I've told you before that I've worked with men my whole life. I've traveled with men, breakfasted, lunched, dined, sat in meetings until 3 AM. I've known their wives, their kids, their dogs, sometimes their grandmothers and aunts, their strengths, their failings. My company had 350 employees, but people like me and the Company President and Vice President saw to it that we respected each other. Setting up your freaky mirror system and binoculars was an asininity so far beneath our dignity, we could not even relate."

So furious, my teeth are gritting, "And one other thing, Romick, you may have not considered. Most of these sailors, men, on this ship make big bucks for their homelands, more than they could ever hope to make there."

"Do you think, DO YOU THINK that they are going to give up that for little more than a fleeting glimpse of a naked sixty-one-year-old woman prancing around in her cabin? One or two peeps because their Captain – their God, their Master, I believe you called yourself - set the stage for a titillating moment, urged them to disparage the American!

Woman! about whom they knew little and disdained as a result of their naivete and forceful former governmental influence. Do you really think that little moment was worth it?" I pull away from him and gaze at the peepers sitting stunned in their chairs. *Was it worth it, you idiots?* All eyes drop to their tables.

"Why, o' co'se, honey, I knew your little schemes. Why, goo'ness, you're not tellin' me anythin' new." Scarlett at her best, stressing the accent that I knew would drive him wild. Then in precise English, "You told me earlier, when we were talking about that ridiculous agent, that I was cargo and needed to be cared for as carefully as the boxes. Is this how you take care of your cargo? Deliberately putting it in danger? Trying to destroy it? Is this what a good Captain does? You thought to make a fool of me, but you've made a fool of yourself."

I pat his head and return to my chair facing him, hoping for one small scratch in the deafening silence. We sit like this, glaring, Stan out in the aisle holding his head in his hands, unmoving, Ion, sitting perfectly still with hands folded in lap, Marius anxious, then doing an absolutely Marius thing – shooting me a brilliant smile.

The Peasant lurches out of his chair, sending it screeching and crashing to the floor. Swaying, in a high-pitched slur, he says, "A very nice party, Mrs. Lindley."

"Thank you, Captain. I'm glad we all got to enjoy the filet mignon." And he's gone.

No sound. Not even the cratching of a roach, which I have never seen, but know must inhabit this ship. No movement, which is even scarier. I stare at The Peasant's chair as if he were sitting there and I could wallop his stupid brains out, my antennae alert to the room.

"There's more cheesecake," I say to The Peasant's chair into the silence. "And more booze. Who wants what?" Not a movement.

I turn and look at the room. "Come on, you people, every time I saw you over lunch or dinner for these last weeks or we exchanged funny discs, what? You didn't think I knew?" (In fact, I didn't, but I'm not going to tell them that.) "You think I was going to give any one of you," and I sweep my hand at The Peasant's chair, "the satisfaction that you had intimidated, perhaps scared me? Besides, I have it on pretty good authority that few, if any of you, actually saw a shriveled-up sixty-year-old naked body." Not a peep or breath.

The ship shifts and creaks. *We are getting into choppy waters. Good sleeping tonight. 2nd Officer, I wish you were here for this one. No worries, you'll hear every word before you go to bed.*

"Come on," and I walk to the side table, pick up a bottle of something (whatever it is) and make the rounds, lightly touching shoulders, saying "Is that enough?" Although I know in my heart they think there will never be enough.

And we're back to it – almost – maybe not as we were before they all knew I knew, but as back at it as we could be now, after all this horrifying and sad disruption – until midnight. Everybody has to work tomorrow.

I do a hasty cleanup. Every scrap of food is gone, not even a cracker.

As I stagger into bed, exhausted and not exactly sober, I wonder if The Peasant will remember all we said. Won't need to. We had lots of witnesses, although whether they will want to remind us or themselves is a whole different ball of wax.

CHAPTER ELEVEN
Dilemma

Monday, November 13. The Gulf of Mexico

Warm and sunny. Force 5: Fresh, 17-21 knot winds, 6-8 foot moderate waves. Many white horses. Spray with small white-capped waves. Enough to keep us on our toes.

0630: I run down to the galley, hoping to catch Cristori before he is busy with breakfast. He is beaming and cackling.

"I'm so sorry I left you with that mess last night." I look around. "I can't believe your gleaming galley."

"Mess? No mess. I eat all the leftover Caesar salad. It was so very good that I just eat and eat. And there was lots of it, remember? So very good."

I smile, thinking of how every acquaintance accuses me of cooking for an army when there are only a few to feed. "I don't want anyone to go away hungry. Besides, I like leftovers," I have defended myself all of my adult life. Caesar salad, of course, could never be a leftover as its dressing turns the lettuce soggy within minutes. It must be eaten immediately after dressing. Good, Cristori.

"Yeah," I say laughing. "Those Mexicans really know how to do it."

"Mexicans?" He regards me blankly.

"Caesar salad, you know, originated at Caesar's Hotel in Tijuana, Mexico. If you ever go there, you'll like it bunches. Every salad is made at table. Very impressive show and delicious salad."

"Oh." Obviously new information to the chef.

"Anyway, last night's dressing isn't quite the original, since the original doesn't have anchovies or a touch of mayo, but I prefer it that way. But, I'm so glad you liked it, Mr. Chef. It means a lot to me. Thanks, Cristori."

He giggles and jigs around the room, singing off-key, "So good, so good." He stops abruptly. "A very nice party, Mum, and I was glad to be a part of it. The filet mignon was outstanding. Easily the best I've ever eaten. Do you know that there was not one bite left on any plate? Not even a slice of mushroom. Not a drop of butter. Thank you, Mum."

"Cari."

"Yes, ah, thank you, Cari."

"And the cakes?"

"All gone." To my shocked face, he adds, "Remember, we do not have dessert except for ice cream on Sunday. It was such a treat that they, like me with the salad, couldn't stop."

I grab coffee and go to the Bridge to see how Chief Officer weathered the garlic and tons of booze. I run up the five decks of outside stairs and am about to enter breezily through the port bridgewing door.

And stop short.

Bosun, who always appears at this hour to get the day's marching orders for the crew, and Chief Officer are in deep conversation. Bosun, an old, wiry, gnarled Filipino, is boring holes into Ion, arms akimbo, looking ready to clobber him. Ion is shaking with anger.

"It must stop," spits from Bosun's nearly toothless mouth. "STOP!"

Whoops! Get out of here! I turn on my heel and start to soundlessly retreat across the bridgewing.

"No! Don't leave! Come in here!" Harsh, commanding, the voice of the person in charge. Ion is striding across the Bridge toward me. "Please come in now!" A tone I've never heard from him.

I turn in a daze and walk across the Bridge to the chart table where Bosun is standing stiffly, watching my every step, his wizened face tight and furious. We stand staring at each other, Bosun's black beady eye's glaring at me. *My God, what have I done?*

"Last night, after the party," Ion begins, "in the middle of the night, Captain went to one of the crew rooms. He…" Ion shakes his head, his body deflated, defeated.

"He," Bosun shouts, "Captain come into the cabin where two of my new boys bunk together. He was so drunk he couldn't hardly stand up, holdin' onto chairs and doors. He had somethin' in his pocket: A tiny black rag doll with eyes, mouth, a few pieces of hair on top. He…" Bosun stops. "You know what it means? You know what it MEANS?"

I bob my head, stunned. I know.

As if he hadn't seen me, he shouts, "Kulam, voodoo, black witch-craft. He shook it at 'em, sayin' all he needed was some blood. Then he laughed and laughed, sayin' he knew the best way to get it. He used his finger to show 'em…"

I glance at Ion, who is watching me, his square face a mask of sad-ness. Tears spring to my eyes.

Bosun hollers, "He fell down, couldn't get up, and my boys, they pushed 'im out the door into the companionway and locked it." Through my shock, I wonder yet again – how many times have I wondered this before? – how he got back to his cabin, up three flights of steep, narrow stairs, crabbing up each step on hands and knees, fat fingers grabbing and slipping. What do I care? I wish he would have fallen and broken his fat no-neck.

Bosun stops, grabs the top of the half wall of the Chart Room, tee-tering in his rage. With visible effort, he calms himself. "My two boys are so scared they won't get out of bed. They're like paralyzed. I need them on deck; they gotta work, but they can't. They can't," he ends with a moan. "*He,*" and he jabs his finger below, "will say they are only lazy and don't want to work. *He* will blame me and Chief Officer for not com-manding our crew. *He* will write us all up for not doing our jobs. *He* will do this and all that other evil again and again, as he's done in the past, and *he* will get away with it. He's the Captain, the Master." Bosun has run down and stands with mouth opening and closing, but no words. It is obvious that he has just spoken more at one time than ever before in his life.

Yet, he has one more outburst. "I've been with the sea, as she would have me, since I was fourteen, Mrs. I've sailed with mebbe a hunnerd captains. Hard men, tough, sometimes mean, but you could trust 'em, even with all that. We had enough to eat, a place to sleep and were OK as long as we followed Chief's," he gestures at Ion, "orders. We were left alone to do our jobs. Sure, Captains came on deck, hollering orders, but they weren't no differnt than Chief's, just louder. None of 'em ever came in the middle of the night and..."

"He wants to stomp us, hurt us, scare us, but we won't let him," Ion says softly. "You, 2nd Officer and I will talk to these men, do whatever it takes to make them go back to work before he can write them up. You must tell them to stay within sight of another worker at all times during daylight, even on deck where *he* never goes. At night, they, everybody, must lock their door. If you organize a kind of watch team at night to help the two boys through this scare, they won't feel or be alone."

"All of your men will want to help as *he* has pulled ugly stuff on some of them, too – if you think they should know. I wish they wouldn't have to know. We've already got too many problems on our hands. What this will do, I don't know. Oh hell, I don't see how you can keep it from them. No, you can't. So tell them and get their help."

Bosun nods, and I can imagine his brain clicking. He and Chief Officer discuss remedial measures for a few more minutes and agree on their tactics. The trust they display for each other amazes me.

I stand rigid as stone, waiting, I guess, for the dismissal order, but it does not come. Suddenly, The Peasant sneaking up behind me during the lifeboat launching flashes into my mind. *Maybe he didn't want to throw me overboard – maybe he wanted a few of my hairs for his little rag doll! Or maybe a scratch to get a drop of blood. Stop it! Stop it now!*

They finish, and both turn to me, the shaved head, solid-as-a-door, young Romanian man-in-charge and the old, knurled Filipino man who has seen it all.

"I'll tell you the truth, Cari. The only reason this ship hasn't," Ion stops and searches for a word and finds it, straight from his *Compendium*, "splintered is because you're on board. All of us want you safely in Veracruz, where we know you have business."

"Just school," I offer meekly.

He nods and continues. "Business. I almost asked you to sign off in Miami, but it was agreed that everything would maintain until Veracruz, hopefully Houston."

"Captain is scared to death of you because you're a passenger, and, also, since Stan and you have become such good friends. He knows that the officers and crew and you have become friendly. But he counts on Stan signing off next round and that he won't do anything – or he would already have done it - and that you are signing off in the next port. You notice how he treats Stan so carefully. You too, although you think he's, uh, gross" (a quick quirking of the lips). "You ought to see him when you aren't here – altogether different. So bad, so bad that… Ask Stan, force him. He'll tell you, Mrs. Lindley, he'll tell *you*. All we can hope is that Captain stays passed out in his cabin.

"He's scared when he's sober, but thinks he's invincible when he's drunk. As you have seen, he gets so drunk that he doesn't consciously know what he's doing. Then his inside being – the really savage, evil side – takes over. But the half-drunk stage, which is almost every day and which he masks by chewing garlic, is every bit as dangerous. It is his mean stage. It is then that he writes reports, issues dangerous orders, goes on rampages," he smiles mirthlessly, "and organizes mirrors and spies on passengers."

"But he's got to know, Chief Officer, how dangerous it is not only for the ship, but for himself too, for his job, for his promotion with The Company he is so hoping for, if Stan should ever talk."

"Or you."

"ME!" My voice rises two octaves with one word. "ME?"

Chief Officer and Bosun, so different yet so alike, trusting work-mates and friends, glance at each other.

"My call from Miami was pretty much brushed off. I will not be surprised if my call from Houston won't be treated the same. Companies normally don't hire crews for ships. They have management companies to do that, and management companies don't like problems and just get rid of problems. As you yourself have pointed out, they will side with a Captain, who is in complete charge of the ship, and simply sweep under the rug (he grins briefly in spite of himself) any interference from inferiors.

"You saw what happened to the first cook. Cook, as you know, reports directly to Captain. He told me many things, many things before signing off, no, being thrown off - for offenses he didn't commit, made-up charges because Cook caught *him* stealing and didn't like being blamed for little or bad food. The reality and what Captain reported are like from two different worlds. My confronting Captain didn't help; it only made things worse. I believe the same thing is happening all over again with the new cook, although he hasn't yet completely confided in me."

"Cristori?" I breathe in horror. He nods.

"You have been absolutely right, Cari, even if I didn't want to admit it, that the one in authority is the one that will be believed, like it or not. Even if we're talking about a Captain, a very bad man, who should not be commanding men on land, where those men can escape, much less at sea, where they are nearly prisoners between ports. Prisoners by virtue of the empty, endless sea, but also prisoners because of their need for work, money, their survival in impoverished countries. Captains are just what *he* said – God – and it is rare, nearly impossible, for them to be stood down by Companies.

He pauses and looks at Bosun, then out the panoramic Bridge windows at the heaving sea.

"But an outsider, a passenger, who can complain and attest to it all? And maybe make statements or inferences outside the seafaring community? Well, now we have a different matter. These Companies, powerful as they are and with complete control over their workers, are very sensitive to outside criticism. Particularly the Germans, who pride themselves...well, they have lots of pride. And this is a German ship. And you are an American passenger. This man is a tyrant, a bully with a depraved cruel streak who should not be in a position of authority, and you've experienced it, seen it, felt it, know it."

I am dumbstruck and stare with round eyes and open mouth.

"Will you help us?"

Again, voice a high squeak, "Me? Me? What could *I* possibly do?"

"Write a letter. Just a short letter. You need only tell a few things you know. Enough for them to at least think about opening an investigation. *He* cannot be allowed to continue. Maybe with both you and I..." (I think meanly, "You mean if *I* do it, you won't have to." And am immediately contrite. *Get real, MsSelf, he is putting everything on the line. Even if he does not make the call in Houston and my letter should prompt an investigation or The Company finds out another way, his spearheading of the drive to get rid of this Captain will be front and center. And he will take all the heat.*)

My wooden legs propel me to the starboard bridgewing door, and I lean back against the frame, holding on with both hands, welcoming the warm, humid breeze, glad for the pitching of the deck, the bright sun glancing painfully into my eyes. How long has all of this taken? Ten minutes? An hour? A lifetime?

"I can't. I've traveled all over the world. I've never mixed in ship's business or interfered with the business of any other conveyance or provider. How would I like it if you, a novice, came into my physics business and mouthed off about my method of producing lasers? Or strode into my restaurant for the first time, and without knowing anything of meat, told me my steaks were of inferior quality? Had you eaten one, that would be different." I am struck by how I sound like Marius. And I realize I have just painted myself into a corner: Metaphorically speaking, I have eaten the rotten steak provided by this Captain.

"Never mind that. I can't, I just can't. It's just not my place to do this. I don't REALLY know anything. Sure, I've seen this asshole at work, seen your paperwork, but... I am just a passenger, for God's sakes! Just like flotsam and jetsam, floating on top of the water with no real purpose. I came for a relaxing ride on a big boat. I didn't know...I didn't expect...I can't."

"Will you just think about it?"

"No. Yes. But I won't change my mind."

Bosun fixes me with his small black eyes, says in his gravelly voice, "OK, we do that," and hurries down the outside stairs.

Do what? I want to scream after him. *There is no "we." I am not doing anything.* Then sag back against the doorjamb. He was probably talking about organizing all that has to be done to protect his terrorized boys. *Oh dear heaven.*

I stagger down the starboard outside stairs, eyes drawn once again to the still- disconnected TV cable.

0805: Good Lord, it is still morning! My cabin is moving around, things beginning to clink and clank, as I ruminate on the events which just occurred, turning them over and over, ending with the ridiculous thought that Chief Officer has certainly been studying his *Compendium.* A speech such as that didn't come out of a Romanian high school English class.

In the Dining Room, a parade of officers, including Stan and 2nd Officer, enter and leave, all full of congratulations for a great party, the exquisite filet mignon, wonderful baked potato, everything perfect. The fracas with The Peasant is not mentioned. Guess they feel my mouthiness somehow didn't extend to them, only The Peasant, who is not, of course, in attendance. They assume he is either drunk or too hung-over to move. At this point, it is obvious that only Ion and I know more. But, as I leave the Dining Room, I see Ion stand and move to the other full table.

I start writing Florin's filet mignon preparation story, but can't concentrate. On the pitching deck as I walk, crew hollers "good cake", wave and smile, but there is an added dimension – a friendly watchfulness, a measuring, an expectation. Bosun has blabbed, probably trying to quiet the angry anxiety, saying something will be done, something, putting a hopeful twist on my 'thinking about' the letter. I also notice that there is a crew member in sight for every step I take, a soft hissing signal as they hand me off one to the other, waving from atop boxes or a smiling body suddenly appearing between boxes. He must have added me to his crew's watch brigade.

The inside stairs and hallways seem peopled with folks I never see outside of the Dining Room or Bridge, including a few Filipinos who seem to be wandering aimlessly, smiling shyly and stepping against the bulkhead as I pass. "Hello, Mum." I want to ask them all what they are doing here. But the officers are prepared, handing me blank discs with their names neatly printed to be filled with computer jokes, slips of paper with addresses, business cards, "Stay in touch, let us know how you are. Send us your book." *Hah! If the damned thing ever gets written.* Repeated thanks and tummy patting for the filet. Requests for copies of Stan's US itinerary. "You'll have to ask Chief Engineer. It is not mine anymore, it is his - to share only if he wants." The same undercurrent of measuring, expectation, hope fills every face. It is unnerving to confront all these people in the normally empty hallways and stairs.

I ride with Marius a few minutes, going out on the bridgewing, trying to get angles as to how The Peasant could see in my window. The mirror setup must have been pretty ingenious, although my shoes in the open window are easy to see. There is lots of glare from the glass. The Peasant has probably made up the naked part, although, behind locked doors, I do admit to walking around in the altogether knowing no one could see, so maybe. I study the angles, two steps this way, three that way, hanging out over the railing. If I were sitting in that tiny spot in the corner, he could view part of me, but then I would be able to see him. How did he do it? All telltale equipment has been scrupulously removed, and the deck and railing are spotless.

Marius comes out laughing. "What are you doing?"

"Trying to see if they could actually see me. And, if so, how."

"Disgusting." He frowns. "So really stupid of them." He raves on, laughter gone.

"Come on, Marius, Captain said that to get my goat. But rather than being mad, I think it is silly. When I think of how careful in dress and manner I've been on this ship of men, then find out about this, it makes me laugh – hard! Although, I admit, in view of everything I now know, it's not as amusing as when you first told me. Not nearly."

Marius looks at me sharply and scowls, then adds a chilling afterthought, "Cari, for your safety, try to be civil to him. You've only two days left before Veracruz."

"Marius, should I be scared?"

"No. Yes." He swallows hard. "Definitely, yes."

An attack on the computer to write Florin's filet story takes up the afternoon. The normal afternoon round of walking inside and out brings a second wave of officers and crew everywhere, waving, smiling, chatting, watching me with slightly narrowed eyes. *Hello, we've already done this. What's up?*

The Peasant never appears, but no one expected him to. Maybe he's dead in his cabin, I think for the umpteenth time. Could there be such luck?

A full company for dinner. I sit with a very quiet Stan and Ion (for different reasons). We start out subdued as each diner realizes we are only twenty-four hours removed from last night's debacle, then pick up and rollick.

"Come up to the Bridge later, and we can look at last night's pictures," Ion invites. "Stan?"

Stan shakes his head. He wants to say something and keeps leaning forward as if it is on the tip of his tongue, but it just won't come out as he regards me with his long face and brown eyes full of sadness and fear.

"It's OK, Stan. I'm all right."

"My cabin is just around the corner from yours. I will leave the door ajar, will be able to hear, in case you…"

"I'm fine, Stan. But thank you." *Are you, MsSelf?*

We eat Cristori's sad little efforts, I picturing him seated last night in his special little chair in the corner of the galley gorging himself on Caesar salad, dreaming of cruise ships and better days.

I look around at the assemblage, marveling at how I have learned to compartmentalize events and my feelings about this ship and its inhabitants. I detest The Peasant and wouldn't be caught within a hundred yards of him anywhere else, yet on this ship I can actually speak in a normal voice to his despicable face. These men hated me on sight, did everything to demonstrate their contempt, yet, here I am laughing and talking with them. The peepers wanted nothing more than to dehumanize, denigrate me, yet, I am making discs of jokes for them. Stan, who is in the best position to help these tyrannized men, will not lift a finger to assist them, yet I love the man for his kindness and gentleness to me. Everything in its own little cubicle: Forgiven, but not forgotten.

Florin hollers as I leave, "Don't forget the filet mignon recipe."

I wave at him. "Tomorrow at lunch."

There is some whispering, then Florin remembers he wants to make sure he left an extra disc at my door, so accompanies me to Superstructure Deck 4, stands at the top of the stairwell and watches me enter my cabin.

"I don't see a disc," I holler back to him.

"Oh, I'll bring it by tomorrow. Are you going to see the pictures? Yes? Think I will, too. I'll just wait here for you."

Ion, Marius and 3rd Engineer are already looking at the computer when Florin and I arrive. They nod at Florin approvingly. They back up the pictures, and we go slowly through a long list, hooting, reliving it all.

A picture of The Peasant appears, and Ion grits, "This is the original fuck-face.' I try not to display shock, but this is the first time anyone on this ship, other than The Peasant, has ever used that word in my presence. *Silly, MsSelf, you know that word and use it under stress yourself.* Still, a little jolt of surprise shoots through me.

"He looks like a gypsy!" They all snort, make spitting motions, although none would dare to actually spit on the Bridge's gleaming surface. "A peasant."

I flinch, wanting to laugh and tell them I've been calling him The Peasant for weeks. But don't. No more fuel to the fire tonight. But their group response startles me. I didn't think....

"Pick what you want," and I select six pictures, which are printed on the ship's 'inferior' printer. Good enough for wonderful memories.

"Think I'll call it a night, gentlemen. Lots of fun. Good night. Safe watch."

"Me too," says 3rd Engineer. "Must go to work." We go down to Superstructure Deck 4 together. He waits on the top of the stairwell until I close my door.

I sit in front of the computer, holding on at times, trying not to roll across the plunging floor. We've run into a good one – a typhoon, tornado, hurricane, whatever. It's having a grand time with MarkShip Mexico, and my "smart ship" is growling.

At last, I'm done and sit back to survey the filet mignon story. Boxes are trumpeting like elly-fawnts, the deck heaving, steel screeching, crashing and tinkling from all sides and my windows are securely shut as I read:

FILET MIGNON

I'm doing this quickly before His Royal Highness throws me overboard, Florin, so please bear with any typos and incorrect English and punctuation. You requested, and I am pleased to respond.

The steak you ate last night, and liked so well, is called filet mignon.

The piece of meat is a beef tenderloin, a long narrow round muscle (at least I think it is a muscle) that lays along the backbone of cattle (indeed, every animal, including chickens, probably even us humans, although we'll probably never know how human tenderloin tastes - ye gods, I hope not!), one on each side of the spine. The muscle, unlike all others in the body, is not regularly used; therefore, it is very tender. Hence, the name "tenderloin."

Please understand that although you might find everything American of substandard quality - at least that's what I have been hearing from nearly everyone on Markship Mexico - American beef is of very good quality. Americans demand it and are willing to pay for it. Even imported beef is raised like American beef in Argentina or other countries if the foreign rancher wants to sell to the US.

The process is this: After weaning, the "cow" (and I'm incorrectly using this word for both male and female cattle - "cow" is female in the crazy English language, but there is no word for both male and female except "cattle" which is plural), it is put out to pasture for a period of less than one year to many years. The best meat is from a male castrated "cow" called a "steer." I suppose that is because the steer spends all its time eating rather than looking at those lovely female cows and using its energies to chew rather than screw. Sorry, couldn't pass up the opportunity to have a little fun here in the midst of such serious discussion. The older the cow, the tougher the meat, of course.

The most important part of obtaining good beef is to grain or corn feed the cow in a small holding pen for two to six weeks. The cow is now fat, the meat marbled with small particles of fat that enhance the taste and tenderness. The next step is careful killing, literally surprising the animal with its own demise. If you excite any animal before its death, adrenalin pumps through the muscles, and the result is tough meat. Therefore, you want a very quiet animal before you kill it. The next step is to "age" the meat, hanging it for a couple of weeks or months in cold storage (not freezing).

The final step is the way the meat is cut. I have a German friend, now a rancher in the U.S., who loves American steaks and baked potatoes so much he probably eats them two or three times a week. Of course, he believes everything German is perfect and THE BEST, everything, that is, except American steak.

Germans, he told me, could have steak every bit as good as Americans, except (he added sadly) Germans don't know how to cut the meat. To my amazement, he pulled out a book that delineated the difference in the way the U.S. cuts meat versus the way Europe (and nearly all the rest of the world) cuts meat. I was fascinated. The U.S., he pointed out, cuts meat for grades of quality and tenderness. The rest of the world cuts meat simply to eat it. I believe Karl, my German friend, is now on a campaign to single-handedly change the world's savoring of beef. In my mind's eye, I see Karl running about the world, huge butcher knife in hand, hollering, "No, no, you are doing it WRONG. This is the way to do it! Believe me, I know, I eat American steak three times a week."

Because beef tenderloin is so tender, it must be cooked at a high temperature, NEVER well done. A good piece of meat like tenderloin wants to be eaten medium or medium rare, pink or red inside. Only inferior cuts of meat need long cooking.

It is possible to buy an entire tenderloin, rub it with garlic, rosemary and salt, and roast it at a high temperature in the oven. Then slice it, surround it on a platter with luscious vegetables, say, asparagus or broccoli, carrots cooked with lemon and sugar, mushrooms sauteed with garlic, butter and sherry wine (like you had last night), cherry tomatoes heated with butter and basil, and whipped potatoes and butter broiled a bit to make the top slightly brown. Served on a wooden or silver platter, it is a beautiful sight. And very tasty. Restaurants call this Chateau Briand, and it is only served for two or more. Very expensive, but wonderful.

Last night's two-inch thick, ten-ounce filet mignon was prepared like this: Wrap a piece of bacon around the steak and secure it with a toothpick. Heat butter in a pan over very high heat on the stove until butter is brown. Put meat in pan. A thick steak like this will take probably twelve to fifteen minutes to cook over high heat. Turn the meat over in the pan at least twice. This keeps the juices flowing within the steak, enhancing taste and tenderness. At each turning, apply garlic salt (which I forgot to do last night - sorry, too much wine in my tummy). The outside should be crispy brown and the inside pink.

The first time you try to cook it, you might want to cut carefully into the side of the steak with a knife, just a small cut, to see if it is done to your satisfaction. Remember that the meat continues to cook internally for a few minutes even after you take it out of the pan. It's the blessing and curse of using such high heat. So don't overcook it. On the other hand, because tenderloin is such a good piece of meat, even if it is well-done, it is tasty and tender. Serve immediately. Steak is not good unless it is sizzling hot. Cooking on a barbeque, if you like the taste, heightens the flavor of all steak. I didn't do it last night because it would have been too much trouble to run in and out. But, at home, you may want to try it.

Serve with a baked potato with sour cream, chives or minced onion and crispy bacon bits, or potatoes in any fashion. American steak and potatoes simply go together. It's just the way it is done. Rice or cous-cous or pasta simply won't do. Save those for another ethnic dinner you wish to serve. American steak and potatoes, and that's FINAL!

Sometimes, particularly if you serve a whole filet (Chateau Briand), you have some left over. Leftover steak is edible, but the taste is not like when you cook it and serve it immediately. My advice is to slice it thin (no more than a quarter of an inch, probably less), heat butter in a pan until it is brown and quickly heat up the steak slices. Do not use oil, only butter.

All right, where are you going to buy this steak and how much will it cost? First, the cost: $12-20 a lb. Let's see, that is $26-40 (?) a kilo. You figure it out. Even with tenderloin, there are grades of OK to excellent. The price will tell you what is excellent. Except in capitols in Europe, you will probably not see it in markets. How about buying a few pounds in the U.S., asking Cook to freeze it for you in the ship's freezer, then take it with you when you sign off. Wrap carefully in a plastic bag and maybe some paper towels or a real towel or jacket for insulation and take it with you on the airplane. It is frozen and will last for many hours without refrigeration. Freezing tenderloin does not deteriorate its quality. When you get home, surprise your wife with your expertise. You liked it last night, she will love it also.

See, there is no magic to any of it. Just buy it and cook it. Filet mignon or Chateau Briand is always a special treat. You could even be funny, like I was last night, and cut that two-inch steak with a fork (Better buy the $15-20 per pound tenderloin if you want to show off.) And cooking it is a snap - nothing to it. But you will impress your wife, I guarantee it. YOU cook it. That will add to your wife's impressiveness. She will think you are a genius. She won't know that the quality of the meat has saved your ass. Do it, you'll both like it.

It's been a pleasure to be with you, regardless of Markship Mexico itself and its many problems. I have really enjoyed getting to know you and laughing at fun stuff. Thanks a whole "bushel and a peck." Meaning, thank YOU very much.

Thank you also for your kindness to me. You could never disappoint me. Only small-minded people (regardless of their position aboard Markship Mexico or anywhere in the world) of inferior quality, like inferior steak, disappoint me. You, like filet mignon, are best quality.

Cari Lindley

I chuckle with satisfaction. Hope he "gets" it all. He's a sharp cookie, no problem.

I check my door and fall into bed.

Tuesday, November 14. Gulf of Mexico

WIND, rain, sun, fog, very high humidity. You name it, we've got it. Including FORCE 9: Strong gale, 41-47 knot winds, 23-32 foot waves. Edges of crest begin to break into spindrift. Foam blown in well-marked streaks.

0645: Whooee! We are rocking and rolling! The desk chair smashing against the wall awakens me. I jump up and look at the savage sea, waves and spume seem to be nearly as high as my window, crashing and regrouping for another assault before the previous crash has even partially dissipated. The sea appears and disappears in ominous clouds of dirty fog. The banshee wind screams in piercing ululations, and the boxes screech in earsplitting wrath.

It's hard to tell, but it feels as though we are not moving.

Coffee! Down the stairs, hanging on tightly and jolting here and there, the intense humidity even in the air-conditioned superstructure giving the sensation of floundering through heavy water, then up to the Bridge with sloshing hot coffee.

Chief Officer, 2nd Officer, 3rd Officer and 2nd Engineer are on the Bridge, everybody doing something that commands their attention, very intent, yet oddly relaxed, low steady words exchanged. I say nothing as I stand by the inside door, but receive quick nods, eyes flicking toward me, returning immediately to the chore at hand.

At last, Marius walks toward me.

"Doesn't seem like we're moving, Marius."

"We are, but very slowly. The sea - plus a problem with the engine."

Oh brother, heavy seas are not an optimum time for engine problems. I'm about to ask about schedule, when he says, "Unless this abates and all goes well below, we'll be a day late. Never good, but manageable. Chief Engineer promises results soon. Although the weather report..." and he glances quickly at the GPS slapped beside the port bridgewing door. He smiles at me as I use the long tail of my blouse to keep from splashing coffee on the deck.

We brace on the bulkhead and try to distinguish the sea through the rain streaked windows and fog, the mammoth wipers barely making a dent in the wind-driven rain and sea streaking with ferocity. When there is a split-second clearing, the sky and sea are a solid mass, and we cannot distinguish at which we are looking.

"We don't all really need to be here. Ion can handle this with no problem. But we want to be, so he's given us chores to keep our idle hands busy." Marius laughs. "Chief Engineer has sent 2nd Engineer up just to keep a double check on engine readings. It's a new ship, and, well…this is the first time we've run into weather of this magnitude, and it's best for the safety of the ship."

Just then Ion turns and hollers against the low background roar, "How do you like the ride, Cari?" The others turn and chuckle.

"I like it a lot. You're a darned good chauffer." We all laugh. 2nd Officer barely flicks an eyelash above his gleaming white teeth. I do believe that young man just winked at me, filling me with a warm little glow.

Marius returns to his 'chore for idle hands,' and I try to drink my coffee, marveling at the effectiveness of the Bridge's soundproofing. It is not quiet, but the tempest outside must be ear-shattering.

Florin takes a minute break and joins me. "Only for a second. Just wanted to say good morning. Got to keep a close eye on everything," he says importantly. I slip him the filet mignon disc. He puts it in his pocket, smiles briefly and returns to his display.

The inside Bridge door opens. It could have banged, but would have been lost in the background noise. The Peasant is suddenly in the middle of the deck, staggering from side to side, barely upright.

"Woman on the Bridge! Bad luck! Woman on the Bridge!" He screams, his high piercing voice crescendoing with a final crack. "Bad luck! Bad luck!"

The officers turn in shock, bodies taut and erect, eyes spitting fire. They are lined up in a straight row right across the deck from me, the displays blinking green behind them; I am looking at them, but they have eyes, livid with rage and disbelief, only for The Peasant.

The Law of the Superstitious Sea: Think it – don't say it! In fact, if you can keep from even thinking it, so much the better. Concentrate on something else so the errant thought vanishes, so the superstition will not sprout wings of its own and become reality. Regardless of position or rank at sea, the dark side is always waiting.

The ship rolls sharply, and The Peasant loses his footing, nearly unheard of on a ship's Bridge and stumbles sideways, arms wind-milling. He is drunk again, very drunk. As he rights himself, he looks malevolently at me, eyes glittering with glee, his puffy cheeks a strange burnt orange. Maybe more than booze. He grabs the bulkhead handrail and sways in and out as if performing a bizarre series of arm and back exercises, his feet jigging in little uncoordinated scrabbles.

I back away from him, staring in horror. The lineup across the way is motionless, spread-legged to absorb the shocks of the violent sea, eyes transfixed on their Captain.

He turns his squinted pig eyes on them with a maliciousness that makes me tremble. "Hawwhh!" He screams, "Woman on…"

I cannot let him say 'Bad Luck!' one more time. CANNOT! The weather, the vagaries of a new ship, the sea caroming in mountainous waves, the shrieking of the wind---He cannot say it again!

"Hey! HEY!" Two sharp shots. He glares at me. "Captain," I yell against the roar, "I have ridden on Bridges very often before, where Captains, just like you, said I could whenever the mood struck me, and the ships returned to berth with everything intact and everyone safe. In fact, prosperous voyages." *Be soothing, calming. Be anything. Do something!*

He falls against the bulkhead, mouth working beneath the unruly bristling mustache, backs up and falls into it again, hitting his head hard. No one moves.

Partially standing, he flails his hands to the side, like a wounded bird trying to take wing, his bushy eyebrows raising and lowering, his slitted eyes vacant, spittle collecting at the corners of his mouth. "No, no, a joke. It was a joke," and he grabs the handrail.

The statues across the deck look stricken, faces tight, lips drawn back. This is no joke to them, in fact, a thunderous slap from a drunken, thoughtless Captain. Their rigid bodies speak louder than words. Never put the Superstitions into words!

I holler, "Hmmph! Some joke, and, of course, at my expense!" *Who cares about my expense? Why can't I think of something to grab his stupified attention? Say anything, anything to keep his drunken rage away from the hapless men under his direct command and get the hell out of here. Every second you're here makes it worse. Go away. Now!*

I glare at him, then turn to the frozen men and smile, "Good day, gentlemen", before turning on my heel and making for the inside stairway. Damnation, I wish I could escape out the bridgewing door, in the opposite direction of this maniac.

I hear a sharp stumbling shuffle of feet behind me. *Dear God, he isn't going to try to stop me!* The ship jerks suddenly starboard, and I turn my head slightly as I right myself, in time to glimpse three men move a few steps behind The Peasant. I put my hand on the knob, hesitate long enough to hear the shuffle cease, fling open the stairway door and walk slowly down the stairs, hearing the door clang behind me, holding the handrail with both hands.

My heart is hammering, and I realize that, for the first time on any ship, I am very frightened – and very angry with that white-hot heat that has become intrinsic to my existence on MarkShip Mexico.

Power walking, which I desperately need, is impossible. 'Power standing' is a miraculous accomplishment on the pitching deck. The morning passes in front of the computer, writing ship notes and lists of things to do when I get to Mexico, blocking my chair with pillows and blankets. At last I'm calm and gingerly make my way to the Dining Room where I sit, not surprisingly, alone, watching the sea smack wildly, beautifully in green and lacy white splashes against the windows. Such power.

At noon, Florin comes in, sits in Ion's chair and takes a few bites, instructing Alex to take plates to the Bridge.

"What happened, Florin?"

"He passed out."

"Where is he now?"

"On the floor of the Bridge. In fact, kicked against the bulkhead in a heap. I wanted to drag him to his cabin, but they wouldn't let me."

"Everyone has come to the Bridge, including Cook, Roberto, Bosun – and Chief Engineer. No one has touched him. A pariah," he adds breathlessly. "He...he looks thrown in a corner – like an overstuffed, useless pile of castoff baggage."

"Is he?"

Florin puts his head in his hands and rubs his forehead. "Yes."

Knowing Florin is friends with Electrician, I ask, "Would Roberto drag him to his cabin?"

He sags. "No. No he would not."

We sit without moving for an eternity. Florin finally rises and starts toward the door. He removes a computer disc from his pocket.

"I have read it swiftly. But I shall read it very carefully later. This, "he shakes the disc, "letter to me is wonderful, just incredible. I can't believe you would do this for me. It will always help me to remember that there is decency and humor in the world. Even when I am convinced there is none. Thank you, thank you." He sweeps the back of his arm across his eyes and is gone.

Pillows and blankets tucked between mattress and bed railing as a barrier against being thrown to the floor, I nap. Such an enterprise in the midst of this dual melee astounds me, but exhaustion rules.

Mute and despondent, Stan and Ion sit at dinner, both disheveled and in need of a shave. We push food around the clinking plates, catching errant salt shakers and condiments on the fly.

"You must be worn out," I say to them. They shrug.

Finally, I ask, "Where is he, Ion?"

"He woke up, but couldn't get up. I ordered him to stand down to his cabin. He crawled, *crawled,* across the deck. Stan," Ion looks at his plate "opened the door for him, then closed it after he crawled through. He's not on the stairs now, so he must have made it."

"Were you able to leave the Bridge, just for a few minutes, to rest?"

"Stan replies, "He couldn't. Only Chief Officer could make the decisions that had to be made. That only a stand-down order was needed was fortunate. But, it was not known what would be required." He drops his head and shakes it slowly. We sit.

Stan lifts his head and fixes me with his keen brown eyes, glistening, tired under perfectly trimmed thick, gray eyebrows. "You understand, Mrs. Passenger," he emits a squeak of a cackle, which lightens the mood dramatically, then plunges us into the depths again, "all of this is not about you. You, Cari, have been on the Bridge daily for a month, and our weather has been perfect, engine humming with only minor problems, vessel sound. You have been welcomed there. A pleasant and intelligent distraction from the tedious routine."

He clears his throat delicately. "It was the inappropriateness of what he said. The sea…we…yes, not at all appropriate. In fact, menacing, dangerous." *Say it, Stan, he shouldn't have invoked the Superstitions in a storm. Or at all.* "And the fact that he was on the Bridge" his lips barely quirk upward as he glances at Ion, "dead drunk, well…" *The Compendium rules.*

"I'm sorry I was the catalyst. I feel so terrible."

Ion grimaces. "That's just it. You might have been the catalyst, but you weren't at fault. Often at the height of his drunkenness, he is most crafty. And his drunken brain recognized the perfect twisted vehicle to lash out at, try to destroy, punish, both you and us." He sits back in his chair. "But his poor pickled brain couldn't get beyond the gallon of liquor to envision the consequences."

"What now?" I ask heavily.

"We don't know yet," Ion grits. "We're going to try to hold it together."

Stan gazes sorrowfully at Ion and shakes his head. Not me, the sad look says plainly, I won't be involved in any initial action or complaint.

And I wonder why not. If there is a complaint and/or action, The Company will surely make their trusted man, their only direct employee on this ship, Stan, the star testifier – up to his ears, like it or not, in the events on MarkShip Mexico.

"Goodnight, gentlemen, I have lots of packing to do."

"You have the whole day tomorrow," Stan says. "We are a day late for berthing."

"I know, but I've got lots of stuff. You know, tins of smoked eels and pickled garlic, flags, reference books." Ion breaks up laughing, Stan looks anxious, then laughs, and I exit.

When I finally negotiate my way to Superstructure Cabin #403, nearly falling twice when the ship zigged and I zagged, I realize I don't have an escort. In fact, the stairwells and hallways are deserted. Problem eliminated for the moment, 'dead drunk' in his cabin.

So I inch my way up to the Bridge. "Marius, how is your head, my dear 3rd Officer?"

He touches it gently and answers ruefully, "Full of things." And I add to myself: *Full of anger, frustration, desolation, fear — fear of Captain, fear of what may happen aboard this ship, fear of the Sirens of the Sea, fear for his job, his career.*

"Will you be all right?"

"I hope so. Will you ride with me a few minutes?"

"Yes." And I giggle to myself that these men now use 'ride' on the Bridge as a given. When I first used it, the contempt was incredible, the sneering rampant.

More importantly, after today's calling up of the formidable Superstitions by the drunken Peasant, a Man aboard this ship is requesting that I, the Woman who inadvertently, but miserably is the cause of the whole mess, spend some time on the Bridge.

We ride companionably in silence, the ship tossing us from port to starboard, bow to stern, the wind complaining loudly.

We hang on, watching the wipers ineffectual attempt at cleaning.

"Safe watch, 3rd Officer." I see his wave, but feel his smile on the dark Bridge.

The ship sleeps. Although if there were a rock band next cabin over, one wouldn't hear it. But at the heart of this wild, scary weather is a strange calm which overtakes MarkShip Mexico like a balm. From top to bottom, we deserve it.

Wednesday, November 15. At anchor off Veracruz.
WIND, rain, sun, fog, very high humidity. FORCE 10! Storm, 48-55 knot winds, very high waves with long overhanging crests. Foam blown in great patches. Tumbling of sea heavy and shock-like. Yesterday, PLUS.

0645: Holding on tightly, I stagger down for coffee. Then debate going to the Bridge, if I can get there. Why not? Can't get any worse. All the damage is done.

We are moving slowly, some fifty miles out, plunging heavily. The intermittent crackling of the radio from the Pilot Station tells us they have no specific information for MarkShip Mexico. We were to have been at berth last night, although it wouldn't have made any difference, we couldn't have gotten in. (No matter, one can be sure we will pay heavy fines for not appearing at least in the roads.) The harbor is closed. (Ports do not want ships alongside in hurricanes. The ships are thrown against the dock and destroy their dock, although no mention is made of what damage would be inflicted on ships.) No information as to when it will open.

We proceed to the roads, dropping anchor well away from the many ships already pitching wildly in the heavy seas. They appear mistily through the gale, then disappear for an hour or more, only to reappear in a moment's respite, complete with an astonishing sliver of sunshine.

We are rolling port-to-starboard only ten to twelve degrees according to the indicator, but it feels like we will tip over at any moment. The deck falls ominously first to port, then to starboard as we top one wave, slide down its side to the trough and are tossed up onto the next. Waves crash alongside, giving the impression we are moving, but we are dead in the eerie green water frothed with fierce white rollers and flying spindrift, which smacks the Bridge windows with a force that seems impossible so high up. An incredible spectacle of unleashed power of the sea. Terrifying, awesome, beautiful.

Now it rains hard, blowing across the boxes in a white sheet, then abruptly stops, then glancing shards of sunshine. Always the wind, tearing across our bow regardless of how we drift around the anchor. The boxes shift and squeal. The combined noise is horrifying, even in the sealed shelter of the Bridge.

A constant parade of officers and crew appear on the Bridge, obviously advised when they requested permission that no Captain is in sight, yet looking surreptitiously from side-to-side. Stunned by the overwhelming panoramic sight greeting them as they push open the inside door, their eyes pop, mouths gape.

We attempt talking, the background roar causing a constant litany of, "What? What did you say? Again?" Lots of tentative smiles, which earn a back-pat from the Chief or 2nd Officer, who is on the Bridge for his own reasons.

The radio crackles: Weather improving. If correct, port open tomorrow. Pilot at 0500. Confirm Pilot by 2200 this day.

No Captain.

2nd Officer leaves, and I am close behind him, lurching down the inside stairs, holding the railing tightly, praying my arms will not be jerked from their sockets.

0900: All lights in my cabin are on. Every movable object secured, actually re-secured after last night's wild ride. I have discovered the securing devices for the desk chair. Should have remembered that from The Other. Guess I just assumed that MarkShip Mexico wouldn't have such amenities.

Between frenzied spurts of packing, I watch the north end of Veracuz, lights twinkling in the dim daylight, come into view, then disappear in a black cloud of roiling fog. If I stand at the window long enough and the tempest permits, I will see the southern lights of Veracruz wane, then the open raging sea, then the many other ships anchored in the roads, bucking around their anchors like infuriated stallions, then the northern end of Veracruz again. I wonder how many 360-degree turns we have already made around the anchor, being blown like chaff in the wind. Hope the anchor chain holds.

Lunch is a really good chunk of roast with buttered canned veggies. (It's lots of fun trying to eat between ship's jolts and falls. I put down the fork with its sharp tines, cut my meat in pieces and eat it with my fingers. Veggies go into my mouth by spoon with plenty of clinking against my teeth.) Cristori has pulled out all the stops. Wonder where he got this stuff. He's probably hoping to re-provision in Veracruz and actually receive at least a percentage of it in his stores, where hopefully he will get the chance to use it before it goes into brown-wrapped, string-tied boxes. He'd better use it fast: Houston is coming.

With my prepared thank you notes and generous tips, I go to the galley and thank Cristori and Alex. They are beside themselves, and much hugging ensues. When I give Alex his money, I say, "Thank you for all you've done for me, Alex."

"And thank you too, Mum." How many times have I heard that over the last month, his smiling little face full of adoration. Oh Alex, I'm going to miss you. I hug him again, and he jigs on the pitching deck. The ship lurches, and I falter. Alex reaches for me and holds onto my arms like precious cargo.

"Chief Officer," I say on the Bridge, "here's your computer disc of jokes."

Just when I thought everyone had handed me their discs when they were acting as escorts, I found another pile of them outside my cabin door, actually splayed across the hallway due to ship action. Notes included: "Just in case the first one is defective." "If you find enough stuff that won't fit on one disc." "This is extra. You can keep it if you want."

Ion hands me a piece of paper with names and addresses of The Company and the Ship Management Company. Also, an address to send my picture of the box we took in Miami. And "Have you thought about it?"

"I can't, Ion. I just can't get involved. It's so far out of the realm of my being on this ship as a passenger. I've thought about it and thought about it. I need real proof."

"And yesterday wasn't?"

"Of an asshole, yes. But we've got lots of that. Real proof of theft, no. I don't personally know what's in those boxes. I've only briefly seen your requisitions, and it's all kind of Greek to me."

"Here." He pulls out a thick wad of papers. "When you get to Mexico and have time, go through them. If you can't write the letter, maybe, if needed later, you can write them what happened on this ship and maybe these requisitions, receipts and payments will help you remember that there was little food to be eaten from this" and he slaps the papers, "pile of food. Any help you can give will assist us greatly. We've got big trouble here, Cari."

He looks so sad that I want to run away. "Ion, if you are successful in opening an investigation, I will help by mail or by phone. But I cannot be the person, the passenger, who instigates it all - if, in fact, The Company would ever do anything, which is very doubtful altogether, but particularly as a result my feeble say-so. They will think me a whiner, one of those women complainers, who try to stir up trouble." I gaze at him meaningfully, "Woman! American! Enough said?" He grimaces. "Remember, as if you could forget, we are talking about a Captain and their possible future choice for an in-house Captain. Do you think a mere passenger complaining is going to get in the way of that?"

"Yes. I don't know. I work hard for my Captains. Whether I like them personally or not makes no difference. But I CANNOT work for a Captain that I do not trust, whose judgment puts us in constant jeopardy, is in constant question not only by me, but by all he comes in contact with, whose drunkenness constantly interrupts ship's business, who undermines me, goes behind my back every day, who steals and cheats and uses voodoo to control my crew." He slumps, then throws his arm to indicate the entire Bridge. "But I do. I do it. Every day on this ship."

"That's because for all intents and purposes you are the Captain of MarkShip Mexico. Everyone looks to you for leadership, for trust, for fairness, for common sense – wisdom, if you like, for human contact from above."

The ship does an astonishing hop, and I grab for the railing, laughing in spite of myself at the suddenness and intensity.

Ion watches me slide across the slanting deck, finally making contact with the handrail. He joins my laughter. "Thank you. See you at dinner, Cari."

"Oh? You're coming down?" He nods. "Good. Thank 2nd Officer for me for relieving you." I stuff the papers in my pocket and leave.

Two lovely cocktails, the end of my booze and maybe all booze on MarkShip Mexico, depending on the contents of the brown box for the agent tomorrow. Without ice - I don't want to grope my way down for a couple of pieces of coldness - sip by sip, hanging onto the window frame and bracing myself against the desk, tilting and lurching, watching the now twinkling, now blacked-out lights of Veracruz. Vivaldi is blaring from my computer, competing with the wind and the complaining boxes.

Stan, Ion and I sit at dinner, holding tightly, as does the other full table, all of us laughing and trying to get a forkful in our mouth (mine, by the way, a nice pork tenderloin slice, whereas the others are eating chicken legs. Yuck!)

The Dining Room door opens with a bang, and I think the vacuum seal must be on the fritz. But, in these seas, who knows.

Enter The Peasant, wine bottle in hand, clean and pomaded, khakis pressed, face shiny. The silence he ignores, comes to table, produces a wine opener from his pocket, says "Good Evening," sits, and opens the wine himself (Alex standing aside, aghast). "For our last evening." Smiling and jolly, he pours four glasses. We all stare at him, eyes round, mouths open, heads cocked. *This guy is a certifiable maniac.*

He toasts, "A good trip for you, Mrs. Lindley and a good voyage for us." He pumps his wine glass at each of us. We do not move. He looks at each of us jovially, sets his wine glass down and says, "Pilot at 0500." Alex arrives with his plate, and The Peasant starts shoveling, arms around his plate, as we regard him speechlessly. Eating at the other table resumes, but it sure is quiet over there.

"Oh," he says through his full mouth, while Stan recoils, "here is the trip comment form The Company wants you to fill out. You can just fill it out, and give it to me. I'll see it gets to the right place." He drinks a gulp of wine. "I'll take care of it." He smiles hugely, but his eyes are menacing, as he hands over the form.

Oh, sure, Mr. Peasant, if you had an idea what I plan to say, I know where the "right place" would be. It's round and full of cookie wrappers – or maybe shit. And from your telltale eyes, you have an idea of how the blanks might be filled in.

"Oh, I'll deal with it later," I say languidly and force a smile.

Still seated, he suddenly is bustling, gulping down the last bites of food, all parts of his body in motion. "Must check with the Pilot Station." He rises hastily, shakes himself and rushes to the door. It bangs violently, and we all jump. *Yup, something wrong with the seal.*

"Mission accomplished," I smile and set the comment form on the floor, holding it down firmly with my foot.

Ion had slavered over the Parmesan cheese at the filet dinner, and, luckily, a good-sized chunk is left over. I lurch to the Lounge refrigerator to retrieve it and present it to him with a flourish. "You said you liked it."

He is deeelighted, squirming all over like a puppy. He holds up the cheese and looks at Chief Engineer. "Stan?"

Stan joins in the happy squirming. "Tomorrow." Then turns to me with a sigh: "He will need this. After you leave, I am sure we will be eating quantities of spaghetti or the equivalent of whatever is cheap, even cheaper than what you have experienced, even though I know you do not think that is possible."

I look past Stan out the window, the lights of Veracruz now twinkling on and off in coordination with the ship's jolting upward and downward motion. *He knows. He knows it all. But true to the sea and his age, he will not say a word against The Master unless forced. Oh crap, Stan! Oh crap, all of us!*

Turning to Ion, I say: "You seem in no hurry to find out what he's doing with regard to the Pilot Station."

"3rd Officer is relieving me. Marius can deal with what little harm he could do, if he were going to the Bridge, that is, which I'm sure he is not. I know this Captain. He's had enough exposure for one night – that is, for nearly two days. He's swilling it down in his cabin right now. We'll see him for Pilot tomorrow. Maybe." Ion examines his hands. "Swilling, what a nice word." He looks at me, and we burst out laughing.

"Come on up to the Bridge, and we'll watch the storm wind down. I think the GPS is right this time. I know Marius will be expecting you." He feels my hesitation. "*He* won't be there. Don't worry."

And *he* is not there. Chief Officer and I jounce around on the Bridge, not exactly seeing, but feeling, the storm lessen. The fog lifts, and the rain lessens, those mountainous waves flattening. When we are in the right quadrant of our wind-driven circuit around the anchor, we can actually view the other brightly lighted ships anchored in the roads bobbing like rubber ducks in a splashed-up bathtub. Quiet sighs of relief.

Chief Officer stays on an hour longer. Ion, Marius and I just laze back and idly chat, listening to the crackle of the radio and the abating howl of wind, watching the green flickering screens. No talk of The Peasant, urging for my participation of what's certain to come, or the undecided futures of these young men who have become my friends.

"Why *did* you put your shoes in the window?" Ion asks, and we howl with laughter.

"You will never know, 'cause I ain't telling."

I learn about hunting stags in the snow; ice fishing from heated huts insulated from the ice to keep it from melting; Marius' long-time surgeon girlfriend ("who sure doesn't want an unemployed boyfriend. She doesn't mind my time at sea – would probably go crazy if I were underfoot all the time." the closest we get to the crisis on MarkShip Mexico); Ion's short perfect wife, a translator for the State bank, who speaks six languages fluently (ah, the real purpose for the *Compendium* jumps up*)*; and his adored son.

They talk of things Romanian and Polish, their hatred of gypsies.

"I always think of gypsies as beautiful women, handsome men with golden earrings sitting around wagons and campfires," I sigh.

"Hah! You sure don't want them in your neighborhood. They steal everything, I mean, everything. Sometimes even land. Once they are on your property for even a short time, they think they own it and are very hard to get rid of. People run them off, however they can, the moment they appear. They're dirty, sneaky and mean – mean like picking fights, killing with knives and broken glass. There is nothing romantic about gypsies." I think of them calling The Peasant a gypsy and spitting on the deck. I see now. I should be calling him Gypsy.

"See you at breakfast. Have a safe watch, Marius."

"I have to go to the Dining Room. I'll walk down with you," Ion says pleasantly. *The Peasant is awake; the escort is back.*

My cabin feels empty, deserted. I tug the cork out of the last bottle of wine, toast the cabin, and drink the two remaining swallows. "Luck to us all." Just one thing left to do – a little note to Ion.

MARKSHIP MEXICO
November 16, 2000

Dear Ion:

Well, Chief Officer, it has been a blast. We have shared laughter, anger, boredom, jokes and ship's intrigue.

Thank you loads and loads for your computer help, the fun pictures, ship facts and items of interest (which I never would have received from The Peasant. Yes, I have secretly been calling him that name for weeks.) Most of all, I appreciate your humor and kindness to me. You are a very funny guy. I have enjoyed myself immensely despite my crappy cabin and marginal food (no fault of the cook's - he's a magician in view of the stuff he gets to work with).

I hope that everything goes as you plan in Houston. I'll be thinking positive thoughts for you. I wish I could help, but...

My best wishes for success in your life. You'll make a great Captain if you decide to continue with the sea. Yet, I hope that wonderful shore job materializes so you can stay at home with your family. Whatever you do, you will be successful and, perhaps, one day be the Master of your very own $4 million yacht. Send me an e-mail when you become Captain of a ship or Master of a yacht, and I will plan to ride along with you just for giggles.

I sign off tomorrow, so you can put the binoculars away. (Yes, I know that was uncalled-for.) By the way, my shoes in the window were a signal to my pirate friends to stay away from Markship Mexico. Had they (and you) seen any lacy garment fluttering in the window, that would have been the signal that I had found treasure on the ship, and they should board immediately. You see, Ion, I can make jokes, too.

A wonderful life, my friend. Hope we meet up again sometime.

If you and your wife ever come to the USA for a vacation, let me know, and I'll help you plan and, perhaps, meet up with you somewhere for a filet mignon dinner.

Best regards, Cari Lindley

P.S. In fact, Ion, I should have put some lacy stuff in the window because I did indeed find treasures on board – you guys. Hugs to you all.

PART FIVE

AFTER THE SEA

CHAPTER TWELVE
HUNGRY

Thursday, November 16. Veracruz, Mexico

O vercast, warm, very humid. Sea very choppy. Force 6, maybe 7: Near gale, 28-33 knot winds, 12-1/2 – 19 foot waves, spray, white crests – wish I had the book. But it's in Poland. I'll buy my own damned book and never leave home without it, going to sea or not.

0438: Telephone rings, scaring me silly, since I have rarely heard it. "Chief Officer here. Pilot in ten minutes."

"Thanks, I'll be right up. Thank you." I look at the phone receiver in amazement. *Where were those courtesy calls in Europe and the U.S.? Gads, MsSelf, you are a pain*!

I am already awake since I heard the engine start, followed fifteen minutes later by a strong blast of the horn. What? Maybe a procedure for at-anchor.

0448: On the Bridge with my empty coffee cup. On the last morning on MarkShip Mexico I can surely help myself to instant coffee, which I'm sure getting used to.

The Peasant is on the Bridge, strutting about with authority, plus Chief Officer, 2nd Officer, Helmsman and a backup Filipino.

0610: Two Pilots arrive, halting abruptly in the middle of the Bridge to stare rudely at the blond. (Where is that Mexican cortesia?) Two Pilots? It's a long way from our anchorage in the roads to port in rough waters, so I guess we need two guides.

"Buenos dias, senores."

"Um, si', buenos dias, senora." Pilots look around as if for coffee. None offered.

0700: Alongside. Not a word spoken between those on the Bridge except for the calling and repeating of headings. Pilots flee, casting me one last look of disbelief.

0715: I'm starved and go down for real coffee, eggs and toast. Cristori and Alex make me promise I won't get off without saying good-bye. Cristori tells me that he tried fishing in the storm while we were at anchor.

"Cristori, no!"

"Yes, Mum, needed some fish real bad. But broke my hooks."

I think of the incredible danger to him out there in the maelstrom, how the wind or sea could have swept him overboard without a whisper. He is certainly an avid, albeit crazy, fisherman.

"Bosun says he is going to town, if he has to jump overboard, to buy me some new hooks for my fishing line." This excites him greatly, and I think yet again of the boredom for officers and crew on a commercial vessel. (I must get used to saying vessel: Ship is out, vessel is in. OK, on this vessel.)

Stan runs in for a quick breakfast.

"Oh Stan, you have been so kind, so much fun. I have loved knowing you. We'll stay in touch forever. I want to meet your Eve, remember. Stan, you are a truly lovely man. I will see you at lunch for a goodbye meal?" I blink back tears.

"Cari, you have made an impossible voyage possible. My thanks to you are deep and heartfelt. A truly magnificent woman. It will be not the same without you. If only I could thank you enough for all you've done." He stands quickly, reaches across the table and takes my hand for an instant, then is gone.

Neither Ion nor Marius appears. Too late, we are berthed, and the outside activity is hotting up.

My last walk on the decks before the cranes start. I constantly look up, poised to run out of the way when they do, even though I stay away from port side.

Near the Hatchcover door, Marius, in white coveralls, hair pulled back in a ponytail under the hardhat, motions to me. Ion, hard-hatted, stands at the door behind him, motioning. Agent wants to see me. Well, good, because I want to see him too. As I walk by Chief Officer, I give him the "Dear Ion" letter.

A tall, lean, bordering-on-handsome Brit greets me in the Visitors Lounge, standing beside the table with a brown-wrapped, string-tied box. I don't have to look at the address, but what else from this vessel could possibly be inside? The cupboard is bare. The Peasant stands in the corner, regarding his agent with awe, and we exchange not a word.

Spare, arrogant, dressed in a pressed, sharply-creased khaki, many-pocketed safari outfit complete with bush hat, brim pinned back with an Australian flag pin, speaking the clipped King's English, the agent greets me warmly, holding my hand a moment too long. He regards me appraisingly. His thoughts in high-definition film flick in Technicolor across his face: 1. Well, looky here. 2. American, how nice. 3. Hmm, possibilities. 4. Too old. 5. Still, maybe. 6. Must have a buck or two, running around on ships. 7. No, too old. Too bad. He drops my hand abruptly.

I explode with laughter.

"What, madam, is amusing?"

"You're English, not Australian. Where'd you get...?" I gesture at his bizarre outfit, worn so pompously in Mexico.

"I am pleased that you can distinguish that I'm not Australian." His distaste at the word 'Australian' infers "from the provinces," which doubles my glee. What a prig! But I've ruined my chance to hear where he got the outfit. From Central Casting?

With merry eyes, I ask: "What information can you give me?"

Thin lips pulled primly back over yellowing teeth (better see your dentista today, honey, because your girl- or boyfriends aren't gonna like that), he tells me that his sub-agent (spoken dismissingly) will pick me up at noon and take me to a hotel of choice. He suggests the Colonial since I want to be near el centro.

The Peasant watches the exchange, his admiring eyes never leaving the agent. He adds nothing, and we ignore him, engaged in our own hilarious (to me) paso doble.

I finish packing, take a short nap, shower and go outside to watch the cranes working. Their precision never ceases to amaze me.

Once, in Tokyo on a hot midnight, I dressed, then opened my forward window and sat on the sill, watching the crane working two boxes over from my window. It was a scene from "Grapes of Wrath," port lights streaking off the crane's window high above, the operator and his bank of levers alight from his computer glow, appearing like Steinbeck's aliens. He lifted the box precisely, swung it high over the superstructure and placed it with a muted bang on the waiting truck below. The crane swung around to just above the next box and stopped. The operator stepped onto the adjoining platform and waved. I waved back. He took off his safety glasses and smiled, teeth glinting, shouting something. I shouted back and waved. One more wave and he disappeared inside, and the crane prongs lowered unerringly onto the box, hooking it and sweeping it upward into the night sky. A fun moment for us both. Another testament to the futility of discrimination: Crane operators the world over do their jobs well - color, religion, nationality be damned.

I walk to the port edge of Main Deck, the cranes working well forward of me. A truck driver sees me and hollers in English, "Where are you from?"

"De los estados unidos."

"What is your name?"

"Cari."

He smiles largely, bright teeth in a brown face. "Thank you very much, Cari."

"You're welcome, and your English is very good." He waves and moves his truck to the loading mark.

At last noon arrives. Marius shakes my hand, cranes roaring and clanging overhead. To my amazement, his hulk towering over me, he kisses me on both cheeks European style. Why should I be amazed? It is pure Marius – all long hair and rumpled shirt, yet with a mindset different from anyone I have ever known.

"I enjoyed, loved, knowing you, Marius, your company on those many nights riding on the Bridge, even the arguments. It was a pleasure.

Much more than a pleasure. You are very special." I can't seem to let go of his hand.

He laughs, then looks serious. "No, Cari, it was MY pleasure. I'm going to miss it, you, a lot. A lot." Tears spring to his eyes, and he turns quickly away to his loading charts. *Ah, Marius.*

I run inside to the Dining Room, hoping to have one last word with Stan, although we kind of said goodbye at breakfast. He is not there, and I know in my heart exactly why. His sensitive mind has become used to a Western body at table with different ideas and manners, to whom he can ask cautious questions, which he has stored carefully in his methodical brain over the years. Although he has come as close as he can, he is unable to say he will miss me. It would simply be too gauche for him to do so. Never would he presume or offend in any way. We have become friends, and he doesn't know what to do about this surprising condition. But I want badly to tell him again that I will miss him and give him a big hug. Short of a trip to the Engine Room, where he is hiding and doesn't want to see me, I am not able to tell him. And, for his sake, will not do so - my parting gift to Stanislov, although he will never know it. Only I mourn the moment.

However, The Peasant sits grandly at table alone. I go in anyway, maybe Stan…

"Good morning," I say with forced cheer. "I'm ready to sign off. Just waiting for the agent."

Some few idle words. I have no intention of thanking him in any way. *Do you thank a goat for being in the pasture?* I rise and say, "Must run out and see if the agent is here," which, of course, is ridiculous. The agent would make his presence known if he knew Captain was in the Dining Room.

I start to the door. "CARI!" his voice commanding. I whirl to glare at him, and he lowers his voice drastically. "Do you have the form? You know, the form I gave you?"

"I have it. I haven't decided what to do about it."

"It is not obligado," he hastens to add in Spanish, smiling slyly, voice full of self-satisfaction. Hah! She is not going to fill it out.

"I know. If I decide to fill it out, I will send it directly." *Not to you, Peasant.*

"Ah, directly." He looks at his plate. I escape.

Who can believe that the agent arrives at 1215, nearly on time. Excuse me, the sub-agent, a round, nicely coifed young Mexican man in a guaya-berra shirt, with a brilliant smile and pleasant manner. This kid works for Mr. Safari?

I step inside the Hatchcover door to the Chief Officer's office, where I shake hands, then kiss him on both cheeks, hug him. He blushes bright red with pleasure – although maybe he has read my Dear Ion letter and is blushing from that. I have seen him five times this morning, and he hasn't mentioned it. Who knows?

"E-mail me about Houston. I will be waiting."

He regards me sadly. "If I can, I will."

One more quick look for Stanislov. Still not in the Dining Room. Definitely hiding. Bloody hell, Stan, I really did want to give you a humongous hug.

The agent wants to tell Captain sailing time is 1700, so Ion goes in search of him, but can't find him anywhere.

"Did you try his bed?" I ask Ion. He laughs loudly, and the agent blinks, startled. "Well, you see, we arrived early morning," I smile. Ion runs off, laughing, for another look.

Cristori comes on deck and admonishes the agent to take care of his mother. I'd like to sock Cristori, who looks every bit as old as me, but I simply laugh. The agent looks perplexed, then frightened, as Cristori grabs his arm roughly and shoves his face up to the agent.

"I mean it, take care of her. She is…Just take care of her." He throws his arm toward the ship. "WE mean it."

Tears well in my eyes. WE, I recognize immediately, means all the Filipino crew on board. He has been elected spokesman for them all and is fulfilling his role for them as well as for himself. I melt, then hug Cristori in his stained white apron, while the agent looks on in amaze-ment. When I step back from Cristori and turn around, the sub-agent is

smiling gently. This is Mexico, and he understands emotion and attach-
ment. My Mexico. I smile brilliantly at him.

Now the agent runs about looking for Chief Officer. We run here and
there and can't find him. My God, I think, Ion has found The Peasant,
and they've killed each other and are spurting blood in the Master's cabin.

Alex, who has spent the morning smiling at me and closing both
eyes as if winking, adding every moment "Thank you too, Mum, thank
you too," is entrusted with the absolutely vital information of sailing
time. The despairing agent looks wide-eyed at me. Holy shit, MarkShip
Mexico, will you ever sail or will the authorities blast you out of port,
The Peasant hanging from the main mast, bottle waving, screeching:
"No es obligado."

The distraught agent now gets another hit. I don't have a visa. Must
have. Don't have and upon inquiry, the returning errant knight, Ion, can't
provide. Much telephoning with The Brit, and it is finally decided that I
will go to the hotel and after checking in, will give my passport to Francisco
(the darling sub-agent), and he will arrange a visa with immigration.

I quickly hug Chief Officer and 2nd Officer again, wave and blow
kisses to all the hard-working men atop the boxes, who wave, smile and
shout to me, then go carefully down the gangway. On land, I turn and
put my left foot up on the first step. Superstition of the Sea. *Luck to you
MarkShip Mexico. You sure do need it!*

I look up. Ion and Marius are standing at the top of the gangway,
watching me. I wave and blow kisses. They smile and wave back. Ion has
my letter to him in his hand and lifts it.

The sun appears, adding its force to the thick, humid air. The sub-
agent and I, jabbering in English and Spanish, ride in his shiny green
Volkswagen to el centro. I keep repeating that I can't believe the lack of
storm damage.

After checking in, I hand him my passport at the hotel desk, arrange
to meet at the hotel at 1700, and he is gone. No sooner done than I
worry: What the hell have I done? I've just given my passport to someone I've never seen before in my life. Oh well, he, the sub-agent of the
agent, I hope, whom I know only by Francisco, is gone, and I am without

passport. Visions of American Embassies, Mexican jails and difficulties jump into my head.

A perfect ending for a leisurely voyage aboard MarkShip Mexico - hugs all around to those of importance on board, but not a word of thanks or goodbye to or from The Peasant, the Master of the Vessel. Wow!

The bellboy escorts me through the lovely hotel to a room that looks at a wall. I am distraught. "No arboles? No flores? Solamente una pared?" I ask him sorrowfully.

He looks at me in dismay. In Spanish, he answers: "I will find you another room immediately A room with trees, flowers, no walls to look at, a room with a balcony.

All right, he gets a very nice tip, and I have a room ten times the size of MarkShip Mexico's with two floor-to-ceiling doors leading onto a balcony overlooking the Zocalo and a spectacular view of the cathedral and Palacio Principal. *Bless you, MsSelf, for being able to speak a little espanol. The noise from the square may drive me nuts at night, but the view is to die for.*

Back on land, which rocks and rolls, particularly after the last few storm-driven nights, without a drop of alcohol, I careen down the street, threatening to tip over. Every sailor knows the curse of the sea on land, where each step is tentative, the body's inside mechanism trying vainly to adjust to a solid, level surface, the gait appearing drunken, swaying from side to side, missing steps and stumbling badly, balance completely askew. We are used to a rolling deck, a rocking ship, standing with legs apart and braced. Dry land makes US roll.

Signed off MarkShip Mexico with many regrets, I am, nonetheless, ready to eat Mexican food.

Randomly choosing one of the many outdoor restaurants on the Zocalo, I sit comfortably in the umbrella's shade and order chilaquiles, frijoles and beer. It will take some time, I know. This is after all my Mexico, so I sip beer and study the tourist map I picked up at the hotel desk.

"Hi, hi, hi." Three different voices. I look up. Good Lord, it's Bosun, he of the gnarled body and few teeth, and two of his Filipino men, "boys" he calls them, from MarkShip Mexico.

"Hi, sit down. I'll buy you a beer."

They look dubiously at each other, the restaurant and at me, then at my repeated insistence, gingerly enter through the wrought iron fence. I insist they pull chairs from other tables, after I have asked permission in my most formal Spanish from the people seated informally at those tables. Pulling chairs is obviously something completely alien to my men, but they do it to please me.

Stares of disapproval all around. To hell with you Mexicanos! Americans and Canadians stare when I sit at YOUR table. Honest to dear sweet Diana, will this never end? I won't allow it. I will associate with whom I please, and the rest of you can go take a flying leap. The waiter looks aghast at these three dark, scruffy people with the blond lady, but brings them beer when I order it in grating Spanish, using a harsh tone I didn't even know I had.

I am so pleased to see them. Familiar faces in the midst of nobodies. What fun! Let's drink beer. Want something to eat?

Bosun looks at his watch and says their time is short, maybe one beer. They exchange meaningful glances, speaking quickly in Filipino, nodding to each other, then in English excusing their rudeness.

My God in heaven, there were surely no secrets on MarkShip Mexico. Even the Filipinos are excusing themselves from communicating in their native language, something I told the officers of MarkShip Mexico was very rude at table, when they very well knew and very well could speak English in my presence, for only a few minutes daily. Not one secret on MarkShip Mexico. Not one!

I begin, "Did you get the fishing hooks for Cristori? I hope so. He really likes to fish and is hoping you could get him a couple hooks since he can't get off board. But, mostly, he really wants fresh fish for you guys."

Silence. Then Bosun produces a package and waves it in the air. They have purchased the hooks. I add feebly, "The food on board isn't so good. Well, I mean, fresh fish would be great. A real treat."

They stare at me incredulously, look at each other and begin to speak slowly and clearly in English. Gnarled, short, wiry Bosun first, of course, then he of the tall body, long hair cut to curl around his neck, then the young one.

"Cook fishes all day. Even at night, he checks the lines. We take turns helping him so he can sleep. Cook fishes so we can eat. He drags in seaweed, too, and dries it. (I picture thin little Cristori dragging in tons of seaweed.) He makes a kind of thick stew with whatever he has. Remember the ship ahead of us that was throwing all kinds of garbage into the sea? Cook saw a box, and we used grappling hooks, finally got it. Tinned vegetables. We ate well that night." He touches the hooks reverently. "He doesn't fish for sport, Mrs. (Bosun is the only one who never calls me Mum), he fishes so we have something to eat."

"What!?"

Carefully – I can feel their utmost care with each English word – they tell me about food and their Captain.

Anger greater than any I experienced on MarkShip Mexico, maybe anywhere, suffuses me, sweat running freely, face frozen white with disgust. This isn't Chief Officer showing me his evidence, this isn't officers grumbling about food like garbage, this isn't officers turning the faces away because they don't want to face consequences, this isn't me railing to The Peasant. No, this is none of those things.

"Does Chief Officer know all of this?"

They hang their heads. "Not most. Not about the fishing. He already has so many burdens. He does everything he can to help us. He is a very good man, Mrs."

So, Ion, you knew some of it. Why the hell didn't you tell me? Did you think I'd go berserk and slit the Captain's throat?

In the sunlit Zocalo of Veracruz, Mexico, they talk of inferior food, not having enough food daily, of being near starvation.

"He is slowly killing us; we are hungry; we don't have enough to eat."

Horror and anguish engulf me..

"He can spend $6 daily, but spends much less, putting the rest in his pocket. We know we are allotted $6 a day to eat. But understand, Mrs., that one of us Filipinos is designated to check food received on board. But, he grabs the list, and we see him checking off items that are not there. Sometimes, nothing or little is received at the provisioning station, although it is all checked off on the list."

Tears stand out in this unattractive man's eyes. Regardless of the disapproving Veracruzanos staring at us, I find this man very attractive. His passion and goal are to direct, take care of and FEED his eleven charges. He is powerless. No one in management would listen to his lone voice, the voice of such an underling.

On and on they talk about sick and twisted things, the beer roiling violently behind my tongue and heaving in my stomach, mostly about lack of food, venting anger without end, while I listen without a word.

"He cheats us, he steals from us, we don't have enough to eat. We see the on-board provisioning and what we are to vouch for. It's not there or if it is there, it and many other things disappear at the next port, in those heavy brown boxes to Poland. He goes and raids in the wee hours. I have personally seen him do it, staggering up the steep storeroom steps with boxes heaped. So has he and he," he jerks his thumbs at his boys. "We watch, we watch, most of all at night when *he* thinks everybody is sleeping."

I stare at Bosun. 'Wee hours?' Not one Polish or Romanian on board would know that phrase. There has been no 'coaching.' I believe him totally. And shake with fury as the afternoon sun gilds the trees.

"Captain Evil! You fucking bastard!" I scream internally, sweat rolling into my eyes.

"We are scared for our jobs," says the long-haired one.

"I understand perfectly," I reply.

"I have five daughters," he moans.

To give a moment's levity to the tension, I say, "Five!"

"He was trying for a son," giggles the young one.

"Ah, don't be disappointed in daughters. Maybe not in The Philippines, but in many places in the world, daughters can make you happier and be more successful than sons."

They regard me dubiously. And then I get to tell them the story of Myrna, my hand-picked replacement at the world-renowned physics company, who drives a red Mercedes sportscar and dresses from only the finest stores. This lady is making a BUNCH of money, much more than her husband. "And she is FILIPINO." They love it, beam at me, would hug and kiss me if they dared.

"She was by far the best qualified. It never occurred to me that she was Filipino or any other thing. She was, and still is, *very* good at her job. So, don't you worry about your daughters, young man, they will outdo you by miles. Just get them a good education. Are you sure you don't want something to eat?"

No, they couldn't. Not 'don't want,' 'couldn't.' How could they explain to the others?

They look at me with trust. I wonder with as little contact on board why they feel this way, then remember the vessel's Jungle Drums, the instant communication. Still, I recall nothing I have done to instill such trust.

"I know you're scared. I understand why you are. I would be too. Yet, if you want to stop this animal, you have to support Chief Officer when he makes his formal complaint. Not only with your signatures but with your verbal statements as well, if required. You may only be sailing with this creep for a few months, but he will be out there doing it to other crews. Do you understand me?"

"Yes. We know he has done it before, for example, on Mayfair Concord. We have people on board now who were with him there. They almost died from no food. One couldn't work for months and is still weak, many problems. You're right, he will do it again. Plus, plus those other things." They exchange fearful glances. "He should not be commanding. He is without honor."

My mouth drops open. There is that word again, that word I insisted upon using to indicate my disgust of Captain Dishonor without cursing him roundly as I so desired to do. So, 'honor' made its way between the two Dining Rooms, wafting through the service pantry, then galley and presenting itself in the crew's dining area – or floating up the inside stairwell and along each corridor, stealthily entering each door of Superstructure Decks #1, 2 and 3. Honor.

"Look, if I had real proof, things I've actually seen myself, I would not only write, I'd be on the phone to The Company. I've seen the requisitions where he signed for provisions on board where you tell me there were no provisions. I've seen the faxes about lashings he didn't distribute that could have caused serious injury. I have personally seen the brown boxes, but I didn't know what was inside. Do you understand, I've heard and seen all sorts of things, but I have not one shred of personal evidence. If someone asked me, 'What do you know for a fact?' I would have to answer, 'Nothing.' What I know in my heart," I lightly thump my chest in a mea culpa as they watch the motion with reverence (all good Catholics) "after spending a month with this guy and what I could swear to in court are two different things."

The defeat in their eyes nearly undoes me. This was a chance meeting, and when I asked them to sit down, they had hoped, they had hoped.

Goddammit all to hell, why don't I just lie to help them? I want to with all my heart, and I know they want what they know so terribly personally for a fact to help me easily lie. But I can't. Perhaps just inference could help them. But I am not skilled at half-innuendos. I want the whole enchilada.

"Let me think about this more. Maybe there could be a letter, but you must understand it would be with (caveats, I want to say, but realize they wouldn't know the word) what I've actually seen and not seen." They nod, praying for the best. I'm not sure I have a 'best' to give them.

Bosun says they have to leave. Sailing at 1700. They have to dash. They stand and each formally shakes my hand, regarding me with hope.

I look at the three forlorn stickmen before me - tall, short, medium. Hungry, maybe starving. Because some depraved maniac wants better towels for his swimming pool in a country where swimming pools are nearly unheard of, only for the rich and privileged – and the corrupt.

No! I forbid it!

"Tell Chief Officer I will write the letter. Tell him I will write it with caveats." They regard me solemnly.

"Say it – caveats." They repeat. "Once more." Each repeats the word. "Tell him to look it up in his *Compendium*. Say it." They repeat twice. "Caveat. Compendium."

"Tell him the moment you are on board. Promise me."

They smile hugely. One of them will get it right.

I sit dismally in the afternoon sun, pushing the just-arrived chilaquiles around on my plate. My favorite, but I can't eat it. I sip my warm beer.

What can I do? Letters and slow actions by management could take months. They might be dead by that time. What can I possibly say to make management take fast action, to convince them that this is not a complaint from a whiney, hysterical old woman?

The world tilts as I rock with the vessel which is no longer under my feet. Somehow there is a clue there, but I cannot pick it out. Jesus-jumped-up-Christ, what am I to do about MarkShip Mexico? Is it really mine to do? Can't the officers and crew take care of themselves? How can I live with this begging for help? What can I, an outsider, really do? Who will listen to me – The Company? The Management Company? I am crazy with the verbal and silent pleas.

Is this like when the drunken Peasant declared himself God on the ship and I retorted, "No, I am. I am paying." And one of the officers appealed to me to be more considerate of his Captain? I tried to be, but to no avail, since his Captain was drunk beyond repair. That same officer less than one month later stood on the Bridge and nearly spat on the photo-picture of his Captain. Still, he appealed, and I tried to respond. No problem to be magnanimous when it's relatively easy; nearly impossible when it's difficult. Do Chief Officer and Bosun, each in charge of the ship's activities, expect me to be what I so carelessly said: Because I'm paying, I am God on this vessel? Do they expect me to make good on my nonchalantly given boast, even after I have signed off? Oh MarkShip Mexico!

As I sit in the fading afternoon sun trying to focus on the plaza, rolling with the vessel even on land, I realize that MarkShip Mexico is preparing to sail without me. I see Ion, 2nd Officer, Helmsman and The Peasant on the Bridge, Pilot standing midships, Marius directing the crew to cast off the four aft ropes from starboard stern, tugs pulling us off. I hear the radio staticking and loud voices reporting positions. The Helmsman's voice is strong, low, repeating instructions: Dead slow ahead. Starboard 20. Midships. One eight oh, suh.

We rock as we leave the breakwater. I see Veracruz becoming only a speck of land.

She points her nose to the sea – and I am not with her. Sadness for MarkShip Mexico and all aboard her, as well as for me left here on shore, wells up, and I swipe tears.

In the lovely Veracruz Zocalo musicians are playing traditional music, the breeze is soft, air warm and humid, waning sun playing tag with buildings and trees.

And I begin to realize I, personally, have indeed actually seen and experienced things on board, things to which I can swear, that I DO have something to say to Owners, The Company, the Management Company. Things I NEED to say – all true, all different, most horrifying. I DO have proof: I lived it!

Where would I start? A letter to top management, not simply filling in the form that would be received at the bottom and slowly work its way up. I would mention some of the other nasty items to set the scene, but the paramount thing – the one that has just now made me wild and crazy – is lack of food for hard-driven men. Save the drunkenness, voodoo and danger of the mirrors for the second round; don't want to overwhelm them at the outset. Ease them into all the problems, make them disgusted or conscience-stricken enough to open an investigation, to talk to my people, hear it all for themselves. The rest will follow. Present it logically, calmly – the simple, unvarnished truth as I know it.

Yes, Starvation! should get action.

How I wish circumstances had been different and I did not have to 'complete the form.' Then I hear The Peasant's sly voice. "It is not obligado."

Ah, but it IS obligado. Faces white and brown, long-haired and crew-cutted rise up before me, smiling at me, treating me with great care and respect after our very rocky start.

On deck, "Good morning, Mum. A good day."

"Good morning. Wow, another beautiful day." Return smiles as spectacular as the day.

On the Bridge, "Good morning, Cari, are you enjoying this sunny day?"

"Very much, thank you." I do a little jig, then make motions as if looking for the U.S. Coast Guard picture book. My silent motions are a joke between us. That book, as we know so well, along with all the other seafaring books on the Bridge, has disappeared to Poland.

"Force 3 today," comes the automatic, amused reply to my unasked question.

"Naw, Force 4." We laugh and watch the oncoming sea.

Yes, I am obliged to complete the form. Heaven help us all!

CHAPTER THIRTEEN
The Letters

Mr. B. Goethe/RR-OPS   November 18, 2000
Ritteer GmbH & Cie. KG\
Van-der-Liesen-Str.10 - C 33676
Hamburg, Germany
Email: Info@Ritteer.de
SUBJECT: Captain Romuald Kiezlcmuzc, MarkShip Mexico
REFERENCE: "HE IS SLOWLY KILLING US.
                  WE DO NOT HAVE ENOUGH TO EAT.
                  WE'RE 'AFRAID TO SPEAK UP.
                  WE NEED OUR JOBS."
                  (Veracruz, Mexico, November 15, 2000, Chance
                  Meeting in Zocalo with 3 Crew Members,
                  Approx. 2 P.M., Two hours after I, a passenger,
                  "signed off" Markship Mexico)

Dear Mr. Goethe:

The above reference is the reason for this letter.

In a lifetime of traveling, I have received and discarded literally thousands of forms to express my opinion of quality, service, etc. Never have I responded, although service or quality may have been dismal. Understand, sir, I am a veteran traveler, moving about the Earth's surface with few complaints, taking in stride most inconveniences. A part of the traveling experience.

This is the first time I feel an obligation to respond to a request for comments. Mixing in ship's business is not my aim. I did not go looking for this situation, prying into matters not my business; I simply got caught up in the tornado of angry emotions. This furious tornado spun me out onto dry land in Veracruz, Mexico and spat its parting words: "He is slowly killing us." No person of conscience could hear those words without seeking redress. I ask only that you read the following, without judgment, until the last word. Thank you.

That Captain K is devoid of charm, wit or grace is not important. Of primary importance is that Captain K lacks HONOR and INTEGRITY, unable to keep his word even to an outsider - a passenger. The crew has learned not to expect it.

It is widely believed amongst people aboard that Captain K is stealing choice provisions and other ship items, sending them in boxes to his home in Poland from different ports. (A direct quote to me from a crew member: "I have personally seen him carrying many, many specialty provisions in the wee hours." An odd expression from a Filipino, 'wee hours.')

I myself have seen these heavy boxes, but unfortunately do not personally know the contents. While at sea shortly after Gibraltar, officers requesting small tinned items were told there were no more. Their astonished faces said "Impossible!" but the reality was no requested items were left in provisions. Where do we suppose they were?

The shocking widespread belief, and the reason for this letter, is that of the $6 daily provision allotment per crew member, Captain K is only spending $4-4.50 and POCKETING the difference. Hence inferior quality and quantity, which I have experienced.

They say they have proof. After a month aboard Markship Mexico, I believe them.

The officers will survive under this despot, but the hard-working deck crew needs food.

As days rolled by, I became horrified by Captain K's crudeness and lack of honor, which literally made me shrink away from his person. I shall detail a few experiences so you can get the flavor:

1. The Barbecue. Twice, Captain K personally promised me a BBQ for all ship's personnel, in front of numerous witnesses. Twice, on the appointed day, he disappeared into his cabin behind a firmly shut (locked?) door for the entire day. No order ever reached the CO

or galley regarding a BBQ. The crew's disappointment nearly made me weep.

A barbecue may be a small matter to thee and me, but to a crew onboard for six months or more, it is a JOY. Captain K was, as usual, unable to keep his word.

(It has occurred to me that he does not hold barbecues for all personnel because he is afraid to walk among them. Unlike other captains, apparently he is only seen in the corridors and stairs between his cabin and the Dining Room or the Bridge.)

2. The Polish Food: Captain K received special food from Poland, brought by the driver who picked up the Polish shipyard technicians in La Spezia.

It was HIS, no question. At table, he hunched over the Polish delicacies, only rarely offering to share a few bites with the Chief Engineer, also Polish. When others requested, the nervous steward said, "Only for The Captain." The Captain told them directly that the food was sent to him by his wife for his personal consumption. Except, Mr. Goethe, the Polish food was paid by MarkShip Mexico formal requisition. I saw it. I don't care that the ship paid for it, only that he lied.

3. Small Food Portions. During my first meal aboard in the Officers Dining Room, I wondered at the small portions. I thought: Perhaps Poles and Romanians eat less. Then I noted the large quantity of bread consumed. Better bread than hungry. The Captain, however, always seemed to have some fish or sausage delicacy as a sort of dessert, while the others watched with watering mouths. More than once 'sadistic' flashed in my mind.

4. Reference Books on The Bridge: When I asked difficult questions, the Officer On Duty would say, "We have books on this subject and we'll consult them." But to their astonishment, the books had 'disappeared.' What do you mean 'disappeared?' Shrugs. Perhaps in boxes to Poland? I wondered.

5. The Television Satellite Disk: Purchased from Crew Fund, the disk's slender white cable snaked across the bridge and over the side to Captain K's cabin ONLY. This expenditure depleted the Crew Fund dramatically. If they want a Christmas tree, they each will have to donate. Again, a seemingly small matter to thee and me. But...

6. The Guitar: Promised by our genial Captain K so the crew could have music and entertainment. Never purchased with money from the crew's own fund. Disappointment rampant. "He promised us..."

Had I known of the guitar matter, I would have gladly traded the $300 I personally expended for groceries in a Miami supermarket in order to provide a very special dinner for the officers and kitchen staff (so they could have at least one quality meal while I was aboard) for a guitar for the crew. The officer dinner and huge sheet cake for the crew that I provided to thank them for their kindness and respect was eaten and gone. The guitar would have lasted for years.

If only a small part of this is true (and I can personally vouch for the astonishment at 'unavailable' and 'disappeared' items), the crew's food issue is paramount and, once again, the reason for this letter.

Even a hint of tampering with crew's food provisions, I would think, should be sufficient reason to investigate. At least from the point of view of those aboard MarkShip Mexico, for his own gratification Captain K is literally stealing food from their mouths. Ask them. If they dare speak up, you will hear much more than detailed above. Much more!

German management and strict standards are the envy of the seas. You are bound by your own reputation to look into this matter.

The whole situation makes a person who never gets seasick want to vomit.

Sincerely,
Cari Lindley
PO Box 3320
Phoenix, AZ 85012 USA, clindley@juno

P.S. Because Mexican mail is notoriously unreliable, I shall re-send this letter from the United States a few months hence.

COPIES: Mr. L. G. Palson, Managing Director
Mr. Ronald Belson, General Manager
Asteroid Ship Management Ltd

***

It's done. I can do no more, having just posted that which I told myself and others I could not/would not do. Now we wait.

Cuernavaca, Mexico, December 5, 2000

Upon arriving at the Spanish school, I check e-mail and am both surprised and excited to find the following:

Mrs. Lindley: Acknowledge receipt of your letter. Investigation pending. Will advise developments.

B. Goethe/Ritteer GmbH & Cie

Four months of school in sunny Mexico with no "advisement." Just as I thought, they had thrown me a sop to shut me up. Behind every "Buenos dias," every "Como esta' hoy?" MarkShip Mexico and its dark problems lurk. I even enter a beautiful ancient cathedral and light a candle, hoping the roof won't tumble onto my head. No further word.

Phoenix, Arizona, USA, April 1, 2001

On the 1st day of April 2001, I return to the USA – and to a stack of mail
months old. Therein lay:

> Mr. B. Goethe/RR-OPS
> Ritteer GmbH & Cie. KG
> Van-der-Liesen-Str.10 - C 33676
> Hamburg, Germany
> December 16, 2000

Mrs. Cari Lindley
P.O. Box 3320
Phoenix, AZ 85012 USA
SUBJECT: Romuald Kiezlcmuzc, MarkShip Mexico
Dear Mrs. Lindley:

To follow up and conclude our correspondence with regard to
the subject, I wish to advise that a formal investigation was instigated
on December 10, 2000 and that Romuald Kiezlcmuzc was discharged
from duties as of December 14, 2000. He will never work again for this
Company in the capacity of Captain or in any other capacity. Where
possible, I am using our influence to bar him from command, in fact,
from the sea.

Mrs. Lindley, I began my career with the sea at a young age as the
lowliest deckhand, slowly working my way through the many layers of
seafaring duties. I know first-hand the requisite for fair treatment of
crew and the absolute necessity of adequate quantities of hearty food
for the hard-working members aboard. As you stated, to 'tamper' with
the food supply is indefensible.

I send you my best regards and hope that you receive this information favorably.

Sincerely, B. Goethe

CHAPTER FOURTEEN
Aftermath

FAVORABLY? FAVORABLY!!!! YYAAAAHHHHOOOOOOO!!!!!
December 14! That wonderful, fabulous, extraordinary Company got right on it! There is Honor, Integrity, Character – Justice in this world. And Mr. Goethe is all of it personified. December 14 – WOW! My people might have been hungry, but still alive!

I rocket around the living room, laughing, crying, hollering, shaking the letter above my head, leaping, yelling, tears rolling unchecked, dancing on air. My sister and brother-in-law regard me as demented. "How nice."

"NICE! NICE? It's fantastic!" I shout at their shocked faces, laughing, dancing, weeping.

My brother-in-law, also my best friend in the world, steps back and faintly smiles. Before the week is out, he will have dragged every detail from me, his quiet intense interest pulling every nuance of what led up to this delirious happiness. And this man of honor will look straight at me, his smile and nod of approval doubling my pleasure.

***

E-mail from Florin: Cari: Thank you for your e-mail. I would have written earlier, but I did not want to intrude.

Captain K is gone, dismissed in a very unfriendly manner, citing accounting irregularities. The new Captain brought on, who lasted only a short time, was nearly as bad with his drunkenness, but at least we had enough to eat. Ion sure got a lot of hours in as acting Captain during his contract. After all of our contracts were over and all of us who you knew had all signed off, we heard the next Captain, making that the second since Captain K, was found dead in his cabin. The Company changed the name of the ship. No, before you ask, I will not sail on that ship again. Nor should you. Perhaps it would be best that you not take a sea-going vessel for a year or two. One never knows where HE might turn up, maybe as a cabin boy. Haha! And one must beware when a ship's name is changed.

My mother invites you to visit in Transylvania. She will write you soon. My wife and I would be very pleased if you could visit. They would enjoy knowing you as much as I.

I have heard nothing from anyone on MarkShip Mexico, but that is not uncommon since our contracts take us in different directions. So I don't know for a fact if Ion ever filed his formal complaint as he would not talk about it at the time, but it seemed The Company started its investigation quite promptly after you signed off - in fact, at our first European port, Valencia, where you had first signed on those many months earlier. They somehow knew the near-mutinous problems on MarkShip Mexico, although, throughout the investigation, they said not a word to anyone (believe me, we were all comparing notes) of why they instigated it. I wonder *how* they knew, Mrs. Lindley.

Hope you will visit. Best regards, Florin

E-mail from Tom: Many months after the fact, we ashore have heard of Capt. K's dismissal. Too bad! If my instincts are correct, I believe congratulations are due you! For your safety, you should probably not travel by ship for a while. Certainly not on MarkShip Mexico. They changed her name, as you probably know, so you really don't want to sail on her. My wife and I extend invitation for your visit to Poland. She wants to meet you. Tom

***

All these years later, I still await a brief note from Stan, Ion or Marius. I don't know if Stan and Eve took their USA trip; if Ion got his coveted shore job; if Marius' headaches have disappeared – if the investigation and its ensuing revelations placed a taint on their careers. Or are Ion and Marius now both in command of their own ships, Captains with honor and humor?

Only silence answers me.

Probably as it should be.

Yes, MsSelf, it was worth it.

About the Author

G erri Simons Rasor, a veteran world traveler, has explored most continents by both land and sea. She loves riding on big boats that carry her to exotic destinations around the globe and has been a passenger on many cruise ships plus two freighters, one of them an around-the-world adventure. *Treacherous Seas* is the fictionalized story of her other freighter trip, a remarkable voyage across the Mediterranean and Atlantic.

A loner and party animal, learner and teacher, clotheshorse and wannabe nudist, she spends winters by the sea in Mexico and summers in the back desert of Nevada. She relishes answering questions about freighter travel: You traveled *alone* on freighters? What's it like? Weren't you scared? Are you nuts?

Gerri lives full time with one grouchy old computer and each summer hosts twenty-some rambunctious "grandkids" (a.k.a., newly-hatched, wobbly California quail).

Made in the USA
Charleston, SC
05 November 2014